PRAISE FOR PETER TEMPLE

*Winner of the UK Crime Writers' Association Gold Dagger,
the Miles Franklin Literary Award and*

'Temple is a master.' Mi

'As dark and as mean, as cool
as any James Ellroy or Elmore whom
you might kill the small or sad hours.' *Age*

'Peter Temple has been described as one of Australia's
best crime novelists, but he's far better than that. He's
one of our best novelists full stop.' *Sun-Herald*

'Temple is the man—the lay-down misère
best crime writer in the country.' *Advertiser*

'The top hard-boiled crime writer on the local scene.'
Courier-Mail

'Peter Temple is, quite simply, the finest crime writer
we have…He has set a standard internationally that few
come near. His Chandler-like ability to capture the dark
corners of our sunniest places is as good as it gets.' *Mercury*

'Temple's work is spare, deeply ironic; his wit, like the
local beer, as cold as a dental anaesthetic.' *Australian*

'One of the world's finest crime writers.' *The Times*

'This bloke is world-class.' *Washington Post*

'Peter Temple is an addiction. Read one book and
you will want to read them all.' Val McDermid

Born in South Africa in 1946, **PETER TEMPLE** is one of Australia's most celebrated writers. His novels—among them the Jack Irish series, *Truth*, and *The Broken Shore*—have been published in more than twenty countries. He was the first Australian writer to win the UK Crime Writers' Association Gold Dagger, and the first crime writer to win the Miles Franklin Literary Award. Peter Temple died on 8 March 2018.

MICHAEL HEYWARD is the publisher at Text Publishing.

PETER TEMPLE
THE RED HAND
STORIES, REFLECTIONS AND THE
LAST APPEARANCE OF JACK IRISH

TEXT PUBLISHING MELBOURNE AUSTRALIA

textpublishing.com.au

The Text Publishing Company
Swann House, 22 William Street, Melbourne Victoria 3000, Australia

Some of the pieces in this book were first published in the *Age, Best Australian Essays, Best Australian Stories*, the *Bulletin, Mystery Readers International, The Broken Shore* (FSG, 2007), *Truth* (FSG, 2010) and *Griffith Review*. 'Ithaca in My Mind' was first published by Allen & Unwin in 2012; 'A Novel of Menace' was first published in the Text Publishing edition of *Wake in Fright* in 2001. 'Reading the Country' is an edited version of the Miles Franklin Oration which Peter Temple delivered at the University of Melbourne on 7 June 2011. Peter Temple's original script for *Valentine's Day* is published courtesy of December Media. Many thanks to Jason Steger for his help in retrieving Peter Temple's extraordinary contribution to the review pages of the *Age*.

Published by The Text Publishing Company, 2019

Book design by Text
Cover photograph by Candy Bryce
Typeset by J&M Typesetting

Printed and bound in Australia by Griffin Press, part of Ovato, an accredited ISO/NZS 14001:2004 Environmental Management System printer

ISBN: 9781922268273 (paperback)
ISBN: 9781925774986 (ebook)

A catalogue record for this book is available from the National Library of Australia

CONTENTS

A CHARISMATIC CURMUDGEON

MICHAEL HEYWARD

WHEN *TRUTH* was published, in 2009, it capped off an extraordinary decade and a half of writing for Peter Temple. His first novel, *Bad Debts*, had come out in 1996 when he was about to turn fifty. Peter had arrived in Australia in 1979, after leaving his native South Africa at the height of apartheid. He had worked in journalism and academia in Sydney, Bathurst and Melbourne. He was and remained in love with Australia. 'I'm Australian by rebirth,' he once said. In 1989, with his wife Anita Rose-Innes and their son Nicholas, he decamped to Ballarat, ninety minutes west of Melbourne, and there he stayed, inevitably with a poodle or two at his feet.

In the thirteen years after *Bad Debts*, Peter published nine novels and a range of stories. He wrote a screenplay, which was turned into the delightful telemovie *Valentine's Day*. He turned out dozens of brilliant book reviews. By the time of his death, in March 2018, at the age of seventy-one, he was an internationally celebrated author, the first Australian to win the Gold Dagger in London, and the only crime writer to win the Miles Franklin.

He was a late starter. Could he write fiction worth the candle? *Bad Debts* was set in Melbourne where Peter had lived for just a few years. Could he bring it to life in a novel? Here is its opening page. It's the first time we hear the voice of Jack Irish:

> I found Edward Dollery, age forty-seven, defrocked
> accountant, big spender and dishonest person, living in

a house rented in the name of Carol Pick. It was in a new brick-veneer suburb built on cow pasture east of the city, one of those strangely silent developments where the average age is twelve and you can feel the pressure of the mortgages on your skin.

Eddie Dollery's skin wasn't looking good. He'd cut himself several times shaving and each nick was wearing a little red-centred rosette of toilet paper. The rest of Eddie, short, bloated, was wearing yesterday's superfine cotton business shirt, striped, and scarlet pyjama pants, silk. The overall effect was not fetching.

'Yes?' he said in the clipped tone of a man interrupted while on the line to Tokyo or Zurich or Milan. He had both hands behind his back, apparently holding up his pants.

'Marinara, right?' I said, pointing to a small piece of hardened food attached to the pocket of his shirt.

Eddie Dollery looked at my finger, and he looked in my eyes, and he knew. A small greyish probe of tongue came out to inspect his upper lip, disapproved and withdrew.

A reader might grow old hunting about for the equal of that final paragraph. All of Peter Temple's books are studded with diamonds cut like this. He wrote spare, audacious sentences that give shape to emotion, like poor Eddie Dollery's fear, for which we hardly know whether to feel compassion or contempt. Pain, grief and melancholy course through Temple's fiction, but there isn't a page without sly humour or where the language doesn't gleam. His heroes—Jack Irish, or Joe Cashin from *The Broken Shore*, damaged, wounded charmers— never lose their dry wit. When Jack Irish isn't part of a scam at the track or planing aged walnut boards in Charlie Taub's workshop, he listens to Mahler and breakfasts on anchovy toast, drinking tea from bone china. Some of Temple's female readers discreetly inquired if it might be arranged for them to sleep with Jack Irish.

Temple wrote four Jack Irish novels, and five standalone novels, including the international thriller *In the Evil Day*. It was *The Broken Shore* (2005) that made him famous and brought him the audience he deserved. It sold over 100,000 copies in Australia, and was published in more than twenty countries. *Truth* was darker and sadder, a long masterly bass note about the futility of things. When it won the Miles Franklin, Peter was astonished. He had already sent me a form guide describing each of the contenders as if they were horses at the barrier. He rated his own chances at 200/1: 'Ancient country harness racer attempting new career. Should be a rule against this. No.'

The Red Hand celebrates all these achievements: it includes a big chunk of an unfinished Jack Irish novel about an art scam, which we have called *High Art*, along with the best of his short fiction, some moving and entertaining reflections about his adopted country, a sample of his book reviews, especially of other crime writers, and the original screenplay of *Valentine's Day*.

It doesn't include any of his emails, but Temple was a master of the form. From the time that we began publishing him at Text, in 2003, every day was spiced with the possibility that Temple was likely to email us, possibly repeatedly. If he did, the day instantly became more entertaining, or terrifying, or both. He emailed when he needed something, when he was bored, when he wanted to annoy me or to make me laugh.

Like Jack Irish, Temple was a skilful debt collector. He had a gift for sending reminders about the folding stuff.

Dear M: Concerning the money, how long is ASAP? So far, it's a week. Of course, the matter could be lost inside the large bureaucracy you now command. Exactly how big is the Text Accounts Department? Best, Peter

If that didn't work, there were other equally inventive approaches:

Dear M: Please send me a test e-mail. Try to say something interesting (such as why your cheque hasn't arrived). Best, Peter

And then there was the nuclear threat:

> Dear M: We need to talk. Or would you prefer Orange? Best, Peter

I always preferred Agent Orange, a fop with a nose for cash and expensive booze who could never be reached on the phone and who inevitably emailed from a prone position on a superyacht moored somewhere off the coast of Mustique while being served margaritas by the improbably named Nurse Flagstaff. Orange was an unusual literary agent. He had only one client, and he liked to resolve matters, as he said, 'at Sans Culotte over a few morsels and a bottle or two of a decent Romanée-Conti'. He was full of fabulous bullshit. He once chastised me for asking to read the new Peter Temple novel we were negotiating over:

> My dear Michael: I must confess to be flabbergasted at your wish to see an actual manuscript. I have not seen an actual manuscript since I sold Scotty's *Tender Is the Night* to Scribner's. Complete waste of time, reading manuscripts. Yours, Orange

Nonetheless, Orange was certain his client was, as he claimed, 'an authentic genius and more versatile than Mata Hari'. He was so much fun to talk to that I would string the negotiation out as long as possible, even when Orange was sulking, which he frequently did.

> My dear Michael: I trust you will not be offended if I say that my client is beginning to wonder if you have any staff left, and, more importantly, any money. Yours in disappointment, Orange

For a man so languid, Orange was most alive to the fact that his author was in constant danger of being poached by rival publishers.

> My dear Michael: As your intelligence service will no doubt have reported to you, Peter has been importuned by two publishers suggesting quote fresh starts unquote. One

of these rascals had the impertinence to say that my client was a proven publishing harlot and the only matter for discussion was price...As always, we send our warmest salutations and look forward to a frank exchange of lies. Yours, Orange

But Orange was not entirely without principles. It would have been a breach of faith for him to accept an opening offer:

My dear Michael: You find me in the last minutes before the flight to Mustique. Here the leaves have lost their grip, the ice is in the air, and I feel a strong sense of the ending of days. I have put your offer to my client and, my word, didn't we chuckle. I look forward to a much improved second proposal. For some reason, other publishers think a new Temple is worth more. Yours, Orange

And Orange disapproved of Temple negotiating directly with me, something we did by accident from time to time:

My dear Michael: My client informs me that he has committed the sin of speaking directly to you on matters contractual. The silly man is engaged in self-flagellation even as I dictate this to my amanuensis. I cannot, of course, accept your ludicrous offer...But now it is time for the dip off one's beach, followed by the pre-prandial jug of gin and lime, the light repast of grilled manta ray, and the nap-nap. Yours in boundless admiration, Orange

After the deal was done, while Orange resumed his comatose condition, we could find other ways to entertain ourselves. When Stieg Larsson was selling squillions of copies, Peter and I wrote to each other for a while in fake Swedish. I asked him to write a novel in which a Swedish detective becomes lost in the Australian desert. I told him it would be an instant bestseller. Peter sent me the opening page of the novel I had commissioned:

The sun was staring from the sky like a monstrous eye when Lars crossed the burning sand to the vehicle. He could not meet the savage gaze of the dog on the back. It appeared to be a cross between a pitbull and an Irish wolfhound and was tied to the rollbar with rusty barbed wire. It was chewing on the leg of a kangaroo. The kangaroo was making small sounds.

'Where ya flamin goin, ya bastard?' said the driver. He was a huge man, wearing only a Speedo bathing costume. His entire body except for his head was covered with brown hair like coir. On his upper lip was tattooed F U C K.

'Darwin,' said Lars. 'I am going across the great Aussie outback to Darwin.'

'Fucken Darwin,' said the man. 'Fuck all in fucken Darwin, mate. Where ya fucken from, ya bastard?'

'I am from Sweden,' said Lars. 'I am Lars Holmsakort, a private investigator from Sweden.'

'Fucken Sweden, hey,' said the man. 'Fucken IKEA. Rootin this fucken sheila on the fucken table, the fucken legs fall off. Fuck fucken IKEA.'

Peter invented Lars to entertain me but he was otherwise the harshest critic of his own writing. He loved complex plots and tortured himself trying to wrestle them into submission. 'The fucking thing has about fifteen strands,' he wrote to me about *Truth*. 'I am like those Telstra men you see in holes by the roadside, except they look happy and they know what to do.' Some of Peter's journalism students still wear the scars of his insistence on craft. Editing him was like editing granite. He loathed it: 'I have done all the corrections AND I DON'T WANT ANY MORE FUCKING EDITING.'

He was curious and sceptical about everything. He gave the impression that he had networks of informers all over the place providing him with the inside story, a capacity he shared with Jack Irish. He had read everything. He was proud, shy, outrageously funny, a charismatic curmudgeon. Writers are sometimes plainer than their books, but Peter's conversation could light up a room. He loved pushing relationships to their limits. 'Michael: Are we breaking bread on Monday night or would you rather break my neck? Yours, Peter.' He could be disarmingly generous and completely ruthless. He knew how to parse both a sentence and a society. He brought the sensibility of a poet to the demands of the crime novel. His incomparable ear gave us dialogue that is a brutal celebration of the way we speak. So much of *The Red Hand* reveals his endless facination with Australian speech.

When we sold his novels to FSG in the US, the American publisher asked him to write glossaries to unlock his Australian idioms. Peter relished this assignment, and I have included them in *The Red Hand*. Defining 'sanger' he wrote, 'Sandwiches. Someone who fancied a chicken sausage sandwich could ask for a chook snag sanger.' Trackies, he wrote, are 'tracksuits, two-piece garments once worn only by people engaged in athletic pursuits, now worn by people who wish they had.'

Peter wanted to write a sequel to *Truth* and to write his fifth Jack Irish novel, but the books eluded him. He became an even more merciless critic of his own work. He worried that he had run out of things to say. He would write a draft, reread it, report to me how awful it was, and throw it away. It would have been unacceptable to submit a novel to his publisher which might fall short. His failure to produce another novel after *Truth* was the price he was prepared to pay for writing books that mattered so much. But if he was tormented by the prospect of a new manuscript it was always entertaining to torment his publisher too. He once emailed me to say that a manuscript was on the way only to send a message the next day headed 'False Dawn'.

He heard us and saw us, our lies, our loves, our corruption and our kindness. His novels will be required reading for historians of Melbourne. He wrote about the city from the inside out: its football, its racetracks, its cafes and back lanes, its bent politicians and shonky property developers. He wrote again and again about men, pummelled by life, for whom humour, carpentry, horse racing and other diversions make the sadness bearable. He caught the signature accents of friendship between men, often separated by culture or race, survivors staring down their grief and rage. This is what connects Jack Irish with a character like the swaggie Rebb from *The Broken Shore*, a man who would otherwise be invisible in our society.

After he won the Miles Franklin, and had been given the award at a dinner in Sydney, the Text contingent flew back to Melbourne together. Our sales and marketing director, Kirsty Wilson, always a great champion of Peter's work, let the flight crew know that the winner of the Miles was on board. As we began our descent, the captain announced Peter's triumph over the PA and offered his congratulations. Our fellow passengers burst into cheering and applause. It was a wonderful moment. Peter pretended to be horrified but got off the plane with a secret half-smile, his response to the folly of things, which is how I remember him.

FROM *HIGH ART,*
AN UNFINISHED JACK IRISH NOVEL

JOE MIRVIC made many marks on society, all of the kind that grew scar tissue.

Now tiny creatures—ants, mosquitos, wasps, worms, and a species of tiny caterpillar with bulbous eyes and scissor-like jaws—were making marks on Joe.

They covered his bloated stomach, the greying chest thicket, his throat and face. They were exploring Joe's eyes, ears and his shaven head.

And birds were standing around. They had been pecking at him. One expected more of birds.

Joe was becoming part of the forest floor, of the rainforest ecology, a contributor to the great chain of being. It was a wonderful setting for him finally to be of some value—a valley full of birdsong with two quicksilver creeks sliding over pebbles, bickering when they merged and vanished into the greenery.

After weeks of looking for Joe, a tip-off sent me to this place. In the shack, I found a gas-bottle lamp, a sleeping bag, dirty clothes, empty vodka bottles, stale bread, and milk cartons with recent use-by dates.

I wandered around for a while and was about to leave when I saw the big black ants.

Ants on the march, ants disciplined as legionnaires, led me to the body.

I had no doubt that it was Joe, but certainty required a sight of his left hand.

Denise Coogan, a brothel queen, had positioned a square whisky glass on the fingers of Joe's left hand and stamped on it with her Italian boot. This made Joe's four fingers all the same length as the pinky.

Denise was known for going too far. Nuded-up, she weighed in at 110 kilograms. Simply placing the weight of a leg and a shuddery sofa-buttoned buttock on the glass would have amputated Joe's digits.

The hand was now covered in tiny feeders. I found a fallen piece of the rainforest, possibly a limb of quandong or the rarer birrabindi, and used it to beat off the creatures.

Bad news for my client's client.

Joe wouldn't be providing alibis for anyone.

I swatted the insects from his mighty stomach. Now I could see what looked like both exit and entrance wounds. Shot in the back, then turned over and shot three or four times in the chest.

More overkill, but it couldn't be Denise because her work on Joe's hand caused him to have her sailor-tossed off a sixteen-storey building.

Time to go home.

I took the swatting branch with me. It would harbour bits of my sweat and serve only to confuse the forensic geniuses who had Joe in their future.

Low gear all the way, I drove the Falcon out of the valley, grinding up the steep and winding road to the junction on the spine of the mountain. You could see the sea from here, the tower blocks at the water's edge and the houses packed in behind them. Soon everyone would live at the sea in Chinese subdivisions and Chinese peasants would farm the outback.

Near Brisbane, I stopped at a service station and rang the number.

'Helloo,' said a man.

I could hear the clicking of pool balls, coarse laughter.

I asked for Collo.

'Which Collo, mate?'

'Pigtail and missing front tooth.'

'Mate, mate, that's all the Collos.'

'Spider tatt on his forehead. Dead centre.'

'Narrows it. And you are?'

'Jeremy. Try Jeremy.'

He shouted, 'Collo, darling, it's a Jeremy. Know any Jeremys, doll?'

I listened to laughter and rude words while I watched a man shouting at two small boys trying to kill each other in the back seat of a station wagon.

'Yeah?'

'Jack. The car.'

'How'd it go?'

'Top machine. Purrs.'

'Done with it then?'

'Dusted.'

'Back where you got it,' he said. 'Ticket on the seat, lock up. Chuck the key down a drain. Got lots of keys.'

I did as I was told, walked three blocks from the parking garage, caught a cab to the airport. All the way, the driver, who told me he was from Pakistan, lectured on the superiority of Queensland to all other states and territories.

'Been to them all?' I said.

'Virtually. But not necessarily.'

At the airport, I loitered until a public telephone became vacant. Wootton answered the third number dialled.

'This matter is concluded,' I said.

'You're sure?'

I'd endured more privations than Scott in his polar stupidity.

'No, I'm not sure,' I said. 'It's all conjecture and surmise. Wild fucking guesses.'

'Steady on, old boot,' said Wootton. 'You may have gone troppo. This news will make someone very happy.'

An ancient woman in combat gear was staring at me, willing me to finish.

I stared back. Why couldn't she use a mobile? Public telephones were for people with something to hide.

'Happy, Cyril?' I said. 'I thought this prick was needed to pull the sword out of the stone?'

'Perhaps I didn't spell it out in block letters.'

I engaged in eye-combat with the whippet-thin woman.

'I'll be around, Cyril,' I said. 'My plan is to make someone very unhappy. It's you, you prick.'

I flew home on the 4.10pm, mercifully between mealtimes, spared the choice between two kinds of tasteless and soggy-bottomed Qantas rolls.

'NO KNOCK, no nothing,' said Charlie Taub. 'She walks around like it's a shop. She touches.'

Silence.

Charlie was applying his own-brand sanding sealer to the top of a hall table, dabbing a huge index finger into a Chinese takeaway container, rubbing the substance into the wood. Applying too much sealer meant scraping it off later, a skill in itself and a complete waste of time. I was permanently excused from the humble task of the sealing before the sanding.

'I'm astonished you saw her do that,' I said. 'You being crouched and holding your breath behind the chisel cabinet.'

I was in the armchair, bottom almost touching the floor, trying to make sense of a drawing Charlie had done for me. It was hard to get him to commit anything to paper and when he did it was on anything to hand—old envelopes, strips torn off the *Age*, the chests of young women in the lingerie catalogues that came through the letterbox. He also wrote notes no Enigma codebreakers could have deciphered. Had Charlie been running German codes in World War Two, the whole world would be eating raw fugu fish on Bavarian-style pickled cabbage.

'A kitchen,' said Charlie. 'That's what she wants.'

'At the heart of family life, the kitchen.' It was easy to drowse, sitting close to the stove burning the fragrant offcuts of priceless timbers from the store in the roof.

'This looks like a place makes a kitchen?' said Charlie.

'Well, it could be a kitchen for all the generations to come,' I said. 'Ancient craft skills applied to two-thousand-year-old timbers. Why not?'

Charlie gazed at me from under his yak eyebrows, head skewed, making it clear that he too feared what the tropics had done to my mental stability. 'Wasted,' he said. 'All my time wasted.'

He went back to rubbing.

'I think we should move to computer-aided design,' I said. 'Streamline this operation.'

'Going bang soon.'

'What?'

Charlie waved a huge hand. 'The Michaelatos grandson was here. Not a Greek to notice the boy. Red hair like that Kerry was on the ABC. I miss that Kerry.'

'What's he want?'

'A nice boy. You could learn manners from him.'

'I'm sure it was like a heavenly visitation.'

'Just a visit. He didn't touch.'

'That's the test now? The touch test. What possible harm could anyone do by touching anything in here? Except to themselves.'

Charlie was rubbing sealer into the grain, gentle movements. 'You never touched,' he said. 'That's why I let you bother me. A big mistake.'

'What's he want to talk about?'

'Superannuation. An expert.'

'Your superannuation?'

'Who else?'

'Charlie, you don't need super,' I said. 'You're not going to retire. What would you do? Drive the family mad?'

'I could retire, play bowls.' He snapped huge fingers. 'Club champion, just like that.'

'Rubbish,' I said. 'You play bowls now when you should be

working. Anyway, it's about sixty years too late to start super.'

'That's why it's time. Before it goes bang.'

I had a feeling about the Michaelatos' grandson and the imminent bang. I rose from my ground-zero position with difficulty, approached the grain-sealing operation. 'What's his name, the grandson?'

'James.'

'I know him. He calls himself Jamie Michaels.'

'Why you looking at me?' said Charlie. 'Do some work. Sit around here, you should be doing your profession. Wasted your father's money.'

'My father didn't have any money. What's Jamie want you to do?'

Charlie found something interesting in the patch of wood he was rubbing, perhaps a grain aberration, a lovely whorl, a twirl. He lowered his head to study it. 'Feed the stove,' he said. 'Freezing in here.'

'Jamie's got a plan, hasn't he?'

'Partnership,' said Charlie. 'Co-developers. Cost me nothing.'

'Just the building,' I said. 'You put in the building. Is that right?'

'Old building. Falling down. Roof leaks.'

'It's not falling down. Triple brick. The roof doesn't leak. I risked my life fixing the roof. I went up there in the rain, in a gale-force wind. I had to attach myself to the chimney with a rope.'

Charlie sighed, a sad deflating sound.

'Jamie wants to build something, does he?' I said.

'Jack, the family. Property goes bang, what's to leave? Like the Depression. Loaf bread, you need a basket of money.'

'Charlie, forget about property going bang, decent bread already costs a basket of money and the family's doing very nicely. They need nothing from you. I wish I'd married Gus when she proposed to me.'

Proposed was probably an overstatement. She had certainly looked at me in an appraising way.

'Jamie doesn't give a damn about your super, Charlie,' I said. 'He wants to make a lot of money out of you.'

The doubting look.

'And that retirement rubbish, Charlie,' I said. 'You hum all day. You whistle. I have to drag you out at night. That's work?'

'Well,' said Charlie, changing tack, 'maybe it's for you I'm whistling. You don't smile anymore. Maybe it's time you retire from looking for rubbish people.'

'This place open for business?'

In the doorway, against the light, Cameron Delray.

'The gambler,' said Charlie. 'At least he doesn't want a kitchen.'

'Brought some food,' said Cam. 'You eat lunch here? Stop the assembly line?'

'What kind of lunch?' said Charlie.

'Could be corned beef, gherkins and mustard. Could be on sour-dough rye, bit of lettuce.'

Charlie said, 'You're a good boy, Cam. For a gambler. Let me wash my hands.'

When he was gone, Cam said, 'You're scarce.'

'Been up north, studying the insect life eating dead people.'

'Dead people up there deserve to be eaten. Big man's going to NZed tonight. Know where that is?'

'Can I ask the audience?'

'Free?'

'I have to kill Cyril. After that I'm free. Never be freer.'

'ROBBY ROSS come to me through a bloke called Len Morton,' said Harry Strang. 'Long ago, just findin the feet again then. Forgot I had em for a while. Nice bloke, Len, a bit like Cam here. Born with the eye. Foaled, really.'

Cam nodded in a musing way, didn't look up from the breeder porn he was reading, a compendium of thoroughbred bloodlines.

We were above the planet in a twelve-seater jet, no sense of movement.

The door ahead slid and a man in a dark suit, neat hair, white shirt and a striped tie took the two paces.

'Sixty-two minutes to landing, gentlemen. Dinner will be served in a few minutes. It's what you had last time. The Crawford River sirloin, rare with sour-cream and wasabi sauce.'

'Bring it on,' said Cam.

'We've taken the liberty of accompanying it with potatoes dauphinoise and minted peas, Mr Strang.'

'A memory on you,' said Harry. 'Got that frog bread?'

Derek said, 'Unfortunately the Paris flight was late, so we've substituted a local loaf for the Poilâne. Made by a Frenchman, though. Out of the oven four hours ago and now digestible.'

'A substitute?' I said. 'Well, I don't know.'

'I can handle a local loaf,' said Cam. 'Loaf anywhere, really.'

The steward smiled at Cam. 'As for wine, sir,' he said to Harry.

'Perhaps the 2001 Cullen Diana Madeline? Mr Ross's favourite Australian.'

'An open mind, Robby,' said Harry. 'That'll do nicely, Derek.'

'Thank you, sir.'

'Robby Ross owns this?' I said.

'A syndicate,' said Harry. 'They've got a quid.'

He moved his shoulders inside his houndstooth jacket, looked at the roof. 'We'll have the crayfish goin home. The fisherman brings em to the plane, the buggers crawl on board.'

Fifty-nine minutes later, the jet touched earth with no bigger bump than a car crossing a cattlegrid, the impact scarcely agitated the last of the silken Diana Madeline in my glass. The brakes howled briefly, our upper bodies were pushed into the red leather armchairs.

'Good driver,' said Harry.

I watched the airport lights stream by. Derek appeared. 'Customs aboard shortly, gentlemen.'

We taxied to a spot well away from the terminal. Inside two minutes, Derek ushered in a man in a blue uniform carrying an electronic device. 'Good evening,' he said. 'Welcome to New Zealand. If I could see your passports.'

He placed each one face down on his machine for a second, then stamped it with an old-fashioned rubber stamp. 'Enjoy your stay,' he said and left.

'The transport awaits, gentlemen,' said Derek. 'Your luggage has been loaded. We look forward to flying you home tomorrow.'

A helicopter, a Bell, was parked a hundred metres away. I got the seat next to the pilot. Like many helicopter pilots, he was a big man and a gum chewer.

'G'day,' he said. He was Australian. 'Name's Geoff. Pity you won't be able to see the scenery. The sheep.'

We rose, the city opening beneath us. Geoff pointed out the landmarks. We followed a four-lane highway for a while, then veered left, the suburban lights thinned and the world below was dark, just a farmhouse here, a one-street hamlet there.

'Not many people,' I said.

Geoff nodded, chewing. 'Bit like the Ghan,' he said. 'Only the sheepshaggers here don't try to take you out with old SAM-7s.'

That was all he said until, twenty-five minutes later, he flicked switches, spoke into his throat mike. A long way off, a small glowing disc appeared in the black world. As we got closer, you could see the lights of what looked like a village and the glassy glint of moonlight on a lake.

It was just after midnight when the helicopter settled on the pad like a mother's hand. A Land Rover drove up and a young man got out, had his long hair blown about.

'Enjoy,' said Geoff. 'Robby's a serious host.'

The young man's red woollen jacket had Ross Estates embroidered above the breast pocket. 'I'm Murray,' he said. 'Hop in. I'll get the bags.'

It was a three-minute drive up a hill and down a dirt road between vineyard posts and into a complex of buildings, brick and wood, some joined by passages, some by covered walkways, some independent.

'What's this?' said Cam. 'He's got his own town?'

The driver laughed.

'A lot of friends,' said Harry. 'He doesn't like to turn anyone away.'

Robby Ross met us at the front door. He was a tall man, ski-tanned, broken nose, full head of grey hair cropped close and eyebrows left to go wild. 'Harry Strang,' he said. 'Come here, I want to kiss you.'

'Steady on, Rob,' said Harry. 'Haven't told me mum about us yet.'

They embraced. Harry was tall for a jockey but it was not a meeting of equals, not by half a metre.

'Cameron Delray,' said Harry.

They shook hands.

'Cam's got the eye,' said Harry.

'Stay as long as you like, Cam,' said Robby. 'In the President's Suite.'

Harry pointed at me.

'Jack Irish, the travellin lawyer.'

'Rather travel with a rattlesnake. But nice to meet you, Jack.'

We went into a room the size of a small parking lot, two storeys high, a fieldstone fireplace with an ox-size hearth. There were animal heads on all the walls: elephant, tiger, lion, cheetah, puma, leopard, buffalo, rhino, stag, moose, antelopes of all sizes, hyena, wild dog. On the floor near the entrance doors stood a man, head back, wrapped in a python.

I went closer. The man's mouth was open in agony, gold teeth glinted within.

'Dennis McGirr, bookie,' said Robby. 'Owes me a million and a half, he goes under, the bastard.'

I looked up at the nearest animal, the buffalo. Something wasn't quite right. It was smiling and winking, one large grey buffalo eyelid drooping. I looked at the elephant. It was smoking a cigarette. The wild dog had a collar and a licence disk and a small teddy bear in its mouth. The tiger had caught a bullet between its teeth. In its left eye, the lion was wearing a monocle.

'Job lot bought in Scotland,' said Robby. 'Got a film bloke to work them up for me. People come in here, give me the look. Animal killer. Never killed anything bar ducks. And fish. They don't count. Jesus was a killer. Killer of fish. Fisher of men.'

'Speakin of fishin,' said Harry.

'Let's go next door,' said Robby.

We went into a rough-plastered white room that could have been the snug of the pub in *The Quiet Man*. Robby opened a humidor.

Harry and Cam took Havanas from the humidor. I ached. It was like saying no to going upstairs with the prima ballerina of the Ballet Rambert.

Robby handed out balloon glasses. He used a silver instrument to draw the cork of a bottle of cognac and poured. I saw the ancient label and the pain of refusing a cigar receded a small distance.

We talked about the affairs of the world, got around to racing.

Then Robby said, 'It's about Prince Gustav.'

'I thought it might be,' said Harry.

Robby's horse Prince Gustav was a million-dollar stayer from Germany. He qualified for the Melbourne Cup by winning the Australasian Stayers Challenge, taking out the Wellington Cup, the Auckland Cup and the Metropolitan Handicap. Then, two days before the Geelong Cup, the last step in his preparation for the big one, he was found dead in his stable at Tower Run, a horse property on the Bellarine Peninsula.

'Got the reports,' said Robby. 'Not easily. All they say is heart failure.'

'Well,' said Harry. 'Not unknown.'

Robby took on a look not unlike that of the stuffed buffalo. 'What brought it on is bloody well unknown. Perfectly healthy horse has a heart attack in his stable.'

Harry blew Cohiba smoke my way.

'Given something, Robbo?' he said. 'Unknown substance? Thought you boys were the experts on them? Such as the Blue Magic.'

'Just because New Zealand is Australia's brain,' said Robby, 'you shouldn't think we know everything. I want you to find the bastards killed my lovely horse. Then I'll deal with them myself.'

Harry studied his cigar. The ash was five millimetres too short to tap off.

'More and more bad people around racin these days,' he said. 'Don't know that we can help here.'

'Harry, I don't care what it costs. Nobody does this to me.'

We sat in silence.

'What's your Melbourne associate say?' said Harry.

'He ruled out the obvious. He's shit-scared, I reckon. I've been in the hands of your racing idiots. Ex-cops, I gather. Probably still on the take. Of course, the brass want the whole thing to go away.'

'Trying to protect racing's good name.'

'In Oz? Are you mad? What good name is that?'

'Being so hard on us, Robbo,' said Harry. 'Handle the bettin yourself?'

Robbo closed his eyes. 'I know I should have come to you, Harry. I wanted to but bloody Gavin Roxley talked me out of it. How'd you think I feel now sitting here asking you for help? Like a proper arse, that's how I feel.'

'Don't feel too bad,' said Harry. 'I'd have turned you down.'

The discussion continued. After a while, I wilted. A stern woman in a tweed suit showed me to my quarters.

'There's a button next to the lamp,' she said. 'Ring if you need anything within reason. There's freshly ground coffee in the kitchen. Goodnight, Mr Irish.'

'Goodnight, matron,' I said.

I SLEPT in silk sheets on a bed that held me as if it cared, woke in the dark, in peace. At first gleaming, I rose, showered, clothed myself. In the kitchen, I filtered coffee, Lost Horizon, by the aroma.

I took the brew onto the verandah and looked upon a world lost in mist. In minutes, the dawn sawtoothed a high eastern range, then the lake below showed itself in dull-silver glints. Soon I could see vines all around. They followed the contours of the slopes, going over the hills to God knows where.

Cam came out in a white bathrobe, carrying a cup and saucer. He took the chair beside me.

'Up early,' he said. 'Didn't know that about you.'

'Only had to ask. First decent sleep for weeks. So what about this?'

'That snake crushing the bookie,' said Cam. 'Harry told me when he was a boy of fifteen, on his first decent chance in the bush, a bloke offered him a sling to pull the horse. He said, won. They come back to find his dad's ute got four flats, the dog's baited. Dog on a chain on the tray. Dying.'

In the lightening day, the vine leaves were darkest green. The nearest were a few metres away, grapes in small, tight bunches.

'What did they do?'

Cam yawned, stretched arms, scratched his scalp with both hands. 'Next meeting, the book's putting his bag in the boot, two brown snakes come up to greet him.'

'Nothing faster than a brown.'

'Bookie. A bookie's faster. But not fast enough.'

I went inside and filtered more coffee. Harry came in wrapped in fluffy white towelling, tiny bare feet.

'Jack,' he said. 'I smelled the coffee in me dream.'

We sat outside, in a row.

'Nice place,' said Harry. 'The boy tells me twenty million's gone in and it's down to losin thirty bucks on every bottle of wine.'

'I can feel his pain,' I said.

'Give the school away at fourteen, Robby,' said Harry. 'Dad was a postie, calves on him like footballs from riding the pushbike up the steep bits.'

He sipped, sighed, looked into the cup. 'Decent drop this, get the sugar in. Robby was in pubs, buyin and sellin. Then it was the junk food, early in there with the Yanks, sellin the pizzas, the hamburgers. Didn't put a hoof wrong in the junk. Now it's your hotels, your resorts, everything.'

Silence.

I became aware of an eerie trilling, at the edge of hearing.

'What's that sound?'

'Weird,' said Cam.

'Horses and boats,' said Harry. 'When your usual idiot's got the mansion, the cars, the boat, the horses, he wants to breed his own winners. No idea what they're gettin into. Robby's too smart for that.'

A man and a large dog were in the vineyard. The pecking fowls ignored them.

'Huntaway,' said Cam.

'What?'

'The dog.'

The man set off between rows. Here and there, he picked grapes, eating some, doing something to others.

'What's he doing?' I said.

'Measuring sugar,' said Cam.

'How do you know that?'

'Everyone knows that. Deciding when to pick. It's late for vintage here. Probably the riesling.'

'Toiled in the vineyard, have you?'

'Worked for the mafia, yes. Nice blokes some of em.'

'Probably led astray by the bigger boys,' I said.

In silence, we watched the man going down the row. He looked up and waved. We responded.

'Rob's narked by what happened to his horse,' said Harry.

'Hard to miss that,' I said.

'Don't know we can do anything,' Cam said.

'No,' said Harry. 'So I'll tell him you boys aren't keen.'

A phone rang. Cam went in, came out again.

'Breakfast in twenty,' he said loudly.

Harry rubbed his hands. 'Best bacon-and-eggs on earth comin up. Eggs from those chooks down there. The man's got pigs eat acorns.'

'So far to come for acorn bacon,' I said. 'We could ask around about the horse, I suppose. Provided Robby's serious about unlimited money.'

Harry looked at Cam, who nodded.

Harry rose, put hands on our shoulders. 'Good boys. It'll be worth it, I promise you. Won't hurt either if some bastards get a kick up the arse.'

JUST AFTER dark, Cam dropped me at the old boot factory. The park was empty and the inner city had lowered its volume for a few seconds, one of the strange moments in the day when all the traffic lights seemed to be on red, when no one hooted, when all the trains stood silent in the stations.

Perhaps the traffic control system had blown a fuse, perhaps the trains had broken down in the stations. This was Melbourne after all.

Then, from the direction of Hoddle Street, there was the vicious squeal-snarl of a car burning rubber, probably a carjacking by a group of unreconstructed Sudanese boy soldiers armed with machetes on their way to rob a jewellery shop.

Semper aliquid novi Africam adferre.

I went upstairs, unlocked the front door and the sight of my accommodation produced a caress of distaste—this was the penalty for spending time in the abodes of the extremely rich. Furnishings that had seemed so clubby and comfortable on my return from Queensland now looked mouldy and sad, all the pictures askew, the feeling of dust in the air.

I did not want to eat rich food again, ever. What I needed was a glass of pineapple juice followed by raw oats soaked in cold milk.

But what I was going to have was a slow bottle of Cooper's Pale Ale and, in time, a toasted cheese sandwich, perhaps two, just bread and cheese, squeezed flat enough to mark the place in a book.

There were ten messages on the machine. Never again would I put off listening to messages. The first was from Linda Hillier in London. The following eight included three from clients with trouble understanding the slow peacock dance of the law, one from my sister, who understood my dancing perfectly, one from a woman who said, '*It's Lyndall, Jack, I'll try again*', one from a man who said, '*Oh, fuck*', one from a man who cleared his throat horribly and hung up, one from Andrew Greer, my former partner-at-law, and one from Kevin Trapaga, mechanic, who thought my Studebaker Hawk Lark needed a 1200-kilometre test drive to the architectural hot spot of Merimbula.

The last message was again from Linda. She said:

Listen, sunshine, your window is now the size of a stamp. Ring any time, night and day. We never sleep. Unless exhausted by the demands of pale unwashed Englishmen. At least I think they're men.

I fetched the Cooper's from the fridge. What was the time in London? Mid-morning? She did evening drive-time, she could be at home getting ready, reading the papers, two television sets and two radios on. I could see the telephone on the table in the deep dormer window. I had often sat there, reading, listening to Linda on the radio, looking at the square below, the Bulgarian, Estonian and Australian nannies walking their babies, pausing to exchange universal nanny-whinges.

The phone rang.

'Jack Irish.'

'This is London calling.'

'Is that Jack London? In the frozen north? Do I hear a dog barking?'

'The dogs are barking, the bells are tolling, the eagle's screaming, the competition's offered to double my salary, a two-year contract, a flat in Chelsea and, take special note here, a golden hello of fifty thousand pounds. How's that?'

'Tell them to get back to you when they're serious.'

'I think you should get your arse over here,' she barrow boys are willing to put you on the payroll.'

'Only if I can do the shortwave Falkland Islands talkback. Advice for those in unhappy sheep relationships.'

'I fought for that. But it's researcher stroke legal advisor. Working ex-office, as in bathtub in Chelsea, at local pub, at Ladbroke's. Then you convey your findings to me in circumstances of our own choosing.'

My gaze had found a high corner of the room and a small spider beginning to rappel down a cliff of air. 'People will say the boyfriend's on the payroll. Doing sweet buggerall.'

'Of course they'll say that. What does it matter? If you don't want the job, I'll put the golden hello in your account, you can give it back some time, you can give it to Oxfam, you can piss it against a wall. I don't care.'

Why not?

I took a deep breath. 'I'm flattered,' I said. 'But I've got some things on the go.'

'Jack,' she said, 'in my halting and stammering way, I'm saying I'd like us to be together.'

I said, 'Ditto. But I can't just walk away.'

Linda sighed. 'Can you ask Cam if he'd like the gig? I've always felt the chemistry between us.'

'Feeling chemistry is enough. Give me a month.'

'Max. Then it's eurotrash by the six-pack.'

We talked about other things, laughed, both a bit hollow, said goodbye.

The tiny spider was going up now, going home to the cornice. I finished the beer, fetched another bottle, and lay on the old leather sofa, feet on the arm, head on a cushion. I listened to the sounds of the reawakened city, an annoyed toothy, snarling creature. Then I put on the television and a world of pain, grief, hatred and inconsequential rubbish was presented to me.

The impulse came.

Ring Linda back. Say I'd be there in two weeks. The worst of winter was over in England. In the spring, we could go to Linda's friend's house on the river in Devon, we could go walking in Wales.

And we could go to Paris.

We could take the top-floor rooms in the battered Hotel Wagram, sleep late, breakfast on croissants and coffee with the papers. Then we'd walk, look at paintings we'd seen before, walk some more, eat lunch in the less-smart places, test the Wagram mattress, nap, read, go out to listen to music and eat and drink, go to bed and plan how to do the same things again, only better.

Was there more to life?

Probably not, but I did know that in the times of indolence and hedonism, I often caught Linda glassy-eyed, saw her write quickly in her notebook, make excuses for catching the television news. And then there were the mobile calls, coming and going, six or seven to the hour.

Linda was paid a fortune to do her job. I would be a bystander, an idler, a person without task or purpose, without a single useful thing to do. Not so much a mature toyboy as a faithful old teddy with a piece of ear missing from the time the dog got excited.

Thank you, but no.

Food.

I had the ancient bread, I had the dehydrated cheese, I had the power to fuse them irrevocably.

The phone rang. I said my name.

'Jack, mate, caught you. Barry Chilvers.'

'You're Oh, fuck, aren't you?'

'Hate leaving messages, I can't do it.'

Barry taught constitutional law at Melbourne University. He should have been a professor but he didn't publish enough. It was remarkable that he published anything at all because, as the years passed, he came to see the shadow of the Gulag in every imprisoning of a parking ticket behind a windscreen wiper.

'People could be listening,' I said.

Barry coughed. 'Some advice on a property law matter needed. A lease a friend of mine wants to enter into. No use asking anyone around here. Not rarefied enough, not a summit-of-Everest property law matter. A foothills matter, a bump.'

'I am,' I said, 'the master of the lower levels of the leasing landscape, of the merest undulations.'

'Coffee tomorrow? What time?'

I gave it some thought. 'Seven-thirty,' I said. 'That's in the pre-noon part of the day.'

A groan. 'Jesus, Jack, have a heart.'

'Seven-thirty,' I said, 'is your pinhole of opportunity. Pinprick.'

In the night, I woke and listened to the city, the pricks, dabs and smears of sound, and I thought about the voice on the phone:

It's Lyndall, Jack, I'll try again.

After three years of silence.

TWO PIECES of dirty plywood had replaced the plate-glass window of Enzio's in Brunswick Street. It was not a look that would encourage passers-by to pop in.

From the service hatch, Enzio saw me enter. I scarcely had time to nod to Bruno the Silent and sit down in the dim and near-empty room when Enzio was standing over me.

'Where you been?' he said, deep frown lines. 'Not at the office, not at home.'

'I've been travelling. Eating in smart places where the cooks shave as often as twice a week.'

Enzio put a hand to his chin and took on the startled look of a man who sees in a bathroom mirror that he has grown a full beard overnight. He recovered quickly, sat down.

'Listen, Jack,' he said, 'There's a phone before yesterday, they tell Carmel to call me, it's business. I think it's the wine reps, no, it's this bloke. He says they can give me twenty-four-hour security.'

'I'm meeting someone here in half an hour,' I said. 'I thought I might eat first.'

Enzio waved his hands. 'Fuck eating,' he said. 'I said I got the alarms, I got the insurance. He says, no, no, we can save your whole business, we can make sure you still got a business. And he laughs, the cunt.'

A tall woman came in, a serious face, strong dark hair

finger-combed, light topcoat: dressed for Paris in the spring. She looked around and our eyes met. For an instant, she thought she knew me. I wished that she did.

Enzio lowered his voice. 'I'm lookin out the window, Jack, I'm lookin across the road, I see two blokes in a black Beemer, the driver, he's on the phone, he's lookin at me. The other one, he look too. I remember him, fat bastard, no hair, no ears. Like a wrestler.'

'Remember him?'

'They sit over there,' said Enzio, pointing at the corner near the door. 'The thin cunt, for him scrambled eggs too soft, sausages got no taste, he doesn't want pesto on the tomatoes. Plus he wants more fucking toast.'

I said, 'I don't think we should dismiss this man's legitimate concerns out of hand.'

'Jack, on the phone he says four hundred a week. Cash.'

Another customer came in, a person known to me and to the arson squad, he would not be daunted by the bombsite appearance of the place. Now there were six paying people on site. Alana, the confident new recruit, was taking orders.

She could take but could she deliver?

'What did you say?' I said.

'What you think I say? Fuckoff, that's what I say.'

'Right. They did this that night?'

'A piece of pipe.' He made a circle with finger and thumb. 'I kill them.'

'What do the cops say?'

'They say nothing. Like it's bad luck, like a storm broke my window. Hailstones.'

'You told them about these blokes?'

Enzio didn't want to look at me, he was glowering at the plywood. 'Can't get glass till this afternoon,' he said.

'You told the cops?'

'What for? Could be the cops.'

'Enzio,' I said. 'Don't be a prick. You report crimes. You put crimes on record. You can tell them what the men look like. Chances are they've got form like Black Caviar. You don't tell the cops, these blokes are laughing. They think you're too scared to tell the cops.'

Enzio stared at me, narrow eyes, raised a hand and tried to find some hairs to run his thick fingers through. 'Scared? I show them fucking scared.'

'Report this to the cops,' I said. 'That's my advice. Do you want my advice, Enzio?'

'Jack, to talk to cops, I don't, I'm not...no. You can do the insurance for me?'

In dealing with some clients, there is a moment when the legal practitioner must encourage them to reflect on why they have sought professional advice rather than relying on, say, the judgement of their friend's sister, who once heard a caller talk about a similar matter on the radio. This seemed to me to be the time for this approach.

'Enzio,' I said, 'make an appointment to see me. Ring my answering machine. And now, my breakfast order is smoked trout on toast, that's newly depackaged trout, one grilled tomato, that's halves of the same tomato, not fried in old bacon fat but grilled, with olive oil and a pinch of sugar and no pesto. Plus another slice of toast, warm toast, if the food-preparation technology makes that possible. And with it all some butter. And a tablespoon of Vegemite, that's not a one-teaspoon plastic container but a tablespoon from a bottle of Vegemite.'

Unhappy, Enzio went to the galley. The food came in ten minutes flat, prepared as specified, which gave me time to eat in peace and read the small section of the *Age* mini-newspaper that contained actual news of events.

Barry Chilvers arrived when I had moved on to a story in one of the lifestyle sections about a course for business executives offered by two bondage professionals. He was wearing a mouldy op-shop suit and carrying a briefcase tied up with rope. The ensemble was topped off by a Fitzroy Football Club beanie, now collectible.

He put the briefcase on a chair, looked around through smudged glasses, removed the headgear. This revealed a severe, self-inflicted haircut. The overall effect was homeless recovering-alcoholic.

'Jesus, Jack, since when did it get light this early?' he said.

'Every day for those who don't live on planet academic. Short black?'

'Please, God. If there is one.'

'There certainly is a short black. That's not mystical conjecture.'

I looked at the maker. Alerted by the sound of my eyeballs moving, Bruno the Silent had me in his gaze. I made the polite sign for two. No response.

'So, Barry,' I said. 'A leasing matter too trivial for the scholars.'

Eyelids narrowed. 'Trigger word and they're recording.'

'Is that your phone or mine?'

Barry made a fluttering gesture, presumably picked up in some culture to which I was unexposed.

'Delicate, Jack,' he said. 'The word is Pel.'

'Oh, God.'

Pel was Pelham College. My former partner-at-law spent his student years in this Melbourne University residence founded in 1879 by Lucas Pelham, whose tallow factory poisoned the Yarra River for sixty years. Pelham was an atheist rationalist, so the college was favoured by the unreligious rich. Their children had dominated the university's academic results and the vicious-loner sports like squash and fencing. A sortie into track and field athletics failed, particularly in the relay races, where Pelham runners were reluctant to hand over the baton.

At games like chess, draughts, go, Scrabble, Boggle, Babble, Stabble—indeed any game favouring mind over matter—Pelhamites crushed all comers.

The place would now be infested with pallid techno-geeks and geekesses busily inventing applications. Whatever applications were.

'I'm trying to keep out of delicate stuff, Barry. So if it's not a little leasing technicality, why don't you…'

'It's a matter of a missing Pel tutor.'

Tiredness claimed me in the sudden and diminishing way it did when you had been up late, indulging without care, perhaps dancing, a bulb aglow with immortality until the filament failed.

I gave him the cross-examination stare.

'Missing for how long?'

Barry looked around as if he had heard ears moving or mice breathing. The arsonist was furiously spooning something healthy out of a bowl. All healthy foods were now served in bowls. Bits of health attached themselves to his moustache like tiny creatures fighting to survive a tsunami.

'A while,' he said. 'A month or so.'

'My, you Pels move like greyhounds. Anyway, I don't care if this involves the Pel dachshund. Go to the police, Barry. Now take up your shabby bag and depart. I've got form to do.'

Silence. He did not leave.

'I'll just have my coffee,' he said.

Alana delivered the glasses in a professional manner.

I sipped, felt a trifle less weak. Chilvers was staring at his small vessel as if he had expected a mug of Nescafe.

'Never got over Pel, have you?' I said. 'Pathetic.'

'Best years of my life.'

'Such a sad confession, Barry. It's worse than saying you loved the altar-boy years.'

'A brotherhood,' he said. 'You wouldn't understand.'

'No I don't and nor do I wish to.'

Barry pulled a clown-like face.

'I'm pleading, Jack. You're a lawyer. Well, of a sort.'

'Whose fees are exorbitant when the rich are paying.'

'Bill by the hour. The actual hour worked.'

'I often work in my sleep,' I said. 'Barry, if you think I can do something the cops can't, you need a mind detox.'

'I spotted you as bright in first year. Too smart for your own good. It doesn't hurt to jolt the complacent. Five-thirty at Pel? Make yourself known at reception.'

Pondering the jolting of the complacent, I went down the side streets of Fitzroy to my office in Carrigan's Lane, which was as far as you could go before you met the front street of Collingwood.

Opening the door revealed a tessellation of cellophane-windowed letters. It took all my self-restraint to refrain from dancing on them and then kicking them into the street.

TONY BARTHE put the phone down. 'Chairman's just parked,' he said. 'Annoyed with himself. A stickler for punctuality is our Geoff.'

The Master of Pelham's study was on the first floor of a three-storey brick and bluestone building with towers and crenellations modelled on Inverness Castle.

We sat in ancient leather chairs, the hides cracked like old oil paintings. Through an oak's bare branches, the view was of a twisted building that appeared to be falling over.

'What's that?'

'Magnificent, isn't it?' said Barthe. 'The Lockyear Wing. Designed by Martin Giudice, an old Pel. You'll know of the Quartermaine building?'

I knew the building. The architectural blight on the city had won awards adjudicated upon by architects who could not unaided draw a cat with whiskers and a tail.

'Of course,' I said. 'The signature twist and lean.'

'Actually,' said Tony Barthe, 'Martin designed our building before the Quartermaine, so we were first.'

'The first to twist and lean. As Chubby Checker was to twist and shout.'

Barthe showed horse teeth. 'Sorry, blank there.'

Gentle taps. The door opened a finger-width.

'On his way up,' said a voice.

'Thank you, June,' said Barthe. 'Coffee, please.'

To me, he said, 'I'll pop down to see Geoff in.'

Barthe rose, not easily, left. I looked at the paintings: undistinguished oils, gouaches and watercolours of the college and the university, presumably the works of artistically-challenged Pelham Pricks.

A big man came in wearing a suit tailored to mitigate thirty years of long lunches and four-course dinners.

'Geoff Lockyear,' he said, expelling alcohol fumes.

I shook 400 grams of moist wagyu fillet.

Lockyear sat, caved the chair, sighed. 'Jack bloody Irish. Your grandfather king-hit mine in 1936. Famous game. We lost by a kick.'

Football nonsense like this came with the Irish name.

'Melbourne,' I said.

'Familiar with the crime?'

'I'm told some minor player ran into my grandfather's hand. Staging for a free.'

Lockyear made a noise like a dog gagging on a piece of bone.

'Minor? Minor my foot. The Demons' captain. An assault seen by seventy thousand people.'

'More than half of them one-eyed Melbourne supporters.'

Lockyear QC barked, as close to amused as he would ever be.

'Well, Geoff,' said Barthe. 'Shall I proceed?'

'Carry on, Master,' said Lockyear.

'Firstly, thank you, Jack, for agreeing to assist us. Barry Chilvers holds you in high regard.'

'I've agreed to nothing,' I said. 'I understand you're missing someone.'

'One of our resident tutors,' said Barthe. 'Mark Ulyatt. He didn't appear for a tutorial six weeks ago and not seen since.'

'Where does he live? Or did.'

'The cottage on the left coming up the driveway.'

'Do I have to tell you the police handle missing persons?'

'We'd like to keep this in-house,' said Barthe.

'Why?'

'To avoid the possibility of publicity. To be frank, our enrolments aren't what they used to be.'

'I thought children were put down for Pel at birth?'

Lockyear scowled, pointed out of the window.

'That ghastly leaning edifice bearing my father's name stands half-empty,' he said. 'Built to house the sprogs of rich Asians wanting to buy Australian citizenship. Now the Orientals have gone else-where, there's no money, and everyone I know has given up on Pel.'

'Pel's what it's always been, Geoff,' said Barthe.

'Tell that to my family,' said Lockyear. 'They've sent their sprats to bloody Ormond and Trinity.'

A tadpole's pulse throbbed in his right eyelid.

'Mark had been doing some work on the Pelham Collection,' said Barthe.

'Which is what?'

'Our art collection,' said Barthe. 'Dating from the founder. Lucas provided a Turner, a Reynolds, a Martens, a Gill, a Piguenit and a Bull, all hung in the Great Hall. Paintings trickled in over the years but the collection expanded hugely when the Pelham Foundation got charity status.'

'Third-rate paintings grotesquely over-valued before being donated to us and the tax benefit claimed,' said Lockyear.

'They went into storage,' said Barthe. 'The insulation of the store-room cost a fortune. The intention was to build a gallery.'

Silence. I waited.

'Mark was big on art, interested in the collection. He got wind of our financial position and suggested we sell some works to tide us over. He offered to do an inventory and a valuation of the collection.'

'And?'

'When he absented himself, we looked everywhere for him. Our housekeeper checked the art storeroom and found about a dozen paintings taken from the racks and lined up against the wall.'

'Immortal works by Old Pels?'

Lockyear gave me a displeased look.

'Gifts from Old Pels,' he said. 'We've been puzzled by why he picked out what appear to our untutored eyes to be obscure paintings.'

My instincts said I should be absenting myself. And, lo, on my wrist I discovered my watch, missing these many days.

'Heavens, hasn't time taken flight,' I said, preparing to rise. 'I hear the siren call of elsewhere. Nice to meet you all but unfortunately I have too many other commitments.'

'Chilvers has such faith in you,' said Lockyear.

'Faith,' I said. 'Unfortunately, I disapprove of the concept in all its manifestations.'

Lockyear leaned over and patted my arm, every inch the scout-master ingratiating himself with a small woggled boy.

'A few hours of your time, Jack, there's a good fellow.'

The fan of bills on my floor came into my mind. It had been a long time since the magpie screamed.

'I generally work the revenge and greed end of the street,' I said. 'And so I charge like a wounded QC.'

'Who will be paying you, since this college cannot,' said Lockyear. 'Up for it then?'

I hesitated.

Make a few calls, trouser two grand?

'Since you press me,' I said. 'Yes.'

'Good man,' said Lockyear.

Barthe offered a folder. 'Mark's CV, a photograph of him in a tutorial. From the Pel magazine. Any other questions, please ring.'

The dark had taken Pelham's quadrangle when I came down the stairs and walked along the verandah, admiring the columns with their protomai capitals. I crossed the sombre entrance hall. The front door resisted me, as it had resisted many thousands of Pelham Pricks.

I pushed harder and went into the failing world. Everywhere, the fires of autumn's show-off trees—the maples, liquidambars, claret ashes and scarlet oaks—were fighting to hold off the dusk.

THE PRACTICE of the law calls for intelligence, judgement, learning, integrity, and persistence. In a pinch, you can get by with persistence.

At the table of the long-gone tailor, folders at my elbows, I attended to business.

It took less than an hour of note-taking and issuing of mild threats to deal with all legal matters requiring my attention. In time, I would have to do it all over again. Since leaving criminal law, I had found that it was much harder to settle a dispute over a few hundred dollars than to go to court and secure the release of vile people deserving of being shackled to bare Bass Strait outcrops until death.

And then, to be on the safe side, chained a bit longer.

Then I read the curriculum vitae of Mark Ulyatt, forty-six, research fellow at the Hilary Lakeman Institute for Modern European Studies and resident tutor at Pelham College.

Born in 1972 in Brighton, England. Educated at the Cairncross School, Hampshire, and Oxford University. He had a blue for fencing and came eighth in the 2000 modern pentathlon world championships in Pesaro, Italy. In 2002, there was a PhD from Queen's University in Canada, followed by three years teaching at a women's college in Virginia called Mary LeMay, and two years as curator of modern European art at the August Freundlich Gallery in Boston.

Ulyatt's book *The Wind from the North: Hungarian Jewry*

1933–1945, published in 2008, won the Charles Lezard Prize for contemporary European history in 2009. In 2014, he joined the Hilary Lakeman Institute as a research fellow and became a tutor at Pelham.

In the photograph of the Pel tutorial, Mark Ulyatt—long faced, floppy hair, a sixties English actor—was sitting in an armchair, chin on his right fist, amused look. Four students sat around him, essays in hand.

I dialled the Greer number. The secretary answered, a voice new to me:

'Andrew Greer Associates.'

'Jack Irish for Andrew,' I said.

'May I ask your business?'

'No.'

'I need to know your business.'

'Nightclubs, drugs and sex slavery.'

'And you wish to speak to Mr Greer about?'

'A private matter.'

'If it's private, please call Mr Greer on his private number.'

'Comrade, three words: Put. Him. On.'

A long silence.

A click.

'You are probably unaware that giving offence is now an actual offence,' Andrew said. 'My new child employee is offended.'

'She needs a benchmark for offence. I'll come around and set one.'

'Jack, no, please.'

'What do you know of one Mark Ulyatt?'

'What's the purpose of your inquiry?' he said, displaying the rusted-on suspicion that is such an attractive feature of those who embrace the law.

'The lords of Pelham say he's missing.'

'Where's the boyo gone?'

'Missing, Drew. Consider the word. It means they don't fucking know where he's gone. And they're reluctant to go to the constabulary. Do you know him?'

Drew sighed. 'Come around six. We'll have a glass.'

I went into the back room to make tea. It had been some time since I'd done that. Rinsing the kettle turned the water yellow. I was forced to repeat the procedure four times. Then, opening the cupboard disturbed a spider. I resisted the temptation to look at the cornices lest I see just how badly this place was in need of a cleaning.

Leaf tea keeps pretty well. It has legs. You could find Scott of the Antarctic's old tea caddy in a glacier and brew something recognisable as tea. Long-life milk, on the other hand, knows when to call it a day.

There was also a lemon. Your lemon does gets juicier with age— up to a point. This one was on its way to being the citric equivalent of a raisin.

After a decent interval of steeping, I poured tea into the precious bone-china cup given to me by my wife, Isabel, and added lemon juice. Then I went to the front door, opened it and leaned against the jamb: a man at his ease, drinking tea in the morning sunlight.

People walked by on their way to the river that was Smith Street. Once Carrigan's Lane was a tributary so minor that in a day no more than a dozen people would have passed my door, most of them looking for an easy break-in.

Across the lane, the door of the red-brick building opened.

My former client Kelvin McCoy appeared. The celebrated artist was naked save for what looked like a sumo wrestler's jockstrap made from an old lace curtain. It was a pleasing textural contrast to the furred expanse above and to what appeared to be yak-hair chaps below.

He gazed at me. Then he spoke in his school-sports loudhailer voice.

'So fucking idle. Standing around, drinking tea, the poor bloody clients rotting in jail due to staggering incompetence of the so-called fucking defence.'

I gazed back at him.

'You should be arrested just for being in public,' I said. 'Imagine the effect on a child.'

'Last child I saw was carrying a television,' said McCoy. 'A sixty-inch plasma fucker. The other little bastard had the speakers.'

I sipped.

'Corrupted youths but still vulnerable to being traumatised. As I am, every time I see a young female art student enter your door.'

McCoy scratched his chest pelt. I thought I saw insect life dislodged, take weak flight. 'Exposing the girlies to my genius,' he said. 'Giving something back to society.'

'The best thing you can do for society,' I said, 'is to burn everything in that cave of horrors and go back to stripping stolen cars.'

McCoy cocked his head. 'Phone,' he said. 'Probably the gallery. Can't get enough of me, mate. Talking about a retrospective.'

'Great idea,' I said. 'Bringing your revolting works together provides a bomber with the chance to strike a blow for both taste and hygiene. I may be that person. Suicidal, if necessary.'

A massive four-wheel-drive was in the lane. When it had passed, McCoy was gone.

HUNGER LUNGED at me. Time to hunt and gather.

I walked down to Smith Street, to the New Turkish Grocery, an enterprise founded in 1983. Its horizons had long since expanded to include, first, the entire Mediterranean shore, even the Grecian shore, and, next, all of the known world.

On the way, my mind turned to old lovers. An old lover had phoned me and left a message.

Lyndall.

The house in Parkville on that first cold night, the warm glow of the fire, the velvet taste of the Hill of Grace, the buttery cheese with ash on it.

I was guilty of phoning lovers past, of catching them unawares, hearing them inject the extra vowels of false delight into my short name, hearing their tinny excuses for unavailability, their enthusiastic promises.

Love to catch up. Look, I'll ring you.

The public telephone was behind a barricade of bags of split peas. I rang detective senior sergeant Barry Tregear on one of his numbers. An electronic voice said to please leave a message.

I did, inspected the shelves nearby. The phone rang.

'Where the fuck are you?' said Barry.

'New Turkish Grocery. At the canned and bottled vegetables. Considering a pickled turnip purchase.'

'Who eats pickled fucken turnips?'

'Those who enjoy a less sweet turnip. A tart turnip. I need an opinion on a Mark Ulyatt. The address is Pelham College, Parkville.'

'Spell.'

I spelled.

'Parkville. All wankers. What kind of opinion?'

'Come to your notice.'

'Someone waste precious time for a prick eats fucken pickled radishes?'

'Turnips.'

'Whatever. I'll see.'

I resumed my culinary browsing, selected a jar of virgin Montenegrin capers, tea grown high above the thundering wildebeest hordes of Kenya, and artisan Italian pasta rolled between the thighs of maidens in the Le Marche town of Pinocchio.

At the counter, I requested the salad and salami roll.

'With the new salami,' said Mrs Osmani. She pulled on a plastic glove with proctological nonchalance. 'From Coburg. The Coburg salami.'

Until the speculators arrived, the suburb of Coburg consisted of a bluestone jail surrounded by the modest weatherboard dwellings of its present, past and future inmates.

'Coburg salami?' I said. 'Of course. The backyard pigs, free-ranging swine, long a feature of local life. They should have a running of the pigs. Down Sydney Road.'

She studied me, concerned. 'Thin, Jack. Need more meat.'

'This is not thin,' I said. 'This is less plump. How's Burek?'

She shrugged. 'Max buy him the exercise bicycle. He get on, he listen to the radio on the earphones. Then he get off.'

'No pedalling?'

Mrs Osmani shook her head.

'Well, it's better than nothing,' I said. 'The getting on and the getting off.'

'Dog bark him all the time too.'

I knew the dog well, a cross between a Jack Russell terrier and a crocodile, it prowled the aisles casually nipping customers in the lower leg until Burek decided to stay at home and work on his fitness.

'Perhaps the dog misses biting the customers.'

Mrs Osmani smiled. 'Jack, you see who come in here now, I bite them myself.'

The public telephone rang.

'Mate,' said Barry Tregear, 'someone'll be around your shithole office. Ever think of offering me money?'

'Quarter pounder with cheese. How's that? Money spoils the purity of relationships.'

'Never spoilt mine.'

'I suppose it makes most of them possible. Lusty Kinkylips charges what these days?'

'Pays, mate. They pay me.'

ANDREW GREER came to the street door, tie fashionably loose, beer bottle in hand.

'Imagine a victim of workplace bullying being met by a drunk solicitor,' I said. 'Trauma heaped upon trauma.'

'Many visitors to these premises remember being met by a drunk solicitor,' said Drew. 'You.'

'Can't move on, can you? That's so sad.'

In his office, I sat in a chair bought from Doug's Furnimart on Smith Street, Collingwood. Doug, his Furnimart and, some would say, Smith Street itself were long gone.

Drew uncapped a beer bottle.

'Craft beer,' he said. 'Made by Boris Kobevko, an artisan unjustly accused and now walking free courtesy of my dismantling of the key crown witness.'

I took it and sipped. 'What's Boris's craft? Cheese?'

'You detect malolactic fermentation, the trademark of Boris's Oblast Ale.'

'Mal as in bad, I presume. On cheese, what happened to Brie? Bresse?'

'Breanna. Fell in love with a client. Now on his family farm tending to the animals.'

'They probably make her look after the livestock too,' I said. 'Then there's the dope crop. Tell me about Mark Ulyatt.'

'Ah, Mark. I know very little about him. Except that you wouldn't want to pick a fight with him. One night, he's left the casino, he's waiting for a taxi, and four young dicks make that mistake.'

'Private-school boys, no doubt.'

'Indeed, hand-reared by the Baptists. The biggest arse, the bully boy, he came away from the encounter missing four front-row teeth. That's about sixty grand in implants. Mark's elbow thrust, I think. Arse number two, right arm pulled out of its socket. Mark threw the third dolt into the cold and septic Yarra. Unfortunately, he could swim.'

'And the fourth?'

'Sprinted home to Toorak, to mummy. Mark was getting into his cab when the filth arrested him. He rang Pel, who rang me. In due course, all charges dropped.'

'Of course. Mark's sexual proclivities?'

'Would I know? Twice married, I understand, which isn't evidence for anything. But Pel doesn't smile on improper relationships between staff and students.'

I tried another teaspoon of Boris's beer. 'It could be a matter of Pel's definition of improper. On the subject, surely it's both improper and illegal to bottle the liquid wrung from bar towels?'

'You've become so effete,' said Drew. 'Palate corrupted by Scandinavian pisswater. I suggest you allow a few days, tell Pelham you can't find Mark, and bill them.'

'Bill them for doing nothing?'

'Surely you're not questioning the billing practices of the entire legal profession? What are you, some mad leftover from communism?'

'Just naive,' I said.

Drew's eyes were on the Oblast Ale's crudely-drawn label. It featured a creature resembling an aardvark with goat horns.

'The saiga antelope,' he said. 'Endangered, so Boris tells me.'

'This swill certainly endangers life. Got any non-craft beer? Perhaps Scandi pisswater?'

Drew sighed, rose, decanted his Oblast Ale into the stained wash-basin in the corner.

'I'm prepared to be effete,' he said, 'if it makes my guests happy. What beats me is how these Pel duffers would know he was missing. In my time, a tutor, a person now Mr Justice Shallbenameless, was on the books for two terms without taking a single tutorial. Met that pompous arse Lockjaw, did you?'

'As it happens, he's paying.'

'Put another grand on the invoice.'

'TALK IN the car,' said the big-jawed man, early fifties, overweight.

I left the office door open, followed detective sergeant Colin Harris of the Homicide Squad to his illegally parked Holden. It was early afternoon, the smell of impending rain somehow seeping through the petrochemical layer.

The car reeked of newness aerosol spray. It didn't say Cop, it said Hire.

'Rain coming,' Harris said.

'Bring it on.'

'Took the lawn out in the drought. Straight off it rains for a month. Still, half of me's not sorry. The fucking mowing.'

Up the street, McCoy came out of his door and looked around like a man in search of a dog: right, left and then a stare at us that said: *Noting your rego.*

'And him?' said Harris.

'Blind bloke.'

'Looks like he's wearing the guide dog,' said Harris.

McCoy went inside.

'So, Mark Ulyatt,' I said.

'Doesn't show much.'

The slightest darkening of the day, no more than the death of a single bulb in a ballroom chandelier.

'Known to get a home-delivered hooker from the Officers' Club,' said Harris. 'But not for a while. Had a fight outside the casino last year. A matter settled.'

He found an envelope. 'There's this.'

It was a professional-quality 8x10 colour print, taken by available light with a long lens.

Mark Ulyatt was standing next to a car, talking to the driver, a man in his thirties, hair combed back, loose tie.

'What's this?' I said.

'Surveillance.'

'The man in the car?'

'Lynton Curtis. Know who he is?'

I nodded. Curtis was a journalist specialising in white-collar malfeasance who also knew more than was healthy for him about Melbourne's criminal underworld and its links to corrupt cops. There would almost certainly be a bounty on his head.

'Can I keep this?'

'Told to give it to you. Date's on the back.'

'I could use a month or so of Ulyatt's phone.'

'Owed big time, aren't you?' said Harris, shaking his head. 'A fucking killer too.'

'Well, just the once.'

'Walked. Not even community service.'

'I was performing a community service.'

'They all say that. Nice to meet you, Jack.'

We shook hands.

I was almost at my door when fifty-cent rainblots appeared on the tarmac, on the gutter stones, on my bluestone doorstep.

THE LIGHT in the Prince of Prussia came through windows not cleaned since the last days of the war in Vietnam. I navigated by instinct through the gloom to the corner where sat three ancient men.

'Anyone know this bloke?' said Norm O'Neill, not looking at me, adjusting his glasses on a nose that, owned by a smaller frame, would pose the danger of a wind gust sending the owner flying off on a broad reach.

'My shout, lads,' I said.

'Tell this bloke we're busy,' said Eric Tanner, the man against the wall.

I raised a finger to the publican. Stan was on the phone at the far end of the bar, back to the kitchen hatch, nodding.

He ignored me.

'Never took a drink from a stranger,' said Norm. 'Never.'

'Take nothin from a stranger,' said Eric in a musing way. 'Drilled it in us, our mum. Mind you, I never actually had to say no.'

'Not a lot of strangers around them days,' said Wilbur, the man in the middle. 'I would have taken something to eat, always hungry, we...'

'No,' said Eric. 'Can't recollect a stranger offerin me nothing. Not a sausage.'

'A sausage?' said Wilbur, meat brain-trigger pulled. 'Can't get a decent snag any more. Used to be go into any butcher, you'd get a decent…'

'Shuddup about sausages,' said Norm O'Neill. His head was turning in my direction at the speed of the container ship Yokohama Global Traveller No 26 changing course.

I had enough time to signal to Stan before the movement was complete.

'So what's the story?' said Norm, every word combining disappointment and menace. 'Given up on ya mates, have ya?'

'It was work,' I said. 'I had business up north.'

It had been my duty for many years, a duty thrust upon me, to take these men to watch the Fitzroy Football Club play, a club they had followed since infancy. Then Fitzroy was declared surplus to the football league's needs and our weekends were free. This lasted until I could no longer bear the ancient supporters' melancholy.

I convinced them to move their allegiance to another club, St Kilda, a side that promised to give them just as much pain. In the beginning that promise was realised on most weekends, but no day passed when I did not regret my impulse.

Six lizard eyes upon me.

'Took a bit longer than expected,' I said.

They nodded, cynical and merciless nods. It was like facing the inquisition at Pamiers in 1318, Norm standing in for Bishop Jacques Fournier.

'There's such a thing as a taxi,' I said, defensively.

'There's such a thing as not leaving your mates in the lurch,' said Norm. 'Particularly on the day we give the Spice Girls from Sydney a bloody good towelling.'

The Saints had beaten the artificially created Greater Western Sydney at Docklands, thrashing them in the last quarter. I'd expected to be back in time for the game. Looking for Cyril's missing person in the torrid zone was pointless and would take no more than a day or two.

And so it proved until hours before the plane home. A message was relayed to me from a retired Brisbane crim called Wogdog

Weech, known to police in three states and a territory. Suddenly there was the prospect of finding Barry.

But it took another week.

For no good reason, I said, 'I saw the daughter's boy while I was up there.'

Added crinkles around the antique eyes. A discernible softening of the inquisitorial demeanour.

'What's his name?' said Norm.

'William,' I said. 'William Sundquist.'

'Bill,' said Wilbur Ong. 'Damn good name.'

'Proper boy's name, Bill,' said Eric Tanner.

'Bill,' said Norm O'Neill. 'Another Bill.'

I could not tell them that the toddler bore no resemblance to me or to any Irish male I had seen in photographs. This was not surprising, given that the boy's father was Erik the Viking from Skalhammer. There just wasn't a lot of Irish in the lovely boy. And what genetic material there was in him the trio of ancients well knew to be sub-standard.

That was because these men had seen my father play football for Fitzroy. As if looking back to the previous weekend, they spoke of marks Bill Irish had taken, of goals he had kicked from impossible distances and unthinkable positions, of brutish opponents he had caused to be carried off the field and have smelling salts waved beneath their noses.

Making matters worse, the ancients carried blood memories, ancestral memories. They spoke as if they had seen my grandfather perform great deeds, seen him almost singlehandedly send dozens of Fitzroy's enemies to sit on cold change-room floors, in their nostrils the pungent odours of sweat, wintergreen ointment and defeat.

Around us, on the nicotine-dark walls of the Prince, hung the old photographs of the Fitzroy Football Club teams. I had always avoided looking at them, not wishing to meet the eyes of the Irish paragons. I needed no reminder of how thin their blood ran in me.

'Had to listen to the wireless,' said Norm. 'Not what it used to be, the wireless. These dickheads, shoutin and screamin, they call the game over, it's bloody ten minutes in the second slice.'

'Worst's that ABC bloke,' said Eric. 'Bloody fortune-teller.'

'No, worst's that Carlton dick,' said Norm. 'Followed by Valves.'

'Not a bad coach was Stan,' said Wilbur.

'Bullshit, cost us a flag. Darren bloody Jarman and that McLeod, run around like foxes in the chook pen. Mr Bloody No Answers, that's Stanley Alves.'

'Steady on,' said Wilbur. 'Got us there, didn't he?'

Norm raised a hand, like a Roman magistrate. 'The boys got us there. Stanley didn't finish the job. Like that Thomas. And that Lyon.'

'I think about it,' said Eric, 'you was the one didn't want to go with the Saints.'

In the brown corner, Norm studied his glass. 'Get a beer here?' he said. 'For Christsakes, Jack, shoutin or not?'

Now I had the eye of the publican. He ended his telephone conversation and sidled down the bar, dry-washing his hands, face glowing with bonhomie.

'Jack, my boy,' Stan said. 'Welcome home. Round's on the house.'

'Free beer? You may need trauma counselling.'

'The old boy's ready to sell.'

Stan's father was behind the bar of the Prince for forty years before wife number two dragged him off to a Gold Coast villa. Maurice owned six other small properties around the city and I acted for him in his endless bickering with tenants.

'Maurie said that to you?'

Stan's eyes stayed on the beer he was pouring. 'Happy to sell,' he said.

'Maurie told you he wanted to sell?'

'Well, not him, no. She told me.'

Maurie's wife had long pestered him to sell the Prince and the other properties. Ten years above the pub had left her with a marked lack of affection for the place.

'I'll wait to hear this news from Maurie's lips,' I said.

Stan planted two glasses on the bar towels, thought to be the oldest textiles of their kind in existence. 'Not himself, the old bloke,' he said. 'She's getting power of attorney.'

'Not himself how?'

'Y'know. Losing it.'

I had spent an hour with Maurie while I was in the sub-tropical zone. Fifty-eight minutes longer than I wanted to.

'Stanley,' I said, 'count yourself lucky if you have Maurie's marbles when you're eighty-two.'

Stan set glasses before Eric and Norm. 'Keep running this place, I won't have any marbles when I'm bloody forty-six.'

'Wonder what happened to my marbles?' said Eric. 'Wasn't nobody could beat me at marbles. Had this bag, took em off the whole street, couldn't hardly carry it.'

'Probably took at gunpoint,' said Norm. 'Relied more on force than skill around your way.'

'One had a little gold ball in the middle,' said Wilbur, eyes narrowed in thought. 'Real gold they said.'

'A goldie,' said Eric. 'The king marble. Had lots of em.'

'Did bloody not,' said Wilbur. 'That's a big porky.'

Stan looked at me. 'See what I mean?' he said. 'Need a bit of advice on another matter, I do.'

'Domestic?'

Stan scratched above his right ear, his right eyebrow. 'In the office will you, Jack?' he said. 'Little chat.'

There are moments when you wish that you were a casual observer unfettered by the gossamer shackles of duty and obligation.

Just moments. They pass.

'I'M HAVING a baby,' said Rosa. 'I'm pregnant.'

'Pregnant is the prerequisite,' I said, in shock. 'At the end of a process, you will be having a baby.'

A faintly humming silence.

'Thank you for that correction,' Rosa said. 'What I would really like to do now is send a bullet of super-condensed pig shit through this telephone line so that it could plaster you and your cruel and callous and pedantic mind all over the nearest wall.'

'I don't think they have that feature on mobiles yet,' I said. 'Who's the co-sponsor?'

A silence, pregnant.

'It's a private matter.'

'So you're not planning on setting up a household with this person?'

'Why should I?'

'It's a silly thing people used to do. Is the child to know its paternity?'

'What gives you the right to cross-examine me?'

'Consanguinity and seniority,' I said. 'I'm your brother and I'm older.'

On our mother's side, the rich side, the other side of the Yarra side, we had a cousin called Laurence. Rosa barely remembered him, arriving as late as she did. He treated me with disdain when I came into his life after my father's death. My strongest memory of floppy-haired Laurence was a tennis match at Kooyong when he thrashed me 6-0 in the first set.

I won the second 6-4.

Then he had me three games down in the third. I fought back, drew level, knew I had him. When I broke his service, Laurence clutched his right shoulder, feigned agony, and called it off.

Many years later, I went into mourning when told he had skied into a ski-lift pylon in Aspen: nose powder and powder snow, a fatal combination.

'No one would detect that we're related,' said Rosa. 'I see you three or four times a year if I'm lucky. If that's being lucky. You show absolutely no interest in me.'

Being deadset guilty as charged, your honour.

I said, 'Hang on, I've taken a keen interest. The sommelier, for instance. And the money-launderer, the man the Feds called Omo. Plus the film producer shonk. And the foreign-exchange dealer. I ran the ruler over all of them.'

'Fuck you, Jack. Is there another way to put it?'

'Not as succinctly, no. I take it your condition stems from an affair?'

'From a fuck with a professional surfer at a party.'

'You go to parties with professional surfers?'

'Not with. At. He was at the party.'

'Congratulations.'

'You do not mean that.'

'I might mean it. I need time to think.'

'Jack,' she said. 'I'm feeling a bit lonely.'

My instinct was to say: *Why don't you ring the surfer?*

But my throat closed.

'Well, my dear, grab your swagette and come over here. Then you'll know the meaning of lonely.'

'You don't mean that either.'

I looked around my quarters, uncleaned these many days. 'On

second thoughts, I suppose you shouldn't. For health reasons. Eaten tonight?'

'It's six fucking fifteen, Jack. I'm not in Barwon Prison.'

'Well,' I said, 'I could paddle across the river with my jarmies. We could have a bite at the Screaming Eagle. The wall of wine. Then I could sleep on your sofa. Tomorrow, a brisk walk on the pre-owned syringes, the gallery crawl, lunch.'

Rosa snuffled. 'That would be nice. There are actually three guest bedrooms here.'

'One will be fine. I'm not coming with the Donner Party.'

'Don't do this because you feel you have to.'

I said, 'My dear, all that separates us from the three-toed sloth is the feeling that we have to.'

'An admirable creature, the sloth,' said Rosa. 'On your bike. I'm now hungry.'

For the first time, I saw something of myself in her.

Oh God.

THE HILARY Lakeman Institute for Modern European Studies was on the third floor of a hideous building resting on concrete stumps in Swanston Street.

I'd rung.

'Coffee?' said the director's secretary. 'It's Aeropress.'

'Is that an instant?'

'No, no, it's a device for making espresso.'

'Black, please,' I said. 'No sugar.'

'Long or short?'

'Short.'

'Derek will be impressed,' she said. 'He's a coffee purist.'

Professor Derek Helm looked like a purist's purist: shaven head the shape and colour of a free-range egg, round rimless glasses, black Mao-collar shirt. His desk was pure except for a red rose in a test-tube vase, an unstained blotter and a stainless-steel fountain pen, capped.

'Mr Irish,' he said. 'Sit.'

'I'm trying to find Mark Ulyatt,' I said. 'On behalf of Pelham College. You know he's missing?'

'I do. We've been worried. Recently he's been behaving in a…well, a disturbed way.'

'Disturbed?'

Helm tilted his head, an egg thinking.

'He went to Germany on a research trip, paid for by us. Came back changed. Morose. Not the joking Mark anymore. No more singing. He used to sing in his study. Good voice too.'

'The research trip. You wouldn't normally pay for it?'

'No. Travel expenses are the fellow's responsibility.'

'Why did you pay?'

'You catch me at a good time for indiscretion,' he said. 'Two weeks to go as director. The background is that Sally Lakeman met Mark at a dinner party in New York. He's of distant Hungarian Jewish descent and so is one wing of the Lakeman family. When she got back, she insisted that we shortlist him for a fellowship.'

'She encouraged him to apply?'

'Indeed. We flew in the three shortlisted applicants for interviews. Sally chaired the panel, two other Lakemans on it, both pass-level commerce graduates. Mark gave a bravura performance. I thought Sally was going to disrobe.'

'That's bravura.'

'Byronic is the only word for Mark,' said Helm. 'The outstanding candidate, a terrific scholar but dumpy with ginger moulting hair and a bad case of the sniffs, he'd have had more chance auditioning for the chorus line of the Moulin Rouge. That or to be the next James Bond.'

'I see. What was Mark's research?'

'Hungary, working on a new book,' said Helm. 'He did his master's on the subject, that became a PhD and then a book. Onanism is unfortunately common in academia.'

'What's your field?'

Helm looked at me through hooded eyes. 'Modern Franco-German history. Why?'

'Just professional curiosity. Are Mark's papers still here?'

'He never kept any papers here. Never used his study computer either as far as we can see. He came armed with a laptop and brief-case. He used the printer though, so there may be papers in his study at Pelham.'

A knock. The coffee entered, in small white porcelain cups.

I sipped.

'My word, the Blue Mountain,' I said. 'Positions vacant here? I can be onanistic.'

'You know your beans,' said Helm. 'Helen's the queen of the Aeropress. I'm told Kenya's now in fashion.'

'Only with untutored palates. So Mark was unhappy after his trip? Cause or coincidence?'

Puzzled egg. 'Impossible to tell.'

'Did he see a lot of Sally Lakeman?'

'More than I did. By a factor of about five.'

'Here?'

'In his study. Of course I'm not suggesting anything improper.'

'Of course not. Will she talk to me?'

Helm massaged his scalp with spatulate fingertips. 'The Lakemans value their privacy.'

I drank the last of the Jamaican nectar, rose.

'Thanks for your time,' I said. 'Talking to me could avoid embarrassment. Pelham wants to find Mark without going to the police. But if they're forced to, you'll have television crews outside. Talking to me could help avoid that.'

Helm nodded. 'I'll explain that to Sally, Jack,' he said. 'Within the hour. Be assured. Leave your number with Helen.'

We touched hands. I left the building and made a call on the device.

Then I set off down Swanston Street for Fortress Pelham.

THE RECEPTIONIST rang.

'He's coming down,' she said.

I paced out the chamber: six metres by eight, estimated the ceiling height. The golden ratio.

Barthe appeared, panting like a large pale dog.

We touched hands.

'I have to ask,' I said. 'Ulyatt's private life. Known to you?'

Barthe squirmed, cocked his head, closed his eyes demurely.

'Well, from time to time a car would park outside our side gate late at night. Mark would unlock it, and escort a woman to his cottage. About two hours later, he'd take her back to the gate.'

'How do you know this?'

'Closed-circuit cameras. We were the first college to…'

'Of course you were.'

He looked beyond me. 'Ah, Betty. Our housekeeper, Betty Fellows.'

We exchanged nods.

'Betty, please show Mr Irish Mark's house.'

We left the main building and went down a gravel path flanked by box hedges to the front door of a bluestone cottage. My guide unlocked it, waved me in.

'Four rooms,' she said. 'Study on the right. Please close the door when you leave.'

It was a small room with a desk, an upright chair, an old armchair and a filing cabinet. On the desk sat a laptop computer, a pad, a printer, two pencils and an old Conway Stewart fountain pen.

I crossed to a wall of bookshelves. Four shelves held a charity-shop collection—travel, biography, bestsellers, classic novels, popular history, self-help titles, games and puzzles, a dozen or so bound A4 notebooks, two red document boxes.

I opened a notebook. The first page was headed, in an architectural hand: *Bundesarchiv/Reich/Weimar 1918-33.*

Notes for Mark's master's degree, no doubt.

The filing cabinet was empty. I took the document boxes to the desk. The first one contained Ulyatt's British passport with Australian and American entry and exit stamps, bank statements, bills, receipts, letters of appointment from the Lakeman Institute and Pelham.

The second box held invoices, receipts and bank statements.

In a short time, I knew that in two years $350,000 had come into Mark Ulyatt's Commonwealth Bank account: two deposits of $150,000 from the Lakeman Institute and a single transfer of $50,000 from a London bank.

Mark cashed cheques for sums from $500 to $2000. In the previous three months, he had paid for flights to Sydney and Flinders Island. The most recent statement, dated two weeks before Pel noticed the scholar's absence, recorded a balance of $144,586.56.

On to the bedroom, which held a double bed, a bedside table with lamp, chest of drawers, and a huge 1950s veneered wardrobe.

Mark's clothes were chosen for the City of London and the Cotswolds: suits (summer-weight greys, dark-blues with a barely discernible pinstripe, a solemn charcoal, a dinner suit), sports jackets of tweed, mohair-silk, linen, six pairs of casual trousers, a silk gown, a trench coat, shoes black and brown, and battered running shoes.

His shirts, all white, Turnbull & Asser of Jermyn Street, were stacked in fours. The chest of drawers held underwear, sweaters, socks and handkerchiefs.

No pyjamas. Mark slept in his natural state.

Next, the bathroom. These chambers often speak more eloquently than other rooms. Mark Ulyatt's said he didn't need pills to sleep or alter his mood and travelled with only the necessities, which included three condoms, well inside their use-by date.

I went back to the bookshelves and began taking down books, three or four at a time. Halfway along the second shelf, I found a leather-bound notebook, perhaps ten by sixteen centimetres.

Why did people think you could hide things behind books?

I put the book in a pocket, took Mark's laptop, left the premises and found Barthe, who gave permission to take away the device for examination.

'Information from computers?' he said. 'Can you do that?'

'I squeeze them like oranges.'

This wasn't quite true. A digital super-sleuth, the handsome Simone Bendsten of Bendsten Research, took care of my squeezing. Once I gave these assignments to Eric, Wootton's computer geek, a man who while giving every appearance of being stoned mindless could extract gold from the teeth of dead computers.

I walked to Simone's office close by the pub in Fitzroy where Drew and I once consorted with legal and welfare guerrillas. They were apostate products of the middle-class suburbs, all sworn to fight for the poor against the capitalist state's apparatus of oppression. Alas, the state's apparatchiks proved too strong and the guerrillas fell back to the leafy suburban fastnesses, there to fret over private-school fees and the ever-rising cost of skiing holidays.

Simone didn't answer her doorbell. I wrote a note and deposited the laptop in her bombproof postbox.

ON MY way home, I brooded over what I'd done with my share of the Savage Glance coup.

I'd stocked up on Pichon Lalande and Hill of Grace, dined out most nights, replaced my fraying wardrobe. I'd given the Hawk a heart transplant and new leather upholstery and I'd made a large loan to a man I trusted, a man who would now walk into the traffic rather than meet my gaze.

Nothing remarkable there by my standards. What was broodable upon, however, was the painting I bought.

I'd seen an oil by Terence Charles Langan entitled *Macedon Autumn* in an auction catalogue. Langan, an Australian painter unduly influenced by the landscapes of Giorgio Morandi, had never been in favour with art collectors.

I didn't intend to go to the auction. But the impulse came after a few sherbets toasting my former partner-at-law Andrew Greer's feat in beating an armed robbery charge for a man who deserved to be stripped naked, handcuffed, greased, rolled in top-grade cocaine and thrown into a junior merchant bankers' end-of-year party.

From the back of the auction room, I watched the price inch up—two-fifty, three, four.

At $450, the betting was over.

I raised my paddle. 'Five.'

Silence.

'Five I have,' said the auctioneer. 'Do I have any…'

Someone offered $520.

'Five fifty,' I said.

Someone added ten. Someone else added thirty.

'Bugger this,' I said, careless. 'Six.'

The dealers made gestures. No responses, it was mine, once, twice…

'Six-fifty,' said a woman near the front. She looked back at me, thirties, severe face under a cap of black hair.

'Seven,' I said.

'Seven-fifty,' she said.

'Eight.'

'Eight-fifty.'

Madness took hold of me.

'One thousand,' I said.

She said, 'Eleven hundred.'

Drew said, 'Pack it in, mate, the dogs are pissing on your swag.'

I said, 'Twelve hundred.'

It went on this way until we were at $1800, the woman's bid.

A long silence.

'Jesus, Jack,' said Drew. 'The estimate's four hundred.'

'And a hundred,' said the woman.

'Two thousand,' I said.

'And a hundred,' said the woman.

'Don't be an idiot,' said Drew. 'She wants it.'

'So do I,' I said. 'Twenty-two hundred.'

'And a hundred,' said the woman.

And so it went on.

In the end, I paid a price for the small Langan would stand until Melbourne was under ten metres of melted polar-ice water.

In the rain-slicked street, traffic blurring past, Drew said, 'Infantile instincts satisfied? You're the prick who won't be overtaken on a country road, it's an ego thing.'

'A cleansing Krug,' I said, system flooded with adrenalin. 'That's what we need.'

'I'm going home,' Drew said. 'I suggest you do the same and take your shitty little painting with you into a cold shower.'

Harsh words, not easy to forget.

Autumnal scenes always touched something in me. And I liked its size. Big paintings overloaded your senses and got away with being rubbish. Small oils call for delicacy and a perfect eye.

But that wasn't why I'd bought it.

The love of my life had given me a Langan dated June 1947, a detailed pen-and-ink of stonemasons working on a Melbourne University building.

Years later, I found out that in June 1947 my father had been working on that building.

By then, Isabel was dead, murdered by one of my clients. The drawing and many other things I loved were gone too, casualties of an attempt to blow me to eternity.

If I'd bothered to study the stonemasons, I might have found that one of them was William John Irish, ex-soldier, stonemason, footballer, communist. And my father.

The Langan didn't please me from the moment I put it on the wall: the dog was fractionally too big, the car too small. I sought out other Langan paintings of the same size and did not see the same failings in them. Perhaps it was a forgery. But the provenance seemed sound: it was from the estate of Langan's godchild, Chester Hawkins.

To hell with brooding, consign the thing to auction this day. Langan's star had risen since I paid the outlandish price. Perhaps the woman still wanted it. When she folded, she strode out, giving me a thin sideways glance that spoke to the anxious child in me.

I parked in the lane beside my office, behind another outlaw who rang me every so often when he wanted to take his car for a spin to charge the battery.

Standing on my big stone doorstep with its hollow that became a bath for sparrows on rainy days, I felt eyes on me. I didn't look. I was in the back room when a single knuckle tapped.

Once I would have opened the door without a thought.

Now I hesitated.

No.

Better again to be king hit, kicked and pissed on.

I opened the door.

The electricity man.

Everything about this matter was displeasing to me. When the meter reader was done, I shut up shop and went around to Taub's. Inside the door, the workshop cold, I called Charlie's name.

Three times I called, ever more anxious, tense in my face and throat and chest.

'What?' said Charlie behind me.

I turned. He was holding a brown paper bag, lunch bought from Mrs Osmani at the supermarket.

'Why is it so cold in here?' I said, composing myself. 'What happened to heating?'

'I forgot,' said Charlie. 'Working for a living. Not like some.'

'I'm ready to work,' I said. 'I'm eager to work.'

Charlie waved at the workshop. 'So? You don't have wood? You don't have tools?'

'Lunch,' I said. 'I don't have lunch.'

IT WAS a cupboard like no cupboard I had seen.

Charlie's drawing was of a piece of furniture four metres long, sixty centimetres deep, one hundred and ten centimetres high. It had thirty back-to-back drawers, five at each end, five in the middle. Between the drawers were frame-and-panel doors, sixteen of them. Behind them were shelves. Except for the shelves, the timber was to be *Nothofagus cunninghamii*—Tasmanian myrtle.

'This top,' I said. 'That's two boards. Four-metre boards?'

Charlie grunted.

'And four centimetres thick?'

'I give you a plan. Now you want me to tell you also?'

'Sorry,' I said. 'Just checking.'

I had learned that using boards this size carried risk. The lovely piece is built, the customer takes delivery. Then there is a change—in temperature or humidity or altitude or latitude or longitude or attitude, any old thing, really—and a board cracks or bows or cups or twists or all these things.

Charlie had no qualms about the stability of his timbers. The myrtle tree from which these boards came was felled in August 1983. Charlie bought it and three other logs in Launceston in 1985 for what would now scarcely buy four cartons of cigarettes. Milled to his instructions, they were shipped to Melbourne. Since then, the boards had lived like cheeses, stacked with space to breathe, turned. In addition, like all timbers in the workshop, they spent long periods standing on their ends. Changing ends required a block and tackle.

I inquired about this practice when I first began to hang around the workshop.

'Trees don't grow sideways,' said Charlie. 'You made that glue? You want I should make the glue?'

No, Charlie wasn't taking a risk in using a slab. The risk was allowing me to make the cupboard that would support it.

'Who's this for?' I said. 'The entire Franciscan order?'

'Just a person,' said Charlie. He was chiselling a slim mortise. 'Doesn't matter who it's for.'

'I like to know where something is going. I can think about it while I work.'

'What you think about while you work is the work. You notice I got them all?'

He waved his hands at me and, since they blocked the light, I could not but see that he had his full complement of fingers.

'I notice. So who wants a cupboard this size?'

Charlie blew into the mortise. 'A man.'

'What kind of man?'

Charlie shook his head, went to the shoebox that served as the business's filing cabinet and, with difficulty, found a business card.

Manalaus

Purity. Masculinity. Elegance.

Christophe Aregno

'Manalaus,' I said. 'That's a spelling mistake. What is this?'

'New shop, Collins Street,' said Charlie. 'Face creams, that rubbish.'

'Manalaus, now I get it,' I said. 'I'm slow today. So this place's too good to make a kitchen, but a display counter for a men's cosmetics boutique? Bring it on. You'll be popping around for your cleansing cream and a pot of skin buffer made from the scales of coelacanth fossils.'

'He saw Mrs Purbrick's library, Christophe,' said Charlie. 'He knows the work I do.'

'And I suppose he doesn't touch.'

'Come here to work or talk nonsense?'

And so to the engine room. I carried in the boards for the countertop. Then I transported the 100x200mm lengths that would be the twelve legs. I switched on the extra lights. The machines stood gleaming, each in its spotless space—German, Swiss, English, American machines, all but the thicknesser made before 1960. Charlie loved them and maintained them to the standard of Formula One cars. I loved them too, in an inadequate, inept and unworthy way.

I wiped the sawbench surface with a rag, wound the eighty-tooth blade to its full height and put a machined-steel block against it. It was true. There had never been the remotest chance that it would not be.

In the rack, I found a suitable piece of scrap, put it on the table, adjusted the machine's blade height so that a small crescent of teeth peeped out above the wood. Some cabinetmakers cut with the sawblade fully raised on the grounds that it makes kickback less likely. Charlie took the view that kickback was the result of operator incompetence.

The first length of myrtle went onto the operating table. It didn't look like much: rough, dun-coloured. I adjusted the outside fence, put on my helmet and a rigger's glove, and ran the timber through, taking off a centimetre.

The saw blade exposed a silky, tight-grained surface.

I adjusted the fences and spent the next hour preparing the parts of the carcass, beginning with six lengths to be cut into twelve legs.

The finished piece would suit a monastery rather than a shrine to male hedonism. But its severity of line and its feel to a sliding hand, it would please everyone who encountered it, for the unforeseeable future.

I RANG Lynton Curtis's newspaper and asked for him.

'Name, address, phone number, I'll pass them on,' said the man.

I gave the information.

'It concerns him personally and it's an urgent matter,' I said.

'Will tell,' he said.

The phone rang inside ten minutes.

'Jack Irish. Lynton Curtis. I worked with Linda as a boy reporter.'

'She's never forgotten you,' I said. 'You meet a man called Mark Ulyatt, now missing.'

'Did I?'

'I've got the photograph.'

'What did that cost?'

'No payment involved.'

'Jack, people want to tell me stuff. I talk to them on the phone. Sometimes they don't want to talk on the phone or they want to show me something. Then I meet them somewhere quiet. What does this pic show?'

'You standing next to a car with Mark Ulyatt. Possibly in a car park.'

'Shit. The bastards tagged me again.'

'Can you say why you met Mark Ulyatt?'

'I'm alive because I don't talk about the people who talk to me.'

'People are worried. Telling me can't hurt you.'

'With respect, you have no idea of what can hurt me.'

'I have no further questions, Your Lordship.'

A theatrical cough.

'Ulyatt wouldn't tell me anything unless I met his conditions. I declined, said goodbye. That's it.'

'Well thank you for talking to me.'

'Cheers, Jack.'

I landed the phone, eyes on nothing, seeing nothing.

Where to now?

Did I care?

If I didn't, what else did I have in my life?

I'd found an occupation in finding people who wanted to erase themselves from the public records, to remove their names from the world's telephone books, to vaporise their lives. Of course, some of them deserved to be dragged out of their caves and clamped into stocks to suffer under a blazing sun.

But I'd also traced people who had every right to be left alone.

Oh, well, the alternative was a life spent drafting wills and taking affidavits. And then there was staring at the wall and thinking about what might have been.

Moving on.

Mark Ulyatt had taken out ten paintings from a huge collection, lined them up against the storeroom wall. Were these the paintings he thought would end Pelham's financial worries?

How much money did Pelham need?

The phone rang.

'Jack, Simone.'

'I am available to be asked out for dinner.'

'Soon. There's a solid obstacle called Callum. Some name like that. Give me time. I've emptied the drive and printed out everything that looks interesting.'

'Photographs?'

'About twenty. Paintings.'

'Can you enlarge them?'

'To any size. Within reason.'

'A4 will be fine. Anything else?'

'A lot of email drafts. Mostly just a line or two. Make no sense.'

'Might help. Can you print them out too and leave the stuff at Enzio's?'

'Inside half an hour.'

'Add the speed premium to the bill, please. Someone else is paying.'

'We only have one speed. AFAP.'

'Lunch then? Leave a message.'

'You've invested in an answering machine?'

'I bought it at the Salvos. In its original box with invoice dated 1984.'

'What can I say? You're always ahead of the curve, Jack. An early adopter.'

I fiddled around for an hour, then, in a good mood, I walked to Enzio's down the lesser streets of Carlton and Fitzroy, thinking about catching a plane to London, moving in with Linda, taking the bogus job.

Why not?

I was no stranger to taking money. You took it from bookies, from the tote, from the internet interlopers, why not take it from some media conglomerate that wouldn't even notice my presence on the payroll?

Why not, indeed?

Because gambling was an honest way to make a quid, a market in which the best-informed won. You relied on knowing more than the people who wanted to take your money, like any insider trading on the stock market.

Did I want to be with Linda?

Yes.

Did I want to be with Linda when she was my patron?

I thought about my departure from a cold and dirty London. At the second-last station of the cross in its terrible airport, a Qantas woman said: 'Upgraded to Business, Mr Irish.'

She smiled, the modest smile of a benefactor.

Did she expect to be thanked?

Upgraded.

The word did not sit well with me. It spoke of an unearned promotion, a favour.

'No thanks,' I said. 'I love economy. The noise and the people. Like Dunkirk. You'd know about Dunkirk?'

'Sorry? Paid upgrade, Mr Irish. An hour ago.'

Linda.

I took the leg-up, enjoyed the legroom, drank undistinguished South Australian wine in a prudent manner. Someone would have to fly the plane when the crew were stacked four-deep in the toilet voiding the virtual food.

Sobriety was not on the mind of Phillip, the moustached man next to me. He wanted me to know that he was a business analyst and that he was celebrating a coup.

'Caught them at a low moment,' he said. 'Pommies sitting on a cash swag, excellent income stream, plus IP and hard assets. And occupying most of a niche. HBTE.'

Phillip waved his flute at a waiter. 'Four layers of paralysed management. Featherbedded old farts. I love that. Peeled the business like an onion.'

I nodded, reading chapter two of my book, a novel bought at the airport called *The King James Bible.*

It wasn't that I didn't care about streams, about the way cash ran downhill, as is the nature of flows. As for IP and HBTE, I often fell asleep thinking about them.

Hours later, as our aluminium tube crossed the deadly airspace of some captive Russian state, my companion finished another tale of his commercial acumen.

'Tracked down the missing five percent to this granny,' he said. 'Paid her about six grand and, lo, we had fifty-two percent.'

'Brilliant,' I said, thinking about Charlie's workshop, the

pleasures, minute as they were, of living alone.

After a while, Phillip sighed. 'I don't think I've got a friend in the world.'

I sipped my Bruichladdich single malt. 'Why is that?'

'Too busy, I suppose. Always busy, busy.'

'Neglect can cost you friends.'

'That's not the reason.'

'No?'

'People go off me,' said Phillip.

I wondered how they got on him in the first place.

'My wife said it. She said, I've gone off you. Just like that. Eleven months married. Both still virgins.'

'Tired of waiting for you to make the move?'

'No, no, I mean virgins when we married. Then my brother's wife says, no warning at all, she says my mother went off me. My own mum went off me.'

Sniffs. Tears were running down Phillip's cheeks, spilling over his neat moustache.

'I would discount sisters-in-law,' I said. 'What about your colleagues, your workmates?'

'Waiting to knife me. Drinking, football, horse racing, golf, that's all they care about. I hate all that. I'm hopeless at golf.'

He sniffed. 'What about you?'

I thought about how to show this lonely man met in the sky that I cared about him and understood him.

'Off a lazy eight now,' I said. 'Love the game, the company, playing with your mates.'

He made a choking sound.

'Well, nap-nap time,' I said.

Anyway, it was all Linda's fault.

THE HEAVY rain came just as I reached Enzio's, its fenestrations reglazed. It was the late afternoon lull: the lunchers had sloped away, the inchoate artists, writers and film directors were back in their shabby quarters talking rubbish and sweating out the time before the next snort.

Bruno the Silent gave me the nod. Before I was seated, Enzio slid onto a chair opposite me. He had several nasty shaving cuts, the blood apparently staunched with Kellogg's Cornflakes.

'They still trying to fright me,' he said. 'The cunts.'

'Which cunts?'

'You know. The window. They come in, they order and then they have a fucking fight, knock over the tables, the customers run out, nobody pays, they all fuck off.'

'The same people?'

'No. Different.'

'Could just be people having a disagreement.'

Enzio looked away, fingered a shaving incision, dislodged a cornflake. 'No, no. He ring again, the bastard.'

'As I said last time, call the police. I don't want to know your problems.'

'I call them, they come. They say they can do fuckall. I told you.'

'Well, what can I do?'

Enzio rose and left, a heavy tread. At the kitchen door, he looked at me, more in sorrow than in anger. It was the look I could not bear.

The coffee came and with it a large envelope. I sipped, watching the street, thinking about the way it was: a shabby runway to the city, trams rattling past gloomy snooker cafes, Central European social clubs, hard pubs, the gun shop, and Baker's, the first cafe in the street to serve breakfast. These days people talked rubbish about Mario's being the breakfast pioneer.

Perhaps I could start a campaign to erect a statue of Baker at the Brunswick–Johnston intersection. Perhaps not.

With difficulty, I opened the envelope with a table knife, extracted a few sheets, looked at them, took out the others. Close-ups of paintings. They were all interesting works but they meant nothing to me. Time for an expert.

Fortunately, I had one.

In the long ago, I'd appeared for Roderick Cattersby over parking fines, 112 of them. He was a careless parker, distracted for many months by his wife being rooted by a kindergarten teacher called Aaron. At our first meeting, I found out that he was the son of a Carlton footballer of note. We didn't have to talk about it.

I rang the illogically named National Gallery of Victoria and asked for Rod Cattersby. He was at a meeting. I left my name and number. I had just got back to my office and taken my seat behind the tailor's table when the phone rang.

'Jack,' said Cattersby. 'Why has it been so long?'

'Probably because you've been paying your parking fines. I need some help with paintings.'

'What kind of paintings?'

'At Pelham College, Melbourne Uni. Can you take a look at them?'

'Pel? Pelham Collection works?'

Oh, God.

'Not Pel, are you?'

'No, thank God. But I know about the collection. Everyone knows about it, no one's seen it. Not the whole thing anyway.'

'How does 2.30pm look?'

'Damn good,' said Cattersby.

'See you at the front gate.'

I moved on to studying the draft emails. Some were to his wife or ex-wife, some were to his children. Like most people, he changed his mind about what he wanted to say.

He also appeared to talk to himself. Notes to the future.

…this is not a good idea. Do these people know?

And if it's done? Pleasure? Satisfaction? What if they're innocent?

Rubbish. Make the bastards suffer. Pay and suffer.

More of the same. Sentences. Sentence fragments. The name Villa Simone appeared frequently.

Mark appeared to be a man in turmoil.

What was the Villa Simone?

WE FOLLOWED Betty Fellows, the Pelham housekeeper, to the old storeroom, unlocked the door and switched on the lights.

'Just close up when you leave, gentlemen,' she said.

I led the way around the central shelves to the line of paintings. Cattersby took two paces down the row, stopped at a small canvas, picked it up and looked at the back.

He read:

'Franz von Defregger, 1922, *Der Bauer*. Gift of Reginald Hall (1963–1967). Date of receipt: February 1997.'

'Let me write that down,' I said, groping for my notebook.

He read it out slowly.

Next painting.

'This is familiar,' he said, turning it. 'Hermann Herzog, 1906, *Lake Bolagen*. Same donor, same date of receipt.'

'Artist known to you?'

'My word.'

He moved on.

'Wilhelm Heinrich Truebner, 1901, *Das Anleger, Ammersee*. Gift of Reginald Hall again. Remains of a sticker here.'

He held the painting close to his face. 'Ah. Hyslop and Giffard. They go back a bit.'

'Sydney, presumably.'

He nodded. 'Sold many a dubious canvas to Sydney's parvenus in their time.'

Next.

'Charles Anstruther, 1927, *Villa Romantica, Tuscany*. Never heard of him. Gift of Reggie again, same date, also H and G.'

And so it went: artist, painting title, date, gift of Reginald Hall, date of receipt. All the frames bore the sticker of Hyslop and Giffard.

Andreas Achenbach, Severin Roesen, Adolph von Menzel, Carlo Zubetski, Renfrew Adams, Wilhelm Maria Hubertus Leibl.

Cattersby knew them all except Renfrew Adams, 1927, *Portrait of Stefano*, also a gift from Reggie Hall.

'Who picked them out?''

'A man called Mark Ulyatt. Pelham tutor. He's vanished.'

'There's a connection?'

'I don't know. I'm scratching around.'

'I wouldn't mind a day or two scratching around in here,' said Catters.

'I'll arrange it.'

I gave him the envelope of prints.

'Estimates of value would be greatly appreciated.'

'Guesses is the word. Estimates is far too specific a term.'

Getting Catters out of the storeroom was much more difficult than getting Charlie out of the workshop. The man was in art heat, breathing heavily, stopping every few metres to take out a painting and examine it.

'Jesus,' said Cattersby. 'How can they keep paintings like these in a shed?'

'Catters,' I said. 'We are leaving. Now.'

In the street, he rang for a cab.

'I have to come back, Jack. You'll arrange that?'

'Locked in. We could go to a Carlton-Lions game this season.'

'Great idea,' said Cattersby. 'We'll be wearing our fathers' jumpers. I'll get mine out of mothballs.'

In time, a long time, the taxi arrived, driven by a Sikh. I got in next to him.

'So,' he said, 'where I take you?'

'Brunswick Street, Fitzroy,' I said. 'Then my friend in the back to the National Gallery, St Kilda Road.'

Silence. Furrowed brow. He groped under his seat and gave me a Melways street directory.

'You show me,' he said.

I gave the tome back to him. I wasn't going to be a willing participant in the turbanised deskilling of the taxi business.

'Go to the corner, turn right. I'll direct you from there.'

At my office, Catters wouldn't take money.

'It's gallery work,' he said. 'Looking at potential acquisitions. I'll ring with the value guesses.'

I WENT inside and, after a time of reading what was once a newspaper and drinking tea, I began to ring car-hire companies, negotiating my way up from the switchboard, telling the same lie.

'I'm a solicitor representing Pelham College,' I said. 'That's the University of Melbourne. It's a small matter of the college trying to verify some expenses claims for car hire.'

Like Masons who'd all taken the same vow, they said they would need a court order. I too had a standard message.

'I'll give you the hirer's name,' I said. 'All I want is day and time of hire, when the car was returned, and the mileage. That is, the kilometres recorded. But I can get a court order and you'll be up for legal fees. It's all the same to me.'

It took a long time and, weakened by the effort, I assumed the thinking position.

Was it possible that the paintings Mark chose from the stacks had no connection with his disappearance?

Every chance.

The day passed in small tasks.

I went home. There was no solace there but drink. I washed a decent-sized wineglass and took a bottle of Cliff Edge to the slippery leather sofa.

The ABC news featured the usual prix fixe menu of posturing politicians, middle-eastern explosions, road accidents, crimes, weeping women, and animal stories. Its presenter would not allow journalists to speak for themselves, interviewing them as if they were sources of news who needed to be prodded.

The whole sorry business ended with a business commentator who specialised in pointless data correlations (ice-cream sales and house prices, cruise-ship passenger numbers and currency movements) and hand-dancing, followed by a weatherman in a sprayed-on suit.

Next was the star performer, a milky-pale bloated woman with strange-coloured hair. Her role was to enact press releases, to help federal politicians recite the scripts written by their teenage advisors and prompt them if necessary.

When it came to news items, she said things like, 'What happened next?' and, worst of all, 'How are people feeling?'

Eight o'clock on a Wednesday night.

Just me and a book.

I should be somewhere else. Chelsea in London, for example.

Phone.

'Jack, Catters. Some value guesses.'

'Jesus, that's quick.'

'Don't muck about around here. Think we spend our time staring at paintings?'

'I had thought that, yes.'

'There's an element of staring, I confess. In the interests of scholarship. The pursuit of knowledge.'

'Pursuing knowledge. I do a lot of that. Knowledge runs away from you. Sometimes you have to tackle it.'

'Ah, Jack, such profundity. Now von Defregger, von Menzel, Herzog, Truebner, Achenbach, Severin Roesen, Leibl. If you got lucky, $400,000 for the lot. That's Aussie dollars.'

'Something tells me that's not enough to bail out Pelham,' I said.

'Doesn't bail out a failing coffee shop these days. If your man was looking to make money for Pel, these would not be the choice. I saw two canvases each worth more than four hundred grand on our way out. And then we get to the mystery pair, Anstruther and Adams. I'm still looking for them but they won't be worth much. If anything.'

I thanked him. We bantered, fixed a date for lunch.

'Venue to be agreed upon. Somewhere in no man's land,' I said.

'My side of the so-called river then.'

I found my notebook. Reginald Hall, inmate of Pelham from 1963 to 1967.

I rang Barry Chilvers. He answered in the manner of a man taking a call in the pre-dawn hour.

'Reginald Hall, Pel 1963 to 1967,' I said. 'Generous donor of paintings. I need to know more.'

'At this time of night? Not billing Pel, I hope?'

'In the morning will be fine. You can get started on the inquiry as soon as they're awake at Pel. On reflection, perhaps I should rephrase that. It may never happen.'

'Uncalled for, Jack. I'll ring you in the morning. Goodnight.'

I drank wine and cracked the spine of a novel from the remainder table called *The Wind from the High Country*, by Tasman Hogues, published by Vexed Publishing. The blurb said he was a former fettler, tree surgeon and winch monkey, which gave me every confidence that he would know how to write a cracking novel.

Alas, the first ten pages revealed that Tasman's occupations had not equipped him with the required skills. An editor, any editor worthy of the name, would have helped, but the manuscript appeared to have moved directly from Tasman's word-processor to the page.

I found food. I called it food. It was to food what Tasman's novel was to literature.

To bed at 9.45pm?

Time to do something about the saggy curtains: every third curtain ring was not attached to the curtain.

Saggy.

My whole life was saggy, sagging, sagged. If only I didn't know so much about the results of lawyers taking drugs, I could make a phone call and banish all negative thoughts.

Perish the thought. I needed something innocent to put me to sleep.

It was on the shelves. It was about a whale.

For the umpteenth time, it put me under in five pages. Thank you, Herman.

I WAS drawing up a sad shopping list when Chilvers rang.

'Reginald Hall,' he said. 'I've got his file. Undistinguished career at Pel. B-plus was his best mark. Died young, 1997, car hit a light pole. He left his art collection to Pel. No heirs, apparently.'

'Address?'

'Um, that was 166 Young Street, Cremorne. In Sydney.'

'What did he do for a living?'

'Nothing, probably. The Master says the records show Hall's fees were paid by the Crowhurst Family Trust. He thinks it was on his mother's side.'

'Well, thanks. Back to the grindstone then.'

'The Master says he should have mentioned that Mark went to the Macedon house to look at paintings.'

'The Macedon house?'

'Renfrew Hall. Left to the college by Colonel Hugo Renfrew-Phillips. Can't sell it in terms of the bequest. They used to let it to other colleges for retreats, that kind of thing.'

'Retreat? Not a word in the colonel's vocabulary, surely?'

Mount Macedon was once a hill station on the Indian model, an escape from the summer heat for Melbourne's rich. They built grand houses, planted exotic trees, and cultivated gardens in the English style.

'The Master now recalls that some Pel Collection paintings went up there,' said Barry. 'And the colonel left a collection. Mostly stags at bay, I recall. He was a sort of soldier-poet.'

'Where have all the soldier-poets gone? Gone to graveyards every one.'

'My Lord, never seen you as a Pete Seeger man.'

'Don't ever change that opinion.'

I finished my list and drove to Piedimonte's, lucked on a park around the corner. It was Fitzcarlton nanny hour, the place was full of them, brat-charges in the front trays, grabbing items from the shelves, screaming. The parents would be at work, thinking about barriers to entry, income streams, IP, niche occupancy, and possibly strategies for being more effective change-agents.

It took only a few minutes of dispiriting trolley-stacking to load the items needed to fight filth for a few months.

A red Mustang was parked outside the old boot factory, two elegantly-shod feet protruding half a metre from the driver's side window.

Cameron Delray was reading the *Age*. He spoke without lowering it.

'Exhaust sounds nice,' he said. 'That Trapanga's got a touch with Studs.'

'A red Mustang. Not quite you. What happened to the HSV?'

With difficulty, he got his legs under the steering wheel, eased himself upright. 'Lent it to my current. Taking her Pommy visitors down the coast. No enough room in the Cooper.'

I went around and got into the passenger seat. Expensive perfume filled my nose. 'I don't like to think who you borrowed this from.'

'No,' he said, 'except that she's much classier than this bucket suggests. Get coffee around here?'

We drove around the corner to a coffee place called Jack and the Beans Talk.

Cam eyed the name, eyed me.

'Never been here before,' I said.

We went in. The staff were earnest-looking coffee scientists in white lab coats. One approached us.

'Two long blacks,' I said. 'Hot milk on the side.'

'That's espresso, filter, drip, cold...'

I stilled him with a hand. 'You can make it an old sock in a bucket. Just don't burn the milk, professor.'

Unhappy, he left.

'They'll put stuff in it, you know that?' said Cam.

'If they have the testicles. So?'

'Prince Gustav,' said Cam. 'I squeezed this prick, he hangs around stables, hears all the goss. Held him upside down for a while, he gets a nose bleed. Charry Equine, the boys from Hong Kong, that's all he knows.'

'Mean anything?'

'I bid against a Charry at the sales two years ago. He was with a Pommy bloodstock parasite. Alan Carter-Leigh.'

'How'd you find out his name?'

'You don't want to know who outbids you?'

'Right. For Harry?'

'One of his friends.'

'Where do we go from here?'

'Thought you might tell me.'

I gave it some thought while studying the other patients, three tables of couples drinking their coffee as it were communion wine.

'Where did the horses Charry and Carter-Leigh bought go?'

'They're not keen on opening the books.'

'That's not because there's so much dodgy money involved?'

'In racing?'

A junior scientist brought our coffees.

'Two old-sock long blacks,' he said, something sinister in his smile.

'Knowing where helps?' said Cam.

'I'm scratching. Who got most out of Gustav kicking it?'

'Paying to the tenth nag, half the field. I've asked about the big winners from people owe Harry.'

'Not many bookies left take big punts.'

Cam stared at me for an uncomfortable time.

'Okay,' I said. 'That's obvious. Don't look at me like that.'

When we'd finished our coffees, I complimented the scientists on their mastery of the old-sock technique.

'We learn something every day,' said the senior scientist. 'Please come back. I've asked the staff to bring in their old socks.'

Cam dropped me at my front door.

'I'll ring,' he said.

GOING TO Sydney was not easy.

First, I cleared the trip with Chilvers.

'Go to Darwin if necessary,' he said. 'Do what it takes.'

'Your language surprises me,' I said. 'So modern.'

'We move with the times here.'

Then there was the agony of getting to the airport, the waiting, the Qantas flight with mothers and snotty offspring, and being in the presence of hungover young men in their puke suits.

At Sydney Airport, things improved. A man held up a sign. He took me outside to a grey limo whose uniformed driver was holding open a door.

'Your office on the line,' he said. 'Phone's in the back seat.'

'Jack Irish,' said the clipped tones of Miss Annabel Creighton, captain of hockey at Benenden, Cranbrook, Kent, and personal assistant to D. J. Olivier, platinum-grade fixer.

'Annabel Creighton,' I said, 'I tremble to think that only a few kilometres separate us.'

'Destined never to meet. Well, perhaps in foggy Vienna one night. A sad bar in the Schweinstrasse.'

'The Schweinstrasse. I remember it well.'

She laughed, a throaty upper-class sound.

'Now, Jack. To business. Hyslop and Giffard, founded 1947, sold in 1996 to an Andrew Searle. He sold it to Carstairs Gallery in 2000.

Carstairs sold it to Quay Gallery in 2006. The driver will take you there. The Rocks.'

'Faultless,' I said.

'Unfortunately, I can't find out what records have been retained. The only person I've been able to talk to is witless.'

'Leaves me something to do.'

'The car's at your disposal. The driver will give you a card. Please call if there's anything else.'

'I can think of something but...'

'Think of the Schweinstrasse.'

'The old drunk with the squeezebox, the *Wiener Lieder...*'

The Quay Gallery was in a small building with one room at ground level. Now showing to no one was an exhibition called *Visions of Immortality* featuring works by three artists.

A taut-faced woman in her sixties emerged from behind a mirror wall.

'Beautiful, aren't they?' she said. 'Important works.'

'Time will tell,' I said. 'Are you the director?'

'I'm in charge,' she said.

I introduced myself. It gave her no pleasure to meet me.

'The businesses that came before you. Have you kept their records?'

'Why?'

'I'm trying to trace some paintings.'

'You're the second person in a month.'

'Can you describe the other one?'

'Why? What's this?'

'Missing person inquiry,' I said.

She bit her lower lip, suspicious.

'Floppy hair, sort of blond. Englishman.'

'That's him. Could you help?'

'I told him and I'm telling you, we began with a clean slate when we took over the business.'

'What happened to the records?'

'I have no idea,' she said. 'Hold on. I think old Searle might have some. He came in one day about five years ago and gave me a lecture on the history of the place. Very boring.'

'How would I find him?'

'Not the foggiest. He's probably dead. Appeared to be about eighty.'

I went into the cafe next door. 'Mr Searle? Lovely man. Came in every day. He's got an office in the Galvin Building in Gloucester Street.'

It was close enough to walk. The board in the Galvin Building showed Andrew Searle, Art Consultant, on the fifth floor. I walked up, a silly decision, made even sillier by the note on Searle's door:

Andrew Searle will be overseas until July 14, 2015.

I wrote a note, tore the page out of my notebook, slid it under the door.

This had been an expensive way to find out nothing.

I WAS waiting for a car when the device made its noise.

'The luck of the Irish,' I said.

'Find out anything?' said Chilvers.

'Mark went looking for gallery records in Sydney, probably didn't find any.'

'Not very helpful then. Plus expensive.'

'Don't push your luck. I don't go to Sydney for fun. And I recall the words do what you have to do.'

'Sorry, Jack, sorry.'

'I suggest we let this matter rest for a while. He'll turn up or he won't. And I have pressing matters to attend to.'

'I'll tell the college you're in waiting-for-results mode. Actual paid work will resume in due course.'

The car arrived.

It wasn't a taxi, it was a man I phoned when I needed to go some-where. Reg had been a taxi driver—he could take you to Camellia Crescent, Montmorency, without consulting a map—but now his life was more predictable. All he needed was a time or ninety minutes of notice.

'Home, office?'

'Office, Reg,' I said. 'The place where dreams go to die.'

Behind the table, my mind turned to Alan Carter-Leigh, blood-stock agent. Time passed. I was woken by the telephone.

'Those horses, they went to Warren Begbie,' said Cam. 'One's Iron Barron, he's 2,3,1. The other one's Leviticus Sunrise, two trials. Debuts at Bendigo next week.'

'Owner?'

'Metronam Racing, manager Regina Falmouth. She's registered. Four members, two from Hong Kong, two from Singapore.'

'Good work, son. I'll look into it.'

I sat back.

Regina Falmouth. A name to stay in the mind.

My phone rang.

'The last of the Irish,' I said.

'There's no end to the fucken Irish,' said Barry Tregear. 'We've got a body could be your Ulyatt.'

'Where?'

'Drain. Dropped down a drain.'

'Cause of death?'

'Two shots in the head.'

'Where is this drain?'

'North Melbourne. Sligo Street.'

'Dead how long?'

'How the fuck do I know? Ask the maggots, ask Homicide, ask the mortuary. We need an ID.'

I studied the wall for a while before ringing Chilvers.

'Someone from Pel needs to go to the mortuary. Look at a body.'

'Oh, God, no.'

'It probably won't be Mark.'

'Can't you go?'

'Me? I've never seen Mark. If it's him, it's a Homicide matter. I'll put in my bill.'

'Oh God, Barthe will have to go. Where is it?'

I told him. 'He'll be expected. Let me know what he says.'

'When? Before or after?'

'Chilvers, I don't care what he says before. I am not an Old Pel. Can you get that into your head?'

Enzio's problem with extortionists came to mind. I hadn't done anything. The police were no use. They had no inclination to take on the mafia. But I couldn't take them on. In truth, I couldn't take on anyone.

Back to the problem at hand.

Who were the bastards? What had the paintings to do with this?

REFLECTIONS, REVIEWS
& ESSAYS

REMEMBRANCE OF BOOKS PAST

I RECENTLY read a piece in a newspaper headlined 'Books—Do They Have a Future?'. It was one of many published in the last few years about books as we know them being replaced by electronic tablets, the words unloaded from a cyber warehouse. The reader's library will be held in a humming server somewhere, paid for and available on demand. Soon after reading this article, I set about the task of unpacking books as we know them, books not seen for a long time and not noticed for a long time before that. I stood in the garage, in a dim corridor of cardboard boxes, unearthing fragments of my life.

Cut the tape, open the flaps, pull out a book. The *Concise Oxford Dictionary*, shabby, binding loose, faded blue cover inexplicably dotted with white paint. Now this is a book that conveys a sense of place. It conveys me. Instantly, I am thirteen, sitting in a classroom in the place I grew up in, a small, dusty village, hundreds of kilometres from the nearest town of any size. The soil was a handspan of dirt, under it, limestone, white, crumbly, porous. In summer, the topsoil baked, cracked, breathed out little dust devils. Brick houses developed fissures that ran from foundation to rafters. The bone-dry, featureless landscape lay at the end of every street. Out there, in the shimmering, hopeless towns lay upside down, and sudden whirlwinds sent to heaven tumbleweeds and dry hollow sticks and the weightless and bleached bones of small creatures. My whole childhood seems to have been one long drought. Each summer day, the clouds came up from the west, pillars of cumulonimbus, cliffs, massive, biblical clouds, humbling clouds, clouds faintly tinged with grey, hinting at water, tears behind eyeshadow. But these clouds carried no water. These huge formations were born far away on a cold and parsimonious shore where the grey Atlantic, the cripplingly cold, numbingly cold Atlantic, broke on the Namib Desert. They were phantoms, sent to tease. The long passage across the barren interior had bled them dry. Still, no one knew that for sure. It had rained from clouds like these before when things were at their worst, the water table gone, the living animals just bones in skin, the windmills groaning and screeching to produce nothing. Each day brought the hope, each day the dimming and then the silence and then the lightning, sheet and fork, that cast a light so white it expelled colour from the world. Thunder followed, cataclysmic thunder that vibrated in your skull, hurt your brain. And then nothing, not a drop of rain, not even a suggestion of damp.

In these summers, the heat inside could not be borne and we tried to sleep on the verandah, hearing the dogs panting, getting up to stand under the tepid trickle of the garden hose, feeling the needle-thin cicada screeches in the bones of your head. And in the reaches of the night, sweaty and unslept, I thought about school the next day because I dreaded school, a school where I was one of a handful of despised *rooineks*, children who spoke English at home.

I open the old dictionary. The flyleaf bears three experimental signatures and the price: eighteen shillings. The English teacher ordered everyone to buy a copy. He was the first pedant I ever met, pedant and sadist. (Are these things connected? Have I been one, in a small way? Was this where it began?) The dirt-poor parents of the farm children didn't have eighteen shillings in cash money, so he sold them the book on credit. Getting paid gave him a lot of pleasure. Every Monday, the pupils had to queue at his table to hand over two shillings, often in small change knotted in a handkerchief, or to offer folded notes from their mothers or fathers, notes written on cheap lined notepaper. If the man was in a playful mood, which was often, he would read out the sad unpunctuated little promises of payment. ('I am sorry we cannot pay today but we are selling some heifers on Friday so Ernest will bring four shillings next week if that is all right.')

Standing in the garage, I can see the man's shiny, bony, bald head, see his spitty lips, his glasses glittering, hear his scratchy voice, the throat-clearing, hear the nervous, eager-to-please laughter of the class. Grown-up people, scared, dignity slipping away, must have laughed like that when eighteen-year-old concentration camp guards made jokes at the Buchenwald siding.

Not a good memory but one attached to this volume, carted around the world, living in boxes, crammed in with trivial companions. I wish I could go out and find the man, inflict some pain on him, but John Richard Calitz, pedant, sadist, hater of the people whose language he loved, is long dead, the final pain inflicted, gone to be with his adored Shakespeare, Keats and Milton, purer Englishmen somehow, poetic men who never shot a starving Boer running and ragged, never burned a desperate farmhouse or butchered, singed and ate the sad-eyed house cow.

Moving on. From the same box, I extract another Oxford, the *Book of Literary Anecdotes*. Am I the only person except for the compiler to have read this volume from cover to cover? Twice, in my case. Trapped on a slow train to Brindisi in a stifling August, then marooned penniless for days in a sleazy hotel, window opening onto a pungent lightwell dripping water, it was all I had. A book of bits of things people have written. Two pages are freckled with dark spots. They immortalise the moment a full flagon of red wine belonging to an Italian family, three generations present, toppled from the luggage rack and broke on my companion's head. The senior generations jumped up, threw their hands in the air, implored forgiveness. Galvanised by the impact, some shocking impulse sent down the spine, the victim stood up involuntarily, swayed, bathed from head to foot in a dark, oxidised liquid. Her own blood, thicker than Italian wine, much, much thicker, ran down her scalp, spilled over the sill of her eyebrows. Eyes losing focus, she raised a hand to the horrified assembly and murmured, 'It's quite all right,' and subsided.

There is no doubt that some people travel better than others and that melting Scots with Dutch produces a hard compound. But that has nothing to do with books as we know them, paper pages contained within covers. Or does it? Will your e-book resonate across the years? Will you be able to find the page that holds the memory?

In the garage, thinking this thought, I pull out another book, Hegel's *Philosophy of Right*. I take it towards the door, towards the light (or, as Hegel's translator might have it, the Light), flip it to look for marginalia, for something written by me, the early me, the young me, the clueless me, a person trying to understand the words, trying to find a fingerhold on the sheer and shiny face of this European intellectual mountain. There is nothing. The book is broken-backed, used, sullied, but not even a phrase is underscored. Why not? Across time and space, vast tracts of both, I can hear the professor, an intelligent man both exhilarated and mutilated by his time spent at Oxford University among people he simply assumed were his betters. He purrs, 'You might *think* about putting a line under that. I always suggest *using* a book, writing in it, making it your *own*.' A gesture, hands bent outwards. 'It's just a *book*. One man's *ideas*, not a sacred *object*.'

I open the work at random, read a few lines, and the very sight of the laboured and opaque prose transports me back to a tutorial. A difficult customer, G. W. F. Hegel. Not the Bryce Courtenay of philosophers. After lunch on a day in high summer, hot, in a small room fogged with cigarette smoke, five of us, four tired students and the tutor, fell asleep in our comfy chairs. Books in hand, we were reflecting on a particularly abstruse passage in the *Philosophy of Right*. Time passed. A bell sounded. But we were beyond the reach of bells. The next tutorial arrived, waited outside, became restive, knocked, to no result. Someone peeped in, was alarmed. From across the way, a lecturer was called, a social anthropologist, no stranger to the exotic.

Later, he said he thought he had come upon an academic suicide pact.

Hegel. What is he good for? I don't know, but I've kept this book when others, many others, have been cruelly abandoned to their fate at fetes, bazaars and op-shops. I didn't write a word in it, but I made it my own anyway. Imperfectly understood—no, hardly understood at all—but my own.

Next book. *Goodbye Dolly Gray* by Rayne Kruger, a history of the Boer War. I sniff it, give it a good weighing in the hand. It has heft. It should have heft. This book has a lot to answer for. It aroused in me the desire to become an historian, caused me to leave my job and go to university, live for years off the kindness and sacrifice of a hard-headed person of Scots-Dutch ancestry. The best reading years those, months immersed in dry and pettifogging detail (for example, a minute examination of four years in the *Age of Anne*), followed by weeks lolling in a deckchair with such reprobates as P. G. Wodehouse and S. J. Perelman. Kruger is therefore responsible for much of the course of my life, good and bad. He is also responsible for my owning the books underneath it: Denys Hays' *The Medieval Centuries*, Marc Bloch's *Feudal Society*, Ladurie's *Montaillou*, E.P. Thompson's *The Making of the English Working Class*, Eric Hobsbawm's *The Age of Capital*, Genovese's *Roll Jordan Roll*, Womack's *Zapata and the Mexican Revolution*. I open other cartons: more history, books on imperialism, on colonialism, on frontiers, on gold mining and duelling and wars and labour and technology and crowds and secret societies and protest and punishment. And the rest. And there's lots of rest, some books so esoteric that I cannot reclaim the impulse of purchase. Why would one want to own a slim account of six years of utterly uneventful governorship of some minute Pacific atoll in the nineteenth century? (Because it's there, that's why.)

In the dirt-floored garage, surrounded by books I own, I think of a work of history I don't own: Lord Russell of Liverpool's *The Scourge of the Swastika*. I was twelve, I think, when I opened the book in the public library, looked at the photographs of terrified people, of mass graves, of living skeletons, of arrogant men in uniform, of pale, dough-faced Ilse Koch, who could dash babies against a wall, and of Heydrich, face and being devoid of all mercy, a plump lower lip, a baby's lip a mother would kiss, take it between her teeth, bite it, gently. Just ordinary people doing their duty. I took the book out and read it. And then I saw the world around me through different eyes. And I never got the old eyes back.

New box. Novels. John Updike, *Rabbit Run*. I was nineteen when I read my first Updike, *The Centaur*, lent to me by an older colleague who was perhaps less interested in furnishing my mind than in other things. But the lender's motives don't matter now. I wish I had never read any Updike. No writer has ever pulled me close like Updike, pulled me close with soft hands and headbutted me. I wish I'd never read any Updike so that I could wake up tomorrow and the collected works would be on the bedside table and I would be able to have another try at growing up.

But. Here's *For Whom the Bell Tolls*. You can't read Hemingway after you're twenty-one because Hemingway never got past twenty-one. But, for a twenty-one-year-old, he could write. Reading a few pages reminds me of how, at eighteen or nineteen, I read and reread the Nick Adams stories, moved by them and filled with admiration for the prose. Easy to parody, easy to mock, but the best of the writing has the irreducible quality of pebbles worn smooth by a cold, swift river.

Joseph Conrad, *Nostromo*, the political novel against which all others must be judged. Costaguana is still more real for me than any real South American country. In my first year of work, daunted by some of the people around me, people who struck me as worldly and widely read, I set myself the task of reading all of Conrad, read him doggedly at night, in trains, on buses, in the sad carbolic corridors of magistrate's courts where the brutal sounds of floggings sometimes came to your ears. I don't know exactly what good this reading did me except that afterwards, and for a long time, I came to find echoes of Conrad in almost all male writers I read.

On I plunge, ripping open boxes, bringing to light Faulkner,

Steinbeck, Baldwin, Stegner, Joyce Carol Oates. To call your child both Joyce and Carol is more than a lapse in taste. A good writer, though, a better writer by far on boxing than Hemingway and, to my knowledge, never pulled on a glove. The problem is output. J. C. Oates writes enough for two people. Perhaps she *is* two people: the Oates girls, Joyce and Carol, a team?

Further into the boxes. Wolfe, Tom, *The Kandy-Kolored* whatever and other titles. The New Journalism. Another man with a great deal to answer for. Show me journalists over forty, take me to where they live. The stuff will be there, thumbed, even underlined, the heavy users. Oh, they'll weep and deny, blame other people, but they've got tracks all over the body. And so has every lifestyle piece in every newspaper and every colour supplement, only the twenty-something authors don't know it. Just Wolfe mules, really, no idea what they're carrying, enter a plea of ignorance.

Open another book. A second Wolfe, Thomas: a little thing called *From Death to Morning*. I sit on a box, it sags into a comfortable bum shape, and read a little and think about how wonderful I once thought this writing was. Yes, well. Echoing the American philosopher, George Costanza, I say, *It's not you, Thomas, it's me.*

Out comes an early Don DeLillo, enigmatic cover, *Running Dog*. This is not a great work but it flags the mature writer to come: absolute American confidence, throwaway, effortless, the John McEnroe of American writing, aces served at will, dazzling groundstrokes, moody, intuitive, brilliant. The writing immediately makes you complicit, found out, two fingers pressing on the pulsing river in your wrist. More than any other American writer, more than Updike, Auster, Gaddis, Carver, Cheever, Fitzgerald, DeLillo seems to me to have displayed the ability to keep the novel fresh and shocking and, in Sven Birkerts' word, dangerous.

In the unpacking of these books, it occurs to me that I don't own them. They own me. Over the years, there have been many moves and many book culls. Colin Wilson went early. John O'Hara got the bullet. Graham Greene survived, Eric Ambler didn't. Kingsley

Amis fell, Evelyn Waugh came through. Norman Mailer was wiped, Carson McCullers too. Nadine Gordimer got packed, Doris Lessing didn't. The books that remain are not there because they've aged well, survived some test of time. No, some of them have aged worse than I have. The reason they are still with me is that they are the ones I could not bear to give up. I have been formed by them. My identity is in these cartons. These books, the books as such, are my youth, my life, my country. I am them. Will people one day say that of electronic books, of books without covers or paper pages, books not adorned with childish signatures, spots of blood or wine, books not marked with old punched bus tickets and scraps of newspaper, books not faded and freckled and redolent in their physical being of other times, other places, other rooms, and of people and passions and loves?

I think not. And where are you, my William books and my Biggles and my *Teddy Lester's Schooldays*?

1999

FAIR GO, MATE

I CAME to love Australia in an instant. It wasn't the beauty of Sydney. You can't love beauty for itself, not for long, anyway. The moment came in a most unlovely place—in the barren suburb of Ultimo. I was waiting for a bus late at night in an empty street, just me and two young printers, leaning against the wall. A drunk man, not young, not tidy, appeared and sat on the bench, fell over sideways, still singing quietly to himself.

Slowly down the street came a police car. It went by, stopped, reversed. Both occupants got out, bulky cops, bored. I looked away, newest of the new chums, uneasy, none of my business.

'Let's see you stand,' said one of the policemen to the drunk man. The man tried and failed, slumped back. The policemen reached for his arms to take him away.

One of the young printers pushed off the wall. 'Fair go, mate,' he said. 'What's he done?'

'Piss off, sunshine,' said the cop.

'Done buggerall,' said the printer. 'Why don't you go down the Cross and catch some real crims?'

'Yeah, leave him alone,' said the other young man. 'He's with us. We're lookin' after him.'

The cops hesitated, looked at each other. 'Watch your big mouth,' said one to the first printer. Then they left, swaggering back to the car.

How could you not love a country where ordinary people were so little in awe of authority, so unafraid of armed men in uniform, so concerned for the fate of a drunken stranger?

On Tuesday, I heard a young woman on the radio talking about spending her Easter long weekend at Woomera. She'd taken part in the invasion of the detention camp that enabled some of the inmates to escape.

The talk-back host was sharp with her. That was criminal behaviour, he said.

The young woman wasn't daunted. We're treating these people like criminals, she said. Putting babies and small children behind fences. They didn't look like criminals to me.

I was pulled back in time. This was the voice of Australia first heard long ago on that sweaty night in Ultimo. For the caller, the issue wasn't whether the people in the camps were genuine refugees or illegal immigrants. The issue was whether they were being decently treated.

She was saying that there is a minimum of decent fairness to which all people are entitled: a fair go. It seems to me that this idea runs deep and strong in Australia, a part of the culture vastly more important than vague and sentimental notions of mateship.

Over the boat people, the image-makers have tried to convey a sense of a brave government guarding Australia against a foreign threat.

The talk-back caller looked at the people caged in a place once deemed excellent for testing weapons of mass destruction. She saw the eyes and the hands, she heard the voices pleading in a language not their own.

She couldn't quite see these people as threatening. She cried for them. What has this to do with the world of writing and publishing?

Nothing.

It is just a good time to pay an inadequate homage to a couple of apprentice printers. And to someone who didn't go to the beach or the mountains over Easter.

It does not matter how this tiny part of a huge and tragic story ends. It does not matter how many people stay in Australia or how many are sent away. What matters is how we treated people who came to us packed in sinking hulks and holding nothing but their children's hands and the hope in their hearts.

'Fair go, mate,' said the young printer. God knows where he learned that kind of disrespect for authority.

2002

THE FITZROY YOUTH CLUB
AT THE 2001 GRAND FINAL

WHEN I came to live in Fitzroy in the early 1980s, it was still a suburb of clothing sweatshops, gloomy central European snooker cafes, printeries, the gun shop, cheap shoe shops. And it had a football team.

I knew nothing of Melbourne or of football.

However, it soon became clear that I would have to have a team or be a social misfit.

The Fitzroy Football Club chose itself. Who else could someone who lived three blocks from the Brunswick Street Oval barrack for?

And so I joined the faithful, then a far from dispirited crowd. How was I to know that it would all end in tears?

Did anyone watching Bernie Quinlan almost beat the mighty Hawks by himself in the 1983 qualifying final think that Fitzroy was doomed? How could a club that could climb the ladder from sixth to joint-second, that could cane swaggering North by 150 points, not have a future?

But the bad times were coming. No one chronicled them better than Barry Dickins. No one better captured the love of a football team, its place in a life. In the 1980s, in the *Melbourne Times*, his weekly pieces on the fortunes of Fitzroy—manic, poetic writings, spotted with beer and cigarette ash and tears—spoke for all supporters of teams having a long bad trot.

Dickins loved; the team lost. He did not cease loving.

By the time I wrote my first novel, *Bad Debts*, in the mid-1990s, the business-suited betrayers with knives were standing around Fitzroy.

Sad and seething with resentment, I made the focal point of the book the Prince of Prussia, a Fitzroy pub that is a shrine to the Fitzroy Football Club. Here the central character, Jack Irish, a gambler, apprentice cabinetmaker, people-finder and occasional solicitor, drinks with three ancient, rusted-on Fitzroy supporters known as the Fitzroy Youth Club.

One evening, one of them, Wilbur Ong, reveals that he has got eight three weeks in a row in his granddaughter's tipping competition.

> Norm O'Neill's huge nose came around slowly, like the forward cannon on the USS *Missouri* swivelling to speak to Vietnam. 'You can only get eight out of eight, Wilbur,' he said slowly and with menace, 'if you tip against the Lions.'
>
> Wilbur gave him a pitying look. 'Norm,' he said, 'if you was forty years younger I'd take you outside for jumpin' to that conclusion. 'Course I don't tip against the Lions. It's the girl. She takes all me other tips and changes that one. She reckons tippin' against the Lions is the only sure thing left in the footy.'
>
> 'I don't think you brought your daughter up right,' Eric Tanner said.

The old codgers live in a world where teams go on forever, loyalty never wavers. A club can have a bad patch, ten or twenty years, but it doesn't matter. They'll come good one day.

It doesn't occur to them that clubs have become businesses that can be closed. That would be like saying that mum and dad aren't paying their way and have to go. Many people still feel that way. They hate the idea of football as business.

When Fitzroy went to Brisbane, I could not follow and I wandered apostate. But that is not a bearable condition, so I went to St Kilda.

In the second Jack Irish book, *Black Tide*, the Fitzroy Youth Club, too, begins to think of marrying again.

Eric sighed, made a gesture of dismissal. 'Stuck in the past, you blokes. Can't bring the Roys back, everythin's moved on. Well, it's round five and I'm not sittin' around here anymore lookin' at your ugly mugs on a Satdee arvo.'

Norm O'Neill took a deep drink, wiped his lips, didn't look at Eric, said at a volume that bounced off the ceiling. 'Yes, well, off ya go. What's a lifetime anyway? St Kilda's waitin' for you. Club's holdin' its breath. Whole stand'll jump up, here's Eric Tanner, boys, welcome Eric, three cheers for Eric Tanner, hip bloody hip, bloody hooray.'

But in the end Norm comes around.

When the last glass was put down, Norm said, 'Well, bloody Brisbane it's not. Never. Nothin' much against the Saints. Few things but not much. Don't mind that little Stanley Alves, gets a bit extra out of the lads. Shoulda won the Brownlow in '75 when they give it to that Footscray bloke.'

Jack takes the youth club to a Saints game and, in the fourth quarter, they begin to give the team some encouragement. The transplantation is under way.

Did I do the right thing by the old codgers? Could the youth club have observed a decent period of mourning and then, however reluctantly, accepted the Brisbane Lions?

After all, Fitzroy itself is changed almost beyond recognition but it is still Fitzroy.

This is what Jack's friend, Drew, says to him:

All we have to do is pretend that the Roys aren't having many home games this season. When they play in Melbourne, they're home. In Brisbane and Sydney and Adelaide and fucken Perth, they're away. That's not hard, is it? Fewer home games. Get a grip on that and we've still got the Roys.

Still got the Roys. Jack and the youth club could be in the crowd this afternoon, wearing their ancient Fitzroy scarves and beanies, seeing many familiar faces around them, enjoying the banter and the camaraderie, feeling the tension build as game time approaches. I had the power to give them that.

Today a football team from Brisbane will run onto the MCG. Humble in football's temple, they will nevertheless know they have earned the right to be there. They will look around, see the great sight, hear the great sound.

Who in that moment will dare to say that these young men are not the heirs of Chicken Smallhorn and Dinny Ryan, of Alan Ruthven and Kevin Murray, of immortal Haydn Bunton and thrice-blessed Bernie Quinlan? Who will be the one to say that?

For will not these men, on this holy ground, on this holiest of days, proudly wear on their chests the lion of Fitzroy? They will. And, therefore, they are Fitzroy.

I was wrong, Jack, Norm, Wilbur, Eric. Wrong, and I am sorry, and I wish I could undo what I have done. Go Lions. Go the Roys. You are one.

2001

AH, THE MELBOURNE CUP

KIWI WON the Melbourne Cup in 1983. It was a day to be at Flemington. Jimmy Cassidy had the horse stone motherless last after 2700 metres, then the boy gave it a lick and it passed twenty-three horses as if their minds were on something else.

Kiwi paid 9/1. People in the know said it would have been a lot more if Cassidy hadn't been tipping it all week to anyone who'd listen.

I know a person who was at Flemington that day. She took two girlfriends to the cup in her boyfriend's car. Since he was a porn entrepreneur, it was a Porsche, canary yellow. They parked in the public car park among the Commodores and the Falcons and the like. Men whistled at them. The women gave them the look.

When the strapless trio got back to the car after the big race, sunburnt through the rub-on tan and a little tired, someone had written CARLTON SLUTS in pink lipstick on the Porsche wind-screen.

The trio looked around. People sitting in, on and around a nearby Commodore were immediate suspects—they were drunk and making comments. The driver of the Porsche then recognised one of these people as an insignificant girl a year behind her at school.

That settled it. She took a bottle of Moët et Chandon out of the back of the car, shook it, loosened the cage, walked across and fired the cork at the revellers.

She was taking a foaming swig of the French bubbly provided

by the pornographer when a full can of Vic Bitter hit the Porsche. It made a big dent.

This could not be tolerated. The Porsche team went over for talks. After a while the police arrived but not before several people and the Porsche's bodywork had sustained much deliberate and some collateral damage.

The next day, the driver was wearing big dark glasses. 'How was the cup?' I asked.

'Great,' she said. 'Terrific. I won twenty bucks and I fell into the roses and I met Bob Hawke and Alphonse Gangitano, what a spunk. I kissed Johnny Farnham. I think it was him.'

She took off her shades. Her right eye was full of blood. 'Also we had a fight and got arrested and Derek's dropped me.'

Ah, the Melbourne Cup. Where else in the world is so much possible within the compass of a single day?

But where else is a country's major sporting event the occasion for an entire city to take the day off? Where else does a sporting event attract the full social spectrum—billionaires, pensioners, tycoons, lap-dancers, religious leaders, drug criminals, neurosurgeons, bicycle mechanics, film stars, beach cleaners, standover men, pop singers?

And this for a horse race. On a Tuesday. What other famous sporting event in the world happens on a Tuesday, a day notable only as the point when reaching Friday begins to seem vaguely possible?

If you come to Australia fairly late in the play as I did, in the second act, it strikes you that horse racing is in the Australian blood at a concentration unheard of in other countries. Everyone has a gambling story, everyone has a favourite Melbourne Cup winner, a favourite jockey, everyone knows someone who owns a horse or a bit of one. This is the country that invented the totaliser, that turned illegal bookmaking into a community service.

It is also obvious that the blood count rises to alarming levels in the weeks before the Melbourne Cup. It gets worse every year. Fifteen years ago, the Cox Plate was a race only the aficionados cared about. Now you can't move in the TAB for mug punters and there's about

$12 million in the pool for the meeting.

No, you cannot but be influenced by the role of horse racing in this country's culture. What is strange is that there is so little about the track in Australian fiction. When I got around to writing my first novel, I thought I'd have a go at remedying this lack.

For the writer, racing has everything. This passage is from the first chapter of *Dead Point*:

> 'Well, isn't this easy,' said the caller. 'Renoir's thrashing this field, drilling the bookies who got caught early, he's in another league altogether and Kathy Gale isn't even…'
>
> I had Kathy and Renoir in perfect focus, all grace and power, an unbidden smile on my face, and then I saw her head drop and her arms in their silken sleeves go forward to clutch the lovely black neck and I saw shining horse and rider falling, falling, falling, all gainliness gone, all grace and power departed in a split second of agony.
>
> They fell and she lay still and he, the proud and lovely creature, struggled to stand and the field had plenty of space in which to part and ride around them so that some undeserving twosome could be declared winners.

Reading this again, I think of gallant Mummify breaking down after trying his heart out in the Caulfield Cup, of the tears in his trainer's eyes, and of the old lady who sent the six dollars she won on him for something to be put on his grave.

For me, the appeal of horse racing lies in its uncertainty, its asymmetry, its beautiful arbitrariness. That's what Flemington's about on that Tuesday in November.

2005

SALUTE THE JUDGE

IMAGINE A cafe, gloomy. At a corner table, a woman is reading a newspaper, making notes on a Think Blot. A man approaches.

'Excuse me,' he says, tentative. 'They tell me you work for the *Macquarie Dictionary* and I just wanted to tell you that I really, really admire the way you've included nocebo and Hollywood tape.'

'Just part of the job,' she says.

'But I have to ask. What happened to pinophile? And low-doc? I mean, they're so everywhere?'

'I'm off duty here,' she says. 'There's a website.'

Compiling a dictionary is a heavy responsibility. Those in charge are the door bitches (term not in either volume under discussion) of the language. We could all handle choosing the ordinary words that little swots want to look up—niccolite, sphygmograph, crepidoma, etc. It is deciding what new words to include that is the wet work (not in). Bestowing the dictionary's imprimatur calls for ceaseless vigilance and fine judgement.

The *Collins Australian Dictionary* is silent on the subject, but the introduction to the *Macquarie Dictionary*'s fourth edition makes it clear that it knows the difference between a perishable coinage by some Sydney advertising smarty (probably a Pom, all the Sydney advertising smarties are Poms, the unit in Bondi, they cannot believe

Macquarie Dictionary (Fourth Edition) Macquarie Library, 2005 and *Collins Australian Dictionary* (Seventh Edition) HarperCollins, 2005.

their luck) and a permanent addition to the gloriously mottled tapestry that is Australian English.

To earn a place, the dictionary says, 'a word has to prove that it has some acceptance. That is to say, it has to turn up a number of times in a number of different contexts over a period of time.'

Right. Let's consider hose rage and jolly bean. Show us the documentation, Susan Butler, *Macquarie* publisher. Show us how many times these terms have been used in public over a period of time (a stunningly imprecise formulation). Convince us that hose rage, in particular, had a life beyond the day it was coined by a sparky (Sydney) newspaper sub-editor.

And if you want to include plays on road rage, what of toad rage? Why is there no mention of this common term to describe the fury of tropical householders fighting off cane toads? Is it because the dictionary compilers live on this island's temperate shore?

One could go on about neologisms not in these volumes (demovate, dessy, sextex). But there could be ego involved. Failing to find a word or a usage that you know exists is like being successfully challenged at Scrabble. It is insulting. You blame the dictionary.

Ego aside, how is one to rate these massive works of scholarship, these word middens, these linguistic coral reefs? Apart from niggles like the absence of chav from the *Macquarie* and the *Collins'* strange omission of DSE (dry sheep equivalent), there is no questioning their general excellence. So, since the *Macquarie* says it is 'Australia's national dictionary' and the *Collins* calls itself *Collins Australian Dictionary*, a short head-to-head match-up featuring Australian content seems in order.

I asked a hand-picked panel to provide a few dozen words or phrases they thought to be distinctively Australian and in common use. Then, without consulting the dictionaries, I culled the most common ones until I had twenty. (Note on methodology: completely arbitrary and unscientific and no correspondence will be entered into.)

Take the test. Define these:
1. Altona bride's.

2. Black aspro.
3. Blood rule.
4. Bomb.
5. Brett.
6. Corridor.
7. Dog.
8. Get-out race.
9. Groiny.
10. Hammy.
11. Hornbag.
12. Low-doc.
13. Parma.
14. Pinophile.
15. Red time.
16. Red zone.
17. Salute the judge.
18. Servo.
19. Spit the dummy.
20. Top shelf.

Definitions:
1. Sheepskin moccasins (allegedly worn beneath the floor-length gowns of brides from the Melbourne suburb). A term with no legs because of creeping gentrification. In neither dictionary.
2. Coca-Cola, thought to be a hangover cure. Neither.
3. Rule that a player who is bleeding must leave the field. Neither.
4. Kick in football. Often a long bomb. As in a coach's famous instruction: 'When in doubt, bomb it to Snake.' (In both, but no mention of Aussie Rules. *Macquarie* says it is an up-and-under kick in rugby league, *Collins* says in rugby union.)
5. Medicinal smell in wine. Short for brettanomyces, a bacterial yeast infection. Easily detected by pinophiles (see below). Neither.
6. Direct passage from goal to goal in Australian Rules football. Neither.

7. Inform on, an informer. *Macquarie* only.
8. Last race on the card or a final attempt to save something. Neither.
9. Common name for osteitis pubis. Neither groiny nor its proper name in the dictionaries.
10. Hamstring injury. *Macquarie* only.
11. *Collins* says a hornbag is a promiscuous woman. The *Macquarie* says it's a sexually attractive person, usually a woman. This is a serious disagreement. What would Kim say?
12. Mortgage loan requiring a minimum of documented credit history. Also lack of scrutiny generally, as in, 'Low-doc job, mate, cash in hand, no ask, no tell.' Neither.
13. Dish alleged to be veal parmigiana. As in: 'Special. Beer and a Parma, $9.50.' Neither.
14. Wine bore besotted with the pinot noir grape variety. Neither.
15. Time-on in Aussie Rules and lesser codes. Neither.
16. Period of danger (from interval before parking meter expires). Neither.
17. To pass the winning post first in a horse or other race. Neither.
18. Everyone knows what a servo is. *Macquarie* only.
19. Ditto.
20. The best or the most expensive or the most sought after. From the traditional position of the most expensive liquor in a bar. Neither.

My guess is that most people reading this will get more than six out of twenty, the *Macquarie* score. A drover's dog would do better than the *Collins*. In fact, using the word Australian in the *Collins* title seems to teeter on the edge of passing off (a term the dictionary does not have).

A clue to the *Macquarie*'s lacklustre showing may lie in its 'Bibliography of Australian texts', the curious collection of printed sources it draws upon for illustrative material. (Included is something called *Flatball News*, presumably a journal for frisbee enthusiasts.) About sixty per cent of these sources date from before 1980.

About eighty-five per cent pre-date 1991, the year of the dictionary's second edition. Given the explosion in book, periodical and internet publishing over the past ten years, this is a worry. Finally, the back cover of the *Macquarie* boasts that it has 'Over 112,000 headwords', and lists five other 'over' numbers. Over should be reserved for spatial relationships. For figures, the term they need is 'more than'.

2005

TRADIES WEAR SUNNIES AND BLUNNIES

TEMPLE WROTE explanatory glossaries at the request of his American publisher to help readers understand the Australian idioms in *The Broken Shore* and *Truth*.

Abo: Abbreviation of Aboriginal. The usage is derogatory except in Aboriginal English.

Access fathers: Fathers allowed by the courts to see their children at specified times after a separation.

Aggro: From aggression or aggressive. (*Just takes two or three drinks, then he gets aggro.*)

All up: In total, final sum.

Ambo: An ambulance worker. (The following sentence is possible: *Mate, the last thing I need is an aggro Abo ambo.*)

Beanie, beanies: Close-fitting woollen cap.

Bickie: A cookie. Abbreviation of biscuit.

Bike: A motorcycle, bicycle or woman of loose morals.

Bikkies: Biscuits.

Blow-in: A term of scorn for a newcomer, particularly one who voices an opinion about local affairs or tries to change anything. (*Bloody blow-in, what does she know about this town?*)

Blowies: Blowflies.

Bludger: Once a man living off a prostitute's earnings, now applied to anyone who shirks work, duty or obligation. A *dole bludger* is someone who would rather live on unemployment benefits than take a job.

Bluey: A workman's hard-wearing cotton jacket. It can also be a blanket, a cattle dog, and a red-haired person.

Blunnies: Work boots made by the Blundstone company of Tasmania. Popular with people who don't work but enjoy kicking things and with people who would like to be mistaken for manual labourers.

Bomb it to Snake: Follow procedure, particularly in an emergency. A *bomb* is a long kick. *Snake* was the nickname of an Australian Rules footballer. Originally an instruction to members of Snake's football team about what to do when no other opportunities presented themselves.

Bong: A device for smoking marijuana, from the Thai word *baung*, meaning a wooden tube. Bongs range from pipes to the necks of broken bottles.

Bonnet: Car hood.

Boofhead: Person of low intelligence, fool, buffoon.

Boong: A derogatory term for an Aboriginal person used by non-Aboriginals.

Branchstacker: Someone who enrols members in a branch of a political party or other organisation, often paying their fees, so as to influence the voting at branch meetings.

Brickie: Bricklayer.

Brumby-hunter: Someone who captures, breaks in and sells brumbies (wild horses).

Budgie: Budgerigar. Someone talking on a tapped phone line.

Bundy: Bundaberg rum, named for the Queensland sugar town. It is often drunk with Coca Cola (*bundy and coke*).

Bunned: Made pregnant, a verb from the expression *To have a bun in the oven* (be pregnant).

Bunnings: A discount hardware chain.

Burg: Burglary.

Bushwalking: Hiking in the wild.

Carked it: Died, as in *He carked it at the servo, two hours all up before the ambo arrived.*

Cattledog: Tough and smart Australian dog bred to work cattle from the 1830s when the native wild dog, the dingo, was crossed with English Smithfields, German Collies and Dalmatians. The dog's oval eyes have a characteristic suspicious and wary glint.

Chook: Chicken. It can also be an older woman or a silly person.

Chop-chop: Tobacco sold illegally to avoid tax.

Collins Street: Melbourne's Wall Street. A *Collins Street farmer* owns a farm but doesn't dirty his hands with farm work.

Cook: Illegal manufacture of drugs, usually amphetamines.

Cop it: To take the blame or accept responsibility. To *cop it sweet* is to take misfortune or blame in a resigned way.

Copshop: Police station.

Corrie iron: Corrugated galvanised iron sheet.

Crack a fat: Get an erection. An extremely sexy woman can be called a *catalytic fat-cracker* (from the process of catalytic cracking where long-chain hydrocarbons are broken down into simpler ones) or just a *cracker*.

Demountable: Prefabricated impermanent structure.

Dill: A stupid, silly or incompetent person.

Divvy van: Police vehicle with room for prisoners belonging to a division of the force.

Dob: To inform on someone, to blame or implicate them. Someone who dobs is a *dobber*.

Drive man: Male radio announcer who does the commuter shift, morning or afternoon, known as *drive time*.

Dunny: Lavatory.

Feeling crook: Feeling unwell.

Fibro: Fibro-cement building material used for cheap housing, garages or shacks. Also used for a house made of fibro-cement. (*Might live in a mansion now, six months ago, it was a fibro.*)

Flannelshirt: A person from the country or the poorer outer suburbs who wears cheap cotton shirts, usually checked.

Flashing: The act of exposing genitals in public.

Flat out: Doing something at maximum speed or being very busy. In Australia, the expression has been elongated to *Flat out like a lizard drinking*.

Footy: Australian Rules football, the world's finest ball game, and the ball used. (*Let's have a kick of the footy.*)

Form: Criminal record but any record of performance, as in horseracing form. (*The way I hear it, the owner's got more form than the horse.*)

Garbo: Garbage collector.

Gargle: Have an alcoholic drink.

Gerry: Old person, from geriatric.

Giss: Give it to me. *Gissit, gissit* is the characteristic sibilant sound of boys playing Aussie Rules football.

Go: To drink (as in *Go a beer*), to fight, as in *Wanna go me, mate? Go for your life.* Also a greeting (*How you going?*) *Might be the go* means might be the thing to do, the course to follow.

Grad-dip: A postgraduate diploma.

Greasy: Fast-food place, from the term *greasy spoon*.

Grunt: Power, as in *Need a car with grunt, mate. Six cylinder is a girl's car.*

Holden: Australian-made car. The company has been owned by General Motors since 1931.

Hoon: Once a procurer of prostitutes but now any badly behaved person, usually a young male. Irresponsible young drivers are hoons who *go for a hoon* in their cars. Mark Twain uses the expression *as drunk as hoons* in *Sketches Old and New*, where it presumably derives from *Huns*.

House-wrap: Thin airtight and waterproof membrane used to insulate buildings.

Hume: The Hume Highway. It either runs from Sydney to Melbourne or from Melbourne to Sydney.

Joseph Rodgers Bunny Clip and Castrator: A legendary clip-point pocket-knife made by Joseph Rodgers of Sheffield, England, for farm tasks such as skinning rabbits and castrating larger animals.

King tide: Ocean tide that exceeds the normal range.

Kneeler: Roman Catholic. Historically, Australian police forces have informally divided on religious lines between Catholic *Kneelers* and Protestant *Grippers*. (Freemasons detect fellow Masons with a secret grip or handshake. All Protestants are deemed to be Freemasons until proved otherwise.)

LA: Local area.

Load: To frame someone with a crime. (*They loaded him up with it, reckoned he was overdue.*)

Lucky dip: Relying on chance or fortune. From the drawing of a lucky number or prize from a barrel.

Mallee: Vast sparsely populated plain in inland Victoria, Australia, covering some 15,000 square miles.

Melways: Popular name of Melbourne's Melway street directory.

Milk stout: A dark beer, sometimes claimed to have medicinal properties.

Milkbar: Small store selling, among other things, milk, newspapers, cigarettes, soft drinks, confectionary, and grocery staples.

Mozzies: Mosquitos.

Munted: Under the influence of alcohol or drugs, particularly ecstasy. To *munt* something is to wreck it or do it badly.

Myxo: Myxomatosis, a disease affecting rabbits. The myxoma virus, first detected in Uruguay, was introduced into Australia in 1950 to combat the rabbit plague. Rabbits came to Australia from Britain in 1788 with the convict fleet but the infestations began after one Thomas Austin released twenty-four imported bunnies on his property near Winchelsea, Victoria, in 1859.

Nod: To be *on the nod* is to be in the dreamy state induced by heroin, opiates or prescription painkillers.

Nose, on the: Foul smelling, out of favour.

Offsider: A sidekick, a junior helper, from a bullock-driver's assistant who walked on the offside of the wagon.

On my hammer: Putting pressure on me.

Pack drill: British Army punishment drill done in full uniform and wearing a full pack (see the Sean Connery film *The Hill*). *No names, no pack drill* means there will be no punishment or other consequences if something is kept confidential.

Panelbeater: Bodyshop worker.

Perp: The vertical mortar between bricks. Abbreviation of perpendicular.

Pillowbiter: Male homosexual.

Piss: Alcohol. Someone *on the piss* is drinking heavily. Someone *off the piss* is abstaining. A heavy drinker is a *piss artist*. To *take the piss* is to mock or tease.

Pollies: Politicians.

Pom: Short for *Pommy*, someone from England. The English are often known as *Pommy bastards*. This has been known to be said affectionately. The term derives from *pomegranate* as rhyming slang for *immigrant*.

Porky, porkies: A lie, the short form of *porky pie*, English rhyming slang.

Pot and a parma: A popular pub meal offer of a glass of beer and meat or chicken cooked in what is intended to be the parmigiana style.

Prac: Practical experience session, as in a *teaching prac*.

Punt, on the punt: A punt is a gamble or wager. To be *on the punt* is to be a serious gambler. *She couldn't get him off the punt, like asking a dog to give up rabbits.*

Punter: A gambler, one who takes a *punt*, but also used to mean a customer or client. (*What this art gallery needs is more punters coming through the door.*)

Quickpick: A lottery ticket that spares the buyer the task of choosing numbers by randomly allocating them. Anything chosen without much thought or care. Also a term for someone, not necessarily a prostitute, picked up for sex.

Ranga: A redhead, from the orangutan's fringe of orange hair. A birth notice in a country newspaper said *Welcome to Thomas Joseph Clancy. A bit of a ranga but we'll keep him.* Thomas Clancy may well end up being known as Blue, a traditional Australian name for redheads (possibly because of the link beween red hair and blue eyes).

Rec reserve: A public recreation area, often with a football or cricket field.

Rego: Vehicle registration letters and numbers. Pronounced with a soft *g*, as in Reginald.

Relly, rellies: Relations, including the extended family and spousal relatives, as in: *Jeez I dunno if I can handle another Chrissie with the in-law hoon rellies.*

Rooting: Having sex. A regular sex partner can be called a *steady root*. An old joke has a man asking a friend setting out by car from Darwin on a long-awaited holiday trip: *What route* (pronounced *root*) *you takin?* The friend replies: *Think I'll take the old girl. She stuck with me through the drought.*

Rotties: Rottweilers. Fairly or unfairly, the dog breed is saddled with a reputation for being vicious and implacable. Only the child welfare authorities have a comparable reputation, witness the joke: *What's the difference between a Rotty and the welfare?* Answer: *You can make a Rotty give your kid back.*

Runners: Running shoes. You can do a *runner* (abscond, take off in the night) in runners.

Salvos: The Salvation Army, which came to Australia in 1880. Because they have always gone to wars with Australian forces— Major William McKenzie of the Salvos was awarded the Military Cross for his bravery at Gallipoli in the 1914–18 war—the Salvos have a special place in the Australian heart.

Servo: Service station, gas station.

Skips: Metal boxes used as giant garbage bins. Also containers used to carry ore. A *skip* goes to the *tip*. From *skep*.

Skun: Past tense of the verb *to skin*. It can also mean rubbed bare or threadbare. *We were so poor, we played tennis with skun balls.*

Slopes: Derogatory term for people of Asian descent. It was probably brought back from the Vietnam War by soldiers.

SOG: Special Operations Group, an elite Victoria Police detachment used for dangerous operations. Known in the force as *Sons of God* or *Soggies*, as in *The dill says he's got dynamite. Job for the Soggies here, mate.*

Spaggy bol: Spaghetti bolognaise. Also called *spag bol*. Italian immigrants to Australia were once called *spags*.

Sparrer: Early in the morning, around dawn. It is an abbreviation of *sparrow fart*, as in *She was up at sparrow fart every day.*

Spot on: Correct, on the mark.

Spruiked: Past tense of verb *to spruik*, to give a sales pitch. A *spruiker* is a barker.

Spunk: Someone, male or female, with sex appeal.

Squeezed: Subjected to pressure.

Stickybeak: An inquisitive person. Also the act of snooping. (*Have a stickybeak around there, see what you can find.*)

Streeters: People on the streets, the homeless.

Stubbies: Small beer bottles. In keeping with the Australian Northern Territory's reputation for hard drinking, a *Darwin stubby* is a big beer bottle. Also used as a measure of distance: *Far? Nah, couple of stubbies.*

Stumps: The end of a day's play in a cricket match when the three stumps at each end are drawn, and, by extension, the end of anything. *Did Janice get out before the company went pear-shaped? No. She's got an unfortunate tendency to stick it out to stumps.*

Suckhole: A vulgar term for one who curries favour with others, an obsequious person. A future leader of the Australian Labor Party once described those in the Liberal Party who looked to America for leadership as *a conga line of suckholes*.

Sunnies: Sunglasses.

Super: Abbreviation of superannuation, a pension scheme.

Superannuation scheme: Investment to fund a retirement income by income deductions during working life. Australia has a compulsory *super* scheme to which both employers and employees must contribute.

Swaggie: An itinerant, a person of no fixed address who carries all his belongings in a *swag*. (A celebrated note passed to a speaker in the Australian federal parliament advising him to change the subject read *Pull out, digger, the dogs are pissing on your swag*.) A distinction was formerly made between *swaggies* and *travellers*, the latter being people looking for work. The expression *Nice day for travelling* means *You're fired*.

Sweet fanny: Nothing at all. The short form of *Sweet Fanny Adams*; the explanation of the term's origin from British navy slang is impossibly complicated and possibly rubbish.

Tabbing: Taking drugs in tablet form.

Tanker: Vehicle carrying liquids in a tank.

The big smoke: The city.

Till: Cash register.

Tipped hair: Peroxided hair tips.

Titsoff: Very cold, abbreviation of *Cold enough to freeze your tits off*.

Trackies: Tracksuits, two-piece garments once worn only by people engaged in athletic pursuits, now worn by people who wish they had. *Trackie Daks* are tracksuit trousers.

Tradies: Tradesmen. *Tradies* wear *sunnies* and *Blunnies*, drive *utes*, often with *skun* tyres, rise at *sparrer*, tell *porkies* about when they will show up at your house to fix the *dunny*, and are fond of a *stubby* or three at *stumps*.

Tucker: Food of any kind.

Tute: Abbreviation of *tutorial*, a traditional and completely ineffective method of small-group instruction adopted in the colonies in imitation of English and Scottish universities. A character in the Jack Irish novels, a Melbourne University academic, refers to his tutorials as 'the pearl-swine interface'.

Ute: Pickup truck, an abbreviation of utility vehicle. An admired ute is a *beaut ute*.

WA: The state of Western Australia.

Wagging: Truancy, playing truant, any form of avoiding duty or obligation.

Welfare: Any social services authority, usually preceded by the definite article. A *welfare sump* is an area in which most inhabitants do not work and receive some form of social-security benefit.

Wharfie: A dock worker, a worker on the wharves. In Melbourne and elsewhere, the occupation is not renowned for helping to enforce prohibitions on the importation of drugs and other valuable commodities.

Whinge: To whinge is to complain in an annoying and persistent way. A *whinger* is not liked, even by other whingers. A *whinging Pom* is someone from England who before clearing customs regrets the decision to immigrate and finds Australia offensively unlike England.

Windcheater: Ostensibly weatherproof jacket.

Wog: Originally a migrant to Australia from a non-English-speaking European country. Also a germ, as in *He's taking a sickie. Some gastro wog that's going around.*

Work experience: The Australian practice of high-school students doing work, usually unpaid, to gain experience.

A NICE PLACE TO DO CRIME

APART FROM *In the Evil Day*, set in Europe, the US, and elsewhere, all my books have Australian settings. I'm proud to be an identifiably Australian writer because I came to the country as an adult—an extremely grateful adult. I've tried to capture my affection for the people and the place in my novels and to tell Australian stories. Becoming an Aussie was helped by the fact that I arrived without a single shred of nostalgia for an 'old country'. My old country was apartheid South Africa and I had a profound distaste for the behaviour of its white population, never missed it, never wanted to go back.

This is not to say that Australia doesn't have a shadow side, that it has transcended its history of transgressions against the original inhabitants. It hasn't. But the good people (and I think they are in the overwhelming majority) care about the past and want reconciliation and a fairer world for all Australians. It's a work in progress. It's also an amazing place where you can be at a rodeo, look over your shoulder and see a cricket match in progress, men in white flannels shouting *Howzat*, the umpire raising an index finger and saying, 'Out.'

I always had the urge to write, but I took early retirement after writing a cowboy novel—of the two pearl-handled Colts variety—when I was about ten. By then, reading hungrily and without discrimination, I had polished off the children's section of the library. I was given special dispensation to take out adult books approved by the librarian. I got around her by getting my innocent mother to take out books like *Peyton Place*.

At school, I was forced to learn poems and chunks of Shakespeare by heart. I think it did some good. I love the slicing one-handed backhands of poetry, the quick, daring artistry at the net, the unplayable aces. In my mid-teens, I discovered American writers who swept me away: Hemingway, Fitzgerald, O'Hara (oh, that high-society sex), Mailer, McCullers, Baldwin, Capote, and, most of all, the silky and unutterably sad John Updike.

Another important thing that happened to me was a friend's mother introducing me to reading plays. If I have any ability to write dialogue, it comes from reading at least thirty volumes of *Best American Short Plays*. This worthy annual introduced me to Tennessee Williams, Albee, Odets, Miller, Mamet, Wilder. I still love reading plays and revere no writer more than the British minimalist Harold Pinter.

Later on, in my early working life and at university, I devised a literary canon for myself, chewing my way through the complete works of writers good and bad. I now suspect that this put a dampener on my creative urges.

I haven't been much influenced by crime writers. One reason I took to writing the stuff was that I found almost everything new I opened to be formulaic. But I have a few old loves and a few newer ones—Margery Allingham, John D. MacDonald, Ross Macdonald, James Hadley Chase, Elmore Leonard (for his wonderful ear and indifference to the props on which so many writers rely), James Crumley, Charles McCarry (without peer in the spy novel, so much better than the indulgent and cloying Le Carré).

I've never had what I felt was a proper job. Sad, really. I've been in reasonably gainful employment—newspapers, magazines, teaching journalism, editing, writing—but I never had the feeling of having a career. I was just waiting for my vocation to announce itself. And one day I began writing and it did.

It's not that writing comes easily to me. Being stuck is the rule, not the exception. In fact, for me writing is one long attempt to become unstuck. I move from one impasse to another. Most of the time, I am convinced that the whole enterprise is a mistake and doomed. This kind of anxiety would be acceptable if I believed I was creating art, but I don't, and that knowledge serves to make matters worse. An ordinary sentence, like an ordinary piece of joinery, isn't dignified by the time it took to make.

I've also found that inspiration isn't something that lasts beyond a paragraph or two. Creative rushes are also to be distrusted. It's the passages that flowed from your fingertips that you have to axe the next day.

The ideas I have for books are also much too vague and ephemeral to be called inspirations. For me, they take the form of images and the feelings that come with them, scenes seen and imagined, usually unconnected, isolated, not part of any narrative. I've usually forgotten them by chapter three. The first Jack Irish book was inspired by seeing two lawyers drinking in a backstreets pub in inner-city Melbourne, worldly men in dark suits talking shop and laughing a lot. Then I created the Irish family history. It fills pages and pages. Most of the detail I've never used but it enabled me to see Jack whole—a man in his place, in his time, in his history. I think it gives a certain depth and complexity to the character.

Jack Irish seems to have struck a chord in Australian readers. I'm delighted to say that people come up to me and talk about him in terms usually reserved for close friends.

Creating singular characters is difficult. And then there is plotting. I must confess to hating plotting. I like travelling without a map, falling into holes, straying down dark alleys into cul-de-sacs, waiting for the electrifying moment when the story wants to tell itself to me, when characters turn their faces to me and speak.

I sometimes think that writing decent crime novels is a higher calling. People will read the most boring and pointless literary novels because they seem somehow improving. They don't expect to be entertained. They expect to emerge as better human beings. Crime receives no such indulgence. So, even in portraying the world at its darkest, the crime writer has to be aware of what the punters have come for. And, the genre limitation aside, I think there is as much good prose in crime as in any other fiction—possibly more.

But I would say that, wouldn't I?

A NOVEL OF MENACE:
KENNETH COOK'S *WAKE IN FRIGHT*

WAKE IN *Fright* was first published in 1961 when Kenneth Cook was thirty-two. It was his second novel, the first having been withdrawn because of a threat of legal action. It was a publishing success, appearing in England and America, translated into several languages, and a prescribed text in schools. It might be forty years since the novel appeared, yet it retains its freshness, its narrative still compels, and its bleak vision still disquiets.

The film version, directed by Canadian Ted Kotcheff and with a cast that included the evil-exuding Donald Pleasence, also met with critical approval on its release. Outside Australia, the film was called *Outback* (and probably set Australian tourism back at least twenty years). Its opening sequence remains in the mind—the 360-degree panorama of a flat, empty landscape, the lonely, flyspotted and comfortless pub, the toy train inching across the plain, the open-faced young man waiting on the crude platform.

Wake in Fright is about a young teacher's five days in a rough outback mining town called Bundanyabba (the Yabba to the locals). John Grant doesn't plan to spend five days there; he is passing through, staying overnight before catching the plane to Sydney, 1200 miles away. He has already come six hours by train from his one-room school in Tiboonda, a name bestowed on a pub and two ant-eaten shacks floating in a dust sea.

In the words of Grant, at the beginning of the story, in places like

Tiboonda, 'a man felt he had either to drink or blow his brains out'. (It has not crossed his mind yet that choosing the former will not preclude the latter.)

One night to pass in the Yabba. One hot night. Then the plane to Sydney, the sea, civilisation, six weeks to impress the delectably unobtainable Robyn. But, on this hot night in the Yabba, Grant goes into a pub, smoky, raucous.

A few feverish hours later, he has nothing. He is stone broke. He has gone from being a man with a cheque for six weeks' holiday pay and twenty pounds in cash in his pocket to being someone who has two shillings and eleven cigarettes to his name.

In the morning, hungover, Grant eats his paid-for hotel breakfast, takes his cases and wanders the streets. By 9.30am the mullock heaps wobble in the haze, the tar is beginning to bubble. Desperate, guilt-ridden, panic in his throat, he goes into a pub, buys a pony, the smallest measure, plans to nurse it. A middle-aged local befriends him. He accepts a beer. A second beer.

The next few days pass as if in a nightmare, an alcohol-induced fog in which Grant is in the company of shadowy strangers whose actions and motives are a mystery to him. When the mist lifts, the educated, Sydney-bred, superior John Grant is no more. Now there is a self-loathing man in a threadbare park, dirty, red-eyed, breath of half-raw rabbit, sitting against a tree and looking at a rifle, one bullet left.

Former Australian Prime Minister Paul Keating once said of his home town: 'If you're not living in Sydney, you're camping out.' The sentiment draws a clean, derogatory distinction between the two Australian worlds, between centre and periphery.

Kenneth Cook was born in Sydney, where he attended Fort Street High School. His fictional town of Bundanyabba is based on Broken Hill where he spent some time as a journalist.

Cook's experience of both Sydney and camping out fixed in him a view that there were two Australias (and two kinds of Australians, two species almost). One is represented by John Grant and by middle-class, white-collar Sydney: urban, educated, sophisticated. The other is the interior, the crude, heat-smacked, beer-swilling blue-collar world represented by flyspeck Tiboonda and by Bundanyabba, both in the middle of nowhere: 'somewhere not far out in the shimmering haze was the State border, marked by a broken fence…further out in the heat was the silent centre of Australia, the Dead Heart.'

John Grant is in the outback because it is the only way he can pay out his teaching bond. He is as much in exile as any English convict. His teaching he looks upon with all the hopelessness of the missionary preaching the gospel to people who do not understand a word he is saying. He combines a deep distaste for the landscape and climate of the inland with a contempt for the white inhabitants. This dislike is spelled out from the opening pages: 'Another year in this apology for a town, himself an outcast in a community of people who were at home in the bleak and frightening land that spread out around him now, hot, dry and careless of itself and the people who professed to own it.'

Cook will have nothing of what historian Richard White called 'the familiar iconography of outback Australia—the homestead, the sheep, the lonely gum and the proud Aborigine'. For him, the place is a variation of hell. And the ability to be at home in the 'bleak and frightening land' is a flaw in the outback's people. There is something wrong with them for enduring this harsh place. They are not the innocent victims of the lonely, arid land; they have made an unnatural choice to live in it that reflects their own stunted, even perverted, nature. Their epitome is Cook's character Doc Tydon. Only in the outback could the drunken, vaguely sinister dispenser of stale beer and benzedrine be accepted.

Of course, Australian writers (and others, notably D. H. Lawrence) have always been unkind about the Australian character in general. In the 1950s, the poet James McAuley wrote:

The people are hard-eyed, kindly, with nothing inside them;
The men are independent, but you would not call them free.

Cook's lip curls as cruelly as anyone's in his distaste, but it is reserved for the white inhabitants of the inland. (He scarcely notices Aborigines.) His character John Grant is a 'coastal Australian', something that sets him above the people of the inland. Sydney, civilisation, escaping the heat and the glare, these are the things in Grant's dreams. And the sea, above all the sea: lying in the sea, soaking out the dust of the outback. 'The sea, twelve hundred miles to the east, had swelled and fallen in its tides, day in and day out, for a year, and he had not seen it.'

Grant's longing for the sea, for the coast, is a familiar one in Australian writing. The coast symbolises home, women, a place where people are civilised, genteel, read books and talk about ideas. It is not like the inland, which is alien and male and devoid of anything resembling cultural life. From the coast the ships sail, and for a colonial to put a foot on the deck of a ship bound for home is already to be home. The sea joins all coasts; thus the coast is tied to the old country; to leave the coast is to stretch further—and possibly to break—the cord that joins the exile to the mother country, to the world.

Once upon a time, London had Sydney. It had lots of Sydneys, one in each colony. The Sydneys aped the colonial metropolis, affected its customs and mores, cloned its buildings and its institutions. And then the Sydneys gained their own possessions—their Yabbas, their internal colonies. Men went to these places to seek their fortunes, dug holes, endured heat, froze. Womanless, they found ways to live with the absence of permissible affections. The law that followed them punished the indigenes to its letter. But it laid its truncheon lightly on whites who followed the unwritten rules. What would be jailable offences in the Sydneys were tolerated or looked away from.

And so the Yabbas, like places of incarceration everywhere, near-total institutions, became their own worlds. The people in them first stopped looking outwards, then they looked inwards, then they stopped looking. They simply *were*.

It is a place like this that Cook captures so well in *Wake in Fright*. The Yabba is a city of men, isolated on the endless empty inland plain, its houses clustered on a slight eminence. At night, from afar, the author sees the town's lights as looking like those of a fleet of ships standing in a vast, dark roadstead. And the Yabba is like a ship—there is nowhere to go, it is an enclosed world with its own rituals, customs and punishments. No one on board can stand aloof. Not to be absorbed, not to seek absorption, is to give offence. It is this desire of the Yabba's people to suck in strangers, to process them, to homogenise them, that the city-bred John Grant finds hard to understand.

But he knows instinctively that he must try to keep these people at arm's length or they will take him over, colonise him.

In a pivotal scene, Grant succumbs to the generosity of his pub benefactor, Tim Hynes, and goes home with him. Here all is stuffy, suburban lower-middle-class normality—the darkened sitting-room, the thick carpet, the armchairs, the cigarettes in an ornate box on the coffee table. Polite Mrs Hynes prepares a meal. Silent Miss Hynes is a dutiful daughter, makes polite conversation with the guest. But for the heat, it could be a home in Double Bay. Yet we feel immediately that it is not an ordinary petit bourgeois household: Tim Hynes's hospitality seems too insistent, too demanding; Miss Hynes may be a succubus. The last thing John Grant remembers is someone asking, 'How do you find the Yabba, John?'

John Grant is finding the Yabba too much by far. But the transient's ordeal is not over; Grant has some way to go before he knows he is at the bedrock. Still to come are the most memorable—disturbing, haunting—scenes of the novel.

When *Wake in Fright* was first published, the respected American critic Anthony Boucher, writing in the *New York Times*, called Cook a 'vivid new talent'. Overall, Boucher was impressed, but he disagreed with the publisher putting the book in 'the genre of the taut novel of suspense'. Boucher saw *Wake in Fright* as 'a perfectly straight mainstream novel of growing up'.

He was half-right about this. It is not a novel of suspense as most people would use the term. It is a novel of *menace*: the land exudes menace; the people seem always half in the dark, exchanging glances, concealing their real intentions behind shows of generosity. There is also the menace that accompanies John Grant's hubris. He is arrogant and disdainful and for this we know he must pay a price.

And what of the 'novel of growing up' that Anthony Boucher identified? In some way, the five days in the Yabba do amount to John Grant's passage into adulthood. He is profoundly changed by the privation, temptation and degradation he experiences. What is more interesting, however, is Grant's regression. Cook, like many Australian writers before him, has no confidence in the durability of civilisation's armour. Grant may be clothed in all the trappings of a more civilised culture but beneath them he is just another brutal and lustful upright animal. Cook recognises that some black flower sleeps in the human heart, waits for the right moment to open its blood petals. In war, many men have found this awful budbloom in themselves, succumbed to it and been haunted by it even to old age as they limp in medal-chinking columns to honour their own dead.

Wake in Fright is a young writer's work: romantic, at times naive, occasionally silly. It also suffers from some uncertainty of character and there are problems of balance. These are flaws but they are outmuscled by the writer's strengths. Cook can make us feel the heat, see the endless horizon, hear the sad singing on a little train as it traverses the monotonous plain: 'The homesteads were just yellow patches of light in window-frames, but the train driver sounded his whistle just the same and, in the darkness, there were children waving just the same.'

And Cook has range too. He captures the icy, flooding charm of the first beer on a heatstruck day. He knows what it feels like to catch luck's eye and hold the gaze across a smoky room, to feel the irrational *deservedness* of it, to hear fortune singing sweet in the veins. And he knows dark things—the frightening chasm that opens when certainty disappears, the savagery in the human heart.

Wake in Fright has the power to disturb, a rare thing in any novel.

2001

CONAN DOYLE AND SHERLOCK HOLMES

HOW WOULD the adventures of Sherlock Holmes be written about in America today?

In the Holmes PI series, drop-out med student Holmes rooms with damaged combat doc Watson. In between bouts of clinical depression, the coke-powered brainiac Holmes solves mysteries that defeat ordinary mortals. As with all good buddies, low-amp Watson's job is mostly to drool in admiration.

That piece of sacrilege will earn the undying enmity of Holmesians everywhere. And they are everywhere: Finland, Japan, Russia, wherever two or three are gathered in his name, they form a society and publish a newsletter and develop theories.

It's not about literary appreciation. It is about apparently normal people pretending that Sir Arthur Conan Doyle's Sherlock Holmes and his flatmate, Dr James Watson, were real and that Watson and not Conan Doyle wrote the stories.

The first piece of Holmes 'scholarship', not to be confused with Doyle scholarship, appeared in 1911. Since then no aspect of the fictions has gone unexamined, in Sherlockian journals and in everything from the *Lancet* (Dr Watson's war wounds) to *Guns & Ammo* (the weapons of Holmes).

Now Leslie S. Klinger, an American Holmesian (the US is the

The New Annotated Sherlock Holmes: The Novels, Arthur Conan Doyle, edited with annotations by Leslie S. Klinger, W. W. Norton, 2005.

cult's heartland) has produced the climax to his study of what the faithful call the Canon. The third and final volume of his annotated Sherlock Holmes contains the four novels: *A Study in Scarlet*, *The Sign of Four*, *The Hound of the Baskervilles* and *The Valley of Fear.*

Klinger has drawn on every last shred of Sherlockian scholarship to illuminate the texts. At 1,878 pages, the work is intended for the Holmes tragics. No one would want to read the novels in this form, attention continually hijacked from the story to the adjoining column of annotations. But wonderful annotations they are.

Here one can learn much about such things as the origins of the modern circus; the vehmic courts; early telegraphy; the Amati family of violin-makers; drinking whisky-pegs; the derivation of the verb 'lag' (from the Old Norse *lagda*, laid by the leg, which should enlighten the Macquarie and Collins dictionaries); the risus sardonicus; the development of the keyless watch; identifying the kinds of calluses peculiar to manual trades; the evolution of handcuffs; and the pseudo-science of phrenology ('the science of picking the pocket through the scalp').

But these enjoyable bits of arcana are there only to supplement the serious Sherlockian discussions—such as the possibility that Watson visited or once lived in Australia (sparked by a comment about seeing the Ballarat goldfields in *The Sign of Four*); whether Holmes's drug addiction was the result of receiving cocaine for dental problems; discrepancies in Holmes's description of Professor Moriarty; or the large number of cases of brain fever in the Canon.

Of puzzles to ponder, there is no lack. Conan Doyle (or Watson) was not one to refer to earlier works when knocking out new ones. The resulting inconsistencies, apparent errors, lacunae and chronological conundrums continue to provoke the speculation so richly documented by Klinger in these volumes.

Was Holmes actually a woman? Was he an American? After he met his temporary end at the Reichenbach Falls in a grapple with his nemesis, Moriarty, did he come back as a ghost or go off to spy for the British in India or visit Russia disguised as a tobacco dealer? Or none of the above.

One scholar has even tried to debunk the assertion in *The Mazarin Stone* that Holmes was humourless by scanning the sixty recorded adventures to produce a table showing 103 smiles, sixty-five laughs, fifty-eight jokes, thirty-one chuckles and seven twinkles.

Good-humoured or not, Conan Doyle came to hate Holmes and to want to be rid of him. By his own account, he felt a great relief when he sent Sherlock down the alpine cliff.

(People in London responded by wearing black armbands and the *Strand Magazine*'s circulation is said to have fallen by 20,000.)

Holmes is definitely not loveable. He is overbearing, smug, pompous, supercilious. He is also the kind of man who beats dead bodies with a stick to check on post-mortem bruising.

But in his conceit that mysteries, no matter how baffling at first glance, are susceptible to observation and deduction, Holmes begins the positivist, empiricist tradition in crime fiction. He is not like the bumbling official detectives. He is a scientist and his method is to seek an explanation that explains all the phenomena: pure mind at work in the world.

To see how far from Sherlock Holmes the detective novel had travelled by 1934, we need only consider the end of Dashiell Hammett's *The Thin Man*. Nora Charles says to her husband, Nick: 'So is that what happened more or less?' Nick replies: 'I don't know. All that I know is that it fits the case, it seems to explain things.'

Holmes would have been outraged by this casual attitude to truth.

Conan Doyle himself was no mean observer. In 1899, aged forty, he went to the Anglo-Boer war for a few months—he wanted to be a soldier but his training and his corpulence meant he had to serve as a surgeon—and dashed off a 500-page account that was a model of acuity and judgement. While patriotic to the core, Conan Doyle pointed out the reasons why small bands of irregulars who wouldn't stand and fight were bringing the British Army to its pale, knobbly knees.

The international Holmes cult has been made possible by the Canon's translation into about fifty languages. It clearly translates well. One unkind commentator has put this down to the prose being so without nuance and the stories so plodding that they resonate with non-English readers whether raised on Icelandic fishing sagas or Japanese bondage comics.

The critic Edmund Wilson was of another mind. 'My contention,' he wrote in 1950, 'is that Sherlock Holmes is literature on a humble but not ignoble level, whereas the mystery writers most in vogue now are not. The old stories are literature, not because of the conjuring tricks and the puzzles, not because of the lively melodrama but by the virtue of imagination and style. They are fairytales and they are among the most amusing of fairytales and not among the least distinguished.'

Fairytales were much on Conan Doyle's mind by the time he visited Australia on a speaking tour in 1920. By then he was firmly convinced of the existence of fairies, gnomes and the afterlife. Watching the grand final between Collingwood and Richmond may have given him a glimpse of the last.

Stripped of all Klinger's wonderful, playful scholarship, the novels remain a damn good read. If some of the puzzles and devices now seem a little shop-worn, it is because they have been tried on by hundreds of mystery writers since they appeared. It is still possible, however, given an idle hour, a deckchair and a leaf-dappled patch of sunlight, to free fall into the world of 221B Baker Street.

2005

ABOUT AGATHA CHRISTIE

FOR ALMOST sixty years from 1920, Agatha Christie cranked out mystery novels, one in a dry year, three or four when the sap was flowing. She also wrote plays—*The Mousetrap* has been running in London since 1952—five literary novels and poetry.

Christie's most famous protagonists, the Belgian Hercule Poirot and the utterly English Miss Marple, dominate the skyline of British crime fiction. In terms of visibility, the likes of Rebus and Morse are foothills, and only the Everest that is Sherlock Holmes stands proud of her creations.

Christie clearly satisfied a need. And satisfied it again and again, selling more books than anyone in history. Only Shakespeare is a better known writer in English.

This kind of fame draws biographers and Laura Thompson is the second. She has the advantage over her predecessor of having the family's blessing and access to all Christie's papers. There can be no questioning the diligence she has applied to her subject.

Christie was born in 1890, the third child of Frederick and Clara Miller. Her father, a cosmopolitan American whose family had business interests in England, lived a life of idleness and steadily but unspectacularly drained his inheritance.

Christie's childhood at Ashfield, the large family house in then-fashionable Torquay, was, by her own and Thompson's account,

---

Agatha Christie: An English Mystery, Laura Thompson, Headline Review, 2007.

a time of bliss. She received no formal education except in music. Later, she dreamed of an operatic career, but had the good sense to accept expert opinion that she didn't have the voice. Madge, Christie's bright and vibrant sister, had gone to school at the future Roedean. She married extremely well, becoming mistress of Abney Hall, a grand, dark Victorian mansion that the envious Christie described as an example of the best 'Victorian Lavatory period'.

Christie's brother Monty went to Harrow. A hopeless incompetent, he then found accommodation in the British army, a traditional sheltered workshop for upper-class dolts. But even the army drew the line at Monty. He was forced to flee to East Africa to escape his debtors. There he found ways of wasting huge amounts of his brother-in-law's money. When World War I began, Monty got himself wounded in a skirmish with the Germans and had to come home to Ashfield.

Mildly deranged and possibly on substances, he amused himself by taking pot shots at the wobbling backsides of the local matrons. True to form, he missed. The family bought him a cottage on Dartmoor, where he took up with his sixty-five-year-old peroxided housekeeper, a mother of thirteen. As one does.

Monty's death, drink in hand, in a waterfront dive in Marseilles, closes by far the most entertaining section of Thompson's book. If only Christie had known more people like her wastrel brother. Archie Christie, the man she married—and she had a few to choose from— was everything Monty wasn't. He was worthy, dogged, ambitious and comes over as an Englishman in an Eric Ambler novel, the kind of dull, middle-class dog who had a decent war and turns up as a machinery salesman cum low-level British spy in some cold, cabbage-scented, 8pm-closing Balkan capital.

Christie lived in a scrimping genteel way with Archie, bore his child, even endured being a Sunningdale golf widow. The high point of the marriage was going with Archie on an Empire Tour for which he was financial adviser. Christie found the nature to be exceedingly grand, the people less so. (Sadly, Thompson thinks Tasmania is its own nation state.)

Christie's first novel, *The Mysterious Affair at Styles*, was published in 1920. She was thirty. She never looked back. Nor, from the evidence Thompson provides, did she do much looking sideways, upwards, downwards or inside. Having money made her more and more satisfied with herself, more and more convinced that the view from an English country house was the only sane one.

It was, of course, written in the stars that Archie, employed by a company with Imperial in its name, would betray her by shagging his secretary. Christie's celebrated response was like that of a child who tries to get attention by holding its breath: she faked suicide. She left her car beside a quarry and booked into a hotel under the secretary's name.

Attention she got. So famous was she by now that the disappearance was on the front page of newspapers throughout England and the colonies. Her reappearance, claiming amnesia, was greeted with a resurrectionist sigh.

Life resumed. Archie departed. Christie kept churning out books and, now seriously rich, married Max Mallowan, an archaeologist, and lived happily ever after. ('I can promise you stiffs all through life,' he wrote; he meant the bodies turned up in his digs.)

It would be nice to say that Thompson has made of Christie's life a riveting read. She hasn't. One reason is her adoption of a style so creamy and cloying, so girlish and gushing that it can only be endured in small amounts.

More irritating is Thompson's wholesale use of Christie's own fiction, particularly the overblown novels written as Mary Westmacott, as scripture. What was Christie thinking at any time? Why, here's a passage that tells us exactly.

And then there is Thompson's view of Christie's books. They are simply brilliant, stunning, clever, perceptive, marvellous. She is blind to Christie's often ridiculous plots and the fact that reading her can be like being trapped in the company of an aged thespian who turns what should be three-minute anecdotes into three-act plays. Christie's was a long and productive life.

Thompson makes it seem even longer.

2007

READING RAYMOND CHANDLER

THE FIRST thing to ask about Raymond Chandler is why his name lives on, when those of best-selling contemporaries such as Erle Stanley Gardner and James M. Cain are forgotten?

Chandler answered the question: 'What greater prestige can a man like me have than to have taken a cheap, shoddy, and utterly lost kind of writing, and have made it something that intellectuals claw each other about?'

The cheap and shoddy writing was the American mystery-detective story. Chandler's achievement was to make the form he didn't 'care a button about' respectable enough to be talked about in polite literary society. When the Library of America published Chandler's collected works, the process of embourgeoisement was complete. (To the point where, more recently, President Clinton named a crime writer as his favourite author. Well, that figures, Americans might say.)

Chandler didn't begin the form's renovation. Dashiell Hammett did this by turning the genre away from English puzzle-solving and semi-literate slam-bang, and aiming it at the corruption at the heart of American city life. But Hammett's equipment was second-rate. His prose was only slightly less wooden than that of most pulp-magazine writers, and there is something naive about his world view.

The Raymond Chandler Papers: Selected Letters and Non-Fiction 1909–1959, edited by Tom Hiney & Frank MacShane, Hamish Hamilton, 2001.

Then came Chandler. He was different. He'd been educated at an English public school, lived the low-level literary life in England, knocked about Europe, seen death in the trenches of France, been an underling to an oil baron. He was a drunk and a womaniser and he brought to the detective novel a cynical intelligence and a literary sensibility it hadn't seen before.

No one who wrote crime fiction before Chandler could have found the words to say of Edmund Wilson's briefly scandalous *Memoirs of Hecate County*: 'The book is indecent enough of course, and in exactly the most inoffensive way—without passion, like a phallus made of dough.'

No one in the genre before him would have been capable of comparing Ernest Hemingway and Cyril Connolly thus: 'The kind of thing Hemingway writes cannot be written by an emotional corpse. The kind of thing Connolly writes can and is…you don't have to be alive to write it.'

The times were right for Chandler, and he for them. His 'hard and clean and cold' stories about the decadent Californian rich and those who would feed off them appealed to a more sophisticated audience, particularly in England, than crime fiction had reached before.

His success was a close-run thing, though. Chandler was not earmarked for fame. Born in America, his Irish Protestant mother took him to England as a boy when she left his alcoholic father. An uncle paid his fees at Dulwich, alma mater of P. G. Wodehouse. On leaving, he sat the civil service exam, worked briefly as an admiralty clerk, then spent five years failing to earn a living by his pen.

At twenty-four, he returned to America. Apart from service in the Canadian army in France, in the trenches, the next twenty years were spent job-changing, drinking, going nowhere. He didn't marry until his mother died in 1924, and then he married Cissy Pascal, seventeen years his senior. She may have concealed her true age from him; then again, she may not have.

In the early 1930s, sacked by his oil boss over four-day weekends in motels with the secretary, he began to write detective stories for the pulp magazines. The publication of his novel *The Big Sleep* in 1939 changed his life forever. Six years later, *Newsweek* wrote: 'Chandlerism, a select cult a year ago, is about to engulf the nation.'

Most of the letters in this third collection are from after 1939, the night letters of an insomniac. Many are mere fragments, sentences gleaned from a voluminous correspondence. Chandler was, in a literal sense, a man of letters. He wrote thousands of them, to all kinds of people, many of them unknown to him, and it is largely through his letters that we know him.

He is not easy to know, a study in contradictions. He was a man who could sound like a clubby English anti-Semite, yet refuse to join a tennis club that wouldn't admit Jews. He could pour scorn on the naivete of socialists, yet pin down precisely the perniciousness of the corporation: 'Beyond a certain point of size and power it is more tyrannical than the state, more unscrupulous, less subject to any kind of inspection...in the end, it destroys the very thing it purports to represent—free competition.'

This collection contains Chandler's observations on many subjects: books, writers and writing, American politics, criticism, war, women, men. Some are trite, some wrong, some wrong-headed, many right on the button.

Chandler was an unhappy Hollywood scriptwriter (the adjective may be redundant) and the film world features prominently in his correspondence. Here he is setting Alfred Hitchcock straight on changes to his script for *Strangers on a Train*: 'What I cannot understand is your permitting a script which after all had some life and vitality to be reduced to such a flabby mess of cliches, a group of faceless characters and the kind of dialogue...that says everything twice and leaves nothing to be implied by the actor or the camera.'

The act of writing, Chandler claimed to enjoy. Being a writer was different: 'It is a lonely and ungrateful profession and personally I'd much rather have been a barrister, or even an actor.'

He could not have been either because he had no taste for work or public performance. In his later life, as we see it through his letters, he was always wrestling with a dialectic. He was not English, not American. He disdained Hollywood and he needed its money. He had elevated tastes in literature, and he practised in a plebeian form. He professed a love for women, yet there is a tortured misogyny in his novels.

Sometimes in these letters we hear the wry, world-weary voice of Marlowe, Chandler's private-eye protagonist. He is clearly what Chandler would have liked to have been: a man without shackles, a man who moved among the rich and powerful and was not impressed, a loner, aloof. He was none of these things.

Towards the close of his life, Chandler wrote: 'It seems that I have had a very severe anaemia—not quite pernicious, but damn close to it. A blood count on the edge of nothing, but that doesn't worry me at all. I have lived my whole life on the edge of nothing.'

Reading these letters, there is a strong sense of the nothing in Chandler's life. His accomplishments brought him no joy because there was no competition. The thoughtless part of his life passed too quickly; the reflective part went on too long.

As we move towards his death, a picture comes to mind· The only house in the street with a light on. In the lighted window, a man sits at a desk, a man with a glass at his elbow. He is passing the small night hours, trying to find something interesting to say to strangers.

A final note, in sadness. That this book is worth buying owes little to anyone involved. The letters cry out for fuller annotation, and the index, to be kind, is cursory.

2001

THE NOVELS OF JOHN LE CARRÉ

IT SEEMS only yesterday since the last one but another John le Carré model is upon us, the first of the new Three Series, taking in all the developments since September 11. Faithful le Carré readers need not fear that the distinguishing features of series one (Cold War), and series two (post-Cold War), have been jettisoned in the rush to update. A few pages will reassure them.

We meet late-fifties Ted Mundy, the hero of le Carré's new novel, in Munich. He is in flight from a failed language school, working as a tour guide in one of Mad King Ludwig's castles, the lover of a young Turkish Muslim woman and foster-father to her son, Mustafa.

Ted is a child of empire, whose mother died giving birth to him on the day Pakistan was born. Marooned by the striking of the Union Jack, his father, Major Mundy, goes into steady decline until finally, in disgrace, he takes the young Ted home to England. Here the major passes the time in pubs, cadging drinks, braying pukka sahib nonsense and lying about his late wife's origins.

Ted is sent to a minor public school, where the masters, perceptive to a fault, forgive him the usual manly misdemeanours of drinking and smoking. He is made a prefect, gets into the first rugger XV, cricket XI, etc. His height seems to be the clue to this, as it is to many things in his life.

By chance—and how useful it is in these matters—Ted discovers

Absolute Friends, John le Carré, Hodder, 2003.

German language and culture. He gets into Oxford, where he meets and roots the diminutive and corrosively intellectual Ilse, who seems to tolerate him only because of his size. She sends him to an anarchist squat in Berlin to complete his education, and here he meets Sasha, the absolute friend who will control his destiny.

Enough of plot. The time has come to face the firing squad of le Carré faithful, to roll a last rough cigarette and consider whether the blindfold is a good look.

It is not a pleasure to say that *Absolute Friends* joins the list of recent le Carré novels that resemble Zeppelins: huge things that take forever to inflate, float around for a bit, then expire in flames. This one's theme is the awful fact that, for the moment, J. R. Ewing and Southfork run the world. It is a windy polemic dressed in le Carré's well-worn tweedy garments.

Perhaps the worst thing that happened to the author was being told he had transcended the spy genre. A self-consciousness of being a storyteller began to creep in—bad pathology in a novelist—and a sense that he saw his audience as captive and captivated. His plots became more and more convoluted, the writing sometimes an irritating Muzak of plummy voices uttering Pythonesque phrases. Each book took longer to wind up to the point where it begins to tick, let alone chime.

All these failings are evident in *Absolute Friends*. The pace has become absurdly languorous, the plot sags like a boarding-house mattress, and there is a pervasive and sticky sentimentality.

That le Carré's writing career would come to this was not obvious when he produced *The Spy Who Came in From the Cold*.

It was a departure, a Cold War spy novel without heroes or heroics, dry-eyed, knowing. One could see the author writing it in a dull office in London where the walls were papered in disbelief and cynicism and nondescript public schoolboys sighed and crossed out the codenames of spies duped, betrayed, deceased.

Acclaimed books followed, notably *Tinker, Tailor, Soldier, Spy*, *Smiley's People* and *The Little Drummer Girl*.

Le Carré's protagonists were the opposite of the priapic and ideologically virtuous heroes of Ian Fleming and his imitators. He dealt not in the simple pleasures of guns and gadgets, villainous apparatchiks and complaisant females, but in a half-lit world of ambiguities, bad faith, messy operations, shabby and expedient trade-offs.

Usually the second-cousins of the establishment, le Carré's characters were aware that ultimately they were expendable. The loyalty they gave to people and institutions was likely to be repaid with treachery and betrayal. But still they served the system faithfully.

A musing on the complexities of character, motive and conduct is the hallmark of le Carré's earlier works. Few British writers have been more perceptive about how family and social class and school and university and empire and defeats and victories have shaped the English. The Cold War was a perfect setting for concerns such as these, a great drama in which action was divorced from morality. When everything is permissible in the service of country and its interests, it is only character that counts.

But that setting has gone and with it much that served le Carré's talent. He does, of course, still do many things well. Brilliance continues but now the flashes are further apart. There is a sense that, intellectually and emotionally, he was at his best as a writer when his mind was not on crusades against arms dealers, multinational drug companies and the new American world order.

These are certainly worthy targets. But they are huge and hard to personify. Le Carré's attempt in *Absolute Friends* reaches its low point in the lecture on the state of the world delivered to Mundy by a character called Dimitri, who cites his sources thus: 'I have in mind such thinkers as the Canadian Naomi Klein, India's Arundhati Roy, who pleads for a different way of seeing, your British George Monbiot and Mark Curtis, Australia's John Pilger, America's Noam Chomsky, the American Nobel Prize winner Joseph Stiglitz, and the Franco-American Susan George of World Social Forum at Port Alegre. You have read all of these fine writers, Mr Mundy?'

Mr Mundy's creator certainly has and the effort has done nothing for his fiction. Le Carré was a better and more powerful writer when his canvases were the rainswept streets and soggy, landmined fields where sad men leaked blood for Washington, Whitehall or the Kremlin.

2003

FROM JAMES LEE BURKE TO KATHY REICHS

FEW PLACES on earth have been as unfortunate in their history and as fortunate in their writers as the American South. Naturally, the two things are causally related. The South's strange history of cruelty, chivalry, feudalism, lust, romance, religion and violence marks its writers, black and white.

Mark Twain, William Faulkner, Flannery O'Connor, Eudora Welty, Richard Wright, Tennessee Williams, Robert Penn Warren, Margaret Mitchell, William Styron, Barry Hannah, Carson McCullers, Lee Smith—they are all distinctively Southern before they are American.

So it is with James Lee Burke. His prose style has strong echoes of other Southern writers, Faulkner in particular, but he is not an imitator. Like Faulkner's, Burke's prose can teeter on the edge of opulence, verge upon the cloying. But it does not. He walks the stylistic line on cat feet.

Someone who does not have cat feet is Burke's series character, Dave Robicheaux, a policeman in the Gulf town of New Iberia. Robicheaux is a decent man, full of sorrows, furrowed with memory. He is as much part of his surroundings as the tepid, fecund sea, the mangrove swamps and deadly sand bogs, the antebellum houses, the Civil War statues, rustling cane fields and flowering trees.

Jolie Blon's Bounce, James Lee Burke, Orion, 2002 and *Grave Secret*s, Kathy Reichs, Heinemann, 2002.

Robicheaux's concern here is the murders of two young women, the innocent teenager Amanda Bordreau and the addicted prostitute Linda Zeroski, daughter of a Mafia hitman. Chief suspect is Tee Bobby Hulin, black musician and hustler, whose fingerprints are found at the scene of Amanda's death. Things look grim for Tee Bobby but there's a sliver of hope: Robicheaux doesn't think he did it.

The scene set, we pass on to the complexities. And because this is the South, they are formidable. Tee Bobby is being defended by Southern aristocrat Perry LaSalle, whose father was the lover of Tee Bobby's grandmother, Ladice Hulin. Ladice was raped by a vile plantation overseer called Legion Guitry, who blackmailed Perry's father and once tried to kill the teenage Robicheaux.

In unwinding this convoluted story, Burke takes his time. He feels no urge to make everything drive the plot. He likes detail and he doesn't care much whether it is telling. His narrative also knows no restrictions of point of view. At one moment, we are seeing the world through Robicheaux's eyes. In the next, we are experiencing an episode from his father's life complete with what he dreamed while drunk. In the wrong hands, slowness can be boring and perspective shifts can be unbalancing and annoying. However, Burke's language makes the difference. He has the right hands for the work. Plus, he knows how to smack a lulled reader with a spring-loaded blackjack.

It is, of course, of no consolation to the oppressed that societies based on ideas of racial or other superiority brutalise everyone. All Burke's characters are victims—at the minimum, they are bruised, many are badly wounded. Some are also truly evil (theologically evil, as Robicheaux puts it), and the worst ones tend to be punished.

In Burke's novels, however, there is no certainty of anyone being punished. It isn't that kind of comic-book moral universe; Burke knows that evil is often an evolutionary advantage in a society that resembles its Delta swamps. Bits are old, bits are new, bits are dead, bits are rotten. Sunken objects send up foetid bubbles from the past. Predators and prey eye one another close up.

And that is the essence of this excellent Robicheaux novel and all the others: the past—all of it, the pure and the putrid—lies heavy on the South and on everyone raised in it. If Burke is not regarded as a writer of literary fiction, the definition of the adjective should be put before the courts as soon as possible.

Kathy Reichs, as I grasp it, practises something called forensic anthropology. It is the science of looking at what remains of the dead with an eye to truth, blame and possible conviction. This is no doubt an honourable line of inquiry, up there with dendrochronology and palaeoclimatology.

Reichs is frighteningly earnest, the science sounds impeccable (if not, the experts thanked are in academic trouble). She could easily make a career out of writing those long pieces on subjects such as seaweed that the *New Yorker* used to publish. But no, she is not content with looking for traces of culture and society in old bones. She writes novels.

Reichs' protagonist is called Tempe Brennan, who is, surprise, a forensic anthropologist. Here Brennan FA is investigating deaths old and new in Guatemala. She shows what a bit of American expertise can achieve, thereby going some way to make up for the CIA-backed coup of 1954.

Since I have read only this book by Ms Reichs, I will not be so silly as to suggest that all her novels are bad. She may have written works that stagger. And it is a fact that many writers peak early and then trundle downhill with the sound this book makes: the hollow noise of empty garbage bins being dragged back to base.

Still, if your interests lie in the stomach-turning details of decom-position and exhumation, this is your book. I can only describe it as forensic porn. That there is an audience for works of this kind testifies to our nature as an inquiring species. We are also playful creatures. A bit of play would do wonders for Kathy.

2002

JAMES ELLROY: THE DEMON DOG OF AMERICAN FICTION

AMERICA HAS a long tradition of writers becoming larger than their work—Hemingway, Kerouac, Ginsberg, Capote, Mailer, Vidal, Hunter S. Thompson. People know all about them without having read a word they've written, their shadows fall before them. So it is with James Ellroy.

Ellroy calls himself the demon dog of American fiction. He has a relentlessly self-publicised past of 'booze and drugs and Mickey Mouse crimes', and the film of his novel *LA Confidential* brought fame to him and others involved. His next book, *American Tabloid*, was hailed as breathing life into the American novel.

No more was Ellroy a cult paperback crime writer who filmed well: he was serious.

This book is the second in the trilogy Ellroy calls 'Underworld USA'. It starts in 1963 with the protagonist, Wayne Tedrow, arriving in Dallas to kill a pimp for the Mob:

> They shook hands. Moore chewed tobacco. Moore wore cheap cologne. A woman walked by—boo-hoo-hoo—one big red nose.
>
> Wayne said, 'What's wrong?'
> Moore smiled. 'Some kook shot the President.'

And so we set off with Wayne Tedrow on a low-level five-year tour of

---

The Cold Six Thousand, James Ellroy, Century, 2001.

America in the time of the Kennedy brothers, Lee Harvey Oswald, Jack Ruby, J. Edgar Hoover and Martin Luther King: the view as seen by the foot soldiers, the grunts, the people sent to do the powerful's bidding. These expendables move in a world of overlapping, interlocking conspiracies, all the threads bound together by the sticky secretions of lusts—for power, money, sex, revenge.

The reader's journey goes on for a long time. The book is as thick as a tax manual. Ellroy's journey too would not have been brief; he reportedly writes in block letters, five hours a day. That fact would be of no importance to the reader, except for one thing. The book reads like that: a block-letter book.

Is that a cruel thing to say? Yes. But, more importantly, is it a permissible thing to say? Can it be said of a writer who has hundreds of thousands of fans, whose publishers pay him million-dollar advances, who is treated with high seriousness by serious critics, that his new book—like all his books—is a block-letter book?

Probably not. Anyway, permissible or not, it is said and it is true. Here is a sample of Ellroy:

> He drove Moore's car to the dump. He stripped the plates. He pulled out Moore's teeth. He stuffed shotgun shells in his mouth. He gas-soaked a rag. He lit it.
>
> Moore's head blew. He fucked up would-be forensics. He dumped the car in a sludge pit. It sank fast.

Is this prose worthy of praise? (It is all like this.) Take this judgement from *Time* magazine on an earlier book: 'The secret, of course, is the language. When it is used well—which in Ellroy's case means being pared down to taut, telegraphic sentences, subject-verb-blooey!—one word is worth a thousand pictures.'

The words to note are pared down, taut, telegraphic. Since Hemingway, these have been the ultimate adjectives for the *Time* magazine school of thought.

They are the code words that say this is man's writing: writing with the vigour of gunshots, screaming marlin reels, the quick throat-punch. Virile writing.

The truth is that it is comic-book virility, mere noise, signifying precious little. Ellroy, the demon dog, has boiled writing down to yaps, incessant yapping, page after page of virile, vigorous, taut, telegraphic, meaningless yapping. Interesting at first, soon it is like being trapped in a tin shed while naughty boys throw stones at it: an endless series of short, sharp noises.

And then there is the plot. It is customary to speak of plot. The plot concerns the Kennedy assassination, a subject that draws American writers like thin dogs to old bones.

But who speaks of plot when discussing Ellroy? One might as well read the *National Enquirer* or the *News of the World* as novels, seek a thread that links unmasked cancer-cure charlatans with the secret love children of actors and the unexplained disappearances on cloudy nights of ships and planes and Cypriot goatherds and fully-loaded Kenworth Double-Bs.

As with these journals of record, Ellroy's principal appeal may be the sexiness of knowing. He gives the impression that, like J. Edgar Hoover, he knows the dirty secrets of the famous. He seems to know where every old used syringe, strap-on dildo, porn film, fired gun and bloodstained sheet is buried.

Ellroy tells us all kinds of things about the Mafia, the Klan, the FBI, politicians, Las Vegas. He names the names and that lends an air of ersatz veracity to the proceedings. (For example, we learn that Rock Hudson, Walter Pidgeon and Sal Mineo were regulars at a queer resort in Vegas.) This is also interesting for a while and then the question bubbles up: who cares? The people are all dead, their fame has not outlived most of them, and they can be defamed with impunity, and where is this going anyway?

In the end it goes nowhere. The book is just a catalogue of psychopathic behaviour—graceless, charmless, witless. There is no moment in all of it when time sticks and the mind considers a sentence, sentences, a paragraph. Nothing induces reflection. The only constant reflex is a vague feeling about the pointlessness of it all.

Still, the book will find its audience. And what does it matter if block letters triumph over joined-up writing?

2001

THOMAS HARRIS AND HANNIBAL LECTER

NOT TOO far into this book, a chapter opens with this paragraph: 'Now that ceaseless exposure has calloused us to the lewd and the vulgar, it is instructive to see what still seems wicked to us. What still slaps the clammy flab of our submissive consciousness hard enough to get our attention.'

For readers seeking instruction of this kind, for those with stomachs made strong by the repeated ingestion of what was once revolting, I commend Thomas Harris's new book. They will surely have their clammy flab slapped before they turn the last page.

This is truly a novel for the end of the century. Its central character is an intellectual, a lover of ideas, of beautiful things, of sensory pleasures. He is a classicist, a sceptic, a sensualist. And he eats other humans, bits of them, the parts some people prize in animals.

Hannibal, two or three people may not know, is the sequel to Harris's *The Silence of the Lambs*. That highly original work widened our experience of Dr Hannibal Lecter, psychiatrist, man of culture, murderer of at least ten, connoisseur of human flesh, whom we first met in *Red Dragon*.

His awful knowledge, teasingly and tauntingly imparted in a maximum security dungeon for the criminally insane, led fledgling FBI agent Clarice Starling to the serial killer called Buffalo Bill.

Now it is seven years since Lecter escaped, killing five people

Hannibal, Thomas Harris, William Heinemann, 1999.

in the process. No confirmed sighting of him exists. But, in the 'phosphorescent swamp of the Web's dark side', he is an object of consuming interest. Agent Starling, meanwhile, has found her capture of the serial killer to be the high point of her career.

Unwilling to play the politics of the bureau, hated by jealous superiors, she is now little more than an FBI gun for loan—jaded, embittered, hard, a survivor. In the novel's bloody opening, she is the last one standing after a raid on a methamphetamine plant goes wrong: all filmed by a television helicopter. Back in the limelight, a candidate for scapegoat, Starling gets a message from Hannibal Lecter. The hunt for the suave and erudite cannibal resumes.

No more should be said about the plot except that Harris is always in control, always knows where he's going. The thread of plausibility may be drawn twangingly tight but it does not snap. On the journey, we learn many things, some of which we may not wish to know. But there is no doubting the author's gift.

Much of the novel is set in Florence and he captures without effort the elusive perfume of the city, that blend of age, decay, art, religion, beauty, blood. Indeed, there is little in the way of literary creation that Harris is not good at. He can write a fine balanced sentence, cast a long line of words, send it floating out with something beautiful and barbed at the tip. He can be short and brutish, sawn-off, explosive. He can be lyrical and evocative and melancholy and philosophical. He is never less than intelligent.

Does it matter that Harris is the creator of repulsive characters, carefully and explicitly depicted in their repulsiveness? Does it matter that his book seems to have no moral stance whatsoever? Does the tongue we occasionally see bulge his cheek mean that this is no more than an entertainment, that one shouldn't take this kind of thing seriously?

No, no and no.

Harris could write books that would make us close them gently, rest them on our chests and look at the ceiling, seeing nothing. He has the mind, he has the words, he has the syntax. He has that power.

It's an awesome thing. Writers of so-called literary fiction can thank their stars he doesn't choose to exercise it. But there is something he can't do. With all his talent, he can't make his characters live, he can't make the reader give a damn about them. The sad thing is perhaps he doesn't want to.

1999

READING THE COUNTRY:
THE MILES FRANKLIN ORATION

I AM astonished to see so many people here. I was led to believe that only the women from Balwyn and the drunk man who used to come to Readings would be here. The purpose of the occasion is to pay homage to Miles Franklin. She loved the novel so much that she provided for an annual prize for novelists. It's a great honour to me to be asked to give the first Miles Franklin oration...there, I've said the word...oration. It's losing its power to terrify me. But I have to say with no disrespect to anyone involved, my negative side—and it's more than a side, really, it's perilously close to being the whole of me—has no idea why anyone would think me suitable to perform this task.

The only explanation I can think of is that when it was found that Peter couldn't leave his Manhattan loft and Roger was off shearing again and David was in Greece and Tim had an unbreakable fishing commitment and Helen—no, perhaps not Helen—thoughts turned to me. Last year the Miles Franklin judges awarded the prize to me for my novel *Truth*. I don't know whether any of them are here this evening to see once again what a rash decision that was.

There is of course no good reason to give novelists prizes. Firstly, one should not indulge a personality disorder that combines narcissism with an unnatural tendency to fantasise. Secondly, novelists have already won a prize. It's called being published. The reward

---

Delivered at the University of Melbourne, 7 June 2011.

begins with the manuscript passing a daunting test. It has to win the approval of a twenty-one-year-old first-year publisher's editor. Someone with an arts degree…preferably from Melbourne University. She's often called Fiona, in my experience. It should be said that Fiona is often both the first and the last person to read the novel.

I've called my talk 'Reading the Country'. It's a talk about me. It's the only subject I know anything about. And, believe me, there are gaping holes in that knowledge too. Weeks, months, at times. I should of course be talking about the state of the novel, the vitally important place of writers in the life of the nation. But I'm not that erudite. And I'm not that stupid, either. I should also be offering a view on why more men than women win the Miles Franklin. I'm not that stupid, either.

Australia has a long history of newcomers failing to read the country. The explorer Ludwig Leichhardt, the inspiration for Patrick White's *Voss*, set a benchmark for failing to read the country in 1848 or thereabouts. The explorer Edmund Kennedy followed. He blundered around Queensland being kept alive by his wonderfully resourceful and brave servant, a man known as Jackey Jackey. How pointless it must all have seemed to Jackey Jackey. Then there was Robert O'Hara Burke of Burke and Wills, explorers who took failure to read the country to another level. This wasn't surpassed until the British chose Anzac Cove for the landings in Turkey. Although the Poms should be given that credit.

Canberra: its very existence is a failure to read the country. But to be balanced there is the Goyder Line of 1865 that divided South Australia into arable and non-arable land zones. George Goyder rode around the countryside for years and years and years looking at the vegetation. And then he marked the line and said you shouldn't go beyond that. And then it rained for two or three years. That was the end of that matter. The farmers stormed over the Goyder Line and from the air as you go over the scrub country you'll see the remains of the farm houses of those who crossed Goyder's Line. They ignored the theory of climate persistence, they were deniers of it, they paid the price.

So, settling in a new country, if you want to write you are going to have to read the country. And coming to a new country in midlife as I did is to become a child again. The grownups around you know everything and they have secret understandings. And while you can easily acquire the factual stuff, you can acquire the dates and all those things, grasping the significance of things to the people, to the inhabitants, is another matter entirely. Even when you speak the language, in my case a form of the language, coming to terms with cultural meaning is a very long process and it's certainly not over for me. It's made more difficult by first-culture interference and all the baggage you bring with you. You're in a completely different environment, with completely different values.

Australia, when I arrived here in the late seventies, was still a small-scale country, I think. A small-scale society like Australia gathers a formidable collective memory. It's something that on the one hand reinforces national cohesion and on the other hand it entrenches tribal loyalties. Everybody knows everything about everything. I don't think there is an Australian baby boomer who hasn't seen a documentary film called *The Back of Beyond*. It's a dramatised documentary made by the Shell company, probably the best thing Shell has ever done in its entire existence and it's about Tom Kruse, the postman of the Birdsville Track. It's a remarkable piece of work. The text was in part written by Douglas Stewart, the poet, when he was literary editor of the *Bulletin*. And more than a million Australians saw *The Back of Beyond* in the first two years after its release in 1954. That's more than a million out of a population of around about 9 million. Astonishing, don't you think? Every school in the country seems to have had a reel in the cupboard along with the chalk and the spare blackboard dusters. I know people who have seen it at least twenty times. A lot of it is dramatised, and there is a sequence in which Sally and Roberta, two little girls—their mother has died on an isolated property—set out pulling a small cart behind them. Behind the cart is a little dog. The faithful dog walks out behind them as they go out into this absolutely aching emptiness. They're walking in circles. And, at a point, the older girl realises they've come round to the same place. It's a marvellous moment. She looks at her little sister and you know she's not going to tell her. They are doomed. And she won't tell her.

The message of all of it is Tom Kruse's courage, endurance, a kind of laconic stoicism. Tom is the platonic ideal of an Australian male, the kind that is set up in heaven or in a place beyond heaven, as Plato put it. In impossible conditions, they go up sand dunes that are higher than this room. They plunge down the other side. They meet floods. They have to drive over the skulls and skeletons of what appear to be enormous dinosaurs. They fall into holes. They keep meeting strange people. It is a harrowing journey.

But throughout this Tom doesn't blink. Tom is an Aussie male like no other. No other country has a person like this. England doesn't have a person like it! You might have a postie riding around in his little van down the green lanes. This is the Birdsville Track. There's nothing to be seen. Until you fall into it. Or it falls on you. There's a memorable sequence in which a cow, the skeleton of a cow, is in a tree! Hanging up there, it's completely desiccated, it's just the skin and its horns and its skull. Tom just drives past in his truck, he keeps picking up these people, these weird people, he's got a couple of people on the top of the truck too. The truck is loaded with everything you could imagine.

And Tom knows that the people of the Never Never depend on him getting through. And Tom will get through. It's his job. He won't fail them. And nor will his truck fail. It's made in England and it's called a Leyland Badger. What a wonderful name. An Aussie bushman and a Pommie truck. The old firm. You can't see Tom crossing the Never Never in a Toyota Deli Boy, a Mazda Bongo or a Honda Duck, not to mention the Suzuki Cappuccino. This is a Leyland Badger.

But little Sally and Roberta, the two little girls, in the end join all the other skeletons in the Never Never. They've gone into that heavenly graveyard. In Australian mythology there are many lost white children. All the way from McCubbin's paintings in which you can see that these children are quite clearly doomed—they're either going to wander further into the bush and never be seen again or a man is going to come out of the shrubbery and abduct them. And then of course there's *Picnic at Hanging Rock*, which is directly in the great mythology of the menacing outback, the innocent people, the girls that live in it and it's going to kill them. Like Leichhardt, Kennedy and Burke, these little girls could simply not read the country.

When I came here in 1979 it seemed to me that everybody knew everything about everything. The governor general's dismissal of the Whitlam government in 1975, coming from where I came from, seemed to be a completely ordinary event. I came from a country where the prime minister had been stabbed to death in parliament. That's an extreme form of dismissing the prime minister. It was well justified, and I was personally delighted, but that's quite beyond the point.

It took me years and years to understand what the dismissal meant in Australian life. I simply lacked the background for it. I needed to understand what winning government after twenty-three years in opposition meant to Labor supporters. And twenty-three years is an extraordinarily long time in a democracy. I needed to understand the legends of Curtin and Chifley. I needed to understand what seventeen years of Robert Menzies meant. I needed to understand the relationship between the Australian communists and the Catholics. I needed to know the difference between kneelers and grippers. I've always loved the idea of kneelers and grippers. I would of course have to be a gripper. I needed to know about the subtleties of class and religion in Australia. I'd never paid much attention to religion at all. I didn't think there was any class division in Australia. Only time teaches you these things. I needed to know about Doc Evatt and Bob Santamaria and about the Petrov Affair and the industrial groups and the Labor–DLP split and the divisions over the Vietnam War and the deeply divided nature of Sonia McMahon's dress. There was no end to what I needed to know and to understand.

I came to Australia with a half-written novel in my knapsack, as it were, and thought I could just switch it over to an Australian setting. But after a few months I put it away. I could never ever, I thought at that point, write a novel that Australians would accept as written by one of their own.

I had been a fanatical reader since a very early age and I had started to demand that I have first go of my mother's English *Woman's Weekly*, probably after the age of eight or so. And in the 1950s no English woman's magazine was complete without a piece of fiction that featured a young woman who travels to a remote sheep station in Australia to care for the children of the newly widowed owner. God knows what happened to the wives. Snakes, I imagine. The female mortality rate in the outback must have been appalling. And these Aussie farmers were all equipped with glints in their steely grey eyes, which is a characteristic of Australians that I expected to find anywhere I went, squinting, steely grey eyes. I was disappointed. Most of them didn't have grey eyes. Anyway, the hapless young Englishwoman was completely adrift, unhappy, until in due course the squatter saved her from being trampled beneath the hooves of a herd of rampaging merinos. The English seemed to believe that merinos were roughly the size of rhinos. Twenty or thirty of them could lay waste to anything. Snatched from beneath their hooves, love was not far away. Now these tales, as you can see, made a deep impression upon me, an impression that some say is on full display in my books. People can be very cruel.

I'd also learnt something of Australia from my uncle, Bern Reardon, who was a farmer. He was the sheriff of a place called Warrenton, which was no bigger than two streets next to the Vaal River, which was just moving mud. And my uncle, in 1940, went to war in defence of the empire, with his brother and the two other men in the small town who spoke English. Only English-speaking people went to defence of the mother country. In North Africa he was captured briefly by the Italians, which he describes as one of the more pleasant experiences of his life. He found them absolutely charming and always wanted to go and live there afterwards. And in the course of this they got to know Anzacs, the Australians and New Zealanders, and one day my brother and I were sitting in the sheriff's office, in his deep old cracked armchairs, the smell of toffee lost beneath the cushions, and old tobacco smoke. He'd have a pipe clamped in his teeth and we'd be reading ancient copies of the *Friend*, a newspaper. He was the correspondent for the *Friend*, and they sent him free newspapers. He opened them about once a year and so we could read all the comics in sequence. We were sitting there reading the adventures of Curly Wee, as I recall, when he made a comment about the Australians that he had met during the war. 'Naughty buggers,' he said in an inflected way, 'you wouldn't bring them home to meet your sister.' And I have found that to be true. It may account for the fact that you had to bring all these English nannies out.

Anyway I moved from the *Woman's Weekly* in due course and onto crime novels. I now know them to be crime novels, Enid Blyton's stories, hard-boiled crime, middle-class children making mincemeat of inept baddies. The stories all involved caves, secret passages. I had never, having grown up in a town of only three buildings, seen a cave and I had never seen a building that could contain a secret passage. I liked the idea enormously. And I also read westerns, pulp westerns. I'm telling you all this to impress upon you how unsuitable I am to have been given this award. Hundreds and hundreds of pulp westerns. Titles like *Ramrod*, *Rimrock*, *Crossfire Trail*, *High Vermilion* (I remember that one well), *Play a Lone Hand*, *Hello with a Gun*, *The Burning Hills*, *Last Stand at Papago Wells*. And then there was the immortal *Hondo*, what a book that was. They were only about thirty pages long. I'd read them in an afternoon. Many novels should be no longer than thirty pages.

And at about that time, I think I was twelve, I was deeply influenced by a pulp western writer called Max Brand, his real name was Frederick Schiller Faust. Max Brand wrote about 500 of these tales. Under his influence I wrote a western, I wrote it in a class workbook, in pencil. It was called *Kid Bellamy, Gun Slinger*. I still think it's the finest thing I've ever written. But I moved on, and at about the same age I read Margery Allingham's *The Tiger in the Smoke*. There were seriously bad people in this book. It had a seriously ornate style, it was set in London, fogs, full of menace. Immediately I managed to extricate myself from the children's section of the library and, having got past the door bitch of the adult section, I started taking out adult books. But she wouldn't let me take out *Peyton Place*, unquestionably the raunchiest novel of the 1950s. She knew this. I don't know why. She didn't look like somebody who read raunchy novels. When I tried to get past her she took it away from me. So I got my mother, my dear innocent mother, to take it out for me.

And I was reading it and my mother said to me, 'What's it about, dear?'

'Nothing much,' I said, drooling over a sex scene.

Much later I learnt that educated people had read great books. I was pathetically eager to join this group and so I read the great books. I made a long list of great books and I read them. Some of them proved to be entertaining. Others less so. Most of them proved to be stunningly boring. In particular those translated from Russian and French. The most highly regarded books I found to be the most boring. This was deeply embarrassing to me. It was obviously me, it was my fault, I was not worthy of these great books. I couldn't tell anyone this and I still haven't, until tonight. I still think I'm totally inadequate, there's something lacking in me.

I resorted to reading books that captured me in a few pages, by people like Graham Greene, and the older Amis, and Norman Mailer, and Updike later and Carson McCullers, Ian Fleming, people like that. Books that I found drew me in quickly, moved me, in some way often changed the way I thought about things. And in a peculiar way educated me about things that I would never have learnt any other way.

The years passed and life changed and I started to try to write novels. I had many stabs at writing literary novels, by which I mean a novel without a dead person fairly close to the beginning. And I abandoned them one by one, exhausted by them, bored by what I was doing, bored by myself, realising I had nothing to say. I had no interior life that was worth relating. How could I possibly have? I still think lots of people should come to that decision much earlier.

And the years passed in Australia and one winter's night, in Ballarat, where we were living—another failure to read the country, I might add—it suddenly occurred to me that I could write a novel set in Australia. By then I'd lived in Melbourne and had a damn good look at the country. And, I thought, I think I may know something about it. I felt I understood enough about Melbourne's character and personality to do it. As you know, Melbourne has no shortage of character and personality. Indeed, Melbourne may have too much personality and character. This is, after all, a city where people go to the museum for the express purpose of looking at a dead stuffed racehorse.

Melbourne's character, I found, was serious, high-minded, moralistic. These attributes are big pluses when you come to write crime novels because, the bigger the gap between people's actions and the things they profess, the more fertile the ground for the crime novel. In truth, much of Melbourne was seriously low-minded but most importantly I found Melbourne to be a city with a very long memory. It's a city of institutions and shrines to sport and war and power and money. Places with lots of shrines don't forget and they don't forgive. And even when you're forgotten you're still not forgiven. In the words, in the immortal words of the song.

Equipped with this reading of Melbourne, and fully confident that I had read the country, I created my character Jack Irish. Jack is a person who is no stranger to pain and love and sorrow. He values friends, he knows about guilt and recklessness and the exaltation and the misery of the punt. And he knows that every last thing has a price and, if you stick by your team long enough, the day will come and then all the years of enduring the jeers of the mongrels will have been worthwhile. Jack is in short a Melbourne person, as I have come to read Melbourne people. In finding my city, I found my vocation. I could enjoy writing and I could enjoy being a savage editor of my own writing, something hitherto reserved for other people. A student of mine recently wrote, 'I remember the first assignment I handed in to Peter Temple and in writing on the bottom of it "If you intend to be a journalist, I suggest you recommence your education in kindergarten."' That's an exceptionally cruel remark. Still, the writer seems to treasure the memory.

There are only a few stories available to us. But there are countless variations. Stories are valuable only and in proportion to the gifts that the storyteller brings to them. I don't know if I have any gifts. I can only say that I've loved words. They haven't loved me back but I've tried to do justice to the language and to its infinite malleability. But my God, I have tested that malleability in my time.

Truth is the end of the road that started with *Bad Debts* and Jack Irish. I have no idea of its worth but it speaks to me. It isn't always easy to read because it wasn't meant to be. It isn't strong on explaining things and it requires a bit of attention to follow what's going on. In part it's a book about people who get up in the morning and go to sleep with violence and death, and are marked and set apart by these things. It's a novel of violence and the bad things people do. It's also a novel of childhood, of family and love and the barbed-wire ties that bind us to our mothers and fathers and brothers and sisters. But it's also a novel about power and influence. About a city and its loss of innocence, its violation by the worst kind of exploitation, that which is done solely for money.

Towards the end of *Bad Debts*, Jack is in serious trouble. His former partner, Andrew, says to him, 'Well, that's the lecture, that's the way the world is now and mate you have been wandering around in it like some yokel from Terang in town for the day. You think you're doing something good, not so. You see it in terms of right and wrong. Justice, that sort of thing. But pardon me, you and I know the system's not about fairness. It's not about good and bad. It's about power, Jack. I know that and you should know that.'

These are the themes that I've been drawn to and which are at the heart of even my most frivolous novels. My most frivolous novel?

They're all fairly frivolous. I suppose I could have written the kind of fiction that Don DeLillo has scornfully described as 'around the house and in the yard'. He was echoing Marcus Aurelius, who I know intimately, who wrote that to wonder about what so and so is doing and why they're doing it or what they're saying or they're thinking or they're scheming 'distracts you from fidelity to the ruler within you'. He means the loss of opportunity for some other tasks. My instincts have all leaned towards writing the world beyond the back yard and the barbecue. And that world is an increasingly nasty and debased place.

Here are the thoughts of Stephen Villani in *Truth*:

> He thought about himself at twelve. He knew many things by then, but he knew little of the intimate physical world of adults, he had only glimpsed the violence. Now, some children that age had seen every last sexual thing, every thrusting sucking beating strangling act, they had seen violence of every kind. Nothing was strange or shocking, they were innocent of trust, honesty, virtue.
>
> What they had was existence in all its careless, joyless horror.

Gertrude Stein saw America as the oldest country in the world, paradoxically, because it was the first country to be truly modern and therefore the first of its kind and the oldest. It invented everything. It invented the assembly line, it invented time and motion study, it invented mass production and mass marketing and mass consumption. The hamburger, the cocktail and it set the standard for pornography. And now it's conspired its own descent into the loss of innocence as the simple logic of capitalist production forces it to try continuously to make everything cheaper and to sell more.

Australia became modern not long after America. It's also a very old country, in that sense. And it has followed America into pointless wars around the globe, against imaginary enemies. It will follow America into economic and social decline. Twenty years of selling rocks and coal to the Chinese will only postpone that. So perhaps it is the task of novelists now to record this late sad period in the life of their country. And that means writing novels that engage with the world, that turn the novelist's gaze on the workings of the increasingly toxic and dysfunctional cities that we are creating.

To the dismay of my publishers and many readers I have been concerned to put language under pressure. To compress it into little bits that cease to squeak and then to put back in only so many words as are needed to restore meaning. My defence in this is that I have been encouraged by my adopted country's ingrained habits of expression. Of saying as little as possible in dealing with one another.

Two tradies in the Golf House Hotel in Ballarat.

'What's she say?'

'Nothin.'

'What'd you say?'

'Ugh, you know.'

'Yeah?'

'Yeah.'

'Bloody hell.'

But is there anywhere a more poignantly laconic and meaningful passage than this one quoted in the voiceover of *The Back of Beyond*. It's from the diary of the Birdsville policeman: 'January 22. Thomas Crowe appears out of his mind. Some Inspector King shot himself while on the police station verandah. Another hot day. The heat.'

2011

STORIES

CROSSROADS

IN SLEEP, the ringing was the electric bell above the primary school's front door, she was always late, always a block away and running, lungs burning, her socks cold, her mother at the scarred ironing board, trying to iron them dry, the iodine smell.

She fought the sheets, stood in the black room, unsteady, walked, the little toe found the bed leg, pain, swore.

'Yes,' she said. 'Hello.'

'Listen, why'd you have to fight over every bloody thing? It's not...'

'What time is it?'

'I dunno, it's just...eleven, twenty...'

'Not here it's not, you prick. I'm unplugging this phone. Fuck off.'

She left the phone off the hook, went back down the passage, head down; she would not sleep now.

'What was that?'

'Nothing. Wrong number.'

'Was it Dad?'

'Go to sleep.'

'It was, wasn't it?'

Unsteady in the dark, Sara put out a hand for the wall, misjudged the distance and lurched. 'He gets drunk and wants to fight,' she said. 'That's what it's about.'

'Did he want to talk to me?'

'No.'

'Mum…'

'Tomorrow, Rachel. Not now.'

Denny's door opened. 'What's wrong?'

'It was Dad,' Rachel shouted. 'He wanted to talk to me.'

'Goodnight,' said Sara. 'Goodbloodynight.'

She went back to her bed and thought about Mick and his legacy. How was it that his boy child turned out to be such a good kid and his girl such a lazy, selfish creature?

From the highway came a thin skidding dental scream and then another, almost in sync, two cars racing, the engine notes turning to howl, gunned in first gear to the limit of tolerance. They changed up, they came closer. *Please God, not tonight, you brain-dead hoons.*

They kept going. Tonight they were Rivervale's hoons. Sleepless people there would be listening to them come. The only people who wouldn't hear would be the cops.

The alarm woke her at 6am. She swung her legs out, sat on the bed for a while, looking at the curtains, the sag where the rings had fallen off. She groaned, rose and went to the bathroom, showered in the cubicle with its missing tiles and leaking tray, stepped out into a cold pool.

At 6.30am she stood at the sitting room window, tea in a mug. Full daylight, the sky like water, moon a bruise above the water towers. At 6.35am, Jude pulled up, hooted. She was tapping the wheel. Today her hair was pulled back like a ballerina's. Cassie was in the back with Carla. From the beginning, Carla insisted Sara have the front seat. There was no reason, and no point in arguing the matter.

'Morning,' said Sara.

'Morning,' said Cassie and Carla together.

Jude crunched the Mazda into first, pulled off. She punched a button. Music. She sang along:

Or you can tell my lips to tell my fingertips
They won't be reaching out for you no more.

'Fuck off,' said Sara. 'Do we have to start the day with this country shit?'

They turned left onto Rokeby Drive, empty. At the highway lights, they watched the big rigs go by, drivers like fat gods in baseball caps, looking down, breathing their own Big Mac and amphetamine fumes, taking them back into the blood.

The lights changed and Jude put her foot flat. She was in second; the Mazda jerked, died. It wouldn't start. She swore, then it caught and she ground it into first. They drove through the lifeless outskirts of the town, saw three homeless dogs, all ribs and snout, an old man sweeping his pavement with autistic precision, the police vans parked outside the station.

'Monday morning,' Jude said. 'One Monday I'm not getting up till I wake up and then I'm goin', no packing, I'm in this heap and it's drive and drive and never look back, never fucking ever.'

'Language, dear,' said Carla.

Carla was a lean woman who had worked at the Panextram factory for more than thirty years. She was older than their mothers, sixty-five, a widow—an engine block fell on her husband, the ambulance took twenty minutes, he'd been dead a long while. The mechanics cleaned up with Karcher, pressure-blasted his blood into the concrete, a dark line appeared at the base of the wall.

'Don't have strong enough language for the way I feel,' said Jude.

'You extra shitty today?' said Sara.

Jude pulled her mouth down. 'My darling husband says he wants his freedom,' she said, for only Sara to hear.

'Don't they all?' said Sara. 'Freedom to be little boys again, that's the ticket.'

'Says his life's slippin' away.'

'That's the life getting tanked with the cretin mates? Or the one on his arsebone in front of the giant plasma?' said Sara. 'Tell him to go for it. You won't miss him.'

'Steady on, Sara,' said Carla.

'Not supposed to be listening,' said Jude.

'Can't help it, can I?'

'All babies, men,' said Sara. 'Born and die babies.'

'Well, babies—it's about babies, actually,' said Jude.

They drove in silence. At the junction they joined four other cars, knew them all, all going to Panextram.

Sara thought about Mick, his golf weekends with Tommo, his new best mate. Spur of the moment, he said; didn't know where they were staying, hadn't booked, see when they got there. Then one Saturday she drove Denny to a barbie on the other side of town, coming back she stopped at a shopping centre, never been there. Tommo came out of the TAB with two blokes, they had the border-line pissed look. She thought she'd be sick.

'Ho, ho, ho and off to bloody Panextram we go,' said Jude.

'Don't say that every day, Jude,' said Sara. 'It jars.'

'Jars?' said Jude. 'That's not a word you often hear. Jars. Well, excuse me for jarring passengers. Excuse me for being the jarring arse that drives the bus.'

'Happy to make my own way,' said Sara, she kept her gaze out of the side window. 'If I can't express an opinion in the free bus.'

She found her bag, groped in it, pretended to be looking for something. Letting Mick bully her into giving up the course, that was what filled her with rage. In the beginning he said yeah, great idea, be a teacher, that'd be good. Then he started complaining, sneering, made her late for classes, made her miss classes. One day she rang the college and said she had to drop out, changed family circumstances. We understand, they said. Come back next year.

Mick had won. There was no going back. You could never go back; no second chances. When she told him, he said, 'Nothin' wrong with bein' a wife and mother like my mum, that's a career, right?'

Her having a bit of life he didn't know about, that was what he hated. One way or another, he'd ruled her since she was sixteen, since she fell in love with him. How stupid that was—she couldn't recapture the condition of being in love with Mick. She remembered only that she hardly ate, started smoking to get thinner, spent hours on make-up, her hair, trying on clothes.

She never gave thought to Mick's silent, sloping father, who came home from his council job, hid in the shed, made ugly wooden objects, drowned kittens, went on long late-night walks. His mother a woman who washed all the curtains four times a year, swabbed the kitchen floor with chlorine twice a day. How could anything decent come out of that mixture?

'You hear where Panextram wants to sell?' said Cassie.

Sara and Carla looked at her. She was reading a book. Cassie was seventeen, looked to be nearly twelve, lived with her mother, a person known to all pension agencies as never having worked a day in her life, a victim of society. Cassie seldom spoke a full sentence.

Sara said, 'Who says?'

'Dean.'

Dean worked in the office, thirties, cracked lips, moon face, hair departing by the hour.

'How's he know?' said Sara.

'Reads the emails,' said Cassie. 'Knows everything.'

'One shit company sold to another,' said Jude. 'Life goes on.'

'Dean reckons they're looking to downsize,' said Cassie.

'That fat nerd?' said Jude. 'Up all night talking on the computer to women in Alabama about his Porsche and his huge cock.'

'Excuse me, I didn't hear that,' said Carla.

'What part?' said Jude. 'The cock or the Porsche?'

'Anyone actually sighted the cock?' said Sara.

'Downsize?' said Carla. 'That's sacking, is it?'

'Such a reliable source, Dean,' said Sara. 'Wait till we see his Porsche. Or his huge…'

'Shush now,' said Carla. 'What's the book, love?'

'Poems,' said Cassie. 'Found it at the op shop.'

Coming up to the lights, Jude tapped fingertips on the wheel, eye-flick at Sara.

'So, back to me and babies…'

'Babies?' said Sara.

'Yeah, well, early on I gave up on the subject.'

'He didn't want kids?'

'Put it mildly. Want a baby, get a sperm donor. The doc took me off the pill, I kept quiet. What'll be will be. Nothin' happened. That's been four years. Not that much chance, mind you. Like blowin' up a jumpy castle to get anythin' to sit on.'

A ute beside them, close. The passenger leaned out, a big boy, ginger, perhaps twenty. 'Real men in here, ladies,' he said. 'Help you out with premium piston oil?'

He showed a forearm like a flattened football, a big fist.

Jude beckoned. He leaned further.

'Come around when your balls drop, Carrots,' she said. 'Meanwhile practice jumpin' your ugly sister.'

Carrots recoiled, blinked, blinked, pale eyelashes. 'Fuck you,' he said. 'Fat bitch.'

The lights changed, the ute growled, fishtailed away. A sticker on the back window: ROOT VEGETABLES? WE ROOT ANYTHING.

'Cassie, hunt that lovely boy down,' said Sara. 'Hunt him down and marry him.'

Hoots all round.

Jude stuck out her arm, gave the finger. 'Jesus,' she said, 'what happened to manners?'

'So?' said Sara.

'He comes in Friday night, two weeks ago, he's three sheets, that's normal, but he's all over me, that's not usual, and he says, c'mon, let's have a baby. I said, well, Davo, nice idea but I don't like the odds. Been off the pill for four years. Macca's or Buster?'

'Buster,' said Sara. 'Coffee's slightly less terrible.'

They were third in the BusterBurger drive-through lane, two tradies ahead, electricians.

'These dorks are keen,' said Jude. 'Never heard of a sparky on the job before ten. Anyway, Davo. First it's like he's taken a bullet, then it's like I've sold his boat, he goes ballistic, really scared me, never seen him like that. Grabs me, shakes me, barren fucken bitch, etc, eyes poppin' out. Thought he'd throw a hearter on the spot. He gets in the car, doesn't come back till Sunday. Not a word between us till yesterday when he gives me the life slippin' away crap.'

'Show him the door,' said Sara.

'He reckons it's me should go.'

'That's cheeky.'

Nothing seemed to be happening at the window. Soon there were eight or nine in the queue. The electrician got out and came their way, tall, lean inside tight overalls, pilot's sunnies.

'Well go, go Superman,' said Jude.

He went in the side door of the building.

'Trapped in a BusterBurger drive-through,' said Jude. 'Got to be more to life than this.'

'Read us a poem, Cassie,' said Carla.

Cassie paged back a few pages. She licked her lower lip. 'It's called The Heavenly City,' she said.

'I sigh for the heavenly country,
Where the heavenly people pass...'

A machine came to life outside Sara's window, almost drowning Cassie's thin voice.

'...dressed in a heavenly coat of polished white...
feet on the pastures are bare...
At night I fly over the housetops
and stand on the bright moony beams,
Gold are all heaven's rivers,
And silver her streams.'

Cassie closed the book, sat head down, face hidden by fine, pale hair. Silence in the car.

'That's beautiful, love,' said Carla. 'The heavenly country.'

'Sounds like a death wish,' said Sara. 'Who wrote it?'

Cassie looked. 'Stevie Smith,' she said.

'No,' said Jude, 'you're not telling me a bloke wrote that, the coat stuff, the bare feet. Bloke couldn't write that.' She paused. 'Well, maybe Elton John could write that.'

'Women sighing,' said Sara. 'That's what gets us into all this shit. Much less sighing needed.'

'Speaking of which, how's Rachel?'

'Same. Lies around smoking, listening to emo junk, won't look for a job. Tells me how wonderful the boyfriend's mum is when what she is is basically she's a junkie. Pills for sleeping, waking, walking, talking. Mick keeps feeding her crap, too: I forced him to leave home, she's his little princess. He can have her. Anytime. I'll shout the plane ticket. One way.'

The electrician came out, stopped at the car, put a hand on the windowsill. 'Somebody flicked the mains,' he said. 'Fortunately I have the technology to fix that.'

'Give this man a free JawBuster,' said Jude. 'Got a card?'

He found one in his top pocket. 'All hours,' he said. 'Specialise in emergencies.'

'Never know when you'll need someone to flick a switch, do you?' said Jude.

'Call me.'

They watched him go.

'Can't help yourself, can you?' said Sara.

'Just teasin',' said Jude. Her eyes followed him. 'Nice bum.'

It took five minutes to get the coffees. The traffic had picked up. Jude had to force her way in.

'Sold my house,' said Carla.

'What?' said Jude. 'Why?'

'Not a happy moment there. Since.'

'Where are you going to live?'

'Don't know, don't care. Just came to me; I rang this mate of Ken's, he brings two kids the same day. Paid up Friday.'

'Well, that's pretty bold, I mean, just doing it.'

'No,' said Carla. 'You know when it's time.'

At the last lights before the turnoff, the Mazda drove into a blind canyon of rigs, sat there like a toy, Sara felt the steel pulse of the diesels throb in her blood, in her bone marrow.

Just audible, Cassie. 'I had a miscarriage on Saturday.'

Sara turned her head and met Carla's eyes. Jude put her forehead on the steering wheel, pressed on it. The hooter sounded, weak, pathetic.

'Cassie,' she said. 'Don't say Dean. For fuck's sake, just don't say Dean.'

The pumping of the huge engines.

'Yeah,' said Cassie. 'Dean.'

Jude raised her head, the rigs were moving, she went with them, edged over, bit by bit, gatecrashed the right lane.

'You like Dean?' said Carla. 'Boyfriend?'

'No, no,' said Cassie. 'No. He just came on to me.'

'Where?' said Sara.

'At home. He's mum's friend. They go to the pokies and that. Sit around and drink wine and stuff. Smoke.'

'So what?' said Jude. 'You said yes?'

Cassie squirmed. 'No. He come into my room. Held me down. Off his face, I couldn't do nothing.'

Carla said, 'So where's your mum?'

'There. I mean, not there in the lounge. Bit off her face, too. Y'know.'

'You tell her?'

'She said oh grow up, think you're so bloody precious, don't you? That's what she said.'

They turned for the factory. 'Your mum's toxic,' said Sara. 'You know that, Cassie? You've got to get out of there, OK?'

'Yeah.' Cassie turned her head to the window, blinking. 'Well, where'd I go?'

Carla patted her arm, big brown hand, 'We'll fix it, don't worry.'

'Jesus, what's this?' said Jude.

Gates closed, cars along the fence, men in blue uniforms outside the main gate, two inside leaning against an armoured money-delivery van. Jude went left, parked next to a Camry with three women in it, the front passenger's arm was dangling, slack, tipped with a cigarette.

'What's goin' on here, Stell?' said Jude.

'Shut down,' said the woman. 'Bastards closed the factory.'

Nothing was said for a long time.

'I'll be…well, bugger,' said Jude. 'Yes.'

'Who'da thought? On the right track, the rapist,' said Sara. 'Just too stupid to get the half of it.'

A man arrived at Jude's window.

'G'day,' he said. He was built like a bouncer, an identity card on a pop-chain around his thick neck. 'Work here?'

'What d'you reckon?' said Jude. 'We come out here at 7.30am to have a park?'

The man offered a clipboard. 'Need you to register, show some ID. They'll start paying in a few minutes.'

'ID?' said Jude. 'Fifteen years here, for what do I need a fucken ID?'

'Just hired for the day, lady, doin' the job,' said the man. 'Name, address and some ID.'

Sara leaned across and took the clipboard. 'Figures,' she said. 'They'll use slaves in China or they'll open again next month, half the jobs for half the pay.'

They wrote down their details. The man took the clipboard. 'Call you in,' he said. 'Alphabetical.'

'Scared?' said Jude. 'Think we might get violent? Rush you?'

He said nothing.

Cassie was first, then Jude, a wait for Sara's name. A security man let her through the gate, in the truck another one checked her driver's licence, found an envelope in a steel box. 'Details inside,' he said. 'Good luck, mate.'

'Fuck you, mate,' said Sara.

On the way back, she passed Carla. In the car, Jude said, 'Three weeks' pay, plus one week for every year. So that's what you get for never absent, never late. Shit.'

'End of life as we know it,' said Sara.

They sat. Jude lit up.

Carla arrived. Jude looked at her watch.

'Quarter to eight,' she said. 'Fair bit of day left. Could park in the main street, watch the traffic goin' somewhere.'

'Could go down to the river,' said Sara. 'Watch it dry out.'

Jude had her head back, looking at the car's bleached vinyl ceiling. 'You know what blokes do when shit like this happens?'

'Yes,' said Sara. 'Get pissed.'

'They get pissed and then they shoot through,' said Jude.

'Where do they go?' said Cassie.

'They just go. Queensland a lot. Port Douglas. Or Darwin. There's a lot end up in Darwin.'

'You need a decent vehicle to shoot through to Port Douglas,' said Sara, she felt numb, something ended, nothing coming.

'Got a decent vehicle,' said Jude. 'Got a Pajero.'

'You mean Davo's got a Pajero.'

Jude was loosening her hair, she shook her head, her hair fell, she was a girl again, for a second, she threw the tie out of the window. 'Person paid for a Pajero, person's name on the rego, person pays the rego, that's the bitch owns the fucken Pajero.'

'What's this about?' said Carla.

'About buggered,' said Jude. 'About marriage buggered, job buggered, everything buggered.'

'It'll pass,' said Carla.

'No,' said Jude. 'Had it with pass. No more pass. I might just go, anyone's welcome to come.'

In the silence, the first heat sounds, tiny metallic clicks.

'Right,' said Carla. 'I'll be in that. Nothing left here for me. Want to come, Cassie?'

'Yes,' said Cassie.

Jude looked at Sara. 'Well?'

'What's a person do for work in…let's say…Darwin?'

'There's work,' said Jude. 'We can do lap, we can do pole.'

'Bit mature, don't you think?'

'Legless, faceless, they miss their mums. Love a flabby tit.'

Sara thought about sending Rachel to Mick, that would be the sweetest, sweetest thing. Denny was his own man, a far, far better man than his father and his father's father. Very likely his father's father's father.

'Can we get out of here?' said Sara. 'This life's over.'

'A minute,' said Carla, eyes on the gate. 'Here we are.'

Dean coming out, dark glasses, a hand through his hair, tossed the snarly strands.

'Just a moment, please,' said Carla.

She got out and walked, intersected with Dean at his car, went close. She said something. Dean pulled a face, her left hand swept his glasses, she stepped back and gave him a full open-hand arm slap. Sara saw his face go sideways, pinheads of shining spit catching the light.

Dean tried to grab Carla. She slapped him again, fluid left hand, right hand, left hand. He went to his knees, slowly, like a penitent.

Carla came back, massaging her right hand. In the car, she said, 'Now we're finished. Let's go.'

Jude started the engine, reversed the Mazda, did a violent swing, she gave a long, defiant hoot. 'Read us that poem again, Cassie,' she said. 'Standing on the bright, moony beams.'

2007

FLIGHT

THE VILLAGE was a long way from the coast, the last thirty kilometres steep, the road narrow, twisting, potholed, not maintained since the fall of Salazar. It was a nothing place—no shrine, ugly, cold. No tourists came.

Sturt and Celik spent two days in the rooms looking onto the *quadrado*, a square designed for a big town, some long-ago dream of prosperity. They listened to Sturt's shortwave radio, played chess. They were of even ability, not very good.

Celik was a Turk from Dogubayazit who spoke many languages badly. They spoke English, Celik's choice.

On the third day, they were playing chess, it was 3pm. Celik's phone made a sound. He spoke to his man on the road.

They carried on playing for ten minutes, then they went to the slit window.

A Mercedes, blue under yellow dust, came into view, parked in the square.

Two men got out, stretched, looked around like health inspectors. Gazzard was the passenger, driven by the thin Hungarian Sturt had once given a package in Vilnius.

'I'll point at you,' said Sturt.

He put the Python into the clamp, went down the back stairs to the alley, walked half a block and turned into the slim passage.

The Hungarian saw him at the last minute, shouted to Gazzard.

Gazzard walked towards Sturt, smiling, right hand out. He had 1950s male-model looks, three days of beard stubble, oiled.

'Hey, man,' he said. 'Fucking shithole, what is this?'

'In the crosshairs,' Sturt said.

He pointed without looking.

Gazzard looked.

'Totally uncalled for,' he said.

'Sit down over there,' said Sturt. To the Hungarian: 'Don't move.'

They sat at a tin table outside the bar, Sturt facing the square. The owner came.

'Beer?' said Sturt.

Gazzard nodded.

'Tuborg. Three.'

Gazzard combed his thin hair with fingers. He had long nails, well kept. 'Listen,' he said. 'Something shorted, I don't fucking know.'

'Who killed Khalid?'

'What?'

'You die right here.'

'I didn't know that, I swear. When?'

'Five, six hours after. The girl too.'

'Jesus.'

Gazzard put fingers to his lips, breathed loudly. 'Well, shit, they must know.'

'Don't be a cunt, Barry,' said Sturt. 'They knew, I'm blown away long ago. Me and the girl. The fact that it fucking happened means they don't know.'

The chainsaw sound. Sturt looked at Celik, who raised a thumb. They waited. The trailbike came into the square, two youths up, did a casual lap, revved away.

Celik's people.

'So,' said Gazzard. 'You can imagine the chaos. Jeez, I need a fucken smoke.'

He went into the bar, came back opening a packet, offered. Sturt took. Gazzard's old Zippo took many scrapes to fire. He lit the cigarettes, hand unsteady.

'Four days,' said Sturt. 'Four fucking days. Who'd you tell? The woman on the switch? The fucking intern?'

'Well, I don't get through to the President,' said Gazzard. 'I'm a nothing.'

The bar owner's idiot son-in-law arrived. Sturt told him to give a beer to the Hungarian.

They watched him deliver it.

A whistle.

Sturt looked. Celik made the signs: something coming.

'What's Katzen say?' said Sturt.

'Number's dead.'

'You've got one number?'

Gazzard put up his hands. 'I've left messages.'

Sturt felt the breeze. It came up in mid-afternoon, disturbed the square's poplars, blew sadly till dawn.

An old Volkswagen Kombi nosed around the corner, its snub front covered in stickers, a mesh shield protecting the windscreen. It parked in the shade, ten metres away.

'Friends?' said Sturt, tingling, left hand in his shirt, on the gun butt.

Gazzard said, 'I'm fucking nuts, am I?'

The Hungarian in the Mercedes was turned to the Kombi, he would have a gun out.

The Kombi's front doors opened in unison. A man and a woman stepped down. Young, tanned, Nordic-looking, both in shorts and white T-shirts with hoods. The man was balding, with a weak adolescent beard. The woman had the face of a clever boy, close-cropped hair, small round glasses. She put her head back into the Kombi for a look, closed the door softly, nodded at the man.

Shapes in the back. Children in safety seats, asleep.

The woman pointed skywards, said something. The man reached into the front seat, took out a big straw hat, settled it on his head, arranged it, asked for her approval.

She laughed: it was an old joke between them.

Sturt sat back, hand out of his shirt.

'Waiting, Barry?' he said. 'For an explanation? Dear sir, we regret we are unable…'

The Nordics were coming towards them, crossing the square to the bar.

In the Mercedes, the Hungarian had lost interest. He was drinking his beer.

Sturt was looking at the woman. Hot in the old Kombi, no air-conditioning, she had a sheen on her face, her arms, her T-shirt was dark at the armpits, under her breasts. He could see her nipples.

Five or six metres away, she put her arms in the air, stretched luxuriously, joined her hands behind her head, elbows out, breasts flattened, moved her shoulders from side to side.

Sports bra, Sturt thought. Nipple cutouts to avoid chafing.

She smiled at him, a friendly, knowing smile. She had blue-green eyes.

Sports bra. Nipple cutouts. Sexy.

Her hands were coming forward over her head.

Hands together.

Oh Jesus, fuck no.

Machine pistol in a bra holster between her shoulder blades.

Hands coming down.

Sturt threw his full beer bottle so hard, his elbow cracked—flat trajectory, head-high, the bottle expelling a curve of liquid and foam.

She didn't have the experience, she couldn't override her instincts, turned her head before she fired.

The bottle struck her full in the face—two more barks, bad unnerved shots that clanged on the bar's tin sign high on the wall.

Sturt threw the small metal table, ran for her, another shot hit the tabletop.

Then he was so close her muzzle flash seared his right ear.

He grabbed her left hand with the pistol in it, turned his hips and swung her, lifted her off the ground, snapped her like a whip.

He heard her arm pop its socket.

He let her go, got her pistol into his right hand, turned.

The Nordic man had the gun out of the crown of his straw hat.

His mouth opened. A large piece of his skull came away, floating in a dark mist. His gun hand dropped, he went down on one knee, pitched forward.

Sturt looked up at the window. Celik's work was done, his barrel lowered.

The Hungarian got out of the Mercedes and fired two shots into the man.

'You cunt,' Sturt said. 'You totally useless cunt.'

He walked over to Gazzard lying against the cafe wall, put his foot on his head.

'A bullet's too good for you,' he said. 'I should kick you to death.'

Far away, a whup-whup-whup.

'Oh Lord, here we go.'

'What?' said Gazzard. 'What?'

'Get up. Help him under the tree.'

They dragged the man.

'Her?' said Gazzard.

'Leave her,' said Sturt. 'Go. Lie out there. Both of you. Quick.'

Gazzard and the Hungarian went out, lay down on the cobbles.

'In the blood,' said Sturt. 'Face down.'

The thrumming closer, the helicopter perhaps thirty seconds away.

Sturt looked at Celik in the window, pointed at the sky. Celik made the sign.

'Look dead, you arseholes,' said Sturt to the men. 'So fucking dead.'

He took off his shirt, dragged the white T-shirt off the dead Nordic's bloody head, pulled it on back to front, felt the stickiness of the man's blood on his face.

He put on the big straw hat, stepped out into the square and stood, the man's pistol at the end of a slack right arm.

The chopper came in a deafening rush, low over the rooftops, cleared them by ten metres.

Sturt saw a face in the door, dark glasses. He gave him the sucking-on-a-joint wave.

Chopper gone.

'Please,' said Sturt.

He heard the chopper coming, from his right—slower now.

He looked up at Celik.

The machine hung four metres over the square, dust rising. It dropped lower, the door man giving the thumbs-up, then the beckon, lazy hands: come to me, come to me.

Sturt walked to him and when he could see the dimple in his chin, he shot him twice, fired three shots at what he could see of the pilot, got off two more as the helicopter lifted.

Last bullet.

Close range, no excuse.

The helicopter reared, horse-like, sank.

Sturt couldn't see the pilot.

Celik.

A boy with three bullets hunting wild goats on the silent mesmerising plains of Anatolia. Three bullets, three goats.

Sturt turned.

'Get up,' he said to Gazzard and the Hungarian.

Gazzard raised himself.

Sturt walked to him. 'Barry,' he said. 'You're a dumb cunt but I trusted you.'

Gazzard got to his knees. 'Gimme a minute, this...'

Sturt shot Gazzard in the left eye, took a pace and executed the Hungarian, he already had his hands in the air, pleading.

Celik used vodka to clean everything they had touched, his prints were on file. His people were waiting. He told them what to do with the Nordics and the Kombi. He made promises and threats. They listened, heads bowed, they had seen what could happen to them. Then he paid them, in US hundred-dollar bills.

They put Gazzard and the Hungarian into the helicopter.

Sturt flew the machine. Overloaded, they rose into a clear sky, into a heaven without end. He was nineteen again, nothing hurt, nothing mattered.

Over the high mountains, Alvoca da Serra to the east, Celik pushed out the bodies, well spaced. They tumbled, opened like skydivers.

There was a brief illusion of flight.

2015

THE STONE HOUSE

THE PAST lies in wait for us, that's what we don't understand when we're young. We can't see that we're journeying towards it. It's in our genes, there and in what we profess to have forgotten but know perfectly: the fears of childhood, the eyes of our fathers, our mothers' fears. And our attitude to the past doesn't matter; knowledge or ignorance, concern or indifference—these change nothing. The past is there, living like a shark in the inner ocean, in the deep pulsing plasma, implacable, outside time, simply the remorseless sum of everything and always. My blood-mouthed shark was always waiting for me. But I couldn't know that until knowing it made no difference.

Before the telephone call, I was sitting in a rectangle of feeble sunlight outside the weights room, sitting in a plastic chair in the pastel corridor smoking a cigarette rolled by Smiling George Da Costa. George was sitting next to me, thighs apart. He was a big calm man who had six years to run for attempted murder and armed robbery.

'Never roll a decent smoke, rich poofs,' said George. 'Gotta learn young. Nine, ten, that's the time.'

'Ten?' I said. 'I didn't smoke before I came in here.'

'Mr Fucking Clean,' said George. 'Your Honour, so my client's been found guilty. Unfortunately. But he don't smoke, never have. That's gotta be worth somethin. Three years off, minimum.' He took a draw and blew a perfect smoke ring, a single ring, resisted the temptation to blow more. It hung in the air like a small, ghostly porthole, becoming bigger and weaker until it met the cold window, shuddered and dissolved.

'How long they reckon?'

'No knowing,' I said. 'Today.'

'Shit,' George said. 'Fucking lawyers.' He turned his head. I had heard nothing but two men in thongs and T-shirts and tracksuits were in the corridor, men with short hair and thick necks and pectorals like fifteen-year-old girls' breasts turned to stone. George watched them come, they came watching him. When they were seven or eight metres away, he put up his right hand. Not a stop sign, more like a blessing. They stopped. George shook his head, left, right, no more. He was smiling.

'An hour,' he said. 'Come back in an hour.'

The man on the left blinked, slow, deliberate blinks. They showed off eyes crudely tattooed in blue on his eyelids. Dale was his proper name. He was doing a long sentence for maiming a taxi driver. 'Says fucken who?' he said. He talked through his nose.

'Stan,' said George. 'Stan's taken up the weights.' He waited, looked from face to face, still smiling. 'He's shy about pumpin in front of strangers.'

The men said nothing, turned and went back down the corridor, bumping against each other as they walked. From behind, they looked like members of another branch of the human race, a branch on an evolutionary march in an alternative direction, towards the insignificant head, the tapered and swollen thorax, the legs like giant chicken drumsticks.

'Quick grasp for Foureyes,' I said.

'Pigshit for brains,' George said. He was watching the pair waddle down the corridor. 'Lucky some things you don't need to think a lot about.'

We sat and smoked. In the weights room, we could hear Stan the Man complaining. Stan never raised his voice but it carried like the whine of a powerdrill. He was talking to his personal trainer, a serial rapist called The Dick. On his first night in A wing, it took five men to hold The Dick down for Stan, hold him face down on a Formica-topped table in the television room. He screamed and cried but no warder came. Once I didn't know about things like that.

Then George said, sadness and resignation in his voice, 'Not guilty. I'd like to hear that. Never found not guilty of anythin. Not in my life. From a child. Charged, I'm guilty.' His eyes flicked again. Now a warder had appeared.

'Cato,' the man said, 'phone.'

I went cold, like stepping into a coolroom, couldn't move for a moment, not even my eyes, couldn't get out of the plastic chair.

George was looking at me. 'What's the worst?' he said. 'Few years sittin around givin free legal advice to people in need.'

The warder, one of Stan's people, a slate-eyed drug courier, skin like old towel, took me through the steel gates to the office. On a bare grey tin desk daubed with bits of pizza and stained with spilled Coke and instant coffee lay a grey plastic handset. Waiting. I picked it up, took a breath.

'Cato.'

'Michael. Sitting down?'

My solicitor, Zelda Saloman, aged at least seventy, gipsy lawyer, mistress of scarves, of face painting. The feeling of cold intensified, my mouth felt cold, my lips icy, my tongue a piece of meat, cold and great meat.

'No.'

'Good. Because as of fifteen minutes ago, my child, you don't have to be in that place. A free man.'

I felt no exhilaration, felt nothing.

'Michael?'

'Zelda. Thank you.' I was looking out of the window, looking at the darkening concrete yard puddled with the afternoon's rain, the wind rippling the shallow lakes.

'Free. You'll get used to the idea, boychick. Maurie will pick you up in, oh, an hour-and-a-half. Thereabouts.'

'Fine. Good.'

'Michael, I've got things to tell you now. Two things.'

'Yes.'

'Your father died two days ago. I asked them not to tell you until we had a result.'

I thought of being on remand, going to see the old man, parking outside the brick two-storey house with its garden clipped, weeded and trimmed into sterility, going down the brick path and knocking. He opened the door, an elderly man in a cardigan. I had once assumed that he loved me, had given no thought to what that loving meant. He looked at me without expression, blinking behind thick-lensed glasses.

'What?' he said.

'It's me, Dad. Michael.'

'I can see that. What?'

'Thought I'd drop in.'

My father sniffed, said nothing.

'Just catch up,' I said.

Silence.

'I've had a bit of bad luck,' I said.

My father studied me, looked up and down the street. 'Read about it,' he said. 'Still got a fancy car.' For all his money, he never went beyond Holdens, waxed and polished Holdens.

'Well, a car's just a car.'

'Rubbish,' my father said. 'You smell of drink. Learnt it God knows where, you and your brother. Billy dead from it. And you've got blood on your hands.'

'I wasn't drunk,' I said.

He looked at his watch, held it up to his eyes. 'Got work to do. What about you?'

I was going down the path when he said, 'Something you'd better have.'

I turned. He was going inside. I waited, not sure that I was allowed to follow him into the house. In a minute, he was back, carrying a large yellow envelope.

'Here,' he said. 'Saved me the postage.'

I'd sat in the car for a minute, hand on the key, looking up at the window of my old room. On the day of my brother's funeral I'd gone up there, just an impulse. Our rooms were empty, stripped bare, as if we'd never lived there, all the things of our childhood gone, thrown out, pale patches on the walls where the pictures had been. My mother had come up behind me. 'Your father did it,' she said. 'I'd never have done it.'

As I sat staring at the house, my father came around the side of the house, garden fork in hand, never looked my way. In the thin rain, he began to dig like a man trying to kill something dangerous underground. I started the car and drove away.

In Carlton, I parked near a pub, went in, ordered a beer. 'Coming up, chief,' said the barman. He had a pigtail and gold studs in his ears.

'Chief?' I said. 'Don't call me chief. You can call me sir.'

He looked at me for a second, considered his options, pursed his lips. 'Sir it is,' he said. 'Sir.'

I took the beer to a table. I was drinking heavily then, in the waiting days, didn't care about drunk driving, didn't care about fights, about anything. I drank half the beer, gulped it, ice cold, tears coming to my eyes. Fifth or sixth of the day and it was late morning. Then I sipped, watched the women with their children in the park across the road, pairs of women with the fruits of their labour, their girls staying close to them, talking incessantly, the boys, prisoners of some male genetic instinct, straying to the edge of the known world, always having to be reeled in by anxious cries. I finished the beer, fetched another one. The barman didn't call me anything. I opened the envelope, and I knew that my father had decided to die, was taking another step in the systematic obliteration of the material remains of his life as a husband and father.

Photographs. I glimpsed Billy in school uniform, his dark-eyed face sardonic even as a child, saw a picture of my mother, impossibly young. Family photographs, perhaps thirty or forty, not many to record twenty-odd years, but we hadn't been a happy snaps family. I had only a vague memory of photographs being taken, of seeing photographs. I didn't want to look at them. I didn't want to see us as we had been, whatever we had been, scared to see myself or Billy, my parents. I opened a second envelope and found waxproof paper holding stamps in compartments, perhaps a dozen. There was another envelope, white, sealed, on it written in my father's strongly vertical hand: Will of R. M. Cato. I didn't want to see that either, put everything back into the big envelope, went on drinking.

'Michael? Michael?' Zelda, anxious. She'd been talking. I hadn't heard anything.

'What's the other thing?' I said.

'I thought you'd fainted. Elaine. I held off telling you this too. She's sold the house, gone to live in Arizona.'

'She's my wife,' I said. I wasn't thinking clearly. It was dawning on me that I was going to leave the place, be free.

'I think that's over. She's joined some sect. She met a man at a personal development thing. We'll talk about it later. Put the screw on, I need to get back to this person who runs the place.'

George met my eyes when I came into the corridor, twenty metres away. The weak sun was on his scalp, filtered through the thinning hair combed back, oiled black strands of hair, strong survivors of a dense forest. His hands were lying on his thighs, mitts, hands too big even for such a large man.

We looked at each other as I walked. I shrugged, raised my right hand, put up the thumb. Leaving home. Escaping. Goodbye. It was all a mistake.

'Fucken tourist,' George said loudly, no smile on his face. He got up and came towards me, holding out his arms.

It was two years and ninety-seven days since I'd entered the penal system at Metropolitan Remand, driven into the yard at 3.20pm on a Thursday, a convicted murderer.

1999

MISSING CUFFLEY

CUFFLEY WAS just a few streets. One pub, a milk bar, a hardware store, the bush hospital, no doctor, a primary school, the bowls club, and two churches, one disused. Around it, the land was rocky, mean, the dams puddles of mud.

Dodge sat at the computer in the winter afternoon, not interested, looking out the window. Almost everyone he saw outside was old. He was fifteen weeks into the sentence. It was indeterminate. 'Here's the options, sweetheart,' Meliss had said. 'One, go to trial with Lee, two, testify against him, three, go somewhere till I say you can come back.'

'I'll quit,' said Dodge.

Meliss put a fingertip into his right ear, wriggled it, closed his eyes. 'Don't be a prick, son,' he said. 'That's the same as option one.'

Outside the milk bar, Rigby was getting out of a silver four-wheel-drive.

He was big, gone to fat. Dodge could see the squatter's English wife put a cigarette to her lips. At the milk bar's screen door, Rigby straightened his back, pulled up his expensive corduroy trousers, showed the crack of his buttocks.

Perhaps he fancied Carol the milk bar woman.

An old Volvo station wagon towing a small caravan pulled up.

Badly. A man got out, sixties, towelling hat, glasses, carrying a zip-up folder. Dodge went behind the counter. Polite knocks.

'Come in.'

A grey safari suit with short pants, long white socks and sandals, not winter clothing but the man had been somewhere warm: his arms were a weathered brown.

A Pom.

'A police station, you can come in without knocking,' said Dodge.

'Good, yes, excellent,' the man said. He held out a hand, all knobs and angles. 'Alan Plumb.'

Dodge didn't shake. You didn't. 'Detective Sergeant Dodge,' he said.

Plumb looked at his rejected hand. 'I'm asking around about my daughter,' he said. 'Being a nuisance.'

He unzipped the plastic folder and took out a sheet of paper, offered it. Dodge looked at a photograph of a girl, not quite a woman, tousled fair hair, pretty, in an immature way. Something about her eyes.

Bold type said: 'HAVE YOU EVER SEEN THIS PERSON?'

'Allison Johnson was last seen in Orange, New South Wales, on July 14, 1989. She was eighteen then. She is English. She has one blue eye and one brown eye. She was wearing a backpack and had a camera around her neck. In a postcard to a friend posted in Narrabri, NSW, on July 16, 1989, she said she had met someone from a town called Cuffley. This was a coincidence because Allison was born in Cuffley in Hertfordshire. Please ring the number below or tell the local police if you know anyone who could be the person Allison met. REWARDS FOR ANY INFORMATION.'

A mobile telephone number.

'The postcard only turned up a month ago,' said Plumb. 'The friend was away. It got lost. Lay in a drawer.'

'Been a while,' said Dodge.

'I didn't even know Allison was missing until a few years ago. No one told me. She's my only child. Johnson's her mother's name.'

'No one told you?'

Plumb's fingertips rubbed the counter. 'I was in Africa. In Zambia. Know where that is?'

'I'm a cop,' said Dodge. 'We don't know stuff like that. Geography.'

'Sorry,' said Plumb. 'Most people don't know where Zambia is. I separated from her mother a few months after the girl was born. You lose touch. Well, her mother wasn't one to keep in touch.'

'I'll put it up,' said Dodge.

'Mind if I put them in the letterboxes?'

'You don't need my permission. Missing persons know about the postcard?'

Plumb had pale green eyes. 'Yes. They weren't very interested. Well, Allison's dead, officially. My ex-wife had her declared dead in 1998. Bit soon, I'd say.'

'Always too soon for some,' said Dodge.

'Well, I'm a father who wants to know.' Plumb pushed back his hat and scratched freckled baldness. 'Are you a father, Sergeant?'

'Good luck then,' said Dodge.

'Thank you. I'll do my house calls, stay overnight. Caravan park?'

'No.'

'Right. Oh, well, the pub, I suppose.'

'Park at the rec reserve,' said Dodge, relenting. 'Turn right after the gate. There's a toilet and a shower. Turn the gas on.'

He took the key off the board and handed it over. 'What do I owe you?' said Plumb.

'Nothing. Turn the gas off and bring the key back.'

He watched Plumb cross the street to the milk bar, shoulders back, open the screen door. Rigby came out, looked at Plumb, he wouldn't covet a terylene safari suit with short pants.

Mrs Rigby had rung in his third or fourth week, 1.37am. She was not coherent. Rigby took the phone from her. He was pissed, slurring, said 'Sorry to bother you, my wife has a strange sense of humour. Goodnight, Constable.'

Dodge had gone back to bed.

'Don't mess with this Rigby,' his predecessor had said. 'No tickets. He's the squatter out here, he's connected. Had a bloke pulled in twenty-four hours.'

'Can't wait to mess with him,' said Dodge.

'Not when you hear where this fella got sent. He missed Cuffley.'

In the shop a few days later, Mrs Rigby introduced herself. 'Sorry about that call,' she said. 'Too much champagne.' She was long-nosed, pale, willowy, much younger than Rigby, wearing dark glasses. When she turned her head, Dodge saw the blood in her left eye.

Near the end of the policeman's formal eight-hour day, Dodge drove out to the start of the sixty-kilometre zone, parked in the shadow of the pine plantation, dark inside, the light going only a few metres. He nailed four speeding offenders, all trucks, one seriously over the limit. Four tickets kept him on quota. He could book any number of sunken-eyed truckies, ute hoons, city four-wheel-drivers having an outback adventure. But his predecessor had warned him about being a big source of revenue.

Driving back in the last light, sky gum-pink in the west, he noted the vehicles outside the pub: four utes, a Kingswood, a LandCruiser, he knew them. If he cared to, later, he could make an example of someone for drink-driving. He didn't care to, he had to live in this shithole, they'd punished punishing cops here before. Also, the seriously drunk tended to punish themselves by slamming into trees or broadsiding into fences and gullies.

The day ended with the paperwork, logging out, shutting up shop, walking through a door to his quarters. At the door, Dodge remembered Plumb's poster, went back and found a place for it on the noticeboard, head high.

He looked into Allison Johnson's eyes. Even in black and white, you could see the difference.

The phone rang when he was in the comfortable chair, heater full bore, plate on his lap, watching a money quiz, fuzzy picture.

'Caught any cattle duffers? Or sheep duffers? Can you duff sheep? He was caught duffing a sheep.'

'You're a priest,' said Dodge. 'Does your confessor know you make animal sex jokes?'

'He tells them. Listen, I saw Ginny today. She says you don't want

Michael for the holidays.'

Acid burn in his gullet, Dodge found a tablet. He was eating half a box a day. 'Steve,' he said, 'no messages from Ginny. Please.'

'It's not a message. It's what she said.'

'What she says to you about me, about Michael, that's a message for me.'

His brother sighed. 'Leaving that open,' he said, 'why don't you want to see Michael?'

'It's not don't want to,' Dodge said. 'He's eleven. Come and see this place and tell me what he'll do all day.'

At ten o'clock, to bed, a long time of lying awake, hearing the wind. He had only a faint memory of what it was like for sleep to steal upon you, of the pleasure of awakening rested. He put the radio off, on, off, and then he fell in and out of consciousness until the light came back.

He rose in the dark morning, put on a tracksuit and left by the back door, went out the gate, down the street, took the narrow dirt road to nowhere in particular, a snaking path through the pine barrens. Twenty-five minutes out, twenty-seven in, there was nothing to see in the dawn light, all the beauty of a lift shaft.

Home, he showered, dressed, ate cereal, two slices of toast, unlocked the station door. Walking by the board, Plumb's poster snagged his eye.

He paid an agency $4000. To do what?

A Pom milked. Not the first one.

Dodge went to the computer. Allison Johnson arrived in Sydney on May 3, 1986, spent four nights at a backpackers' hotel in Maroubra. On May 7, she caught a bus to Canberra and stayed at a youth hostel for two nights. Then she was gone.

At 10.47am, the computer said that no matching Allison Johnson came up in births, deaths, marriages, customs, tax, the electoral roll, the social security files, not in bank records, drivers' licences, vehicle registration, credit agencies, real-estate tenants' lists, video shops, customer reward schemes, the share registry. She did not have a licence to be a taxi driver, a prostitute or an abalone diver.

Allison Johnson was dead, bones somewhere, in a forest, in a hole.

The door opened. Mrs Garrity. She had swung at her neighbour of twenty years, missed, but he fell over and broke a rib. The immediate issues were a collapsed fence, cross-border poultry raids, a vegetable patch ravaged.

'Complaint withdrawn, what's this rubbish?' she said, menacing gargoyle face, lower lip like a water spout. 'Want the old bastard in court, then you'll hear what's bin goin' on. My word, your hair'll stand up.'

It took twenty minutes to get her to leave.

Plumb came in, same outfit, put the key on the counter. 'On my way, Detective Sergeant,' he said. 'Been to every house in town, can't do more. Thank you for your kindness.'

'Ran your daughter's name,' said Dodge. 'There's nothing.' Blinks, short rake-like eyelashes. 'I appreciate that,' said Plumb. 'Restores the faith. No one else took the trouble.'

He held out a freckled hand, arthritic, fingers pointing down. Dodge hesitated, took it, didn't squeeze much. 'I'll ring you if anyone comes in about the leaflet,' he said.

The morning passed. At 12.45pm, Dodge crossed to the milk bar. Usually he made a sandwich or heated a can of soup.

'Don't say salad roll,' said the woman, Carol.

'You have a way with salad.'

'Not a meater,' Carol said. 'Never heard of a cop wasn't a meater. Live on hamburgers, cops. Free hamburgers.'

She had a large frame but she was thin, small ears, nothing breasts, her hair bleached stubble. A local, but the form was Sydney, Rockhampton, Darwin, small stuff: drink-driving, drugs, assault, fines for speeding. Bored, he'd looked her up the first week when he'd seen the signs of removed tatts.

'I'm no ordinary cop,' said Dodge. 'I've been to the opera, the ballet.'

'Shit,' she said, ripping discoloured leaves off a lettuce, 'and here I was hopin' for a root.'

'No beetroot, please,' said Dodge. 'Drips on your shirt, looks like blood.'

She sliced the lettuce, clean, vicious cuts. 'Don't want to be thought to have used undue force on some poor bastard. Which never happens. That Pom, I liked the outfit.'

'Worn by all the spunks in Africa,' said Dodge.

The slack face of Bernie Stebbing appeared at the edge of the cafe window. He was in his forties, balding, mentally about six, apparently harmless.

'Why does every town have to have one?' said Carol. 'Is that written somewhere?'

He went back to the station and ate, reading the day before's newspaper. Then the phone rang.

'Fucken' animals,' the caller said. 'Firin' guns like a war, bloody racket never stops, there's comin' and goin' in the middle of the night.'

'Animals, guns,' said Dodge. 'That's country life. Want me to go around and tell 'em you're pissed off?'

'Jesus, mate, have a heart. City criminals. Got kids here.'

'Come in and make a complaint and I'll see what I can do,' said Dodge. A silence, a breath.

'Only get off your arse if bloody Rigby rings, that right?' Click. Another satisfied client.

Dodge didn't give a shit, he wasn't going to mess with the bikies. The general strike rate against them was a joke and they took revenge, wouldn't blink at killing a boy. If they were cooking pseudoephedrine out here, they'd bring in the ingredients on the night, it would be done before dawn, nothing left lying around. When Rigby complained about them, special operations raided the three houses, using a helicopter. Result: 240 grams of dope, sixteen ecstasy tablets, one unlicensed .222 rifle, and a bayonet.

No wars with bikies. His life was stuffed enough, sent to rot in this hole for doing what amounted to reducing the number of illegal whorehouses. Hardly a crime. Most of the money went on Ginny's dream kitchen, stainless, marble, which never produced anything edible and which he would never see again. A shitload went on the trip to Italy to see the family, to be sponged on or sneered at. The arsehole cousin in Turin, the architect.

The missing eighteen-year-old, Allison Johnson, was looking at him from the noticeboard. She would have been in her early thirties now, probably still looking under-age from a distance, in a certain light. Her smile wasn't right. He went over: it wasn't a smile.

Time for the drive. He went out to the car, logged in, west for sixty-four kilometres at the limit. When he pulled over, he was heading a convoy of seven, drivers afraid to pass him.

Home in the day's closing, shadows across the road, he touched 150, he was his own law. Behind the station, engine ticking, he thought that his stepfather wouldn't have been impressed. Mick Dodge did thirty-five years, got shot by a crazy, was stabbed twice, hit with many things, including an electric guitar, needed skin grafts after saving a child from a burning house. Also, he brought up two stepsons, single-handed.

'My advice is don't,' Mick said when Dodge told him he was joining. They were in the garage, Mick trying to fix the lawnmower. 'Too many turds on the take. I liked a lot of the crims more.'

Later, in the kitchen, Mick touched Dodge's shoulder. 'Do it if you have to. Got a bit of breedin', you'll be your own man. Sleep straight at night.'

If Mick knew he'd taken money. He didn't want to think about Mick, about being his own man, sleeping straight in his bed. He thought about how Alan Plumb could still hold out hope about someone missing so long. Finding out that she'd met someone from Cuffley wasn't a breakthrough.

Tomato soup and a cheese sandwich, flickering television, the evening drifted. Bed. He fell asleep trying not to think about his boy, about Mick Dodge.

Then he was jerked from a dream of being in a broad, swift, shallow river clear as glass, seeing the pebbled bottom, shooting along in the cool water, propelled by the swift current. He rubbed his eyes, tried to read the clock: 11.57pm.

'Cuffley police,' he said.

'Tessa Rigby. Can you come? My husband's been shot.'

Glass and blood everywhere, the man had been shot through the window, sitting in a captain's chair at his desk.

Dodge stood in the doorway of the panelled room. Blood was congealing in a pool under the chair. Tessa Rigby was in the passage.

'What did you hear?' said Dodge, not turning. He was looking at the polo mallets on the wall, the old silver cups, the photographs of polo teams and horses and players holding champagne flutes.

'Nothing. I was in the back sitting-room, it's a long way, there was music on. I was reading.'

Dodge turned. They went down the wide passage to the sitting room, passing dozens of paintings. They didn't sit.

'Rang straightaway?' said Dodge.

'Of course. It was such a fright, I can't tell you.'

'No dogs to bark?'

She swallowed twice, a slender neck, he saw the tendons move.

'No,' she said. 'The bikies' dogs killed our labrador. Brian wanted to get a puppy, but I was too scared it would happen again.'

Dodge went to the car and spoke to the city.

'Wait,' said the sergeant.

He got out, wished he still smoked.

Tessa Rigby came out, smoking a cigarette, showed him the packet. He walked around the car, up two steps, stood a shallow step below her, took one. How could it hurt?

She came closer, offered a light from her burning tip. Their cigarettes docked uncertainly and he drew the fire from her.

Crackles from the car. He went back.

The sergeant said stay in place, touch nothing, we need directions, grid references.

'Grid references?'

'Coming by chopper, mate. Map handy?' Dodge found it, read out the coordinates. 'Sevenish. Give 'em a wave, will ya?'

He got out and told Tessa Rigby. She pushed her hair back. He thought she was an attractive woman.

'Come inside,' she said.

He followed her to the kitchen, a huge room, a table like a runway. She went into a pantry, came out with a bottle. 'Whisky?' she said.

'No thanks.'

She poured whisky into a cut-glass tumbler, three fingers. 'I'm trying not to think about Brian being in there,' she said. 'I don't know how to get through this.'

'It'll pass,' said Dodge. He explained her rights.

'Ask me anything,' she said.

'Homicide'll do it again when they get here,' he said. 'Can we sit down?'

They sat at the table. Dodge filled in the incident sheet, then he went over the event with her, wrote down everything. He didn't want to stuff this up, too many black marks already.

Details taken, he said, 'No one else on the property?'

'Ron Bruder comes from town three days a week, just for the garden and odd jobs. This isn't a farm. It's a kind of Rigby family museum.'

'Kill your husband, who would want to do that?'

Tessa Rigby swallowed neat whisky, he saw her tongue. 'Want to?' she said. 'God, I don't know. He put a lot of people's backs up, but they don't kill you for that.'

'Any backs up recently?'

'Well, he shot two bikie dogs a few weeks ago.'

'On your land?'

'They breached the Rigby Wall, two barbed-wire fences with a ploughed no-man's land. Brian would've mined it if he could.'

'Why would dogs do that?'

'To get at the rabbits. This place is infested with rabbits.'

'The same dogs that killed yours?'

'I don't know. Probably.'

Dodge thought he should change direction. 'I suppose you can handle a gun?' he said.

Her eyes widened. 'Me? I'm terrified of guns. I've never had a gun in my hands.'

'You're calm. Why's that?'

Tessa Rigby closed her eyes, pale eyes, pale face, she looked older, lines visible. 'I don't know. Shock, I suppose. I feel as if I've been in an accident.'

'The time you rang, what was that about?'

Eyes open. 'So embarrassing. Many too many drinks. Brian, in typical Brian fashion, decided he'd had enough cold, leave immediately for Noosa. We've got a place there. I said it wasn't a great idea, he said, "Bugger you, I'll go on my own." Being drunk, I said I'd phone the police and tell them to watch out for him. He said I wouldn't dare.'

'How long have you been married?'

'Six years this year.'

'Was Brian married before?'

A joyless smile. 'Twice. Expensive divorces. He's never stopped complaining.'

'Children?'

'No.'

Dodge looked into her eyes. 'Do you inherit?'

A slow blink. 'I don't know,' she said. 'I have no idea, the subject never came up.'

Dodge got up and went for a walk around the room. 'Well, I don't have to ask this stuff,' he said. 'I'll leave it to homicide. You should get some sleep.'

She ran fingers through her hair. 'I won't be able to sleep. Can I stay here?'

'Of course. It's your house.'

'You won't go away?'

'Here for the night. What's left.'

'There's a television next door. Brian didn't sleep well at night, he watched CNN.'

'We could do that,' said Dodge.

They went into the room and sat in old leather chairs. Dodge accepted another cigarette, little was said, glances exchanged, he looked away instantly. She fell asleep like a child, her body sliding down the big chair, her head coming to rest on its broad arm. She was lovely in sleep. He turned down the sound, drifted in and out of sleep and suicide bombings, floods in India, riots somewhere, a building imploding, weather for the globe, stock market reports, a burning tanker. Waiting for the light. No stranger to that.

He went outside to see the dawn, came back to wash his face and hands at the kitchen sink, outside again, walked around. Now he could see the tunnel of pines he'd driven down, the gravel square in front of the house the size of two tennis courts, clipped hedges around it.

He walked down a path until he came to a gate and saw a flat paddock beyond it, went back and spoke to the city on the radio.

'Helps if they can see you,' said the woman operator. 'About five minutes.'

First, the dot in the sky, then the throb. The chopper came out of the south, Dodge waved, turned his back, he hated helicopters, their sound. The noisy insect settled.

Four men in city black, carrying bags, got out. Then came a man in overalls with a dog. All this for one rich dead arsehole, thought Dodge. In the city, a lot of the dead were lucky to get one tired cop. Where was the justice in that?

It was late morning and there were four police vehicles at the homestead gate before he could leave. Driving into Cuffley felt like coming home, and that surprised him. He ordered a bacon and egg sandwich from Carol.

'Out early makin' the roads safe!' she said, taking out bacon at the fridge.

Dodge waited until she turned. 'Someone killed Brian Rigby,' he said.

Her mouth opened, she stood, bacon in hand. 'Jesus Christ,' she said.

'Don't ask me anything,' said Dodge. 'On the other hand, you can tell me anything.'

She went to work, hiss of bacon fat, her back to him, sharp shoulder blades. After a while she said, 'Helped my dad with some gardenin' out there. Twice. Also he's a customer. Milk and the papers and chips. Salt and pepper?'

'Pepper.'

Just before 3pm, the station phone rang. Dodge was at his desk, falling asleep, ground glass in his eyes.

'Been over the place,' said Burton, the homicide boss, 'no shells, found zero except three unlicensed firearms, none fired recently. Went to see the bikies. Going to be hard to stick this on them.'

When he came to town, Burton said they'd found one bikie, three women, and two kids at home. The man had a broken arm, the three other men who lived on the properties were in the city and had witnesses galore. Burton flew off, underlings stayed for two days to interview everyone vertical in the area. Then nothing.

Weeks later, on a Monday, a day of wind blowing dust across the land, Tessa Rigby came into the station. Her hair was pulled back, she looked tired. Dodge thought of them in the room, her falling asleep, lovely in sleep, the violent pictures on the television.

'No one tells me anything,' she said. 'I'm only the wife. The widow.'

'They don't tell me much either,' said Dodge. 'I'll ask again. How've you been?'

'Well, the cremation was just me and the two nephews, and they didn't acknowledge my presence.'

'The will have anything to do with that?'

'They get half of everything,' she said.

'Greed,' said Dodge. 'Half is never enough.'

She smiled, 'I'm not still a suspect, am I?'

Dodge's scalp itched. 'I'll give you a ring,' he said.

She touched her lips, no lipstick. 'You know it wasn't me.'

'Drive carefully,' said Dodge.

He went to the window to watch her cross the road. Narrow hips. At the milk bar door, she looked back. She couldn't see him looking but he knew she knew.

Don't mess with this Rigby, Dodge's predecessor had warned. No tickets. He's the squatter out here, he's connected. Had a bloke pulled in twenty-four hours.

Dodge had asked. Brian Rigby's grandfather had been deputy premier, his father's companies were big donors to the major parties. How much was half his estate worth?

In mid-afternoon, Dodge put away the files, boiled water for tea. The milk was sour. He crossed the road, no one to be seen, a ghost town. Carol was in the back room, on the phone, hunched. Her vertebrae stood out against the T-shirt like a row of stones.

'Just keep it together,' she said. 'Don't turn into a weak-kneed little bitch on me.'

Carol felt Dodge, ended the call, came out.

'Jesus, I miss my mum,' she said, making change without consulting the till. 'She could listen to whingeing kids. Now it's my turn to cop the shit.'

'Family?' said Dodge.

'My sister. Learnt bugger all. Still thinks there's a Brad fucken Pitt and a Porsche out there. Now she's weepin' cause her second dud husband's jumpin' some tramp.'

Dodge went back, remade a cup of tea. A couple came in with passport applications. In the small, square photographs, they had the eyes of spot-lit animals.

'Never bin to England,' said the man. 'Our girl's met this bloke, looks like she's stayin' on.'

'Just for a while,' said his wife. 'She'll miss home too much. Sunburnt country. Wide brown land.'

'Have a nice trip,' said Dodge.

Sunset, pink on the panelboard wall. Dodge couldn't recall seeing many sunsets before Cuffley. You didn't see the last light in the kinds of places he'd been around at sunset. He put his head back, thought that he'd never been on his own for so long before, not talking much to anyone. He'd see the boy every day when he got back, try to be what Mick had been to his boys, always there, never blaming, quick to praise.

He rang homicide in the city. Burton said he'd been flat chat, sorry, Rigby took three from a 9mm pistol, almost certainly a Tanfoglio P-19S.

They were working on that. Forensic had found nothing of interest.

'Could take forever, mate,' said Burton, 'but the bikie feel, that's still strong. A prick in PNG used to run these shooters into Queensland by the slab. Bikie gun.'

'And the wife?'

'No. Not unless I'm brain dead. Still, jury's out on that count.'

In his kitchen, Dodge ripped open a packet of chips with his teeth. He took it to the sitting room and sat on his spine in the comfortable chair.

Rigby married twice, perhaps there were grudges, hatreds. No. Women didn't wait fourteen years to kill their ex-husbands. On the other hand, to stoned and Jim Beam-fuelled bikies, at a certain moment in the evening, the idea of going over and wasting the man who shot your dogs would have great appeal.

And then bikies, shitfaced, crawling around the verandah looking for the three expelled 9mm shells?

That was the puzzle, that wasn't the bikie way. Pissing off laughing and worrying about the shells later, chucking the gun into deep water or a concrete pour, that was the way.

Dodge had his hand on the phone to ring Tessa Rigby. Then he went to the car and drove out to Rigby's in the twilight. Just something to do, he told himself, make the evening shorter. The four-wheel-drive was standing where he'd parked the night of the killing.

She came out of the front door when he was at the foot of the stairs, her hair loose now, no shoes, red socks.

'The sound of a vehicle sends my heart racing,' she said. 'Please come in.'

Dodge hesitated. 'Coming this way,' he said. 'I thought I'd stop off for a minute and tell you.'

'Come in,' said Tessa. 'Can you have a drink?'

'A beer would be good. Quick beer.'

He followed her to the kitchen, sat down at the table. She uncapped two bottles. Dodge put away half of his at a swig.

'They're working on the weapon,' he said. 'That's the line they're following. It might take a long time. And they're not pointing in your direction, you're not of interest.'

'Thank you,' Tessa said. 'John.'

She drank, offered a cigarette. He shook his head. They talked about the weather.

'I need to get away from here,' she said. 'I'm having nightmares. I'm scared to go to sleep.'

'That's understandable.'

She was leaning against the counter, looking at him, head on one side, hair on her shoulder, she looked away, looked at him.

'He was a terrible man,' she said. 'I feel I should tell you that. He broke my arm, broke four ribs once, locked me in a cupboard for two days, I almost lost my mind.

'He was mad. At times, he went mad. He did things to me, I can't tell you the things he did.'

Dodge didn't know what to say. He said, 'Not sorry then?'

'No, I can't be,' she said. 'I ran away once but he brought me back. He said next time he'd kill me. I believed him.'

Dodge looked away, drained his beer and stood up.

'Got to go. Thanks for the beer.'

They were in the hallway, Dodge ahead, when she put a hand on his shoulder. He turned.

'I wanted to say,' said Tessa, close up, 'I wanted to say you're the only one who hasn't treated me as if I had something contagious.'

She put her hands on his shoulders and kissed him on the mouth, not a polite kiss either. Afterwards, going home, he could smell her, taste her, he wanted to turn back.

The days passed, weeks, the days lengthening. Dodge thought about her a lot, almost rang, drove out her way, almost dropped in. He looked out of the window often, hoping to see her car. She didn't come to town.

Should he tell Burton what she'd said about Rigby? Why? She hadn't done it. She was a victim.

On a Thursday he went trapping, caught a BMW at 155 kilometres per hour. It held a smooth man and a woman, he was forties, she was around twenty-five, both tanned caramel.

'It's not open slather out here,' said Dodge. 'This isn't the testing ground for German cars.'

'Just the ticket,' said the man. 'The lecture I don't need.'

Dodge gave them the blow bag, the full vehicle search, ran the rego. An address in Double Bay, Sydney. He watched them arguing, her right hand accusing. The man knocked it away.

Face of stone, Dodge let them go, turned the cruiser for home. Knock-off time.

Daylight left, it was full light now when he came out for his morning run. He parked behind the station and walked across to get the newspaper.

Carol was closed. The note on the door said: 'On holiday. Papers at shop.' He got a paper, went back and sat at the desk, read about a man charged with insider trading on the stock market. How could the basis of the whole system be an offence?

The door opened. Mrs Garrity. He'd forgotten to lock it and pull down the blinds.

'Saw that Rigby vixen come in here,' she said. 'Should be in jail. Killer.'

'I'm off duty now,' said Dodge. 'This an emergency?'

'Idiot's pervin' again.'

'The fence problem?'

She screwed up her face to the point where it had no obvious openings.

'God, no,' she said, 'not talkin' about that. The Stebbing dimwit, that's who. Lookin' through the bathroom window. Again.'

Dodge thought Bernie might need trauma counselling. 'I'll have a talk with him,' he said.

'Bugger talk,' she said. 'I'm layin' a charge.'

'You're making a complaint,' said Dodge. 'I'll investigate it. Now, I'm off duty, this station is closed.'

He came around the counter, went to the door and held it open. She left, a thin-eyed look. 'Not careful, the bloody law'll be in my own hands,' she said.

In the morning, he went around to where Bernie Stebbing lived with his mother in an old fibro, with dead lawn and dead plants and a cracked concrete path.

Mrs Stebbing was in a pink housecoat. She didn't open the screen door. He told her he wanted to see Bernie at the station.

'Whafor?' she said. 'Never done no harm.'

'If he wants you or someone else with him, that's fine, Mrs Stebbing,' said Dodge. 'Ten o'clock, please.'

Bernie came alone, wearing a dirty, grey windbreaker fully zipped, blue trousers, a solemn manner, no fear. Dodge showed him into the interview room.

They sat at the table.

'Mrs Garrity says you were looking in her bathroom window, says you've done it before,' said Dodge.

Bernie leaned forwards, earnest face, 'Lookin' for sinners,' he said softly. 'Be the Lord's witness.'

'Who told you to do that?'

'I am not came to call the righteous, but sinners to repentanance.'

'Your mum teach you this stuff?' Bernie looked away.

'The Lord,' he said. 'Bruder's a sinner, but she gives me chips.'

'How's she a sinner?'

'Rigby.'

'What do they do?'

'Forcinate.'

'You've seen them?'

'My word,' Bernie said. 'I am the Lord's witness.'

Dodge stood up. 'Listen, Bernie,' he said, 'Mrs Garrity's house: don't go there again or I'll lock you up and you won't be able to see your mum. Understand that?' He stood at the window and watched Bernie go, chin down, a splay-footed walk.

Carol and Rigby fornicating.

Did he pay her? She'd been around—Sydney, Rockhampton, Darwin; convictions for drink-driving, drugs, assault, speeding fines—but she didn't come across as a hooker. Go to homicide with this? With what? He turned, staring blankly at the noticeboard. When he focused, he was looking at Plumb's poster.

Allison Johnson. A postcard from Narrabri. She'd met someone from Cuffley. Dodge walked down to the bush hospital. The nurse was doing paperwork.

'When did Carol Bruder's mother die?' he asked.

'Exactly?'

'Yes.'

She looked it up. 'July 9, 1992. Funeral was on the thirteenth.'

'Whole family come?'

'Oh yes. Stephie was still at home. Dawn and her, mark one came from Melbourne. Carol came from Queensland. Didn't hang around after, mind you.'

Dodge went back to the station and rang Rockhampton; got the cop he'd asked about Carol.

'The arresting officer's here,' said the woman. 'I'll put him on.'

Dodge explained to Sergeant Cassar.

'Carol Bruder, yeah, know her well,' said Cassar, 'the lesbo commune, more dangerous than bikies, some of them, I can tell you.'

'Lesbo commune?'

'Feral lesbos, out there in the jungle. Carol's full of shit. What's she done?'

'Nothing,' said Dodge. 'I'm just after some background.'

'Yeah, well. I almost nailed her on firearm charges, but the girl-friend took the bullet, so to speak.'

Dodge swallowed. 'What kind of charges?'

'Two unlicensed handguns. In the ute.'

'Remember the make?'

'Italian. Can't remember the name.'

'Could it be Tanfoglio?'

'That's it, yeah. How'd you know?'

'Just guessing,' said Dodge. He closed his eyes. 'One more thing. Any unidentified bodies up there?'

Cassar laughed. 'Jesus, getting messages from above? We found some bones yesterday. Tip-off.'

'Female,' said Dodge. 'Young. Eighteen.'

'Could be. They say female. There's no teeth.'

A draught seemed to come from somewhere to touch the back of his head, a cold hand. He went to the map and traced the quickest route from Cuffley to Rockhampton. It went through Orange and Narrabri.

July 16, 1992. Allison Johnson in Narrabri, posting a card. Carol was on the road that day, Carol was nearby, Carol got a speeding ticket outside Cowra on July 16, 1992.

Was Carol waiting in the car for Allison? Did she take her to Rockhampton, to the commune in the jungle? Dodge brooded the day away, into the evening. How many Tanfoglio pistols had been smuggled in from PNG? Hundreds? Why would Carol kill Rigby? Should he tell homicide? Yes. He rang. Burton was out, no mobile contact, could it wait?

He should tell Tessa. Did she know about Carol and Rigby? Surely she would have told him? He got into the car, drove east, the sun's last glow in the mirror, the high clouds ahead a sad, kewpie-doll pink. Unease came upon him. He took the speed up to 130, 140 kilometres per hour.

It was dark when he got to Rigby's, turning into the driveway was like going underground.

Lights in the house, Tessa's vehicle in its place. He got out, heard the music, felt relief come over him. At the front door, the music was loud, classical, he didn't know anything about classical music.

His knocking didn't bring her. Dodge opened the door, went inside, called her name, there was no point. The music was coming from the right, where the study was. He went down the passage hung with paintings: this was the way to the back sitting-room where Tessa had been that night, reading, music playing loudly.

He understood why she hadn't heard the shots.

A door into a small room, a connecting room, stone floor. The music was very loud, rising, cymbals clashing. Dodge crossed, opened the door.

Tessa was standing in the middle of the room, back to him, standing on tiptoe. 'Tessa,' he said. 'Sorry to…'

She was turning, her head on one side.

He saw that she wasn't touching the carpet. He saw her tongue.

He saw the light gleam on the thin nylon line that went to the beam above. Dodge turned, walked, left the house, drove. He got Burton.

'Wait,' said Burton. 'First thing in the morning, we'll be there.'

'No,' said Dodge. 'I quit. I should have quit before. I should never have come here.'

Cruiser howling through the night, he heard Carol: 'Just keep it together. Don't turn into a weak-kneed little bitch on me.'

Cuffley in sight, twelve sad street lights. Bernie Stebbing and his mother were watching TV, eating out of bowls.

Dodge took him outside, spoke slowly. 'Bernie, you said you saw Bruder and that Rigby sinning.'

'Sinning,' said Bernie, nodding, pushing out his lower lip.

'Mr Rigby, Bernie?'

'No. She.'

Dodge went to the station and packed. There wasn't much. You didn't bring much into Cuffley and you didn't leave with much.

2003

ITHACA IN MY MIND

FROM THE terrace, the eye was led down the thin lap pool edged with Castlemaine bluestone pavers and flanked by box hedges to the stone bench in front of the ivy-clad brick wall.

Vincent Duncan was sitting in a cane chair, naked beneath a blue towelling dressing gown, a telephone in his left hand. With his right hand, he was toying with grey hairs on his chest.

'Sorry, say that again,' he said.

'Carter wants to pass.'

'Pass what?'

Duncan pulled a hair. It hurt in a pleasant way. He studied the tiny pale root that had lived in his flesh. What did hairs feed on?

'He doesn't want it,' said Marjorie.

She had the voice of an upper-class English twelve-year-old. That was in part understandable because she had once been an upper-class English twelve-year-old. She lived in London with a man called Rufus who had certainly once been an undersized twelve-year-old. Now he had a moustache like Neville Chamberlain and wrote over-sized accounts of British military disasters involving acts of heroic selflessness, mainly by the officers.

Marjorie and Rufus lived in a flat in what had once been a power station. Architects were engaged to make the place even more cold and brutal. Duncan had spent a night there. It was like living in a missile silo designed by the Bauhaus.

'I don't think it's quite Carter,' said Marjorie. 'Well, it's probably not so much him as the new lot wanting to prune the mid-list.'

'The mid-list's got what to do with me, Marjorie?' he said.

'Of course it's silly judgement on their part,' she said, 'but there it is. I'm afraid you are mid-list, darling, and we probably have to live with it.'

'Marjorie,' he said, 'Carter's a stupid prick. I never liked him. Let's go elsewhere.'

'Vincent,' said Marjorie, 'I've shown the book around.'

'Talked to Random?'

'I've spoken to Random, yes. Vincent, things are not what they were, tastes change, you know that. We may have to batten down. In the long term, your...'

'Well, how much?'

'It's not actually about the money.'

'It never is. Random. They're offering what?'

'Random passed on it too.'

Duncan felt the cobweb tingle of pain across his scalp. It was cold, he pulled at the dressing gown to close it and saw the veins on his feet. Since when had they been big, so grotesque, that revolting colour?

'Well, stuff Random too,' he said. 'Stuff Bertelsmann, stuff the Germans. Let's go to Revanche, he wants me, that pretty boy.'

Marjorie made a throaty sound. 'To simply say it, Vincent, I've walked both sides of the street. I've been offered five thousand pounds by Flashman and it is the only offer and I'm not sure how long it's open.'

'Ludicrous,' Duncan said. 'Insulting.'

'You mustn't take it personally. That is really important.'

'Marjorie,' he said, 'I take it very personally. I cannot tell you how important this book is to me. I am in a position where if...'

He took a deep breath. 'Marjorie, if this book doesn't attract the best advance of my career, I may never write another novel.'

Marjorie was talking to someone. 'Sorry, Vincent, the other line. Yes, your career. Well, it's been pretty good, hasn't it, darling. I mean,

Ithaca, what's that added up to over the years?'

'Gus consumed the proceeds of *Ithaca On My Mind*,' he said. 'The tax office and then Augustine.'

'You insist on marrying them, Vincent. And without pre-nups. That really is unprotected sex.'

Duncan wanted to ask the podgy parasite what she knew of pre-nups and unprotected sex. Any sex. The historian almost certainly had his saggy bottom caned elsewhere.

But he needed Marjorie as never before. He needed her even more than he needed to find Hugh Merill-Porter, formerly of Toorak, the accountant who insisted he put everything, including the house, into the share market.

'Gear,' said Hugh. 'Gear and grow very rich, Vincent. That's all I have to say. You will thank me.'

When he found Merill-Porter, believed to be in a Philippine bolthole, he would say, 'Pain, Hugh. Pain. That's all I have to say.'

Then his hired help would torture Hugh Merill-Porter. It would not bring back the one million-plus bucks lost by investing in house-of-cards property companies now insolvent. Nor would it restore ownership of the terrace. But watching it on video late at night would be satisfying.

At least he'd stopped marrying them after Gus.

'Marjorie,' Duncan said. 'I need the sort of advance I got for *The Taint of Speech*. In that vicinity. Or I may never write again.'

Shrill laughter in the background.

Was he on Marjorie's speakerphone?

She would die. He would travel to England and kill her.

'Sorry about the noise,' said Marjorie. 'It's Emily's birthday.'

And Emily too would die. Enjoy, Ems. This is your last birthday.

'The *Taint* sort of advance,' he said. 'Or I may never write again.'

A sigh.

'Darling,' said Marjorie, '*Taint* was on the back of *Ithaca*. You were hot, darling. But *Taint* tanked, there's no other way to say it. And *Rough Forked Beast* didn't find a readership either. And so we are at the point where, dare I say it, there may not be an enormous amount of pent-up expectation. Forked, really.'

She'd been drinking.

'Have they actually read the actual book?' said Duncan.

'There is no way of knowing, my dear. Short of waterboarding them.'

'But you've conveyed the, ah, essence? The man and the polar bear and the woman and the girl and the journey to the cave full of books? The...'

'Yes, dear. We wrote a compelling blurb. Not an easy work to encapsulate, I have to say. Em did it brilliantly. Marquez, Coetzee, McCarthy, the tiger thing.'

'Oh God no, Marjorie, not the bloody tiger?'

'With respect, Vincent, the tiger was huge. We have tried to put *A Seducing Fire*...'

'*A Reducing Fire*, Marjorie. *Reducing*.'

'Yes. We've tried to put it in the company of hugeness. Associate it with hugeness.'

'And?'

'They didn't make any specific comments. Just said pass.'

Shrieks in the background.

'Darling,' said Marjorie. 'I'm being summoned, have to go, ring you back, not today, that's chockablock. Pecker up.'

The sudden fire in his brain.

'Marjorie,' he said, 'it occurs to me that I might need another agent. How does that sit with you, darling? You've lived a fat life off me and now you come along with this pathetic confession of inadequacy and just plain bloody stupid and hopeless...'

Duncan thought he could hear sluglike marine creatures crawling over the cable at the bottom of the Indian Ocean.

'Thank you for making this easier, Vincent,' she said, voice of the headmistress of Mallory Towers. 'I've had enough of you. I am terminating our agency agreement, backdated to before you delivered this fourth-rate piece of sentimental rubbish. You will have the email within five minutes. Goodbye.'

The connection was ended. Duncan held a piece of moulded plastic in his hand.

Haig's voice from behind him.

'Bye, be back late,' she said. 'You really should go to the gym.'

He turned, saw only a gleam of bare shoulders, hair, she was gone. Gone.

He sat. He heard her car coming out of the garage, heard it gunned down the street, around the corner.

It was an Alfa.

'I have to have an Alfa, darling,' she had said. 'It makes me feel sexy.'

Who was the beneficiary of that? Not the mug who paid for it, paid the exorbitant repair and service bills. He calculated that every time it went in to the dealer, he paid the weekly wage of a mechanic and two slabs of beer.

Well, it wouldn't be going in at his expense again. The letter from StronzoItalia or whatever it was called said they'd handed him over to the lawyers.

A magpie landed beside the pool. Its first contemptuous act was to defecate. From on high, this arrogant bird had chosen this sliver of land to descend upon in order to shit on his hand-cut Castlemaine bluestone pavers.

Hand-cut. The twinky little landscape designer brought in by the skeletal architect had used the term.

Rock pavers cut by hand? Men sitting around with hammers, tapping away? Rubbish. They were cut with massive howling power saws, kryptonite-tipped blades came down and sliced the ancient olivine basalt.

Duncan showered in the marble-floored glass box, talking to himself. 'The swine,' he said. 'The ignorant swine. They can't do this to me.'

He blowdried his hair. He'd left it too late for plugs, that was a major regret. While you still had enough, you could hide them in the real hair. Leave it too late and you looked like a vain buzzard. He cinched his belt until it hurt and felt the small roll of fat with loathing. He made toast in the machine she bought: $540. The bloody thing had twelve settings. Numbers one to six barely warmed the bread, seven and upwards charred it just as effectively as some $25 piece of shit from Target.

He spread the blackened slices with cholesterol-lowering margarine and blood pressure-raising anchovy paste. Then he couldn't eat.

He went to his desk and switched on the computer. He didn't have to be at the university until eleven-thirty. What to do until then?

He had always written best at this time of day. It had come without effort.

What was the point of writing? He was a reject.

Rejected by the publishing world after fourteen novels. He had never been rejected. Published at twenty-three, never rejected.

Was Carter mad? What about the others? Of course, they'd taken their cue from Hillary & Woolfe. When Marjorie came around, they knew H&W had dumped him. If he wasn't good enough for H&W, why should they touch him?

What had Marjorie told them? He should have asked her. She wasn't dumb enough to tell them Carter didn't want the book. Why hadn't she told him before she went hawking the thing around? He could have told her what to say: 'Vincent's unhappy with H&W. He now thinks it was a mistake to listen to Adam Carter's promises. He's been shockingly published for one of Australia's modern masters.'

For a modern master. If the *New York Review of Books* called you a modern master, you were one, even if the reviewer also mentioned two vastly overrated pricks. And one of them was a one-book wonder and only that because his nauseating title, *The Lost Philosophy of Sock Knitting*, had for some reason appealed to thousands of cretins.

A reject. Writer of a book that wasn't good enough to be published unless he accepted an advance of five thousand pounds from some obscure porn publisher. An insult. Haig's bloody studio had cost ten times that.

Beloved of the French critics, winner of the Prix de Goncourt. Deserved favourite for the Booker passed over in favour of a vapid English navel-picker. Three times cheated of the Miles Franklin by parochial, provincial idiots. How could it end like this?

The postman on his infuriating machine. Duncan went out. Four letters. The telephone bill. The power bill. A letter from the bank. They wanted the mortgage reduced by two hundred thousand dollars or he would be handed over to Collections.

Oh Lord. You couldn't write in circumstances like these. Between them, Gus and Merill-Streep had destroyed a major talent.

This could be from Brown. He loved the attention he got there, the intelligent, attractive young people. Sharp, in awe. Not Brown. The Mountain Workshop hadn't asked him back yet either.

Did the Americans know? Shouldn't the invitations have arrived by now? Age was a terrible thing, everything telescoping, accelerating. March. The annual US trip was only four months away. Haig said she didn't want to come this year.

Vincent, I hate being an appendage.

Well, she'd been pleased to be a bloody appendage in the early days. She'd hung onto him, touched him, kissed his cheek, his ear, put a hand in his pocket, she'd made sure the students knew who was the lover of the modern master, who was the chosen woman.

Duncan focused, found himself looking at the two-metre-high painting on the wall opposite, the painting from Haig's joint exhibition after she finished art school. He'd had his eye on her since they were introduced at some lit festival thing. She'd been dressed like a French roadmender, a very appealing look. On opening night, he bought all five of her works. The next night, he took her to dinner and later to the suite in the Connell.

All that remained was to ease Gus off the scene. They barely spoke anyway. He couldn't waste any more of his life on her.

He made her a very generous offer. In an email from New York. That seemed to be a sensible way to do it. It avoided the unprofitable emotions that could be generated in a personal encounter.

How could he have known that the dreamy palely loitering poet would in an instant turn into a slit-eyed money-grubbing vixen? Her solicitor, frightening feminist Alvina Raicheva, kicked off with an ambit claim to half of everything he had. Fortunately, the man-hating lawbitch's search for concealed assets failed to turn up his foreign earnings in the Banque Petain.

But Gus ended up with half of what they could find. He had to borrow six hundred thousand dollars to buy her alleged share of the house.

Two hundred thousand dollars or Collections?

Duncan stared at Haig's painting. It was crap, a piece of imitation Keifer, which made it second-generation crap. Some of the brownish blobs stuck to the canvas had hairs in them and bone fragments and what looked like pale bits of sinew too tough for stomach acid.

Haig thought she owed her career to talent. She didn't know that he'd arranged for two dealers to bid against each other when he'd put two of her paintings into an auction at Looby's. It cost a fortune but the sharp operators of the art world sat up. Suddenly she was collectable. Her career took off. And he got his money back with interest when the ghastly things were bought by art dupes for large sums when auctioned again a year later.

They hadn't screwed in some months now, more like three. And the last time was pretty perfunctory stuff, she'd been in the shower inside four minutes. You got more time from a hotel hooker.

Now that he thought about it, sex and her use of the studio upstairs had tapered off at around the same time. She'd fallen out of love with the studio he'd had built, the bloody thing cantilevered out into space, the light controlled by electronic blinds. She now did her creating in a former asylum, a building full of talentless canvas-defacers, mostly young, a few ancient poseurs wearing neckerchiefs.

He would have to ring Marjorie. She was his only hope. A quick apology would do it. Shock, heat of the moment, grovel to her. He pressed the numbers. She answered at the second ring.

'Marjorie, my dear…'

'Bugger off, Vincent. Don't call me, I'll call you.'

His computer pinged. Email.

From Marjorie.

It is with regret that I inform you that I have decided to terminate our agency agreement as of...

He'd have to sell the house. Rent? Vincent Duncan renting a house? His precious furniture, his books in a rented house? That was not thinkable.

The phone rang.

Marjorie, the cow, she'd be full of regret now, he would be in charge. He let it ring, stroked his stubble.

'Yes,' he said.

'Roberta from uni, Vincent. Just a reminder you've got Sarius Godber's one-on-one at eleven. And Dr Truss wants a minute after you've finished.'

'I'll see him if I've got time before lunch,' said Duncan.

'He wants to see you today.'

'Wants? Wants? Do I detect a command?'

Roberta sighed. 'He asked me to tell you to see him after your student meeting.'

'Truss told you to *tell* me?'

'Ah, yes, Vincent.'

'Well, *tell* the acting head of department to make a bloody appointment to see me.'

He put the phone down.

The brainless, illiterate little poseur.

No newly-arrived twat from Adelaide who'd published a book called *Contestation and Transcendence: The Body in Siejin Manga* was going to summon Vincent Duncan like a junior lecturer. The whole department should fall to its knees every morning to give thanks that Vincent Duncan was on the staff. He gave respectability to the degrees they awarded to sensitive pop-eyed, dirty-haired late-developers for writing sub-David Foster Wallace tripe.

You couldn't fail the unread scribblers because that meant reading their rubbish and commenting on it. And if you did fail them, they went sobbing to the likes of Truss and he had their efforts re-examined by some lickspittle guaranteed to pass them.

Duncan made the journey to the university. The feeling of power the small, thrusting Mini John Cooper Works gave him always cheered him up. He parked in the deputy vice chancellor's space. Why not? She wasn't using it.

In his office, he read the first four pages of Sarius Godber's second draft of her novel. It was like eating deep-fried cheesecake, but, to his amazement, there were three of four acceptable passages. Even a hint of irony. Sarius arrived, dressed like a rock climber. He gave her his twenty-minute lecture on irony, told her the work was promising but the mid-section needed re-imagining. Novels turned on their mid-sections. Etc.

She nodded throughout, taking notes, and went off glowing. She really wasn't bad looking. A hard body.

A day's work done.

He found Dr Leon Truss toying with his earring. He was wearing a black T-shirt with the words LOVE YOURSELF A LITTLE on his chest.

'Vincent, mate!' said Truss. 'Thanks for dropping in.'

'I'm not dropping in,' said Duncan. 'I was ordered to present myself to your Royal Acting HOD Highness.'

'Oh nonsense,' said Truss. 'Complete misunderstanding. I simply wanted to have a little chat. About things.'

'What things?'

'A couple of things, actually. Trivial stuff.'

'Don't trifle with me. I've seen your PhD. *Humiliation, Pain, Pleasure and the Quest for Personal Identity.*'

'Vincent, that is pure, pure aggression. Can you bring yourself to not see every one-on-one we have as a cage-fighting bout?'

'It would be a bad mismatch,' said Duncan.

'Yes, well, firstly, we were thinking, just thinking idly, you under-stand...'

'The idleness of your thinking,' said Duncan, 'I understand perfectly.'

Truss's right hand stroked the left in a loving, comforting way.

'Vincent, we were thinking that since you only use your large office a few hours of the day, an average of 1.6 actually and that's during term...'

'Have you been spying on me, Truss?'

'Please, don't be paranoid,' said Truss. 'It's Rump.'

'Rump?'

'The Resources Utilisation Monitoring Program? It's been discussed at staff meetings, Vincent. Where colleagues meet. The cornerstone of the collegial tradition. We'd so love you to pop in on one when your outside commitments allow.'

'Rump my arse. Spying on the staff.'

'So. We were thinking that, going forward, your office would comfortably house four staff units. That's you and Meredith, Jude and Roberta.'

'Who the hell is Roberta?'

'Ah. When he gets back from long-service, Bob is Roberta. Didn't he tell you?'

'We've never talked about quests for personal identity,' said Duncan, 'that end with the subtraction of two testicles and the addition of a single vowel.'

Truss smiled showing an alarming amount of gum.

'Cruel wit undulled,' he said. 'That's so good to see in older people. So it's settled then. On the same page re resource utilisation.'

'My answer, Trussboy,' said Duncan, the words hissing through his teeth, 'is that I will not share *my* office, that's *MY* office, with Meredith, Jude or anyone else, surgically and chemically regendered or not. Is that clear to you? Are we on the same bloody Adelaide Protestant guilt-ridden hymnsheet?'

Truss put his palms together and bowed his head in a humble eastern non-Protestant way.

'Vincent,' he said, 'I'm really, really sad that you can't embrace the department's inclusive and egalitarian ethic. So it's my sad, sad duty to say that we will have to discuss whether to renew your contract.'

Duncan controlled his need to lean across the desk and take the man by his long lizardy throat and squeeze the life out of him, see his tongue come out, his face turn purple, the capillaries in his face pop.

'I think that you'll find,' said Duncan, 'that my contract has years to run.'

'I think you'll find that the years have slipped by,' said Truss. 'It has one term left to run. I can say that the feeling in the department is that its expiry presents an opportunity for change and renewal. For both parties, of course.'

Duncan tried to slam the door on his way out. But Truss had placed a little rubber wedge against the door jamb.

In the Mini, Duncan considered his situation. A brilliant career in the balance. No: ended. Usurers demanding two hundred thousand dollars or his house. The prospect of sucking up to the entire department, man, woman and those on the plane to Thailand, or losing the large sum that appeared in his bank account every fortnight.

Haig. She could provide the breathing space. Two sell-out exhibitions, forty-odd assemblages of animal, vegetable and mineral substances shifted to the gullible at ludicrous prices. Even subtracting the criminal commission taken by her gallery, she'd have a stash of several hundred grand. She certainly contributed nothing to the household.

A loan. He would propose the transaction as a loan, a short-term loan while accountants were dragging their heels transferring massive sums to him.

He rang her mobile: the answering service. He would have to go to her chamber of horrors in the former asylum.

The Alfa was in the parking area. He couldn't find a space, so he occupied the loading zone. He'd been here once for some art-world function.

Except for two Coles shopping trolleys, the entrance hall was empty. Up the stairs and last door on the left was his recollection.

The place smelled of dope, turpentine, burnt pasta sauce, welding gases and, faintly, of ancient urine containing old-fashioned pacifying drugs. From somewhere came weird electronic music with an unsettling pulse beat.

A card on the door: H. Alexander.

He tried the handle. Locked. He knocked. Knocked again. Again and louder.

It opened a crack. Haig, sleepy, wearing a T-shirt and track pants.

'Having a nap,' she said. 'What do you want?'

He should show interest. 'Thought I'd see what you were working on,' said Duncan.

'Vincent, you know I don't like...'

'Oh, come on,' he said, 'don't be shy.'

He pushed the door open and went in, began a tour of the works in progress. One featured thick-painted male figures wearing plastic shopping bags, bubblewrap and strips of hessian. Another appeared to be composed of blowtorched plastic toys—dolls, cars, guns—and what were possibly sex aids of a phallic nature.

'Interesting,' said Duncan. 'I sense change and renewal.'

He was passing a door and he opened it.

A pale-skinned young man was lying on a blow-up camping mattress. He was naked, tumescent, smoking a cigarette and reading a comic book.

'Hi,' he said.

'Vincent, this is David,' said Haig from behind Duncan. 'He, ah, he's modelling for me. David, this is Vincent Duncan.'

David gave a little wave with his cigarette.

'My mom loves your books,' said David, in a respectful way.

Given a gun, Duncan would have left him bleeding on the deflating mattress, dying in his own blood, cadmium red, deep hue.

'Enjoy your comic,' said Duncan and closed the door.

He continued the tour. Icy calm was required. This could work to his advantage in several ways. At the door, he said, 'See me out.'

They went down the stairs in silence, into the day.

'I see a very powerful show coming up,' said Duncan. 'Very, very strong. An added depth and maturity. Painful with insight.'

Haig was combing her hair with her fingers. 'Thank you,' she said.

'My pleasure. Listen, I need a little loan from you,' he said, no hint of neediness in his voice. 'The bank's being awkward and the accountant's two months behind with a very large cheque.'

'How much?' said Haig.

'Just two hundred grand. Short-term loan. Bridging finance. A few weeks.'

'Two hundred thousand dollars?'

'That'll do. Two hundred, two-fifty.'

She stared at him. When had her lips become so thin?

'Vincent, I can't lend you *twenty* thousand,' she said. 'I've bought a place in Liguria. Somewhere to escape to. Liguria is very expensive.'

She turned and went up the stairs. Barefoot. He hadn't noticed that. At the top, she turned and flashed teeth at him. 'Ask the bank for time, darling.'

Duncan drove home. It was lunchtime, no breakfast, he should eat.

He opened a bottle of Mumm's and took it and a glass onto the terrace. Waiting for the end.

Shall I pluck a flower, boys, shall I save or spend?
All turns sour, boys, waiting for the end.

He sipped and watched the light on the water. Betrayed by everyone. All the wasted years, the words torn from his soul. Tears formed in his eyes, swelled, broke, ran down his cheeks.

The phone. He went in, sniffing.

'Vincent, dear man.'

Marjorie.

'Vincent, marvellous, marvellous news,' she said. 'You've won the Claris Buckhard Prize for Uplifting Fiction.'

'The what?'

'The Claris Buckhard Prize for Uplifting Fiction.'

'For what?'

'For your fabulous new book. For *A Reducing Fire*.'

Uplifting fiction?

A Reducing Fire uplifting fiction? Were they barking mad? It was a cry of existential despair, it was the plaintive hopeless howl of the last polar bear on the last, melting ice floe.

'I know, I know, a prize under the radar, darling,' said Marjorie. 'Our clever Emily had the bright idea to send them all our unpublished manuscripts. It's new, this is the first year. It's Canadian.'

Oh Lord. The Canadian Country Women's Association Prize for Uplifting Fiction. A framed certificate, a LumboJack chainsaw and a case of Brownie Bear's Best maple syrup.

'It's one million Canadian dollars, Vincent,' she said. 'And one million dollars to the creative writing institution of your choice.'

It took time to register.

Oh Lord, in your wisdom and mercy, you have given us this woman Clovis Hardbuck, whatever.

'But hold your breath,' said Marjorie. 'We're on a roll, darling. Cal Braverman at Random and Cissy Cowling at Harper both heard about it and they're in a dogfight.'

'A dogfight.' He was trying to be calm.

'Yes. A dogfight. Cal offered one million, Cissy said one-five and now Cal's coming back to me.'

Ah, the exquisite timing of it. The fearful symmetry.

'Marjorie,' he said, 'dear Marjorie, let me read something to you. It is with regret that I inform you that I have decided to terminate our agency agreement as of…heard enough, Marj, old girl? Old sausage?'

'Oh Vincent, don't be silly, just an impulsive foolishness. We've had so many little tiffs, haven't we? But we're still together. I've sent you an email on the subject, darling.'

'Fourth-rate piece of sentimental rubbish,' said Duncan. 'As I recall, darling, those were your words. Well, darling, since you've terminated yourself, you won't be getting fifteen exorbitant per cent of my earnings derived from the fourth-rate piece of sentimental rubbish, will you?'

He listened to her pleading for a while, then he said. 'Kindly redirect Claret Hardacre and Random and HarperCollins to me. Goodbye, Marjorie. And my best to your boob of a husband.'

Back to the terrace with his mobile. Another glass of Mumm's. How sweet the song of the magpie. He dialled Truss's number.

'Hello, Painboy,' he said. 'Vincent Duncan. I thought you'd like to know that my new novel has won the Mavis Hardsuck Prize.'

'Very nice, Vincent,' said Truss. 'Some rural thing, is it? I'm in a meeting, so if…'

'It comes with a million dollars for the creative writing institution of my choice. That's a million dollars, Trussman.'

'A million dollars?'

'For the institution of my choice.'

'Lunch, Vincent, let's do lunch. I've just been telling the people in this room that I will fight to my last breath for the renewal of your contract.'

'Bye, bye, Trussiewuss.'

A refill. The golden liquid, the minute bubbles of gas entering the bloodstream. He rang Haig's mobile. She answered.

'Vincent Duncan,' he said. 'I want to say to you, you talentless bitch, that people only buy your hideous rubbish because I rigged an auction.'

Haig gasped.

'I also want to say, art harlot,' he said, 'that I am throwing all your possessions onto the pavement. Get your dickboy to park the Alfa outside my house or I'll get a court order.'

Duncan went to his study and found his list of students with phone numbers. Sarius Godber. A rock climber's body. Perhaps an invitation to supper at the Enoteca. They could talk about writing. His, hers. His, in the main.

His computer pinged. Email.

Cal Braverman? Cissy Cowling? Which dog in the fight? What advance on one point five million?

Marjorie, the poor cow.

Vincent: I'm afraid there's been a mistake. Manuscript cover pages swapped. The Buckhard winner is Amerine Panikbar for *A Quest of Flamingoes*. Sorry about that. Marjorie.

Through the window, he saw another magpie alight on the hand-cut Castlemaine bluestone paving.

2009

CEDRIC ABROAD

CEDRIC MARCHANT left England for the first time at the age of forty-one. He travelled to France by train and boat at the insistence of his sister, Freda, who had gone to live in the Dordogne with a painter from Leeds who called himself Roberto.

Freda, who was forty-three, seemed to think that Roberto was a younger man. How she could tell was beyond Cedric because Roberto had a shaven skull and an orange beard covered his face up to his small close-set violent eyes.

The hairy artist came with two offspring, a cheerful boy of eight and a fat teenage girl with rings in ears, nose and lower lip. She communicated by snarling and was not seen to eat anything except a breakfast cereal called Poppo, taken directly from the box. Cedric avoided looking at her lest this appear provocative. He enjoyed his short stay abroad, although he formed the impression that there were more French people living in his own village of Lower Roebuck than in the hamlet of La Bastide-St-Maurice.

When he arrived home, Cedric found the letter from Australia waiting. It was addressed to the school and re-addressed by Mrs Cuthbert in her slashing, vindictive hand. Cedric was surprised that she hadn't returned it to sender marked: NOT AT THIS ADDRESS.

He dated Mrs Cuthbert's antagonism from the day he politely declined an invitation to speak to her book group on the subject of the postmodern English novel.

'I didn't know there was a postmodern English novel,' he said. 'Isn't modern now?'

She stared at him. 'For some reason,' she said, 'one expects senior English masters to be abreast of their subjects.'

Cedric saw the hand of the treacherous sycophant Mathis in this. 'Mr Mathis,' he said. 'He's your man. Person. I saw him with a copy of The Line of something. Won the thingy prize. Least Resistance?'

'It's called *The Line of Beauty*,' Mrs Cuthbert said, showing her upper teeth and a broad vista of pink gum. 'I can see that you have no interest in widening the intellectual conversation.'

Cedric had no idea what the intellectual conversation was and he was sure that he would never get a word in anyway. But, because he didn't like any exchange to end on a sour note, he tried to start a new topic. Mrs Cuthbert was determined to be offended, however, and he limped away.

Letter from Australia in hand, Cedric thought about the looming term at the Gollop School. The prospect gassed him with the same gloom and foreboding he had felt as a boy on the last day of the holidays. He went down the dark and narrow passage into the kitchen and sat at the table.

The envelope bore two bright stamps, Australian stamps, featuring a child's drawing of a sheep and a cow. The animals were the same size. Had the faraway country produced a super-sheep? Or was it possible that the cows were smaller? The place was said to be very dry. It could be an evolutionary adaptation.

He opened the letter with the breadknife. Two sheets of paper with the letterhead:

Girton, Thomas & McGnarr
Barristers & Solicitors
St Arnaud VIC 3478

Dear Mr Marchant,
The occasion for this letter is the official declaration of the death of our client Mr Cyril Rodney Marchant, of Orpheus

Downs Station, Victoria, Australia. Mr Marchant disappeared from his boat in the Gulf of Carpentaria in September 1999. He was then seventy-six years of age, divorced and without issue.

In our client's will of July 1996, Mr Roger Marchant of Manchester or his oldest male descendant is named as the sole beneficiary of his estate. We have ascertained that the aforesaid Mr Roger Marchant is Mr Roger Clement Marchant, formerly of 23A Ludlow Street, Chorlton-cum-Hardy, Manchester, deceased 15 October 1998. Our inquiry agent informs us that you are the sole male heir of Mr Roger Clement Marchant and, therefore, the heir to Mr CR Marchant's estate.

We would be grateful if you could forward to us certified copies of your birth certificate, passport, driver's licence and any other documents that would assist us in confirming your identity.

The letter went on to say that Mr Cyril Marchant's estate contained 'the freehold of the unencumbered property known as Orpheus Downs; the freehold and contents of the business premises known as the Guardian building at 12 Carbine Street, Halls Well; $133,654 in cash on deposit at the Bendigo Bank, St Arnaud; a 1983 Toyota LandCruiser; a Jeep of unknown date; a Massey Ferguson tractor; a four-metre aluminium boat; two trail bikes; workshop equipment, farm equipment and sundries; seven firearms, thirteen fishing rods, assorted other fishing equipment, six saddles and assorted saddlery, household and personal effects, including furniture and books, a stuffed crocodile, nine large stuffed and mounted fish, and a buffalo head.'

It was signed BJ Thomas, LLB.

Cedric looked out of the window at a dismal scene: rain falling on a small overgrown garden, running down the roof of a listing shed held up only by ivy and other creepers.

A stuffed crocodile.

He was the owner of a stuffed crocodile.

And many stuffed fish. And a buffalo head. And guns, saddles, trail bikes, a LandCruiser and a boat.

Thank you, Uncle Cyril.

Cedric's father had often spoken of his brother, always in tones of mild disapproval. Cyril had gone to sea at sixteen. As far as Cedric knew, he never came back. He could clearly remember his father reading out letters from Uncle Cyril, commenting as he went:

'Dear Roger (no comma) Hope this finds you and your's (apostrophe mistake) well. Im (no apostrophe) on a ship on the Sydney Yokohama (no hyphen) run and genarally (spelling mistake) living the life of Riley (spelling wrong, no comma) at least when Im (no apostrophe) on shore (no punctuation) nudge nudge wink wink take my meaning (no commas).'

Cedric's father's occupation as a typesetter and proofreader had given him an eye for lapses in spelling, syntax and punctuation. Every evening, Roger Marchant brought home copies of *The Times* and the *Daily Telegraph*. After supper, he sat at the kitchen table, glass of Hinchbottom's Old Tawny Port to hand, and examined the newspapers line by line, column by column, crying out at a discovery of a mistake or infelicity.

'That's a bloody who, not a bloody that. Tory illiterates. Born to bloody rule, the buggers don't even have a grip on the English language. Come here, boy. Look at this.'

Cedric had always sat with his father at the table and done his homework. His sister, Freda, always sat in the front room, watching television.

One hundred and thirty-three thousand Australian dollars. How much money was that?

And a station called Orpheus Downs, Victoria, Australia. A station. He liked the sound of the word.

O Lord, could he stop teaching at Gollop's?

Well, why not?

Cedric felt a surge of joy at the prospect of never again driving up the Gollop School's dripping avenue to park the Austin A40 on the balding gravel behind the toilet block, of never again tiptoeing fearfully past the headmaster's office, of never again opening his own cell-like chamber's door to release the sad smell of a suitcase closed for fifty years.

Cedric got up, paced the room. Goodbye to trying not to offend people: the flushed and venomous headmaster; the dreadful Mrs Cuthbert; the parents who somehow believed that paying school fees made him responsible for turning their dim offspring into what Mathis called 'fluent communicators'; and Mathis, the oleaginous assassin.

Could he do it? Could he write a letter saying that he would not be returning next term? Gollop's was the only job he had ever had. It was the only school that would give him a post when he left York with his miserable second-class degree. He was offered a term's teaching, then another, and another, and finally a permanent position.

Resign? Oh yes he could. He got out a lined pad and dashed off a letter.

Dear Mr Purdon,
It is with pleasure that I inform you that I will not be returning to the Gollop School next term. My solicitors will be in touch regarding my entitlements.
Yours faithfully,
Cedric Marchant

He read the letter, put it aside, and thought for a while. Then he wrote another one.

Dear Mr Purdon,
It is with great regret that I write to inform you that, for personal reasons, I will not be returning to the Gollop School next term. I would like to say that my feelings towards you and the school are of admiration and gratitude.
My solicitor will be in touch regarding my entitlements.

Roger Marchant had always cautioned against bridge-burning. You never knew. You might have to ask for your job back.

Cedric put on his raincoat and walked down to the high street. In the butcher's window, he glimpsed himself: thin face, wet seaweed hair, sad-dog look. He stopped, pushed his floppy hair off his forehead, lifted his chin, smiled the bold smile of an adventurer—a man setting out for Australia to claim his inheritance.

Going to Australia? What a lunatic idea. But looking at himself in the window, he thought, for the second time in half an hour: why not?

Cedric became aware of something ghostly beyond his reflection. It was the butcher, Bertie Stockton, inside the shop, moving his head and waving a hand like a fan of pork sausages.

Cedric passed on quickly, bought a stamp, put spit on his finger and transferred it to the stamp, pressed it down, went outside and, with a flick of the wrist, sent his resignation into the post box. Halfway in. He had to give it a little push.

Cedric walked down the street feeling like a free man. A man of private means. A man with seven firearms, two trail bikes and a stuffed crocodile.

Cedric had never been on a plane before and, waiting to board, he felt a terrible anxiety. Scalp prickling with sweat, he was considering fleeing the terminal, going home, when he became aware of a boy in an Arsenal bomber jacket staring at him.

The brat had detected his fear. Cedric had much experience of this phenomenon among boys, the bullies. Without thought, he fixed the child with a gaze of pure slit-eyed menace.

The boy packed it in smartly, turned sideways and went back to his electronic game. Cedric found that his anxiety had abated, and then his flight was called. Rising, he thought of a line from *Henry Esmond*: 'The wine is drawn, M. le Marquis…we must drink it.'

That was the spirit. Wine drawn, dies cast, swords unsheathed,

Rubicons crossed, eggs scrambled. There was no going back.

Inside the plane, shuffling along behind an extremely fat young man wearing a slouch hat, stooping to avoid bumping his head, a child pushing at him, Cedric wished very much to go back. Given the chance, he would have undrawn, uncast, sheathed, uncrossed and unscrambled in an instant. It had never occurred to him that aircraft could be so frighteningly narrow, so crammed with people, so lacking in air.

He walked right past his seat and, panicking, had to fight his way back against the flow.

When he found his place, Cedric's small but heavy bag fell on his head as he tried to put it in the overhead locker. He put it back and it fell on him again. The third time it remained in place. Tears of pain in his eyes, he was climbing over a fat man and a woman with a big head of frizzy blond hair to reach his window seat when his stomach rumbled thunderously in the way it always did when he was creeping past the headmaster's study. Cringing with embarrassment, Cedric sat and tried to obey the instruction to fasten seatbelts. But he couldn't find the buckle.

The plane would take off and he would be thrown from his seat. Cedric felt alone and scared, the way he had felt on his first day at school.

'Jesus, I'm sitting on something...' The woman put a hand under her right buttock and extracted the buckle.

Cedric took it gratefully and joined the two bits. Then he clasped his hands, put them on his chest, closed his eyes and tried not to think about the roaring engines.

'I wouldn't give a bugger if we crashed on take-off,' said the woman.

Cedric was not cheered by this devil-may-care attitude to a flaming death. He wanted to be at home in Lower Roebuck, listening to the BBC early evening news on the radio, sipping a glass of the excellent homebrew of his neighbour, Mr Barrow.

'Not a bugger,' said the woman. 'No, I don't really care...'

'This is my faith's time of prayer for the souls of dumb animals,' Cedric said without opening his eyes. 'I would appreciate silence.'

He had no idea where the words came from but they shut the woman up until the aircraft was definitely airborne and on an even keel. Cedric opened his eyes. The woman patted his forearm.

'You're spiritual,' she said. 'I'm like that myself sometimes. I can feel at one with nature.'

How long did it take to get to Australia, thought Cedric. He should have asked the travel agent.

'Jesus, I need to be spiritual, the stress I've had,' said the woman. 'Stress you will not believe.'

'Stress,' said the man on the aisle in a rich Irish voice. 'My dear child, people often don't understand the toll it takes.'

Cedric got a look at him. He was wearing a dog collar, he was a priest, a large Irish priest.

'Father O'Brannigan,' said the priest, offering his left hand to the woman. 'Father Camus O'Brannigan.'

'Cindy Tomacic,' said the woman, taking his fingertips in her right hand. Cedric thought she was going to kiss the ruby ring on O'Brannigan's middle finger.

The priestly hand disengaged and was offered to Cedric.

'And you are?' said O'Brannigan, a tilt of head.

'Cedric Marchant.'

Cedric hated shaking hands. Roger Marchant once said that you could tell a lot about a man by the way he shook hands. Cedric had long regretted not asking him for more information. And this hand-shake was even worse than usual. He was being offered a big hand, palm down. Then it turned sideways. He gave it a glancing feel, knew he'd got it wrong again.

'Welcome aboard, Cedric,' said O'Brannigan, as if he owned the aircraft. 'Off to the penal colony, possibly for the term of our natural lives.'

'Not long enough,' said Cindy. 'Sorry, Cedric. I don't actually mind England. Except for the bloody Poms. Joke.'

O'Brannigan said, 'And a fine joke, my dear, but I sense pain in you.'

Cedric felt pain developing inside his head. He found a magazine in the pocket below his knees and opened it at an article headlined: 'EXTREME HOLIDAYS: CRASHING THE FEAR BARRIER.' Was that what he had embarked upon?

'Pain,' said Cindy. 'You are so on the money, father. Absolutely. I'm up to my…chin in pain.'

'Unburden yourself, child,' said Father O'Brannigan. 'Cedric will be a sympathetic listener. In him I sense the compassion that only sufferin can bring. Not so, Cedric?'

Cedric didn't respond, looked at his magazine. He would not be drawn into this.

'Cedric?' The name now had a steely sound.

Cedric's resolve melted. He felt compelled to look at the priest.

'You are a listener, are you not?'

Cedric tried to use his face to be non-committal without speaking. The Sri Lankan cleaner at Gollop's had been able to say yes while shaking his head.

Failure.

'Of course you are, Cedric,' said the priest. 'Today so few people want to form the bond of listenin.'

Cedric didn't want any such bond. Father O'Brannigan was welcome to form it. Catholic priests were probably trained in bonding. The Catholic Church had always been a mystery to Cedric. As a boy, he had asked his father what the Holy See was. 'Well,' said Roger Marchant, 'there's the Holy See and the Holy Hear. Then there's the Holy Taste and the Holy Smell.'

Cedric had probed no further. Early in life, he developed an instinct for when his father's answers were not to be taken seriously.

'Tell us, Cindy.'

Once Cindy got going, Cedric found himself caught up in her story. A New Zealand girl working in Brighton—well, she wasn't exactly a girl—met an Englishman called Derek in a pub. In what seemed to be an indecently short time, he had moved in with her.

'He wanted to be a personal trainer,' said Cindy.

'A what?' asked Cedric.

They both frowned at him. Cedric realised that the question revealed his ignorance. 'I meant to say where.'

'In London,' said Cindy. 'He reckoned London was full of rich fat people who needed someone to kick their arses around a park. Sorry, father.'

Cedric nodded, no wiser.

'Anyway,' said Cindy, 'he wanted me to be a partner in the business. I'd do the books and a bit of training. When I got fit. He was going to get me really fit.'

She was silent. Cedric peeped at her. She was looking at the roof.

'Jeez, Derek, what a bod,' Cindy said wistfully. 'Rock pecs, six-pack. Manta lats. Bench-press a fridge.'

Cedric looked at her uneasily. *Rockpucks. Sexpeck. Mentalets. Bunchprussafrudge.* What did these terms mean? Was this why Purdon had dismissed Wayne Watkins, the sports master from New Zealand, after only five weeks at Gollop's? Perhaps the boys couldn't understand him. Although Mr Barrow had told a story about Wayne taking off all his clothes in the Prince of Orange and running around the green with only a rugby ball to hide his privates.

Father O'Brannigan was nodding at Cindy, interested.

'I'm an idiot,' she said. 'I put in my six thousand quid.' She sniffed, tried to smile. 'All I had. That's four years of savings. Thank Christ, I had the return ticket.'

'Derek?' said Father O'Brannigan. 'Are you sayin…'

'A total shonk,' said Cindy. 'Took off with the money. The cops say I'm number four. And that's the ones they know about.'

She was really rather pretty, thought Cedric. She had a brave, sweet smile. 'You poor dear,' he said without thinking.

Cindy squeezed Cedric's left hand and held it. He blushed but his attitude towards the long journey had improved immeasurably.

On the last leg of the flight, Cedric found himself reluctant to have it end. Once he had got used to the cramped space, he enjoyed being immobile and having food and drink brought to him. It reminded him of being mildly ill as a child, when his mother was still there to look after him.

He also found himself enjoying the company of Father O'Brannigan and Cindy. They included him in their conversations, asked him lots of questions, and they both told funny stories. Some of the priest's were quite rude, which made Cedric even more puzzled about Catholicism. A film was shown about a man who turned into a woman but was actually still a man, which was interesting even if he didn't catch all the jokes. But he laughed along with Cindy and Father O'Brannigan, and enjoyed being part of the laughing.

Cedric also listened through his earphones to music, some of a kind that he did not know existed. Some of it probably should not exist.

It was true, Cedric concluded as he savoured the last meal's main course, Veal Krakatoa: travel did broaden the mind. The veal came with dwarf vegetables, something else new to him. He had not even reached anywhere and already he was broader in the mind.

'Ceddy, I'm going to miss you so much,' said Cindy, putting a hand on his thigh and looking at him with her big blue eyes. 'Where were you when I needed a man I could trust?'

Cedric almost choked on the veal. Only his mother had ever called him Ceddy. 'I'll miss you too,' he said before he could think about it. He felt a blush rising and it didn't go away until they were almost on the ground in Melbourne.

After they had collected their bags from the conveyor belt and were looking after Father O'Brannigan's while he went to the toilet, Cindy said, 'Well, Ceddy, I walk from here.'

'Walk?'

'This's where my return ticket's from,' she said. 'And I don't have a cent to my name.'

'But you've got to get to New Zealand.' Cedric wasn't sure how far that was from Melbourne but the water in between certainly ruled out walking.

'I'll find a way.'

This poor wronged and brave woman, thought Cedric. All the way from England, she had known that she would be destitute when she arrived in Australia. And she had never breathed a word of it. She had joked and laughed and pretended that all was well.

'How much does it cost?' he said.

'The plane ticket? It's just a few hundred dollars. Four or five, I suppose.'

'Wait here,' said Cedric.

He had traveller's cheques, it had all been explained to him. He found the exchange booth and cashed four hundred pounds.

'Fifties okay?'

'Fine.'

The man gave him far more notes than he expected. Cedric went a short distance away and counted out ten of them. That would pay for the plane ticket. He added two. Three.

He went back to Cindy. 'Here you are,' he said, offering the money. 'Put this in your purse.'

'Ceddy, don't be a dill.'

'You can repay me,' said Cedric. 'It's just a loan.'

'You darling man. I can't.'

'Yes, you can. Please.'

Cindy blinked rapidly, touched his cheek. 'Well, I feel like blubbing. You are just so, just so…'

She took the money, put it in her bag, scrabbled around and found a scrap of paper and a pen. 'Give me your address, Ceddy.'

Cindy wrote down Cedric's address and then wrote hers on the paper, tore off the piece and gave it to him. 'I'll pay you back as soon as I get a job,' she said. 'And then I'm coming to see you.'

She took him by the shoulders and kissed him on the lips, a long kiss of a kind Cedric had never experienced. He felt weak in the legs, giddy.

And then she walked away. At the sliding doors, she looked back and blew a kiss and then she was gone. Cedric looked around to see if anyone was looking. He adjusted his trousers.

Father O'Brannigan appeared.

'Cindy's gone,' said Cedric.

'And isn't that what always happens with the darlins,' said the priest. 'Love you and leave you. Not that I'd know anythin about it. Now, how're you gettin to this property of yours?'

'I thought I might take a train,' said Cedric. 'Or a bus.'

O'Brannigan laughed, slapped his shoulder. 'Train? Bus? It's out the back of buggery, man.'

'The back of…'

'Bloody miles from anywhere. No buses or trains out there. You'll need a reliable vehicle, the four-wheel drive, the bullbars, the water tanks, the extra fuel tank, the snorkel exhaust for the flooded creeks. The flash-flooded creeks.'

Cedric had not considered anything like this. He had thought of Australia as a much bigger England. And drier. Much drier. With larger moors. As in the fabled Outback. A large and dryish moor was the way he had seen the fabled Outback. Sunny too. Obviously. There was no dryish without sunny.

'Well, I don't know,' he said. 'I'm not a very good driver.'

'Nothin to it. What's your car?'

'It's an Austin A40.'

'A fine rugged conveyance. Perfect preparation. Now you want to be careful where you buy your vehicle, a world of sharks out there. I'm goin to do you a favour, put you on to a former parishioner of mine, honest as the Pope. Fella's a beacon of honesty in a sea of duplicity.'

'Thank you,' said Cedric. 'I'm very grateful.'

'What I suggest,' said Father O'Brannigan, 'is that I give the boy a ring, see what he's got in stock. And if there's a suitable vehicle, one of them never left the city, your doctor's wife's car to pick up the kiddies from school, we might be able to snap up a bargain.'

'Why would she need water tanks and extra fuel tanks to pick up the children?' said Cedric.

'Very cautious people, doctors,' said Father O'Brannigan. 'Take no chances with the nearest and dearest.'

'And what are bullbars?' said Cedric. 'I don't...'

'For the animals generally. There's a massive death wish in the local fauna. They travel for days and weeks to find a road to die on. And the bigger ones, the hoppers and the like, well, they can take you out with them. Come right through the windscreen, a bloody huge great thing like a cow with a big tail. Lands on your lap.'

'I see,' said Cedric. 'Yes.'

Father O'Brannigan nodded. 'Dangerous place, Australia. Probably better never inhabited. Now you put your bones down over there and I'll be on the blower to this fella of mine.'

It took no more than two hours for Cedric to be on the road to the interior, albeit in a state of high alarm.

Father O'Brannigan's parishioner turned out to be a dark man called Shane, thin, with gold rings in his long earlobes and on his thumbs. Cedric had difficulty understanding him because it was hard to detect the words that conveyed meaning in the torrent of speech.

Motorlikeafuckenformulaonematenevermindacouplafuckenscratches-thisfuckenthinglltakeyatofuckenbuggeryandbacknofuckenprobs...

The yellow vehicle he brought certainly had the snorkel exhaust and the bullbars. It also had a roof rack reached by a ladder, a winch, four aerials, six spotlights, seats for at least a dozen, and far more dents and scratches than one would expect a doctor's wife to incur on the school trip.

Cedric had looked helplessly at Father O'Brannigan. 'How many children did the doctor have?' he said.

'A good Catholic family, practisin the rhythm method,' said the priest.

'It doesn't look very...cared for,' Cedric said.

The priest nodded in agreement. He took Shane aside and spoke to him in what looked to Cedric like a teacherly manner, finger wagging. Shane looked contrite.

When he came back, Father O'Brannigan said, 'Nothin to worry about, my son. Shane's been naughty, loves the vehicle so much he's been takin it bush himself, runnin into a few trees and animals and the like. As you do. So he's now givin a written guarantee, thirty thousand kilometres, any mechanical trouble, your money back, no questions asked.'

'Um, how much?' said Cedric.

'He was askin twelve. Reckons the tyres are worth three.'

'Three what?'

'Thousand. Amazin, not so?'

'I don't think,' said Cedric, trying to speak firmly, 'that I can afford more than the tyres.'

'Course not,' said the priest. 'Outrageous sum. I've had the word with him and it's now eight thousand, your GPS thrown in.'

'Your what?'

'Magic of technology. There's a satellite watchin over you. Tells you where you are at any given time.'

'I usually know,' said Cedric. He had no idea what Father O'Brannigan was talking about but it sounded vaguely religious.

The priest put a hand on Cedric's shoulder. 'Well, son, I've done my best to save you from the mongrels. But Shane's got another buyer wants this magnificent vehicle so you'll have to get a wriggle on.'

Cedric hadn't bargained for his savings vanishing at this speed, but he went back to the foreign exchange desk, got the money and handed it over. Then Shane gave him a driving lesson.

'Hop in,' said Shane. 'Giveyafuckendrivinlesson.'

Driving the old A40 around Lower Roebuck had no more prepared Cedric for the troop carrier than riding a tricycle prepared a toddler to enter the Tour de France. During the lesson, and afterwards, Cedric thought that he would have nightmares about the experience for the rest of his life: the unnaturally bright daylight, the deafening noise of aircraft seemingly passing metres overhead, the bumper-to-bumper traffic, the near-collisions—four or five of them—the yellow monster stalling, the hooting and the rude shouting and the gesturing of fellow road users.

And, all the while, Shane shouting incomprehensible instructions about changing gear. Cedric had not known that a vehicle could have so many gears and in such a complicated arrangement. Changing them required standing on the clutch pedal to get it to the floor and desperately pushing the gear lever around in search of the right place. Often the stick went into the wrong notch, engaging the clutch brought a loss of power or a hideous scream from the engine. Shane would shout, Cedric would panic, stand on the clutch pedal, try another slot.

Usually that too was the wrong move: the same things happened or the vehicle jerked and the engine stalled.

The end finally came.

Father O'Brannigan and his parishioner departed. Seated side by side, they waved as their bright-red open convertible spun its wheels, left marks on the ground and the smell of burnt rubber.

Cedric was now alone, blinking rapidly, a middle-aged English schoolmaster sitting at least four feet above the greasy tarmac of an Australian airport parking lot, sitting behind the wheel of an old yellow troop carrier with many aerials and spotlights and a ladder to the roof and a steel barrier before it, designed to protect the machine and all who rode in it from the country's suicidal fauna.

In his recent decisions, he thought, was there the possibility of some errors of judgement? Too late.

The wine is drawn, M. le Marquis…we must drink it.

Cedric studied the maps for a long time, plotted his course. Then he sat up straight, moved his shoulders, turned the key. The monster whined, shuddered into loud life. 'Oh Lord, make haste to save us,' he said and stood on the clutch pedal.

The first part of the journey was much worse than Cedric had believed possible. He was bound for a town called St Arnaud, about two hours' drive from Melbourne, but he soon despaired of ever reaching it. Across the city's freeways he blundered, always in the wrong lane, always taking the wrong exit, always in panic, hooted at, many drivers making rude finger gestures at him, their faces contorted with rage.

After what seemed like hours, a hopelessly lost Cedric found himself in a street of low brick houses without fences, trim lawns, a suburban backwater, nothing moving. It was a cul-de-sac with a big circle to turn in. He turned, drove a short distance, pulled to the kerb and switched off. 'Shit,' he said, and put his head in his hands.

Knocking on the window.

Startled, Cedric looked into a face. He recoiled in fright, then realised it was an old woman wearing a knitted skullcap pulled down to where her eyebrows had once been.

She knocked again. He found the winder and rolled down the window.

'What's wrong with you?' she said.

'Ah, nothing,' said Cedric. 'I'm just a bit, ah, lost. Yes. Lost.'

'Lost? How can you be lost?'

Cedric thought that she had remarkably good teeth, wash-basin white, for someone so ancient. 'Don't know my way around,' he said. 'I'm English.'

The woman stepped off the door platform, back to the pavement, retreated a few paces and looked at the troop carrier. Left, right, up, down. She was wearing mechanics' overalls and she had a plastic bottle with a nozzle in her right hand.

'Pom,' she said. 'Where'd ya get this vehicle?'

'A priest sold it to me,' said Cedric. 'No, that's not correct, the friend of a priest. Well, not so much his friend as one of his...'

The woman looked at him with eyes so knowing that Cedric felt no need to say any more. She knew that he was a complete idiot, she had known it from the moment he spoke his first word.

'Where ya goin?' she said.

'In the first instance, a place called St Arnaud.'

'Where?'

Cedric repeated the name. The woman shook her head. He took the map book off the seat next to him, held it out the window and pointed at the dot that was St Arnaud. She came close and peered at the page.

'Snarnid,' she said. 'Why didn't ya say so?'

'Snarnid, yes,' said Cedric. 'That's the spot.'

'Hang on,' said the woman. She turned and went up the driveway of the house.

Cedric wasn't sure what to do. Perhaps she had gone inside to draw a map for him. Yes, that was what she was doing. How helpful. He felt much better. At least all the driving around was giving him the hang of it. He studied the street. Very neat. Not so much as a leaf or a twig or a scrap of paper to be seen. He hadn't expected Australia to be like this.

The old woman came down the driveway. She was carrying a small suitcase and a long leather case. She went around the front of the troop carrier, just her headgear showing, opened the rear passenger door and put her bags in. Then she slammed the door, opened the front one and climbed in, fixed Cedric with her commanding gaze.

'Get movin,' she said. 'Had enough of this place.'

Cedric obeyed, started the machine.

'Down to the corner, turn left, first right, keep goin. I'll tell you what to do after that.'

With a profound sense of relief, Cedric did as he was told.

Guided by the curt commands of Mrs Dot McPhee, as she announced herself to be, they were on the freeway, heading west, in fewer than twenty minutes.

Cedric found himself in a mood he had not experienced since sitting on his grandfather's lap on the small grey Massey Ferguson tractor. Up and down the field they had gone, ploughing the chocolate soil, Cedric's hands on the bottom of the wheel, his grandfather's at three and nine o'clock. From time to time, his grandfather took his hands away, put them on Cedric's shoulders and Cedric was in charge of the machine, steering.

In charge but with grown-up support on hand.

That was the way he felt now, tooling down the highway in the massive vehicle, looking down on most of the traffic, windows open, Mrs Dot McPhee beside him with a small cigar in her mouth, knitting. She hadn't asked him if he minded but that didn't matter. He would have said no, that's perfectly all right. It was all right. He rather liked the smell of her smoke.

'What's ya business in Snarnid?' she said.

Cedric told her about the need to see his late uncle's solicitor in St Arnaud concerning the will.

'A will, eh?' she said. 'Need ya wits about ya when it comes to wills.'

Cedric brooded. 'Why, exactly?' he said.

Silence. Mrs McPhee's smoke drifted past. 'Pass this bug,' she said. 'Idiots clutterin up the road.'

Cedric did as he was told, overtook a small purple car, alarmed at the speed he had to reach. He sighed with relief when he could return to the left lane.

'Little Jap cars,' she said. 'Made of tin.'

'Isn't this a Japanese vehicle?'

'Cruisers are different,' said Mrs McPhee. After a while, she said, 'Not exactly unknown for ya solicitor to be on the fiddle. Trade's got more'n its fair share of shonks and shicers.'

Nothing more was said until they were approaching a town called Ballarat. 'Keep right,' she said. 'Don't have to go through this place, always rainin, mystery, like that Bermuda Hole.'

The sky was blue, cloudless. It could obviously change in an instant. A micro-zone of climatic instability. Cedric had heard about these places from Fiona Greentree, one of the science teachers at Gollop's. Fiona asked him around for a drink once but, frightened by her moustache, he had made a very clumsy excuse and offended her.

'Gotta be careful with lawyers,' said Mrs McPhee, reinforcing her point. 'Could be a shonk.'

'Shonk,' said Cedric, trying out the word. He liked the sound. *Shonk.*

It had everything you wanted in a short word: the sibilant opening, the consonants closing like a safe door slamming.

Shonk. Cedric said it to himself a few times. *Shonk.*

'Knew this fella, his nanna left him the house in Goondi. Bloody lawyer charged him more'n the place's worth.'

'Charged him?' said Cedric. It had not occurred to him that he would have to pay the solicitor.

'Charge like Mallee bulls, some of em.'

Malley bulls?

A vicious strain of bull bred by someone called O'Malley, the O lost at some point. An O'Malley would have surrendered the O to move up the pay queue. Cedric's grandfather had told him of being in the army with a Patrick O'Dowd who became Dowd and jumped from near-last to near-first.

Malley bulls. Irascible animals, prone to charging. Did they have the running of the Malley bulls?

A signpost said St Arnaud was forty kilometres away.

'Will you be staying on in, um, Snarnid?' said Cedric.

'Snarnid?' said Mrs McPhee, opening her window and flicking out her stub. 'Gotta be mad to stay in Snarnid.'

They travelled in silence, Cedric thinking about what the staff of Gollop's would think if they could see him in charge of this massive vehicle, cruising along this Australian highway, overtaking purple Japanese bugs, Dot McPhee's needles clicking.

St Arnaud arrived. There was not a great deal to the place: houses with flaking paint and straggly gardens, a main street with shops that did not appear to be prospering, a war memorial of pitted volcanic stones topped by a piece of marble.

'What's the address?' said Mrs McPhee.

Cedric saw a long piece of unoccupied kerbside and eased the Cruiser in, hit the kerb, mounted it with two wheels, jerked the steering, returned to street level with a bump, stood on the brake pedal, stopped. He expelled all his breath loudly.

Not bad, he thought, all things considered. He looked at Mrs McPhee.

'Shoulda bin a hearse driver,' she said. 'No danger to the passengers.'

Cedric found his papers and the address of Girton, Thomas & McGnarr, Barristers & Solicitors. 'Twenty-seven Napier Street,' he said.

Mrs McPhee lowered her window and waited. An elderly man in a grey double-breasted suit came shuffling along the pavement. 'G'day, mate,' she shouted. 'Where's Napier Street?'

'What?' said the man. 'What?'

'Napier Street,' shouted Mrs McPhee.

'Yeah,' said the man. 'What about it?'

'Well, where is it?'

The man came closer, inspected Mrs McPhee, peered at Cedric, stood back. 'Bloody innit,' he said. 'What's bloody wrong with you?'

'No need to swear,' said Mrs McPhee. 'Be on your way.'

The man walked off, shaking his head.

'Want me to come with you?' said Mrs McPhee.

Cedric was now seized with the fear that it was all a hoax, that he had made a terrible fool of himself. There was no inheritance. He had thrown away a secure job, spent huge amounts of money. He could be ruined. He would have to go home and live in the dank cottage, on the dole, grow his own food, starve.

'No thanks,' he said. 'I think I can manage.'

'Don't sign anythin. Tell em you need a think.'

'Yes.' Cedric hesitated, uncertain whether to ask about her plans.

'I'll be waitin,' she said. 'Might get a few pies. Gotta be a half-decent pie in this place. I'll ask around.'

'Fine. I enjoy a pie.'

'If only everything in life were simple,' said Bertrand Thomas, barrister and solicitor. He was a thin man of unguessable age with a deep cleft between his sprouting eyebrows.

'Indeed,' said Cedric. 'In the matter of my uncle's will, I'd like to know...'

'But it's not simple,' said Bertrand Thomas. 'The web of our life is of a mingled yarn, good and ill together.' He eyed Cedric. *'All's Well that Ends Well.* You'd be familiar with the Bard, wouldn't you, Mr Marchant?'

'To some extent. Not entirely.'

'Not in his entirety, you mean?' said Thomas.

'Definitely not in his entirety.'

Cedric was no longer anxious. His anxiety had gradually lessened during his half-hour wait in a room with nothing to read except a publication called the *Weekly Times*. It had a picture of a cow on the front page and many mentions of something called dry sheep equivalent. Cedric brooded over what could be the equivalent of a dry sheep. Finally, the ancient horse-haired woman behind the desk responded to some silent signal and rose to open a door with BJ THOMAS BA LLB painted on it.

BJ Thomas now looked at the page in his hands. 'A teacher of English language and literature.'

'I am. I was. Well...'

'To teach English language and literature, you'd need to be pretty well up on the Bard, I imagine. A bit of an authority, really.'

Cedric coughed. 'There's actually quite a lot of other writing in English,' he said.

Thomas took on a narrow-eyed wolfish look. 'And well there might be, Mr Marchant,' he said, 'but what's it built on, what's its foundation, man? Answer me that.'

Cedric couldn't think of another foundation, couldn't think of a single brick in any alternative foundation. 'You may have a point,' he said. 'My uncle's will…'

Thomas rose behind his desk and took up the declamatory position, hand on heart.

'Farewell the plumed troops and the big wars
That makes ambition virtue! Oh, farewell!
Farewell the neighing steed, and the shrill trump,
The spirit-stirring drum, the ear-piercing fife,
The royal banner, and all quality,
Pride, pomp and circumstance of glorious war!'

He stood silent, eyes on Cedric.

'*Othello,*' Cedric said.

Thomas wasn't pleased. 'All English writing since Shakespeare,' he said, 'is a poor, halting postscript to the Bard. I quote no less a personage than Sir Morpeth Hardwicke QC.'

Cedric had never heard of Sir Morpeth Hardwicke QC but he sounded like old Mr Plowright at Gollop's. Plowright thought Western history was a poor, halting imitation of what the Chinese had done. He credited the Chinese with discovering everything from toilet paper to nuclear power.

'Old hat,' he said when someone in the staff room remarked on the news of a British breakthrough in gene technology, whatever that was. 'Chinese were manipulating genes by two-sixty BC. Earlier probably. Much earlier.'

'I have someone waiting outside,' said Cedric. 'So if it's possible…'

Thomas sat down. 'Yes, well, can't sit around nattering about Shakespeare. To the matter at hand. Your identification, please, Mr Marchant.'

Cedric passed over his passport, his driver's licence and an envelope containing a copy of his birth certificate. Thomas put on large glasses and made a show of examining them, holding them to the light from the dusty window. Cedric looked around the room. It was like the library of a Victorian mansion, piles of folders and document boxes on tables, dusty glass-fronted cupboards, shelves holding peeling leather-bound volumes. Two moulting stag heads looked on the room from the wall behind Bertrand Thomas, and on a deep wooden windowsill stood a stuffed creature. Somewhere between a small bear and a large badger, thought Cedric.

'Apparently in order,' Thomas said. 'Apparently.'

Cedric found that he was holding his breath. 'Well, that's who I am,' he said, short of air.

'Documents,' said Thomas, 'can be obtained.'

'Yes,' said Cedric. 'I obtained these.'

Thomas had another go. He held up the passport, looked at the photograph, studied Cedric over the top of it. Then he did the same with the driver's licence. 'This could be anyone,' he said.

'It didn't look much like me when it was taken eight years ago,' said Cedric. 'At least I didn't think so. Although I suppose one isn't much of a judge.'

Next the copy of the birth certificate. 'A copy,' said Thomas. 'Could be unauthorised.'

Cedric found himself sighing. 'On the other side,' he said, 'it's been notarised.'

'Ah,' said Thomas. He put on glasses. 'Well then, I will now read the last will and testament of Cyril Rodney Marchant, late of Orpheus Downs station, State of Victoria, Australia.'

It was a short document but Thomas made it last, pausing between words, stalling between sentences, meditating between paragraphs. Finally, he said, 'Do you understand the import of that, Mr Marchant?'

'Um, I have to live on the property for twelve months?'

'That is correct. You are to receive an allowance of five hundred dollars per calendar month from the estate for the period. As executor, it will be my duty to establish that you are in fact in residence throughout the aforesaid period. Short absences will be permitted. Longer absences will require my permission.'

Thomas took off the glasses and rubbed his eyes. 'Are you willing to abide by this condition, Mr Marchant?'

Cedric thought it didn't seem like an onerous condition. A year on his outback station before he inherited it and the money. And then he might choose to stay on, round up the animals on horseback. He would have to learn to ride of course. He could start on a small horse, an older small horse. Perhaps a retired horse, small and placid. Gentle. Yes...

'I am,' he said. 'When does it start?'

'Now, if that suits you.'

'It suits me, yes.'

Thomas opened a drawer and from within counted twenty fifty-dollar notes onto the desktop. 'We will begin with two months,' he said. 'If you supply me with a bank account number, the allowance will thereafter be paid into the account.' Pause. 'While I am satisfied that you are in residence.'

He pushed the stack of notes across the leather. 'An interesting man, your uncle,' he said.

'His spelling wasn't too good,' said Cedric and regretted it.

'Yes. He wasn't a bookish person. I suppose you know he narrowly escaped prison on a number of occasions.'

'Uncle Cyril?' Cedric felt a tingle of alarm. 'I didn't know.'

'Never out of trouble, really.'

'What kind of trouble?'

'Oh, prohibited substances, firearm charges, driving under the influence, goods believed to be stolen, arson. Attempted murder. And kidnapping. The prosecution dropped that early in the piece, though. She changed her story.'

Hesitant, bewildered, Cedric said, 'I somehow thought he was a farmer.'

Thomas looked around his chamber as if seeking something. 'Not a great deal of agricultural activity on Cyril's property, Mr Marchant. Of a conventional kind.'

He rose, offered a hand like a plucked wood pigeon. 'Good luck,' he said.

Cedric stood up and took the hand, determined to assert himself.

He squeezed. The hand was cold. It was also hard. And it did not yield. He desisted instantly. Oh God, he thought, another handshake failure.

Then the hand squeezed him. Cedric thought his knuckles were collapsing, the pain went up his forearm.

Thomas released his grip. Cedric choked a sob of relief.

'Miss Smolett will give you a copy of the will and the inventory and a map,' said Thomas. 'Goodbye.'

Cedric was at the door when he said, 'I take it your own affairs are in order, Mr Marchant.'

'I beg your pardon?'

'Your will, that sort of thing? Since you're so far from home.'

'Of course,' Cedric lied.

Mrs McPhee was in the Cruiser reading a paperback book and eating an apple. Cedric got behind the wheel.

'Well?' she said. 'Well?'

'There's this property,' said Cedric, 'and I have to stay on it for a year.'

'What about yer inheritance?'

'I get it after the year. The property and the money and the…the belongings.'

'Shoulda come with you,' she said. 'Sounds shonky to me. Where's the place?'

'I've got directions.'

'Let's see.'

Cedric handed over the photocopied page from a map. Someone had circled a dot at the end of a thin snaking line.

Mrs McPhee whistled.

'Far from here?' said Cedric tentatively. Despondency was descending.

'My oath.'

'That's about how far?'

Cedric thought he saw pity in Mrs McPhee's antique gaze. 'Bout as far as you can go, goin that way.'

'Ah. That far.'

'You hungry?'

Cedric realised he had not eaten since the plane. How long ago that seemed. How safe and comfortable. He was ravenous, his belly was concave with hunger, he felt lightheaded. 'I am a little peckish,' he said.

'Got us some pies. Lady at the op shop put me on the place.'

They ate their pies sitting on a bench in a small park outside the municipal offices. The ground was covered in dark pieces of bark. Mrs McPhee provided paper napkins and plastic cups from her bag. During his ingestion of pie number one, Cedric had to remind himself to chew before swallowing.

'Don't know pastry from a pig's bum,' said Mrs McPhee, handing him another pie. 'But not bad for a town like this.'

Cedric nodded, bit. He was slowing down and his spirits were improving. After a bout of chewing and some milk, he said, 'My uncle seems to have been a bit of a character.'

Mrs McPhee gave him the eye. 'What kind of character?'

'In trouble with the law a lot.'

'What, out there?'

'Apparently.'

'Dunno how they'd notice. Wouldn't be a copper in cooee.'

Was that the nearest town to his uncle's property? Cooee. Cedric liked the sound of it. 'Cooee,' he said. 'Cooee.'

Mrs McPhee looked at him with one eye narrowed, swallowed the last of her pie. 'You all right?'

'Why isn't there a copper in Cooee?'

She recognised his ignorance. 'No, no, not a place. Cooee. It's a sound. Hear it to buggery.'

Mrs McPhee made a trumpet with her hands: 'COOOEEEE. COOOEEEE.'

The thin vibrating sounds went up and down the street, freezing the few pedestrians in mid-stride.

'From the war,' said Mrs McPhee. 'The first one.'

Cedric thought that there was much more to learn about this country than he wanted to learn. And he was far from sure that he wanted that learning to include travelling a great distance into the parched interior and spending months there, alone.

Alone. He was no stranger to being alone. He was alone at home in Lower Roebuck. He could handle being alone. He had been alone all his adult life, really. It wasn't a problem.

Alone in Australia? On a property hundreds of miles from anywhere?

That was not quite the same thing as being alone in Pringle Lane, Lower Roebuck.

No.

On Orpheus Downs, there would be no nipping down to the village to buy a few pork bangers from Bertie Stockton or a loaf of bread and a carton of milk from the surly Mrs Bull at the shop.

Alone. He would be quite alone in a strange land. Cedric shivered. This was the time to make an excuse and go home.

Mrs McPhee stood, crushed the brown paper bag in both hands, rolled it tight. 'Well, let's get goin,' she said. 'Be long dark before we get there.'

A cloak of relief draped itself over his tense shoulders. He would not be alone. In the short term at least, there would be Mrs Dot McPhee.

They were walking when Mrs McPhee spun on a heel and kicked the balled bag back. It travelled four metres, hung in the air, dropped into the dead centre of the litter bin.

'How do you do that?' said Cedric, consumed with admiration.

'Practice,' she said. 'Talent and practice. We need supplies. Flour, yeast, tea, sugar, that kind of thing. Should be a bit of meat out there. Your burrow chooks. Live off the land.'

'Right,' said Cedric. 'Live off the land.'

Burrow chooks?

Three hours from St Arnaud, Cedric saw the body from a great distance. 'My Lord,' he said.

'Give him a lift,' said Mrs McPhee.

'What?'

'Just nappin. Stop.'

'Does he want a lift?'

'Course he does.'

Cedric knew all about Britons being murdered on the back roads of Australia. 'Is it, um, safe?'

'Don't be silly,' said Mrs McPhee.

He slowed the Cruiser to walking pace before he edged onto the shoulder. Outside St Arnaud he had found out what happened when you put two wheels on the gravel at speed. For a terrible moment he thought that they were going to die hanging upside-down in a flaming wreck.

Cedric stopped about twenty metres beyond the man. In the rear-view mirror, he saw him get up. Then a shock of ammoniac-sour wind rocked the Cruiser, bringing tears to Cedric's eyes. When he opened them, he saw a B-double sheep transport disappearing over the rise.

'Gidday.'

The man was at the window. He was tall and thin, sallow-skinned, somewhere north of fifty, his mouth marked off by deep cuttings. An impossibly battered hat was pulled low.

'Good afternoon,' Cedric said. 'May we offer you a lift?'

'Decent of you,' the man said in a deep, ruined voice.

He walked around the Cruiser, opened the passenger-side back door, put in a canvas-covered roll and a guitar case and got in. 'Name's Oliver,' he said. 'Greg Oliver.'

'Cedric Marchant.'

'Dot,' said Mrs McPhee. 'Where ya goin?'

'Same way you're going,' said the man.

'How far?'

'Drop me when you turn off.'

'Headin for the scrub, us,' said Mrs McPhee.

Cedric had to wait for three trucks to go by before he could get the Cruiser back on the road. Then he had to worry about a truck tailgating him.

A hillock arrived, a mere incline. Cedric put his foot down, left the truck standing. He felt relieved and more than a little smug.

Mrs McPhee punched the radio, fiddled with the controls. Classical music filled the vehicle—Beethoven.

'Happy with this?' she said.

'I'm very happy,' said Cedric, thinking of home. He listened to classical music on the BBC every night, tucked up in his bed with a book and a mug of hot milk and honey.

'Ollie?'

'Me?' said Oliver. 'Don't have to ask me.'

'All in here together.'

'Then I'm happier than I can say.'

With Beethoven and Brahms, Schubert and Mozart, Mahler and Chopin, they drove through the day and into the encircling gloom. They passed through towns that grew smaller and more desperate— one street, a pub, a few pinch-faced people, an old dog or two. When, in the last light, they stopped at a settlement that was just a garage flanked by two sagging houses, Mrs McPhee had to knock on the garage's dirty glass door, go around the back. She returned with a man in a dressing-gown who unlocked a pump and filled the Cruiser without saying a word.

At 7pm, Mrs McPhee ordered a stop and produced cheese and tomato sandwiches and three bottles of Victoria Bitter.

'Kind of you,' said Oliver. He had a snowline across his forehead where his hat sat.

'Extra sanger never goes wasted,' said Mrs McPhee. 'Dry around here.'

'Not godzone, no,' said Oliver.

'Bin this way before?' said Mrs McPhee.

'Not that I can remember. But there's lots I don't remember.'

'Why's that?'

'There was the drink,' said Oliver. 'And the drugs.'

Mrs McPhee gave him a look and a few nods.

They set off again. Oliver went to sleep, his head on his canvas roll. Mrs McPhee gave directions, reading a map on her lap by a dashboard light. As they approached a crossroads just beyond a dark farmhouse, she said, 'Stop.'

Cedric pulled over. Oliver sat up instantly, wide awake.

'Turnin off here,' said Mrs McPhee to Oliver. 'Not much chance of lifts after this.'

'Don't need lifts,' said Oliver. 'I like a walk.'

'Left,' said Mrs McPhee to Cedric. 'There's Turnback Creek, be a coupla shacks, and then, far as I kin work it out, it's first right after that. Sign should say Home Rule Road.'

'Home Rule?'

'Ireland,' said Mrs McPhee. 'You Poms bin oppressin the poor bloody Irish for centuries. Of Scottish descent myself.'

Cedric thought himself innocent of oppressing the Irish but made no comment, drove. He seemed to have sand in his eye sockets, the skin on his face felt tight, he had a headache, his shoulders and his forearms ached, and a dull pain in his right ankle was moving up the calf.

It took another forty-five minutes and the clock on the dashboard said 11.47pm when they passed through Turnback Creek. There was no discernible creek but more than a couple of shacks. A dozen or so shops and a pub stood dark.

Five kilometres out of town, a sign said Home Rule Ro. The end of the sign appeared to have been shot off. After four dead-straight kilometres, the Cruiser's headlights lit up tree-trunk gateposts at least three metres high. A rusted arch of welded steel bridged them. Cedric could make out the remains of letters—an initial O, the top of a P, the bottom of a U, a D, most of an N and the middle of an S.

'What's the place called?' said Mrs McPhee.

'Orpheus Downs,' said Cedric.

'We're here.'

Cedric jolted over a cattle grid and drove down a long rutted avenue of gum trees. It curved and the headlights passed over tin sheds of all sizes and then revealed a huge ramshackle house with a deep verandah. He stopped on the packed-dirt forecourt.

'Someone livin here,' said Mrs McPhee. 'The lawyer say that?'

'No,' said Cedric. 'How do you know?'

'I kin feel it. Hoot.'

Cedric hooted, a surprisingly feeble sound. Nothing happened.

'Reverse a bit, switch off the lights, keep the engine runnin.'

Cedric backed up five or six metres, cut the headlights. The world went black. They sat in silence, the diesel thumping. Then Mrs McPhee reached up.

'Look over the right,' she said.

Cedric looked into the darkness. Mrs McPhee clicked something.

Pure white light violated the inside of a tin shed. For an instant, Cedric saw something.

A face. Pale as a lily.

They got out, the spotlight on the shed entrance. Oliver leaned against the Cruiser, yawned. Mrs McPhee came around the front of the vehicle and advanced towards the shed, a small and slightly bandy-legged figure.

'Come out, dear!' she shouted. 'Nothin to be scared of.'

They waited. Cedric became aware of a cold wind pushing his hair. It smelled of something. He sniffed and the connection came: his old gardening jumper, never washed and holding in its fibres the smell of every autumn bonfire until the practice became frowned upon.

'Come on then!' shouted Mrs McPhee. 'Don't muck about, girl.'

The face appeared at the left of the opening, an anoraked woman with dark hair pulled back, squinting against the glare. 'Whaddaya want?' she shouted.

Mrs McPhee looked over her shoulder at Cedric. 'Tell her who you are,' she said.

'Who am I?' said Cedric.

'You're the owner of this property.'

'Yes. I am. In a sense. I will be. All things being…yes. I am.'

'Come over here and tell her,' said Mrs McPhee.

Cedric advanced into the light, eyes on the woman. She looked frail, unwell. 'I am the, ah, owner of this property,' he said. 'Since my uncle's death. I am the owner.'

'Who's your uncle?' said the woman.

'Cyril Marchant. He owned this.'

'Sailor?'

'I beg your pardon?'

'The old bloke. Sailor.'

'Well, he was a sailor once.'

The woman turned her head, offered her hands. 'Come, it's okay.'

Two children in pyjama-like clothing appeared, different heights, both long-haired. They took her hands.

'Why you hidin?' said Mrs McPhee.

The woman looked away, her hair flicked. 'Bit nervy,' she said. 'Just me and the kids here.'

'What's your name?'

'Erin Donelly.'

'Doin what here?'

'Livin here.'

Mrs McPhee turned to Cedric. 'Squatters on yer land,' she said.

Cedric looked at the threesome, motionless in the icy light: a tall adult and two small ginger-headed children, all blinking, standing stiffly.

'I'd love a cup of tea,' he said, tired beyond endurance. 'Perhaps we could sort this out in the morning?'

'How many bedrooms in there?' said Mrs McPhee to the woman.

'Heaps. Like five, six, I dunno.'

Mrs McPhee put back her head, tilted it in an inquiring way.

'Dogs?' she said.

'Yeah.'

'How come they're quiet?'

'Boy can keep em quiet.'

'Let em go.'

'Big one'll rip your heart out.'

'Let em go,' said Mrs McPhee.

'Ben,' said the woman.

A slight figure appeared at the right of the doorway, curly hair on his shoulders. He held three dogs on leashes, straining but silent. The one in the middle was table-high, head like a petrol can. The others could pass beneath it without touching.

The big dog showed its canines: boar tusks.

Cedric said, 'They don't look friendly, I think.'

'Just dogs,' said Mrs McPhee. 'Let em go, son.'

The boy bent, unclipped the big dog. It came at them, all open mouth and gleaming hog teeth.

Cedric was returning to the Cruiser at maximum speed when he heard Mrs McPhee say, 'Good dog, SIT!'

He did not look until he had almost reached the Cruiser. Then, shamed by the way Oliver was leaning against the bonnet and smoking a cigarette, he stopped and turned.

Mrs McPhee was standing over the big dog. It was seated and trying to lick her hand. The smaller dogs had also arrived and were dancing around trying to get her attention. She turned her head.

'Pull it up next to the house, Ceddy,' she said. 'Let's get the swags out and have a cup of tea and a bikkie.'

Cedric dreamt he had fallen into a giant bin and was being buried alive in old clothes that smelled overpoweringly of camphor. He awoke in sweat and panic.

He was on his back, sunk in a mattress, impressed in it.

A shaft of sunlight from an uncurtained window went to a wall a good five metres away, to the base of a bookshelf whose upper reaches were in darkness.

He fought his way out of the mattress's clutches and put feet on the floor. No feeling in his feet. Oh God, some antipodean virus. He looked down. Shoes. He was wearing his good leather shoes, the once-bright toecaps now dull and a little scuffed.

He had been too scared to go to sleep with bare feet. He had sat on the edge of the bed and thought about the possibility of an emergency in the night, something that could call for quick action. Indeed, flight.

Cedric felt shame. He had slept with his shoes on, afraid to be caught bare of foot.

'The foot,' said Mr Plowright one morning in the common room, pitilessly observing the gym mistress hopping into the room with a foot in plaster. 'Most neglected body part, the foot.'

'Usually found in matched pairs,' said Mr Carstairs, the science teacher, not raising his eyes from a paperback with a gold swastika embossed on the cover.

'Ignored until it's too late,' said Mr Plowright.

'Not by the Chinese though, I'll be bound,' said Mr Carstairs and laughed, sniggered, really.

But for the violence of the pigeons on the roof, there was a silence so deep that when Plowright ran an index finger across his brutally disciplined moustache, Cedric could hear the knife-sharpening sound.

'How silly a wordplay, Carstairs,' said Plowright. 'You epitomise British society. Under-educated and insular. A dim light in a small room.'

'A dim light should be enough for a small room, shouldn't it?' said Carstairs.

'So proving my point *ad unguem*,' said Plowright.

Keeping his shod feet on the floor, Cedric lay back on the mattress. It claimed him like quicksand, but now in a comforting way. He studied the ceiling. It was a shade of pink, with dark patches where bits of plaster had fallen off. He saw a woman's face, just an eye and a nostril and a fall of hair. And breasts, not the same size. Big breasts.

He felt removed from the world. He was certainly removed from the world of the Gollop School and the cottage in Lower Roebuck. Not insular he, not any longer.

What did *ad unguem* mean? Was he under-educated too? Well, he'd tried to be educated. He was probably the most educated Marchant of his line. But what did *educated* actually mean? Knowing about China? About the postmodern English novel? Latin? How much did you have to know before you were sure you were educated?

Dogs barking, on the verandah. He turned his head and dimly saw the big animal looking at him through the windowpane its breath was fogging.

In the sitting room, by the light of a gas lamp, Mrs McPhee had interrogated the pale woman. Erin's smaller children pressed themselves to her like leeches, the boy ignored the proceedings, sat on a cracked leather sofa and tried to pick out a tune on a guitar with two missing strings. Oliver had taken his tea outside.

'How'd you get here, Erin?' said Mrs McPhee.

'Came with these blokes. Vern and Starrey. And this girl. Donna. Yeah.'

'Came from where?'

'Met em in Sydney. Met Vern and he said there's this place we can stay, be a good place for the kids. In the country like. So we came here. Didn't know it was gonna be this. Back of buggery. Yeah.'

'How long ago?'

'Four months. Near that. Yes. Kids should be in school.'

'And where are these blokes now?'

'Took off. About a month ago. Goin on. Just got up one mornin and Vern, he said, goin to town, see ya later. They done that before but they came back in a week or so. Yeah.'

'That's enough yeah,' said Mrs McPhee. 'And the girl?'

'Went off with em the first time, she never came back. Didn't miss her, I can tell you.'

'No one here when you arrived?'

'No,' said Erin. 'Vern said Sailor didn't mind people stayin here. Generous old bloke. Yeah. Sorry.'

Mrs McPhee got up and prowled around the room, stretching her arms above her head, fingers interlocked. 'So,' she said. 'These little ones, they got a dad?'

The boy stopped picking at the guitar.

'No,' said Erin. 'He drowned. Fishin. This Christmas four years.' She was about to say yeah when she caught herself.

Silence.

'Livin off soup and baked beans here the last two weeks,' said Erin. 'There's like twenty boxes of soup packets. Just mushroom and tomato.'

'Town's not far,' said Mrs McPhee.

Erin wouldn't look at her. 'Got no money,' she said.

'What about the pension? Bein a single mum.'

'Don't want the pension.'

Cedric had not been able to keep his head up or his eyes open. 'I think I might toddle off to bed,' he said. 'Find somewhere to toddle off to.'

'Give us a tour, Erin,' said Mrs McPhee. 'Got any candles?'

'Lookin to have a hot shower?' said Mrs McPhee. 'Somethin wrong with the boiler. Doesn't get water from the tank. I kin tell you nothin much works in this place.'

Cedric looked into the bathroom. He could see a yellowish cast-iron bath and, above it, a shower rose the size of a dustbin lid. There was a loud noise from the roof, then a series of clangs.

'Ollie's up there,' said Mrs McPhee.

'Does he know much about plumbing?'

'We'll see. No knowing what he knows.' She went into the room and turned on a shower tap. Nothing happened.

A faint keening sound grew, accompanied by serious hammering in the pipes.

'Ah,' said Mrs McPhee.

Water descended from the shower like a small rust cloud bursting.

'Could know somethin about plumbing, Ollie,' said Mrs McPhee. She closed the tap. 'Get out there and fire up the boiler.'

Cedric obeyed. He found the boiler in a room off the verandah. It was a massive riveted thing that could supply a hotel. He could hear water running into it. Firewood was stacked against a wall. He got to work balling copies of the *Inland Guardian* from a pile in a cardboard box.

'What you doing?'

It was the boy, Ben, tentative.

'Making a fire,' said Cedric. The date on the second paper was May 12, 1997. Did hot water stop around then?

'Why?'

'So that we can have a hot shower. Should we wish to do so.' He opened the boiler door. The ash inside was at least a foot deep. He took a piece of wood and poked around until he could see the grate. He put paper on top of it. 'Pass me some of those twigs,' he said.

'What's twigs?'

'The small branches.'

Ben handed him kindling. 'Mum hots water on the barbie,' he said. 'Have to wash with a rag.'

'This will be an improvement,' said Cedric. 'See any matches?'

The boy found a box with three matches in it.

'Very small margin for error,' said Cedric. He opened the bottom door. 'Going to need all the oxygen we can get.'

'You talk a bit funny,' said the boy.

'Really? Here goes.'

The match snapped at the head. 'Situation perilous,' said Cedric.

The second match fizzled glumly, died. 'Now desperate.'

Match three flared. The paper and twigs ignited like rocket fuel. 'An inflammatory organ, the *Inland Guardian*,' said Cedric. 'Hand me some larger pieces.'

It took fifteen minutes to get a big enough fire going, the boy silently handing over wood. Cedric closed the door and stood and became aware that Oliver was leaning against the doorpost, adjustable wrench in hand. Leaning seemed to be his natural stance, he could probably lean without support.

'Good work on the plumbing,' said Cedric. 'Excellent work.'

'Losing my head for heights,' said Oliver. 'Inner-ear thing.'

'I thought that was balance.'

'That's right,' said Oliver. 'What's your name, boy?'

The boy looked down. Cedric thought he saw a shiver in him. 'Ben.'

'How old?'

'Ten.' He didn't look up.

'Man of the family?'

Silence. 'Dunno.'

'Dad not with you?'

'He's dead. He drowned.'

'Sorry to hear that. Lost my dad when I was your age, bit older.'

'Did he drown?'

'No, he shot himself. Well, shower time. Got the boiler in the shearers' quarters going. Christ knows when that last happened.'

Oliver left.

'You might want to tell your mother there is now water that is hot,' said Cedric. 'Hot and running.'

'Mum's pretty scared,' said Ben.

Scared was a terrible word, a child should not speak it. 'Why's that?' he said.

'We got nowhere to go.'

Cedric thought about this. These people had no right to be on his land. They had no right to be on the place when it was his uncle's. It was like coming home from France and finding a family inhabiting his house in Lower Roebuck.

'Tell her not to worry,' he said. 'You can stay here if you like.'

2010

VALENTINE'S DAY

VALENTINE'S DAY tells a charming and improbable story about an itinerant musician who is the namesake of an AFL star and ends up being dragooned into coaching the local football team when he is arrested for assaulting a police officer. The screenplay was commissioned by December Media, and was eventually adapted for television by the ABC, directed by Peter Duncan, starring Rhys Muldoon as Ben Valentine and Roy Billing as Kevin Flynn. As much as anything Peter Temple ever wrote, *Valentine's Day* reveals his fascination with the patterns and rhythms of Australian speech.

EXT. BEN'S TRANSIT VAN. LATE AFTERNOON

OUT OF BLACK

TITLES THROUGHOUT

Silhouette from the rear of a clapped out Ford Transit van. Ben Valentine is drink-driving and listening to a country and western radio-station. An old Fender twin-reverb and a stack of patched-up guitar cases loll around in the rear. He pulls over for a hitchhiker and meets Jimmy Kennedy. There is little talk.

TITLES CONTINUE

A flashing red and blue glow looms from around the next bend. Ben pulls over and Jimmy prudently takes the wheel.

TITLES CONTINUE

EXT. LEVEL CROSSING. NIGHT

The transit van approaches the scene of a level crossing accident. There is no urgency as a body is wheeled to the back of the ambulance. The van is waved through, we finish on a sign saying 'Welcome to Cardigan, Population 4500, Tidy Town 1968'. We pass the wreck of a delivery van with DICK'S FAMOUS PIES painted on the side.

EXT. MAIN STREET. NIGHT

Ben comes out of a public toilet on the edge of a park, staggers, collects himself, looks around, sees a police car and two policemen and Jimmy at the open back door of the vehicle parked at the kerb. Jimmy's guitar cases and his bag are on the pavement.

JIMMY: That's it. That's my stuff. Rest's not mine.

SMALL COP: Take it out, sunshine.

Ben comes up.

BEN: What's this, what's going on here? My vehicle this.

The policemen look at him.

BIG COP: You drivin?

BEN: My friend here's driving. Sober as a judge.

BIG COP: Licence.

BEN: Why? What's the problem, constable?

BIG COP: Hearin me, dork? Licence.

BEN (*in measured drunken tone*): Constable, I hope you've heard the term harassment.

BIG COP: Heard the term arsehole. Got a licence?

JIMMY: The problem is I'm black and I'm in a vehicle.

BIG COP: Shut yer mouth or it's another fucken death in custody comin up. Turn round, boong. Face the vehicle. Put your hands on it.

BEN: Jesus, watch your language, constable. You're dealing with citizens here.

Ben puts out an arm to the vehicle to steady himself, misjudges, staggers forward. The policemen look at each other, look up and down the deserted street, approach Ben.

BIG COP: Listen, pisshead, yer mouth's too big. Get yer fucken licence out.

Ben looks at the cops, takes a decision, shrugs.

BEN: Okay. Okay. But you don't scare me personally, boys. Just respect for the uniform. You might be racist bastards but I'll respect the uniform.

BIG COP: That right? Not enough respect for the uniform, pisshead.

Big Cop clubs Ben on the head with the inside of a clenched fist. Ben reels backwards.

BIG COP: Have a go, pisshead. Show me how you do it, you fucken hero.

Ben shrugs.

BIG COP: Not such a hero, are you pisshead? All fucken mouth. Too scared to have a go, aren't you?

INT. MAGISTRATE'S COURT. DAY

We see the Big Cop. He now has a plaster covering his nose and a black eye. Ben, hungover, unshaven, bruised cheekbone, plaster on his chin, is escorted to the interview room. A rumpled man comes in and sits down opposite him, gives him his business card. He is Clem Adcock the duty solicitor. He reads the charge sheet.

CLEM: Ben Valentine of seventeen Hancock Street, Glebe, Sydney. Drunk and disorderly, resisting arrest, serious assault. (*he looks up*) They're looking for a jail term, Ben. You've got a prior for assault.

BEN: Jesus. Years ago. Anyway, I wasn't resisting arrest. The big one punched me. What are you supposed to do?

CLEM: That's Senior Constable Perry. He's got a broken nose and a black eye. Saying you want to plead not guilty?

BEN: You think I attacked two cops?

CLEM: Mate, it doesn't matter what I think. Plead not guilty, the case gets postponed, the cops'll oppose bail. Good chance you'll end up in Remand for six months.

BEN (*uncertain*): What if I plead guilty?

A woman's head pokes around the door.

WOMAN: Clem, the mago wants a word.

INT. MAGISTRATE'S COURT. DAY

The magistrate is Kevin Flynn, lifelong supporter of the Cardigan Football Club. He is seated behind an imposing desk. There is a knock on the door.

KEVIN: Come in.

Clem comes in, stands in front of the desk.

KEVIN: This won't take long. This assault client of yours. He the Ben Valentine played twenty-odd?

CLEM: Of what, your worship?

Kevin closes his eyes.

KEVIN: Football. Tigers. In the early nineties.

CLEM: Dunno.

KEVIN: Could you ask him?

CLEM: May I ask why, your worship?

Pause. Kevin swivels in his chair and looks out of the window.

KEVIN: Let me put it this way. If I were that Ben Valentine, I would want my solicitor to ensure that the magistrate knew.

Clem comes in and Ben turns around.

CLEM: Did you play football for, shit, I can't remember.

BEN (*uneasy*): Why?

CLEM: The mago wants to know. Don't ask me why. But if you're the Ben Valentine who played league football, I think it'll help.

Ben hesitates.

BEN: Yeah, Ben Valentine, that's me.

INT. COURTROOM. DAY

Clem is delivering a plea in mitigation of sentence.

CLEM: Finally, your worship, the defendant's prior conviction for assault. Unlucky to be charged at all over the incident, I think it can be fairly said. In any event, he has not reoffended in eight years and has a serious career as a musician and…

KEVIN: I get the picture, Mr Adcock.

CLEM: Yes, your worship. In the circumstance, your worship, I'm sure you'll find that a fine is an appropriate…

KEVIN: Thank you, Mr Adcock. I take an extremely dim view of attacks on the police and seriously considered a jail term. However, given that your client has saved the court the trouble of a trial, I will postpone recording a conviction and issue a community-service order of two hundred hours of work to be done within six months. I understand Mr Valentine has some knowledge of playing fields, so I direct that the service be at the discretion of the Cardigan Football Club. I believe it has a playing field. Mr Valentine, I suggest you put your back into any tasks you are given. If you don't, you and I will meet here again. Report to Mr Stump Woods at the Cardigan Oval at 5pm today. Now, most of us have a memorial service to go to, so this court is adjourned for the day.

EXT. COURTHOUSE. DAY

Ben and Clem are standing on the steps outside the court.

BEN: Cardigan Football Club? Community service? I've got to stay in this shithole? What've you got me into?

CLEM: Mate, you're lucky you're not in the slammer.

BEN: At least you're out of the rain. And they feed you.

CLEM: That's what you want, drive away. Then you'll be out of the rain. And fed. And humped by big blokes with tattoos on their pricks. Good luck, Mr Valentine.

Clem goes down the steps.

BEN: Thanks.

Clem stops and turns.

BEN: Thanks, mate.

Clem nods and continues on his way. Ben looks across the road and sees Jimmy leaning against the van. Ben crosses the road.

JIMMY: Bail?

Ben looks at him in silence for a moment.

BEN: Community service. Two hundred hours.

JIMMY: That's good. Thought you were gone.

BEN: Can I have my keys?'

Jimmy hands them over.

BEN: Get your stuff out.

JIMMY: Didn't just stand there.

BEN: Dunno what you did.

JIMMY: Comin to give you a hand, the little one pulls the gun on me.

Ben eyes him for a while.

BEN: Got a smoke?

Jimmy takes out a packet. They light up.

BEN (*softening*): Just as well. Touched a cop, you'd probably get life.

JIMMY: That's about three weeks for blokes my shade.

BEN: Phone around here?

Jimmy points to a callbox. Ben goes over, dials, waits, dials again, feeds the machine.

EXT. PHONEBOX. DAY

A funeral procession passes down Cardigan Main Street. Lights are on and the Cardigan Football Club colours are flying. Ben is on the phone.

BEN: Over? Over? Gina, is this me you're talking about? Me? Now that's not quite right…

The phone goes down. Ben looks up and down the small-town street.

BEN: What the fuck have I done to deserve this?

INT. DICK'S PIE FACTORY. DAY

Inside Dick's Famous Pies factory, Delvene and Cyn and other women in overalls are at work applying pastry Ds to the tops of pies. Cardigan players Wayne and Beak come in to collect pie trolleys.

DELVENE: Lovely bloke, old Clarrie. Pinch any bum, mind you, but a lovely man.

CYN: My dad says Clarrie only ever fired two people. A bloke wouldn't stop wearin a Lucan beanie, had three warnins. The other one put gravel in a batch of pies.

DELVENE: Yeah. And Clarrie wanted to give the gravel bloke another chance.

CYN: Bet it wouldna happened if we'd won last Satdee. Clarrie must've bin that depressed he didn't see the train.

DELVENE: Jesus, Cyn, bein hopeless's bad enough, now you want to make em into hopeless killers.

WAYNE: Mornin ladies, we're here today to recruit mattress testers. Any of you...

DELVENE: You two flabby dorks'd be better off testin pillows. And you'd know about lyin down. Satdee was an exhibition of lyin down like nobody's seen since that busload of whores came...

WAYNE: Please, ladies present. Some ladies present. Naturally, you won't have noticed that Cardigan's performance was greatly helped by a certain person's brother missin three sitters and developin a mysterious thigh injury now cured.

Mel appears in the doorway. She wears office clothes.

MEL: Gary's been dealt with, believe me. Who deals with you and Beak?

CYN: Hard side to follow, Cardigan.

BEAK: You don't follow Cardigan. That's like sayin yer family's a hard family to follow.

DELVENE: So? That'd be right for my family. Expect a bit more from my footy team.

BEAK: Well, why don't you come and bloody play for Cardigan. Show up at bloody trainin, you'll get a game. Dog comes twice, it gets a game.

WAYNE: Mind you, don't expect you're gonna be exempt from the squirrel grip.

The men find this remark amusing.

MEL: They'd be grippin and findin nothing there, wouldn't they? Much like when they grip you fellas. Find two raisins.

Beak calls from the window.

BEAK: Vultures gatherin.

They go to the windows. We see a man in a dark suit, Bruce Somerville, Dick's solicitor, walking towards the factory.

MEL: Been goin through the books for a week.

WAYNE: What's happenin?

MEL: Clarrie wanted to sell a bit of Dick's. Maybe it's still on. Who knows what Claire'll do.

CYN: Clarrie sell Dick's? Over his dead body.

WAYNE: Exactly.

MEL: Who wants a lift?

EXT. BEN'S TRANSIT VAN. DAY

Ben and Jimmy driving past Dick's Famous Pies.

BEN: How hard can it be to find a football field in a dump this size?

JIMMY: We're gettin there. They said it was past the pie factory.

BEN: I hate pies. How far's the city from here?

JIMMY: About two hundred kays.

Ben is silent, looks at the fuel gauge. The tank is three-quarters full.

JIMMY: Don't even think about it. You think those cops aren't prayin for you to try a runner? Believe it, baby, believe it.

EXT. DICK'S PIES. DAY

Mel, Delvene and Cyn are getting into Melanie's battered car. It has DREAM TEAM: DIE FOR CARDIGAN stickers on all windows.

DELVENE: What'll happen if they sell Dick's?

MEL: There's a South African company wants to buy it. God knows what'll happen then.

Silence in the car. They stop at a light. The delivery van of Papa Franco's Smallgoods pulls up beside them. The driver is Shane wearing a Papa Franco's baseball cap.

SHANE: Hey, girls, got special on Papa Shane's mega-salami. Enough for all three of youse. To choke on.

MEL: Jesus, Shane, you must've swapped organs with somebody. Who got the cocktail sausage?

DELVENE: Not called the smallgoods business for nothin.

SHANE: Your girl team shouldn't play when they got the rags. Why don't you go for a proper team? Lucan. Man's team.

MEL: I'll tell my brother. Might come round with some of the girls for a bit of kick to kick. With your head.

The lights change. Mel turns right.

CYN: Well nothin can happen to Dick's. Dick's is Cardigan. Bin goin for eighty-five years.

MEL: Cyn, big companies won't give a shit about eighty-five years or this town.

They drive in silence for a while.

DELVENE: I heard Papa Franco's is going to be layin off. This whole area's dead. No jobs anywhere.

CYN: Marg met this fat girl does phone sex. Earns heaps.

DELVENE: Before that I dance naked on the bar at the Great Western with a live tiger snake.

MEL: Thought you'd done that. What was his name again?

CYN: Love to dance. Always ads in the paper for exotic dancers.

DELVENE: They mention you have to have tits?

CYN: You bitch.

INT/EXT. DAWN'S HOUSE. DAY

Mel's stepmother's house. Mel pulls up; a ute belonging to Melanie's brother, Gary, is in the driveway. Mel goes in the front door and finds her hulking sibling drinking beer and watching a game show on television.

MEL: Christ, how can you watch that shit? What's this beer? You not trainin anymore?

Gary slumps further down in his chair.

GARY: Team's bloody hopeless, what's the point?

MEL: Don't pick your nose. Team's only hopeless cause of people like you.

GARY: I hear Clarrie'd owed the bank a shitload of money, Conway woman's goin to sell Dick's. That right?

MEL: Just get changed.

GARY: Dick's is rooted, Cardigan's rooted, whole town's rooted. What's the point?

MEL: The point's tryin to win some games so that we don't have to merge with mongrels we hate. THAT'S THE FUCKING POINT!

Their stepmother appears in the doorway. Dawn is a brassy redheaded woman in her mid-forties. She has a wine glass in her hand and she is slightly the worse for drink.

DAWN: Christ, you're a bloody nag, Melanie. Boy's entitled to a bit of unwind.

Mel ignores her.

MEL: You goin? Late now. Missed three sitters, you're a disgrace.

GARY: Don't feel like trainin today, okay?

MEL: Feel? No. It's not about feel. It's about puttin in for the people who love this team. It's not your feel. Get goin, yer bloody lump.

DAWN: Melanie, leave him alone. Bloody bossy.

MEL (*ignoring Dawn*): Get your gear, fat boy.

Gary groans, gets up.

GARY: Shit. They should make you coach. I hate you.

EXT. CARDIGAN OVAL. DAY

Ben gets out of the van at the Cardigan Oval, a ground ringed by trees. Half-a-dozen players are kicking balls about without much enthusiasm. Stump Woods and Donkey Donchi, a wizened man the size of a jockey, are watching.

BEN: Stump Woods?

Stump nods.

BEN: Ben Valentine. They tell you? The court?

STUMP: Kev give me a buzz, yeah.

BEN: Kev?

STUMP: The mago. Kev Flynn. Played for the club. Best and fairest three years in a row, seventy to seventy-two.

BEN: Right. So he picked this gig at random.

STUMP: This's Donkey Donchi, trainer.

Ben shakes hands with Donkey.

DONKEY: Saw you in the Grand Final.

Ben doesn't respond.

BEN: You want me to mow the grass, what?

STUMP: Mow?

Stump and Donkey laugh.

BEN: What?

Stump and Donkey look at each other.

STUMP: Donkey'll find gear for you.

BEN: Gear? What gear do I need?

The two men laugh again.

STUMP: Just the usual.

BEN: For what?

It dawns on Stump. He takes on a wary look.

STUMP: Captain-coach? For the season?

Ben is at the crossroads. He runs a hand through his hair, finds a cigarette, lights it with a plastic lighter. He walks away, watches the players kicking to each other, shakes his head, comes back.

BEN: Big misunderstanding here, boys. Your Kev, he's put the wrong foot in the stirrup. I haven't put on a boot for years, couldn't coach under-twelves. Also I'm generally on the piss, most days.

DONKEY: Look reasonable. No gut.

BEN: That's cause I don't eat. I'm puffed just talkin to you. Talkin puffs me. You want to ring your Kev, explain this? Tell him I'm good with a mower. Precision ride-on man. I'll give him his fucking two hundred hours. In the saddle.

The men look at each other again.

STUMP: You could give it a try. Just a try.

BEN: No. I couldn't.

STUMP: We'd be grateful. Blokes'd listen to you. This club's bloody near a hundred and twenty years old and if we don't win four of the last six, they're closin us down, stickin us in with another club. Lucan. Hate the bastards.

BEN: No. Can't be done. What happened to your coach?

DONKEY: Spat the dummy. Useless mongrel, anyway. Just come for the dough. Three useless mongrels last few seasons.

BEN: You don't want to make it four. Ring Kev. Tell him I'll mow. Mow and weed. Paint. I can learn to paint. That stand could use some paint. That's my limit.

Stump goes off.

BEN: This is everyone?

DONKEY: Don't get more than a dozen at trainin these days.

Jimmy, who has been hovering, comes over.

BEN: Donkey, Jimmy Kennedy.

DONKEY: Kennedy bloke had a few games for the Tigers. Country bloke, from WA, coulda bin a star. You know him?

Jimmy is watching the players.

JIMMY: Some relative.

Stump comes back with a mobile phone.

STUMP: Kev wants a word.

Ben takes the phone.

BEN: Yes?

KEVIN (*V/O*): Mr Valentine. I accept that it would be unfair for the Cardigan Football Club to expect you to play. But if it wants you to coach the seniors, that's what you do. If the club wants you to ride a pig naked around the field at halftime, that's what you do. Clear on that? Otherwise, I can resentence you tomorrow morning. You'll be behind bars before lunch.

BEN: Can I choose?

KEVIN (*V/O*): Choose what?

BEN: Between coaching and the pig thing.

KEVIN (*V/O*) (*pause*): Hah, hah. Put Stump on.

Stump exchanges a few words with Kev, puts the mobile away.

STUMP: You'll need somewhere to stay, earn a quid or two. Know anythin about oddjobbin?

BEN: Use my hands? No, can't risk my hands. I'm an artist.

STUMP (*not listening*): Don't spose it matters. Mouse knew buggerall about anythin.

BEN: Mouse?

STUMP: Bloke used to work for Clarrie Conway. Lived in the cottage. Christ knows what he did, place's a jungle. Clarrie asked me to get a replacement. Wanna have a go?

BEN: I know as buggerall about anything as the next man. Sure. Why not?

INT. BUTCHER'S SHOP. DAY

Stump Woods is behind the counter, trimming a piece of meat. Two elderly women, Muriel and Jessie, come in.

STUMP: G'day, ladies.

JESSIE: Movin ceremony for Clarrie, Stump.

MURIEL: Hear you're the new president.

STUMP: Not a lot of competition for the job, Muriel.

MURIEL: And what's this about a new coach?

STUMP: Bloke called Ben Valentine. Played for the Tigers.

JESSIE: Reckon he can turn it around?

STUMP: Time'll tell, ladies, but there's a bitta hope there now. What about some lamb chops, grow hair on yer chests.

JESSIE: Only six games left. Four outta six's a big ask.

MURIEL: We'll just pray, dear. Can't bear to think of us goin in with Lucan. My Laurie'll be spinnin at the thought.

JESSIE: About Dick's? You heard?

STUMP: Yeah. Dunno how much there's innit.

JESSIE: Can't believe the girl'd sell Dick's. Dick's without a Conway?

MURIEL: Somethin else to pray about. Day's not long enough for all the prayin you need.

STUMP: Put on a night shift, love.

INT/EXT. CLAIRE'S HOUSE. DAY

Ben, bag and guitar in hand, standing at imposing gates. The driveway is flanked by a dank, overgrown garden. He walks down the drive, feels eyes on him. Claire Conway is on the balcony.

BEN: The football club sent me. I'm replacing Mouse.

CLAIRE: Good day.

BEN: My name's Ben. Ben Valentine.

CLAIRE: I'm Claire Conway. The cottage is at the end of the drive. Next to the garage.

Ben keeps going, finds the overgrown but tidy cottage, puts his luggage down and sinks into an armchair. He sits in the gloom, smoking. After a while, he goes outside, looks up and sees Rick, a gangling boy of about twelve, on the balcony. Rick withdraws from sight.

INT. PUB. DAY

Ben is sitting at the bar of a near-empty pub. Stump is behind the counter with a beer. Late afternoon.

STUMP: Two games in three seasons we won. One of em, the other lot had the runs from this prawn barbie the night before. Blokes chargin off the field, never seen anythin like it. I said, don't cry to me, blame Paul bloody Hogan, stuck to good red meat, you'd a thrashed us.

Stump has a long, reflective drink.

STUMP: Anyway, this season the league says, you're not a viable club in this competition, win four minimum or you're Lucan–Cardigan.

Stump drinks beer.

STUMP: Be plain bloody Lucan no bloody hyphen Cardigan inside a season. Six games to go, closest we come to winnin is seven kicks behind. Didn't look like we had Buckley's.

Stump fixes Ben with a fierce stare.

STUMP: Till now. Bloke like you…

A long silence. Stump stares at Ben.

BEN: Don't look at me like that. I'm not the man for the job. I'm here because I don't want to be in jail. Told you, your Kevin's made a big mistake.

Max Cottee and Sid Hanley come through the door.

STUMP: Boys, meet the new coach, Ben Valentine, played for the Tigers. Needs no introduction. Ben, Max Cottee, Sid Hanley.

Ben shakes hands.

MAX COTTEE: Now yer bloody cookin with gas, Stump. Haven't had a decent coach since Wally Pigeon.

STUMP: Only half-way decent, Wally.

Max leans across to Ben, conspiratorially.

MAX: Sorted out that cop Perry. Goodonya. Arrogant bastard. Like sortin out Dermie, was it? Gotta video of you and Dermie. Titanic bloody battle. Titanic. You'd think about that one a fair bit, woodnya?

BEN: Never. Never give it a thought.

The men have a good laugh.

SID: Ya bin coachin where, Ben?

BEN: Nowhere. I'm not a coach. I'm a musician. (*ruefully*) I was a musician.

The men exchange glances, nod.

MAX: Well, a man's got to have a career after footy. Yes. Now, what the team needs, Ben, is…

SID: A game plan. Bobby Cringle wouldna known a game plan came up and bit him in the arse. Who hired him anyway?

STUMP: Same committee bought this pub. Gonna make us a fortune, this pub. Look at it. Like a millstone around our necks. Well, I'm off. Where's Linda?

MAX: Now, Ben, about the team…

INT. PUB. NIGHT

The pub clock shows 8.50pm. The pub is empty except for Ben, at the bar, Linda, the manager, nodding over a paperback (*Shooting Star* by Peter Temple), and two youths, playing pool. Jimmy comes in, nods at Ben, inspects the place. He finds a drum set and three guitars and amplifiers behind the curtains on a small stage in the lounge.

JIMMY: Whose stuff's this?

POOL PLAYER: Fucken awful band. Got eighteen months.

SECOND POOL PLAYER: Nice little crop though. Milford, over there from the footy field.

POOL PLAYER: In a tunnel with the vegies. Irrigation and all. Bastard neighbour dobbed em.

LINDA (*to Ben*): Friend of yours?

BEN: Very good friend. Why?

LINDA: Nothing. That stuff belongs to the pub. Careful.

JIMMY: Treat it like a Stradivarius.

Jimmy switches on an amp, plugs in and tunes a guitar and starts playing. Ben listens, looks away. He doesn't want to join in but he's had a few drinks and can't resist. He goes over and plugs in, tunes the guitar, plays rhythm to Jimmy's lead. Mel, Cyn and Delvene come in. Ben breaks off.

DELVENE: Play some more.

Ben shrugs. They go back to the song.

BEN (*singing*): Yesterday is dead and gone…

The trio come closer, look at one another.

Between the five of them, in the near-empty pub, they produce a rough but powerful version of a classic. The pool players lean on their cues, transfixed. When it's over, they clap. The atmosphere is shattered by the entrance of Gary, Mel's large brother, visibly drunk, with two other young men, only slightly less so.

GARY: Where's a fucken barman? I'll be a fucken barman.

Gary climbs onto the bar counter. Linda, who has been checking a fridge, stands up.

LINDA: Hey, hey, take a seat, mate. Gedoff there.

GARY: Jeez, good view from here. Bundy, that's what I need. Double Bundy. Set em up.

Mel walks across, stands looking up at him.

MEL: Down.

Gary looks at her, hesitates.

MEL: Down.

Gary, shamefaced but surly, gets off the bar counter.

MEL: Arsehole. Playin tomorrow, pissed. Shouldn't be in the team. Arsehole.

GARY: In the team? Playin for fucken Cardigan. Right. Like there's blokes queueing up. One-legged fucken man comes to fucken trainin, he's playin for fucken Cardigan. One leg, one ball, one fucken eye...

On the stage, Jimmy is picking out a sad tune. Gary focuses on him, walks around Mel. Fat youth goes with him.

GARY: (*Southern accent*): Hey, boy, you must be from the South. Gissus some of that delta music.

Jimmy doesn't look at him, looks at Ben, goes on playing.

FAT YOUTH: Not from the Deep South. Where's yer fucken didgeriething, thing ya blow, suck. Suck it to us, man.

Jimmy stops, leans the guitar against the amplifier, switches off, turning his head to Ben.

JIMMY: You comin?

BEN: Yeah, coming.

Ben starts putting the equipment behind the curtain. Jimmy leaves the stage, walks around the two youths, heads for the door. Gary steps into his path.

GARY: Mate, mate, on yer fucken high horse now, listen, listen, got nothin against a fella knows his place...black fella, any fella...

Jimmy looks at him, contempt in the look.

JIMMY: Nothin against white trash knows where he should be.

GARY: Where's that?

JIMMY: For you, on your knees lickin my boots.

FAT YOUTH: Punch his fucken lights out, Gary.

Gary hesitates. Jimmy offers his jaw. Gary takes a swing at him. Jimmy ducks, the punch goes over his head and Gary ends up half-turned, facing his sister. Mel is quick and violent, pushes her brother in the chest, slaps him four times, hard slaps, smacks, forehand, backhand, two from each hand. Gary staggers backwards, holding his face.

MEL: Hoon. Where'd you learn that fucken rubbish?

She turns on Gary's companions, fire in her eyes.

MEL: Get this idiot home, you let him drive, I'll kill you. You won't hide from me.

They back off, escort Gary out.

MEL: I'm sorry. He's not a bad bloke. It's just the drink.

JIMMY: Not your sorry. I can look after myself.

MEL: I wasn't savin you from him. Just wanted to hit him myself. And I said sorry cause he's my brother and you might think…

JIMMY: Think what?

MEL: Nothin.

EXT. CLAIRE'S HOUSE. DAY

Ben walking around the garden. It is choked by unchecked growth. The house is vanishing under creepers and roses. He finds the tool shed and hedge-clippers, gets to work letting daylight into his cottage. Then he stands, clippers in hand, looking down the overgrown driveway, thoughtful, clicking the shears. He looks up and sees Claire on the balcony.

BEN: G'day. Thought I might trim the edges of the drive.

CLAIRE: If you like.

She withdraws. Ben goes to work.

About half-a-dozen people in the big room. Ben is at the bar. Jimmy comes in with another young man, his cousin Luke.

jimmy: My cousin. Luke. Ben Valentine.

BEN: Luke.

They shake hands.

JIMMY: Haven't seen this bloke for years. Plays sax. Played in a band in Adelaide.

BEN: Got live bands over there? Thought it was all recorded. On vinyl.

LUKE: Have to know where to go, join the live music underground.

BEN: Under ground is right. Where musos go before other people.

Mel, Cyn, Delvene are at a table. Mel comes to the bar to order.

MEL: Hi. Not holdin my brother against me?

JIMMY: Against you? No.

MEL: Gonna play again tonight?

JIMMY: Ask Ben.

She introduces herself.

MEL: I'm Melanie Croker. Bit shy to meet a legend. Didn't know who you were the other night.

BEN: Legendary something.

MEL: Three vodka madonnas, please. Play again tonight?

BEN: Not me. The other night was a mistake.

JIMMY: C'mon, Ben. Won't hurt.

Ben hesitatingly asks Linda.

BEN: Mind if we play a bit?

LINDA: Go for yer life.

MEL: Can we sing?

BEN: Is that can or may?

Mel frowns.

BEN: You want my opinion or my permission?

Mel smiles.

MEL: I get it. Permission.

BEN: Sure you can sing.

Ben tunes up with Jimmy and Luke. He beckons the pie-factory trio and they feel their way into 'I Want to See the Bright Lights Tonight'. Ben plays with his back to the small audience, talking to the musicians with his eyes and head. Luke plays a mean sax. They improvise the first verse. It is hesitant but promising.

A hand taps Ben's shoulder. It is Barassi, a large woman with close-cropped ash-blond hair, drink taken.

BARASSI: Want someone on skins?

The men look at one another, cynical.

BEN: Played before?

MEL: Her dad played with Johnny O'Keefe for a bit, lots of rock bands. Taught her.

BEN (*introduces himself*): Ben Valentine.

BARASSI: Barassi. Barassi Smith.

They shake hands.

BEN: Don't mistake us for a band. People in a band have usually seen each other before.

Barassi, cigarette in her mouth, is no slouch, Jimmy turns out to have a powerful, earthy voice, and the pie-factory trio aren't bad either. There is some eye contact between Mel and Jimmy. Gary comes in alone and sits at the bar. He doesn't look too happy. They finish the number, then Ben takes off his guitar.

BEN: Coulda been worse. I'm off. Can't keep my eyes open. Must be the air around here. Too clean.

JIMMY: One more. C'mon.

BEN: Done bands. I'm an odd-job man now.

They watch him leave.

DELVENE: Thought he was just a footy player.

MEL: No such thing as just a footy player.

INT. BEN'S COTTAGE. NIGHT

Ben is slumped in a chair looking at the ceiling, drinking beer out of a stubby, smoking. Jimmy is on the sofa, playing an acoustic guitar.

JIMMY: Girls can sing, naturals. Drummer's not bad either.

Ben doesn't say anything.

JIMMY: Could be a band. What d'ya think?

BEN: Think I've had it with bands.

Jimmy picks out a tune.

JIMMY: Could be an OK band. Work on the sound. Take it to the city.

A long silence.

JIMMY: How'd you get into bands, anyway?

BEN: Didn't get into bands. Only way I could get into a band was start my own.

JIMMY: How many you started?

BEN: Dunno, too many. Time to do something else.

JIMMY: Like what?

BEN: Fruit picking's an option. Steady work. All you need's a basket. That or armed robbery.

JIMMY: Armed robbery's easier. But you need more gear. You need a gun and a basket.

Jimmy plays.

JIMMY: Band'd pass the time while you have to coach these dorks. Make a buck. Must be gigs around here.

BEN: Bands don't pass the time. Bands chew the time. Chew you. Spit you out. Had enough of that.

EXT. CARDIGAN OVAL. DAY

First training session. The players range from fifteen-year-olds to overweight balding veterans. Ben and Stump survey the ill-assorted group, including Gary, Wayne, Beak, Bean, Runt, Robber and Jodie. They look at Ben expectantly.

STUMP: Fellas, this's yer new coach, Ben Valentine, played footy with the best of em. Club's bloody lucky to have him.

Ben doesn't move to shake hands.

STUMP: Right, drills. Got drills you fancy, Ben?

BEN: Just do what you usually do.

The players look at one another.

WAYNE: That's it?

BEN: Expecting something else?

WAYNE: Thought you were the coach.

BEN: Work it out for yourself.

STUMP: Right, let's get on with it. Forwards, get some kickin practice in.

The players kick balls around without any enthusiasm. Ben goes for a walk, smoking.

Stump comes up to Ben.

STUMP: Reckon they were expectin a bit more. Biggest turnout this season.

BEN: What do I know about coaching?

STUMP: Coached by some of the best.

BEN: I'm a guitar player. Why don't you sack me? I can get on with mowing the grass, that sort of thing. Be of some use.

STUMP: Not here voluntary. Know that. Kin you find it in yer heart, Ben? Help us. Won't cost yer anythin.

Ben can't hold his gaze, looks away. On the field, Wayne Lance says to the players near him:

WAYNE: This bastard's useful as a spare arsehole.

EXT. CLAIRE'S HOUSE. DAY

Ben comes out of the tool shed carrying a stepladder. Rick is standing in the garden.

BEN: Hi, I'm Ben.

RICK: I'm Rick.

BEN: Do me a favour, Rick. Get the big clippers in there. On the bench.

Ben positions the ladder beside an overgrown archway. Rick arrives with the clippers.

BEN: Thanks. No school today? Wagging?

RICK: Don't go to school. My mum teaches me.

BEN: Yeah? Why's that?

RICK: Don't know.

Ben goes up the stepladder.

BEN: Hold on to this thing will you, mate? Promised myself I won't die outdoors.

INT. CLAIRE'S HOUSE. DAY

Bruce Somerville is seated in the huge sitting room of Claire Conway's house, a study in chintz. Claire is standing at the French window looking onto the garden. She can see Ben at work, Rick holding the stepladder.

BRUCE: Three hundred and twenty thousand dollars. Clarrie stood surety for a loan to your late husband. Do you, ah, know about that?

CLAIRE (*sighs*): No. But I'm not surprised. Clarrie bailed Richard out several times. Richard moved from dream to dream.

BRUCE: The estate's cash assets are minimal. Is there, ah, some way you could, personally, I mean…

CLAIRE: I don't have a cent. We've been totally dependent on Clarrie since my…since coming here.

BRUCE: Um. This house is in your name.

CLAIRE: Is it?

BRUCE: Yes. Clarrie transferred ownership to you a few months ago. Plus business premises he owned.

CLAIRE: He was such a kind man...

BRUCE: Yes. Well, that, ah, doesn't leave us with much in the way of choice. Selling is probably the, ah, the only option.

CLAIRE: I don't want to see the family business sold.

BRUCE: No, no you wouldn't. Been in the family for generations.

Silence.

BRUCE: Um, well, yes. Unfortunately, the estate has to pay Clarrie's debts. It can't do that without realising the assets. The valuer tells me the business isn't terribly profitable and there's, ah, the prospect of it losing value.

CLAIRE: Why's that?

BRUCE: Well, there's no management to speak of. None at all in fact. It's, um, sort of being run by a clerk at the moment. As we speak.

CLAIRE: A clerk?

BRUCE: Yes. Melanie Croker. Nice girl. But I'm not sure she's quite up to...

CLAIRE: Couldn't we get a manager?

BRUCE: I doubt that. No. Claire, the problem is the bank will apply to put Dick's into receivership if we don't give them a date when we'll pay the money. And the town depends on Dick's. Selling is probably the only way to save the workers' jobs. Plus ensuring that there's, ah, something left over for you and the boy.

Claire is watching Ben and Rick in the garden. Ben turns his head, their eyes meet. He looks away.

CLAIRE: There's no other way?

BRUCE: Believe me, I've, um, I've agonised over this.

Bruce gets up and comes over to the window, sees Ben.

BRUCE: I see you've got the forced labour.

CLAIRE: What?

BRUCE: Ben Valentine. Famous footballer. He's a legend. Got community service for assaulting two policemen. He's coaching the footy team. The magistrate's idea of justice.

Claire goes onto the balcony.

CLAIRE: Rick, get out of that jungle. Snakes and spiders, all sorts of dangerous things.

INT. PUB. NIGHT

Early evening at the pub. Ben enters to find the rest of the would-be band tuning up.

LUKE: C'mon, Ben.

BEN: Tired. Man who works in the outdoors.

In spite of himself, Ben goes over.

BEN: Arrange this, did you?

JIMMY: Never. They just arrived.

MEL: You were waiting for us.

JIMMY: All my life.

BEN (*succumbs*): Okay, let's do something simple, get warmed up.

Luke plays a few bars.

BEN: Doesn't get simpler. Know that song?

The trio sing the chorus.

BEN: Okay. Take it from here…

When they finish, Ben nods.

BEN: Not too bad.

BARASSI (*to Ben*): Got a gig for us, you want it. Me mum's weddin. Weddin number three.

LUKE: They have a band at number three? Thought they just played old Elvis tapes.

BARASSI: She's movin up this time. Marryin the clerk of the courts Satdee week.

CYN: Left it a bit late to hire a band.

BARASSI: Had a band, bastards got a better gig, cancelled today.

BEN: We're not a band. Three numbers doesn't make you a band.

BARASSI: Me mum says she don't care if we do the same number fifty times. They're that desperate.

Silence.

BARASSI: Whole club'll be there. They're doin out the hall in Cardigan colours.

BEN: That's persuasive.

MEL: Ben?

BEN: A thing I'm strongly against. Making a fool of yourself. Can't think why.

MEL: Last band in town only had three numbers. Couldn't count past three. Too wacked.

LUKE: Played in a band worse than this after a year on the road. Bit worse.

Luke looks at Barassi.

LUKE: Drummer was worse.

BARASSI: Very glad to hear that.

MEL: Please, Ben. Take a chance.

BEN: Same money as the other mob, right?

BARASSI: Plus twenty-five each. I told her, last-minute don't come cheap.

BEN: You can be the manager of this band.

INT. MEL'S CAR. NIGHT

Mel, Delvene and Cyn driving home.

DELVENE: Bit of a spunk, that Jimmy. What d'ya reckon, Mel?

MEL: Didn't notice. Concentratin on the music.

CYN: Could've sworn you was concentratin on him.

MEL: Could've sworn you were tryin to rub your tits against Ben Valentine. Your chest, anyway. Where your tits would be if you had any.

DELVENE (*lights a smoke*): Bitchy, are we? Now that's a sure sign, Cyn. What's happenin at work?

MEL: I think they're goin to sell.

DELVENE: So we'd just work for someone else.

MEL: So we'd could be out of a job in six months.

CYN: Could be in a famous band by then. We'd be like the Spice Girls.

DELVENE: Yeah. We could call ourselves the Vegie Girls. You'd be Potato Vegie.

CYN: You'd be…you'd be, you'd be Catty Vegie.

DELVENE: I rest my case, Your Honour.

MEL: Jesus, supportive. So what about me?

DELVENE: Spinach Vegie.

MEL: Cactus, they eat the cactus. You'd be Cactus Vegie. Full of pricks.

DELVENE: You will die for that.

INT. CLAIRE'S HOUSE. DAY

Claire and Rick are sitting at a table. Rick is doing arithmetic problems and Claire is reading something he has written, makes notes in the margin, correcting spelling and grammar. She stops and goes into a reverie, looking at nothing. Rick looks up.

RICK: Mum.

CLAIRE (*startled*): What?

RICK: Are you always going to be sad?

CLAIRE: I'm not sad. I was just thinking. About…about lunch. What we're having. For lunch. What would you like?

RICK: You used to laugh a lot.

CLAIRE: I still laugh at lot. I laugh. Don't I?

RICK: You never laugh. Why don't I go to school?

CLAIRE: School? Well, I didn't know how long we'd be here, so it seemed sensible.

RICK: We've been here for quite a long time. I liked school.

CLAIRE: Yes, well, we'll have to see. Work out what…our plans. Work out what we're going to do. We'll do that soon. Soon.

Claire gets up, comes around the table and kisses Rick's hair. She closes her eyes and we see the love and the sadness.

EXT. CARDIGAN OVAL. DAY

With Ben smoking on the sidelines, the players put a little extra into their kicking and marking and organise a few practice drills. Stump and Donkey sit in the stand.

EXT. CARDIGAN OVAL. DAY

Saturday, at home, Cardigan plays Kitchener. Stump, Max Cottee and Sid Hanley survey the crowd.

STUMP: Best turnout in years.

MAX: New coach, always brings em out.

Stump goes down to the dressing room. Donkey is massaging Wayne's calves, Ben is leaning against the wall outside the door. Stump hands Ben the coach's board showing the players' positions.

STUMP: Usual lineup.

Ben doesn't look at it.

STUMP: Thumped us last time, this lot. No bloody good but too bloody good for us.

Ben shrugs.

STUMP: You'll want a few serious words with the blokes.

Stump stands in the doorway, claps his hands for silence.

STUMP: Have a listen to the coach.

Silence, all eyes on Ben standing behind Stump.

BEN: Only a game. Not the end of the world. Sun'll come up tomorrow.

The players look at one another uneasily.

EXT. CARDIGAN OVAL. DAY

Ben, Stump and Donkey in front of the stand. Stump is looking down. Three-quarter-time siren goes. The scoreboard says CARDIGAN 26, VISITORS 60.

STUMP: Rooted again. Let's talk to em, Ben.

BEN: What's the point?

STUMP (*pleading*): Ben?

They go out to where the players are standing in a depressed huddle. Stump speaks to Ben out of the side of his mouth.

STUMP: Changes, Ben, changes. Got to do somethin.

Ben looks over to where the pie factory trio are standing. They are looking at him. He becomes aware that all the Cardigan supporters are looking at him.

BEN: You want to make changes, make them.

STUMP: Ben, can you just say somethin to em? Give em somethin.

The players become aware of Ben and Stump and all eyes turn to Ben. They wait expectantly. Ben looks at them in silence for a long moment, looks at the crowd, clears his throat.

BEN: Just do what you usually do at times like this.

Ben turns and walks away. Stump sighs, follows, head down, beaten. The players stand silent, humiliated. Wayne speaks.

WAYNE: Why don't he just piss on us?

The players look at one another.

BEAK: Superior bastard.

RUNT: Don't need no has-been to tell us what to do.

The players all look at him. There is a general straightening of shoulders, lifting of chins.

WAYNE: Yeah, right, bugger him. Let's show the smartarse. Bean, that dork ruckman. Jesus, you can do better than that.

BEAN: Yeah, well, the little bastard keeps comin up my arse.

RUNT: I'll fix him. The rest of you, show some bloody fight willya.

GARY: Damn right. Let's stick it up Mr Bloody Big Shot Footy Star Valentine.

PLAYERS: Yes!!!

The players go back onto the field. The opening exchange shows that this is not the Cardigan side that came off a three-quarter time looking at the grass. Three quick Cardigan goals follow.

In the stands.

MAX: Jesus, what's Valentine done to em?

SID: Some bloody slow-release horse drug.

MAX: Go on like this, can't be stopped winnin.

AT THE FINAL SIREN, THE SCOREBOARD SHOWS
CARDIGAN 66, VISITORS 60

The Cardigan supporters are behaving as if they have won a grand final: hugging, shouting, punching the air. The players are embracing, patting each other's bottoms, ruffling hair.

Ben and Stump walk between the playing field and the stand. The supporters stand to applaud them. The muddy Cardigan team raise their hands above their heads and clap Ben and Stump.

Down below, Stump punches Ben's arm.

STUMP: Half of me knew it, other half said, he don't bloody give a stuff. You smart bugger. You knew how to fire em up.

Wayne has an arm hooked around a teammate's head, the other in the air. He comes up to Ben.

WAYNE: Punched our buttons, didn't you. Bloody psychologist.

Ben walks the applauding gauntlet, looking straight ahead. As the crowd break into the club song, we see something in his eyes we have not seen before: fear.

MURIEL (*blinks back tears*): Lovely modest fella. Thank the Lord he's come. Into the valley of death rode the five hundred. Not a snowball's but a few blokes got there, got to the top, jumped right over the guns. Sheer bloody guts.

BEN: Triumphing over brains.

MAX (*to Stump*): Had a look at that video last night, game where Ben took on Dermie. Hadn't looked at it fer years. Funny how blokes change.

STUMP: I dunno. You haven't changed a bit since you gave away that free cost us the premiership in '54.

INT. BUTCHER'S SHOP. DAY

The shop is crowded, customers of all ages. Ben comes in the door. They give him a round of applause, part, usher him to the counter. Ben nods apprehensively.

STUMP: Reckon we can let this bloke jump the queue.

Chorus of approval.

STUMP: One down five to go, eh?

BEN (*hesitates*): Ah, piece of rump, please.

STUMP: Comin up, kilo of premium rump.

He wraps an extravagant quantity without weighing it.

STUMP: Plus a little somethin.

He wraps a large number of sausages.

STUMP: Woods' pork sausages. What every pig wants to be.

Stump hands over the package.

STUMP: Dollar fifty.

BEN: Dollar fifty?

STUMP: It's on special.

BEN: You could regret this.

STUMP: Never.

EXT. STREET. DAY

Ben parks. The camera goes to the poster outside the newsagent. It says:

NEW COACH

BRINGS

HOPE TO

CARDIGAN

We see the weight of the town's expectations sits uncomfortably on Ben's shoulders. He doesn't get out. Rests his head on the steering wheel.

EXT. COURTHOUSE. DAY

Clem Adcock, the duty solicitor, comes out of the court front door.

Ben is waiting on the steps.

CLEM: Mr Valentine. The mago's so pleased with your community service he's letting the deadset guilty walk free.

BEN: Listen, too late for me to change my plea?

CLEM: What?

BEN: Plead not guilty.

Clem eyes him.

CLEM: You're not in jail, mate, because you pleaded guilty. Hit a cop in front of another cop. I don't think you've grasped how lucky you are.

Clem walks away before Ben can say any more. Ben follows, catches up.

BEN: I only hit him after he hit me. I've got a witness.

CLEM: Is this so difficult to grasp? It's too late to change your plea. It was always too late to plead not guilty. The cops don't lose these cases. You got a really good deal. No jail and it'll all be over in a few months.

Ben looks away. It is clear he is resigned to his fate. He looks back at Clem.

BEN: Don't suppose you play the piano?

Ben watches him go, walks to the van. Jimmy is in the driver's seat. Ben gets in.

BEN: Seen any place rents videos?

INT. BUTCHER'S SHOP. DAY

Stump, behind the counter, gives Ben his pay packet.

STUMP: Mel drops it off. Saves ya goin around to Dick's.

BEN: What's my job exactly?

STUMP: Bein there. That's yer job basically.

BEN: Basically, that's not a job. Being somewhere.

STUMP: She's a bit funny. Clarrie liked havin someone there.

BEN: Meaning?

STUMP: Nothin.

BEN: A bit funny?

STUMP: Yeah.

BEN: What's a bit funny mean? Around here? Dangerously disturbed? Criminally insane?

Stump turns, wrapping meat, doesn't look up.

STUMP: Sorrowful. She's had a good bit of sorrow. The hubby and the boy.

BEN: What about them?

STUMP: They had a bit of a domestic, she told him to clear off, he took the boy. In England. They were livin in England. She's a Pom.

BEN: The boy? Rick?

STUMP: No. The first-born. Car ran off the road.

BEN: And?

STUMP: Killed, both of em.

BEN: That's reason for sorrow. Rick doesn't go to school.

STUMP: She's a bit fearful. Loss can take wimmin like that. You should show the boy the pictures.

BEN: What pictures?

STUMP: Club pictures. In the committee room. The teams. Conways in em back to buggery.

BEN: I don't think his mother would approve. Good sausages those.

INT. BEN'S HOUSE. DAY

Ben concentrates on a football video. Rick's head comes through the window.

RICK: Mum says you're a famous footballer.

BEN: Shouldn't you be doing your homework?

RICK: No. Did you play in games like that? In front of all those people?

BEN: I've played in front of crowds.

RICK: They had long hair then. Did you have long hair?

On the screen is a close-up of a player flat on the ground. The camera goes to a player jogging away, trying to look innocent.

BEN: It was the age of long. Long hair, long nights. You seen the football club photos, all your family in them?

RICK: No. Will you take me?

Claire appears behind Rick outside the window.

CLAIRE: Rick, stop bothering Mr Valentine.

RICK: I'm not bothering him. He's watching a footy video.

BEN: He's not bothering me.

CLAIRE: Go inside, Rick.

RICK: Why?

CLAIRE: Just do what I say.

RICK: Bye, Ben.

BEN: See you, Rick.

Rick goes down the path, looking back.

CLAIRE: Mr Valentine.

Ben comes to the window.

BEN: Mrs Conway.

CLAIRE: I hope you won't take this the wrong way but I don't think it's a good idea for Rick to hang around with a grown-up man.

BEN: You're absolutely right. Who's the man?

CLAIRE: This isn't a laughing matter.

BEN: No. I'll send him off every time he comes near me.

CLAIRE: Well, that's a bit…perhaps if you didn't encourage it.

BEN: I'm not encouraging it now.

CLAIRE: Yes. Fine. Please don't encourage it.

She turns and walks down the path.

BEN: Mrs Conway.

Claire turns.

BEN: I'm doing time in this town for assault, not child molesting.

EXT. CARDIGAN OVAL. DAY

A thin rain is falling. Ben and Stump go over to the team.

STUMP: Boys've come alive. Few words, Ben?

Ben lights a cigarette.

BEN: Winning on Saturday, what happened?

Long silence.

WAYNE: You know. Prove somethin.

BEN: What was that?

Another long silence.

WAYNE: Show we're not useless. Stick it up you.

There is a murmur of agreement.

BEN: So what'd you easybeats do right?

BEAK: Come out like mad men. Put em in shock. Six goals in ten minutes.

BEN: Lucky at the end. Clapped out. They'd have had you in another minute.

Wayne: Don't do much runnin after half-time. Well, quarter, mostly. Given up by then.

BEN: Got to change that. Five weeks to go. From now on, you run four days a week, Monday to Thursday. That's stamina. Friday is sprints. Sunday's a rest day. Go to church.

The players look at one another in disbelief.

BEAK: Bit late, innit? Get fit before the season, that's the idea.

BEN: I reckon you skipped that bit. Six-thirty tomorrow.

BEAK: Have me tea at six-thirty.

BEN: In the morning. Before breakfast.

GARY: Punchin cops don't make you a coach.

Ben looks at him for a long time. Gary moves his mouth uneasily.

BEN: Want to be coach? Say the word, the position's vacant.

STUMP: Shuddup, Gary.

GARY: How long's it?

BEN: What?

GARY: The run. In the mornin.

BEN: Around the lake. You all finish. Doesn't matter how long it takes.

GARY: Jesus. Seven kays. What about all day?

Some uneasy laughter. Ben lights a cigarette, takes his time

BEN: It's voluntary, running.

BEAK: So's playin for this club. So you'll be runnin? Coach?

Ben is drawing on his cigarette. His face shows that he never considered this. He takes the cigarette out of his mouth, looks at it, drops it and grinds it underfoot.

EXT. PATH BY LAKE. DAY

Rainy early morning beside the lake. Ben waits, looks at his watch. Finally, three of the younger players arrive in a hoon car, with Wayne close behind. No one says anything. The four do warm-up exercises. Ben follows suit.

WAYNE: Reckon that's all that's comin. Let's go.

They run together for a while. We see the pain on Ben's face as he flags, drops behind. Wayne lasts a lot longer, falls away. The three youngsters string out.

EXT. PATH BY LAKE. DAY

The three youngsters come in, spaced by twenty or thirty metres.

They stand panting, hands on hips. Wayne comes in, exhausted, leans against a boathouse, utterly spent. After a while, Ben runs/staggers into view, finishes. He is ashen-faced, goes behind a tree. We know he is being sick.

EXT. PATH BY LAKE. DAY

Misty morning. The same four arrive. They are about to set out when Beak and Robber show up. The same thing happens. Wayne keeps up a little longer than the newcomers. Ben is sick again.

INT. BEN'S HOUSE. NIGHT

Ben is lying on his bed reading a football coaching book. On the floor beside the bed are half-a-dozen books on football. He reaches for his cigarettes, looks at the packet, throws it across the room. He opens a window, sits down with his guitar and plays something haunting.

INT. CLAIRE'S HOUSE. NIGHT

Claire is at the sink, hears something, goes onto the balcony and listens to Ben playing. Rick comes out. She puts an arm around him and they both listen.

RICK: Like it?

CLAIRE: It's beautiful.

RICK: Why don't you play the piano anymore?

CLAIRE: I suppose I got out of the habit.

EXT. WOLSELEY OVAL. DAY

The final siren goes at a country field. The exhausted Cardigan players stand disconsolate, hands on hips, sniffing, sucking teeth. The scoreboard shows WOLSELEY 82, VISITORS 72.

Ben, Stump and Donkey are leaning against the WOODS QUALITY BUTCHERY: WOODS MEANS MEAT delivery van.

STUMP: By Jesus, bloody near done it. Hammered us by a hundred and twelve last time.

DONKEY: Coulda won that. Lost in the middle, this game.

STUMP: Lovely bloke, the Bean. Bit shy of the physical.

Ben walks across the field to the players, to Robber.

BEN: Four goals. What's it feel like?

ROBBER: Mate, that's four goals in a career. Can I stay up front?

Ben hesitates.

BEN: For life.

Ben surreptitiously turns the tactic board upside down.

EXT. CLAIRE'S. DAY

Ben is clipping a rampant box hedge. Rick's head appears.

RICK: Have you got brothers and sisters, Ben?

BEN: No. Your mum's worried about you talking to me. She tell you that?

RICK: She worries about me a lot. Where's your mum live?

BEN: Don't know. Lost touch.

RICK: Didn't you live with her?

BEN: Not for long. Lived in children's homes, with other people, lots of other people.

RICK: What about your dad?

BEN: Can't remember him. He died when I was little.

RICK: My dad died too. And my brother. In a car accident.

BEN: I heard that. I'm sorry.

RICK: Sometimes I can't remember them too well. I think Mum thinks about them a lot. All the time.

BEN: Yes. She would.

RICK: Will you take me to see the photos?

BEN: Ask your mum.

RICK: Can I do some of that?

Ben looks at him for a while, uncertain.

BEN: There's another pair of these in the shed. On the right, where the spades are.

INT. OFFICE. DAY

Bruce Somerville on the telephone, feet on desk, tie loose.

BRUCE: Run like a charity. Carrying more passengers than the Titanic, wages too high, suppliers paid top dollar, amazing generosity to creditors, money handed out to every cause that knocks on the door. Props up the whole district.

VOICE ON PHONE: So it's a better buy than it looks?

BRUCE: Major understatement. Market share's huge for a business in the back of buggery. Could be a top five brand, bigger maybe.

VOICE: And the valuation, they accept that?

BRUCE (*wryly*): I got an independent valuation.

INT. DICK'S PIE FACTORY. DAY

Mel is working at an early-model computer, consulting piles of invoices, making notes in a ledger. Runt comes in

RUNT: Runnin out of flour.

MEL: Deliverin today, this afternoon. What's the meat position?

RUNT: Dunno. Clarrie did all that.

MEL: Clarrie did everythin. Check for me will ya, Runt?

Beak arrives.

BEAK: No apple pies without apples.

The phone rings. Mel answers.

MEL: Dick's. Yes. Yes. No. I'll get it out today. Promise. Yes. Thanks. Bye. (*turns to Beak*) What've you got left?

BEAK: Two days, I spose. Shortenin's short too.

MEL: I'll get onto it now. What about the other fillings?

Beak shrugs.

MEL: Can you look and give me a list?

BEAK: Clarrie…

MEL: I know. Clarrie did all that. Well, Clarrie's not in this week. And they're not takin calls up there and I'm the accounts clerk.

BEAK: Okay, sorry. Do it now.

He leaves. There is a polite knock at the door and Bruce peers in.

BRUCE: Sorry to disturb. Thought you might like to know. We've had an offer from Consolidated Baked Goods. They've met the independent valuation.

MEL: Is that good?

BRUCE: Excellent. We had, ah, fears of…well, Dick's has got a future. We can sleep easy.

Mel nods and smiles but she doesn't radiate joy.

EXT. PATH BY LAKE. DAY

Early. The running group has grown large. They are about to set off when Gary's ute pulls up. He is getting out when Wayne shouts.

WAYNE: Comin to watch, Gary?

GARY: Shuddup.

Ben, Wayne, Beak, Robber, the Bean and the youngsters run as a group for longer before Gary flags. Ben is in pain but he keeps up longer. Wayne, Robber and Beak stay with the youngsters much further now.

INT. CHANGING SHED. DAY

Saturday. Another away game. Despondent players slumped on the benches, sitting on the floor of the small tin shed. Ben stands in the door, paper cup of water in his hand.

WAYNE: Sorry, coach.

BEN: Could've gone either way

GARY: No one defendin. On my lonesome, bloke's got a beard like fucken barb wire, other dork's trying to squirrel-grip me from behind.

ROBBER: Usin tweezers.

GARY: What? What's that?

BEAN: Loved the handballin to the other side. That was good. Beak was extra good.

BEAK: From the fucken saint never learnt how to kick a fucken football, fucken thing goes anywhere, left, right, fucken anywhere.

GARY: Play people where they should be, be a fucken start.

ROBBER (*undoing laces*): Jeez, Crocker, you're a whinger. Twice your age, the bloke. Fall in a fucken heap, that's your problem.

GARY (*stands*): Problem? From you? I'm gonna take that from you? Think your fucken age'll protect you, dickhead?

ROBBER (*at the ready*): Mate, mate, don't get me in court for hurtin a juvenile. Fat juvenile.

GARY: Hurt me? Old fart like you? You'n your whole fucken family couldn't hurt me.

ROBBER: Blubber. All mouth and blubber. Teenage fucken hopeless whale.

GARY: Fuck you, you little…

Ben steps behind Gary, pours the contents of his paper cup down Gary's back. Gary freezes. Wayne comes between Robber and Gary. The whole room is silent, electric with tension.

BEN (*quietly*): Listen, fellas, I'm just passing through but I thought we were trying to do somethin here. Not much. A little thing. Small thing. Save a club that's been going for more than a hundred years. Maybe we can do it, maybe we can't. One thing's for sure though. We can't do it unless we stand together. In good times and in bad times. That's called being a team. You do your best all the time. You do what's best for the team not yourself. You don't blame anyone. If we don't play the game like that, we're not a team. And if we're not a team, well, what are we? We're just a rabble. And we deserve to lose to real teams.

Long silence. Then Bean speaks.

BEAN: Scuse me?

Ben looks at him.

BEAN: What's a rabble?

Laughter, tension broken.

INT. DONKEY'S CAR. NIGHT

Ben, Stump and Donkey are driving home in the dusk, Donkey at the wheel, Stump beside him, Ben in the back.

STUMP: What you said, Ben, that was good. They heard that. Saw it in their eyes.

Ben says nothing.

STUMP: Competitive. That's what I'd say we were.

BEN: Competitive's not enough.

STUMP: Yeah. Come a long way quick, but three from four? Dunno.

Long silence.

DONKEY: There's bin miracles. Bin a bit of a miracle already, you ask me.

STUMP: Hear the news? Claire's sellin Dick's to pay the bloody bank. Bloody huge outfit, won't give a bugger about the town.

BEN: What is it with this place? I've fallen into some kind of zone of failure. (*reflective*) Maybe I've come home.

EXT. BEN'S VAN. DAY

Ben driving to training. In a school ground, he sees Jimmy and Luke playing one-on-one basketball. Nearby, two boys are kicking a football. Ben stops to watch. It is clear that Luke has a big leap and that Jimmy has terrific ball skills. One of the boys kicks the football towards them, a thumping misjudged kick. Luke marks it easily at a great height, and without pause or effort kicks the ball a good thirty metres onto the chest of one of the boys. The boy kicks it back. Luke and Jimmy grapple, Luke gets in front, Jimmy takes a one-handed mark around Luke's body, kicks the ball back left-footed, a high, singing kick. The kick-to-kick goes on long enough to show that both Jimmy and Luke are skilled footballers. They see Ben, come over to the van.

LUKE: Pervin on us?

BEN: Where'd you learn to play footy?

LUKE: Don't learn. Footy's like breathin. This fella…

Luke slaps Jimmy's head.

LUKE: …coulda bin bigtime. Good as his brother.

BEN: Your brother?

JIMMY: Played a bit. Bout your time. Pub tonight?

Ben looks at them appraisingly.

EXT. CARDIGAN OVAL. DAY

Practice is over. Ben and Stump are leaning on the fence.

STUMP: They turnin out in the mornin?

BEN: Some.

STUMP: Wayne and Beak've dropped some blubber. Robber's lookin a bit trimmer too.

They hear a car pull up behind them and look around. Claire and Rick get out.

CLAIRE: Hi. I wondered if we could see the photographs? Is this a bad time? It's not…

STUMP: This way for the guided tour.

INT. CARDIGAN COMMITTEE ROOM. DAY

The dim Cardigan committee room, not a fancy chamber, with photographs of all the Cardigan sides on the walls and other memorabilia in frames and glass cases. Ben, Stump, Claire and Rick come in.

STUMP: History of the Cardigan Football Club. Now at its moment of maximum peril. (*leads Rick to a picture*) Look at this. Your great-grandpa, that's him there, that's Clarrie. And that's me dad.

Rick has a good look. Stump points to another picture.

STUMP: The year Clarrie and Bongie tied for best and fairest. (*shows another photograph*) Who'd ya reckon this goodlookin bloke is?

RICK: He's the fattest.

STUMP: Muscle, just relaxed muscle. My best season that. Kicked seven goals. Ya grandpa kicked a hundred and six. You gonna play next season?

RICK: Um, I don't know.

STUMP: Proud line yer in. Can't be a Conway and not play footy for Cardigan. (*to Ben*) Still, can't be a Conway and play for Lucan either.

BEN: Hasn't happened yet.

STUMP (*to Claire*): This bloke's all that's standin between this (*gestures around*) and the grave.

Ben looks around the room and we feel Cardigan's future weighing even heavier on his shoulders.

STUMP (*to Claire*): Mind you bring this young fella to Satdee's game.

RICK: Will you, Mum?

CLAIRE: Well, we'll see.

INT. PUB. NIGHT

Ben, Jimmy and Luke fiddle on guitars throughout the scene.

JIMMY: Cardigan Football Club. Bit of history passin away. Wipe the tears from my eyes. Took me mum thirty years to find her family.

BEN: What's that got to do with Cardigan?

JIMMY: Lucky to have some history to pass away.

BEN: Okay, forget it.

JIMMY: Play footy with the white boys? This club ever have a black player? Could play my didgeriething too.

BEN: I'm not pursuing the matter, okay?

LUKE: Anyway, you're just doin your time. Two hundred hours on the clock, off you fuck. Not your history, Ben. Blow in, blow out.

BEN: The train's gone. Moving on.

JIMMY: Anyway, I'm like my brother. Didn't like people callin him a black bastard.

BEN: Without the talent. (*plays*) Moving on, moving on…what's that from?

JIMMY: What's that mean? Without the talent?

BEN: Nothing.

EXT. PATH BY LAKE. DAY

Early morning. The running group has grown from eight to twelve. At the five-kilometre marker, no one, not even Ben, has dropped off.

YOUNGSTER: Jesus, who gave you old folks the Viagra?

WAYNE: Pickin up the pace, little one. C'mon Beak, Robber.

EXT. PATH BY LAKE. DAY

Running in the misty morning, a full turnout now. The original five run at the head of the pack, setting a fast pace. At the six-kilometre marker, eight runners, including Ben, are still going stride for stride, the rest strung out behind them. Gary is last.

WAYNE: C'mon, Ben, kids holdin us back.

The men surge, running three abreast, pulling the others with them. With the final marker in sight, the fittest youngster goes past them, gets twenty metres clear.

At the finish, they stand, exhausted, some hands on hips, others bent over.

WAYNE: Your time is comin, toddlers. The eatin of the dust.

EXT. CARDIGAN OVAL. DAY

Cardigan supporters out in force. Claire and Rick leaning against her car on the boundary. Stump, Donkey and the committee on the edge of their seats.

DONKEY: We can do this, pass the time faster, O Lord.

We see the ruckmen coming in, the Bean outjumping his opponent, taking the ball, coming down. He disposes of it and, vulnerable, is charged by an opposition player and knocked to the ground. In the melee that follows, the Bean has his right knee stomped on. We see the agony on his face. Jodie spins the culprit around and punches him full in the face in plain sight of the umpire. Donkey helps Bean off, Jodie is reported. The final siren goes. Cardigan scoreboard in the dusk: CARDIGAN 74, VISITORS 69.

INT. CARDIGAN CHANGE ROOM. DAY

Ben appears in the change room doorway. The players are slumped. Jodie has his head in his hands. Donkey is strapping the Bean's knee, watched by Stump. Ben goes to the Bean.

BEN: How bad?

BEAN: Bad.

WAYNE: They still here? I'll kill the bastard.

STUMP: Siren's still goin and the mongrel's in his ute, drivin in his boots.

Ben goes over to Jodie.

BEN: That wasn't so smart.

JODIE: Did it for the Bean, didn't think.

Ben ruffles his hair.

BEN: Heart in the right place.

EXT. HALL. NIGHT

Barassi's mother's wedding reception. We see the band standing outside the side door of a hall, waiting to go in, formally dressed, men in dinner jackets, pie factory trio and Barassi in slinky black outfits.

JIMMY (*eyes for Mel*): First for me, this gear. Black on black. Think it works?

Mel looks him up and down.

MEL: You'll pass. What about me?

The eye contact is long.

JIMMY: What about you? Wear a blanket with a hole for your head you'd be all right.

MEL: That's an answer?

JIMMY: Breathtakin. Better answer?

MEL: I like that more. I'm so nervous I could pee.

BEN: You'll be fine. Well, let's go. Barass, remember the drum roll for the speakers.

INT. HALL. NIGHT

Drum roll in a hall draped in the Cardigan colours. Everyone is there. On one wall, a banner says:

TWO TO GO.

CARDIGAN CAN DO IT!

CHARGING THE GUNS!!!!

The magistrate, Kevin Flynn, is on his feet proposing the toast to the bride and groom.

JIMMY: That's your life, Ben. That's your life.

The speech fades out, replaced by a bridal waltz. We see the bride and groom take the floor. We see snatches of the band playing cheek-to-cheek, rock, country, blues. In the first break, music is played on a sound system. Jimmy dances with Mel, Barassi with Luke. Ben dances with Delvene. An attractive woman, Lorna Flynn, cuts in.

LORNA: I'm Lorna Flynn, Kevin's wife. Kevin the magistrate. Dancing with me is compulsory.

BEN: The best thing I've been forced to do in this town.

LORNA: Kevin thinks you can be successfully rehabilitated.

BEN: It's all in the mind. How come the magistrate lets his wife dance with crims?

LORNA: Part of the rehabilitation process. Besides you're not really a crim. You've got nice hands.

They dance. Stump and Donkey are at the bar, backs to it, drinks in hand, watching.

STUMP: Losin two players in one hit. And being so close. (*sighs*) That Ben can dance. Used to be a bit of a Fred Astaire myself. You dance, Donk?

DONKEY: Only with wimmin. Ya notice how shy the blokes are with the grog? Before Ben half of em woulda bin outside yawnin at their boots by now.

Ben and Lorna dancing.

BEN: This is like a family occasion for me. Lawyer who appeared for me, magistrate who sentenced me. All we need is the cop I punched.

LORNA: In the corner to your right. Assaulting the police doesn't seem to go with music. Is it your gentler self?

BEN: No. Assaulting the police is my gentler self.

LORNA: You're a good dancer.

BEN: Only with certain people. Do you rehabilitate many crims?

LORNA (*suggestively*): Only certain crims. Hand-picked crims.

BEN: What's the success rate?

LORNA: Depends on how you measure success. I like to think they go away happier people. (*a look*) They certainly look happier.

BEN: The look is a good indication of happiness. I'd ask you outside for a cigarette if I still smoked and if I didn't think it'd retard my rehabilitation.

LORNA: Tonight it would. On the other hand, save the Cardigan Football Club, I think Kevin'd be happy for you to ask me outside for just about anything. Correction, anything.

BEN: Funny old game, football. Brings out the best in people.

INT. MEL'S CAR. NIGHT

Mel and Jimmy outside Jimmy's aunt's house.

JIMMY: Thanks.

MEL: My pleasure.

JIMMY: Well, see you…whenever.

MEL: Yes. See you.

JIMMY: That was good, not bad for a pick-up band. Well…

MEL: Good, great, it was great. I like the feeling…

JIMMY: Yeah, great feeling…well, pretty late…

MEL: Late, yes.

Jimmy gets out, walks around to the driver's window. Mel winds the window down.

JIMMY: So, goodnight…

Mel puts out a hand, takes him by the bowtie, pulls his head down into a long, passionate kiss. Jimmy is the one to pull away.

JIMMY: This isn't a good idea, very nice but…

Mel pulls him down again, his arms go in the window to hold her.

MEL: Get in. We can go to Delvene's. She's got a spare bedroom.

Jimmy hesitates.

MEL: Shuddup and get in.

EXT. CLAIRE'S HOUSE. NIGHT

Ben in dinner suit, bowtie loose, is walking down the driveway. He hears piano music and goes around the side of the house. Through a French door, he sees Claire, in a nightdress, hair down, at the piano. The light is falling on him and she looks up, gets a fright, recognises him. She opens the door.

BEN: Sorry. Wasn't peeping. Heard the music.

CLAIRE: You look so…formal.

BEN: A wedding. Played at a wedding.

CLAIRE: By yourself? The guitar?

BEN: No. In a band. Just a pick-up band.

CLAIRE: I played in a band for a while. When I was a student, it was…

Claire tails off, they stand in silence, awkward.

CLAIRE: Would you like to come in? Have a glass of something?

Ben hesitates, a long pause.

INT. BEDROOM. NIGHT

Jimmy and Mel in bed after making love.

JIMMY: Thought you were somethin right from the start.

MEL: Liked the way I hit Gary?

JIMMY: Yeah. Not many women can use both hands.

MEL: You'd know, would you?

JIMMY: Sure. Usually they're fightin other women, of course. Over me.

Mel slowly makes a fist, punches his arm.

MEL: Love yerself, don't you. I could see that from the start. Sit on yer bum and the women come to you.

JIMMY (*pulling her onto him*): You can sit on my bum too.

MEL: Too scrawny for me. Anyway, what's the point?

JIMMY: Well, I'm on my bum and you're…

MEL: Okay, I see the point.

INT. CLAIRE'S HOUSE. NIGHT

Claire at the piano, playing. Ben is singing, low voice, glass of wine in hand. She looks around, eyes meet. Rick appears.

RICK: I woke up.

CLAIRE (*startled*): I'm sorry, darling...

BEN: It's my voice. I'm off. Need my sleep.

RICK: Can I help with the wall, Ben?

BEN: All help gratefully accepted. Goodnight all.

Claire comes to the door with him.

CLAIRE: That was nice.

BEN: Yes. Goodnight.

CLAIRE: Goodnight.

They exchange a long look. Claire closes the door.

RICK: You looked happy, mum.

CLAIRE: Did I? Back to bed. It's late.

INT. BEDROOM. NIGHT

JIMMY: Ben wants me and Luke to turn out for Cardigan.

MEL: Didn't know you played footy. Any good?

Jimmy doesn't reply for a while.

JIMMY: Good enough.

MEL: So?

JIMMY: Nah.

MEL: Why not?

JIMMY: Don't want to get too close to blokes like your brother.

Mel raises her head.

MEL: He was just pissed that night. And tryin to impress those two slimebags.

JIMMY: Yeah, sure.

MEL: Jimmy, he's not like that.

JIMMY: He's like that. You can always tell.

Mel sits up.

MEL: No, you can't tell. He's just twenty, for Christ's sake, says what he thinks the older hoons like to hear.

JIMMY: Yeah, well, life's too short to find out what Gary's really like. Could be even worse.

MEL (*tightening*): I'm tellin you. I'm his sister.

JIMMY: Not a reliable witness.

MEL: I'm good enough to sleep with, not good enough to believe. Is that right?

JIMMY: Listen, can we change the subject?

Mel gets up, looks for clothes.

MEL: No, to hell with you. You won't even play in a fucking football team with my brother, what the fuck am I doin in bed with you?

JIMMY: Dunno. Maybe lookin for new experiences.

MEL (*icy*): How wrong can I be about someone?

Mel gathers up clothes and goes out, slamming the door.

INT. LIBRARY. DAY

Mel is at the small library's sole internet computer. Mel types Consolidated Baked Goods into the box and clicks the Search button. A page of references comes up. She clicks the top one.

EXT. CARDIGAN OVAL. DAY

Thursday practice, playing a version of touch footy. Ben is on the field. Stump is standing at the fence with Donkey.

DONKEY: Totally buggered now. Without Bean, no tall at all.

STUMP: That fella's tall.

DONKEY: What fella?

Jimmy and Luke, in tracksuits, walking from the carpark. Ben looks around. He walks to meet them, holding Jimmy's eyes.

JIMMY (*quietly*): We'll play.

BEN: That's nice. What brought this on?

JIMMY: Getting bored on Satdee arvos. Rang my brother today. He says he remembers Ben Valentine at the Tigers. Says Ben Valentine punched out some maggot called him a coon.

BEN: Is that right?

JIMMY: You understand I'm not doin this for the fucking club?

BEN: Any old reason is fine with me.

Ben walks back to the players.

BEN: Boys, meet Jimmy and Luke Kennedy, cousins. Helping us out. Played a bit of footy in WA.

The players eye Jimmy and Luke with suspicion.

GARY: Thought this was a footy team? We all in a band now?

Jimmy looks at Luke, looks at Ben. There is a long moment when we think he will walk off.

WAYNE: Jeez, Croker, save yer mouth for stuffin in food, will ya?

BEN: Give us a ball up, Donkey. Wayne, Beak, you're against Luke. Harry, Col, change sides.

Donkey bounces the ball. Luke out-jumps Beak by about a metre, takes the ball, comes down and handballs ten metres to Jimmy over the heads of players. Jimmy goes for a run, bouncing the ball on a string. Gary tries to get to him. Jimmy avoids him casually, contemptuous, baulks another tackle, and kicks a goal from forty metres.

Donkey walks over to the fence, looks at Stump.

DONKEY: Sweet Jesus, the redeemers cometh.

EXT. CLAIRE'S HOUSE. DAY

Ben is laying bricks, rebuilding a piece of collapsed wall. Rick is helping him, chipping old mortar off bricks, passing them to him.

RICK: Ben, think I could play football?

BEN (*buttering a brick*): Anything you set your mind to.

RICK: But football?

BEN (*laying the brick*): Why not? Football runs in your family. You've got footy in your blood.

RICK: I'm not tough.

BEN: Well, what's tough?

RICK: You know, tough.

BEN: Tough's in your mind. Tough's not believing other people when they tell you you're not tough.

RICK: You're tough. You fought two cops.

BEN: Who told you that?

RICK: Someone told Mum. Said you were a legend.

BEN: No. Fighting with cops isn't tough. It's stupid. Laying bricks is tough. Come here, I'll show you how to lay bricks. Only five to go.

Rick has just laid the last brick and is standing back with Ben admiring his handiwork when Claire comes along the path.

RICK: Mum, I laid these bricks. Ben showed me how.

CLAIRE: Exceedingly neat. I didn't know musicians could lay bricks.

BEN: I've had a lot of day jobs. Well, got to get to training.

RICK: Can I go with you? Watch?

Ben looks at Claire. She is uneasy.

INT. DICK'S PIE FACTORY. DAY

Bruce Somerville and a man in dark suit, the buyer, on the busy bakery floor. We see Wayne and Beak, Mel, Cyn and Delvene and other members of the football team among them. The man, a South African named Cromie, speaks to Bruce.

CROMIE: Seen one bakery, seen em all. Where's the office?

Mel comes out of her office and approaches the group of visitors. Bruce sees her.

BRUCE: Ah, Mel. This is someone you should meet. Melanie Croker, she's been, ah, keeping the business afloat single-handed since...

Cromie looks at Mel without interest.

CROMIE (*politely*): Pushed for time. Where do...

MEL: Mr Somerville, I wonder...if people are worried about the future and…if they knew Consolidated Baked Goods wasn't going to close Dick's.

Cromie looks at Bruce.

CROMIE (*to Bruce*): What's this, fucken ambush?

BRUCE (*softly to Mel*): Back to work.

MEL: I think Dick's owes this much to its workers, Mr Cromie.

Wayne switches off all machines. Absolute silence.

MEL (*loudly*): I've just asked these people from Consolidated Baked Goods to tell us they won't close Dick's.

BRUCE: This isn't the time for this. We're engaged in business discussions with…

WAYNE: You're what?

BEAK: Thought Clarrie left Dick's to Claire?

BRUCE: Well, ah, Dick's is part of Mr Conway's estate and, ah…

CROMIE: Where's the office?

Bruce escorts Cromie away.

MEL (*shouts after them*): New Zealand, Mr Cromie, tell us about New Zealand. Bought eight bakeries, closed the lot. Tell us about that, will you?

EXT. MEL'S HOUSE. DAY

Mel arrives in her car, parks behind Gary's ute and goes into the house.

INT. MEL'S HOUSE. DAY

Mel goes into the kitchen, opens the fridge and takes out a stubby, twists off the top and has a big drink. Gary appears in the doorway.

GARY: What's this? Mary bloody Poppins drinkin in the day?

MEL: Shut up, you goon.

GARY: And what was that shit-stirrin at work?

MEL: Just tryin to save your job. You wouldn't understand.

Their stepmother, Dawn, appears, wine glass in hand.

DAWN: Bloody band's gone to her head. Thinks she's Madonna.

MEL: Why don't you go back to bed? Daylight doesn't suit you.

DAWN: Well night-time suits you, doesn't it? Playin in a band with darkies, don't come home till bloody dawn.

Mel's eyes narrow. For a moment she seems likely to hit Dawn.

MEL: Listen you half pissed...

GARY: Shuddup, Dawn. No one asked you to chip in.

DAWN: Christ, what's happened to you? Since when did you bloody side with her?

EXT. RAGLAN OVAL. DAY

Cardigan run out to a roar from the crowd. Every Cardigan supporter still alive is there. Claire and Rick (wearing a Cardigan scarf) are in the stand.

We see a montage of shots showing the Cardigan footballers playing like they never have before.

When the final siren sounds, the scoreboard says RAGLAN 42, VISITORS 102.

The Cardigan players stand, hands on hips, looking at one another. Wayne ruffles Robber's hair. The pie factory trio embrace Ben. Stump takes Ben's face in his hands and, for a moment, seems set to kiss him. Ben sees Claire and Rick. Their eyes meet. She touches her lips, blows him a kiss, they are both startled by what she has done.

INT. RAGLAN CHANGE ROOM. DAY

In the clamorous changing room, crammed with supporters, the players form a circle to sing the club song. Ben is dragged in. He beckons Jimmy and Luke. They are pleased but reserved.

BEN (*shouts*): Running Monday. You bloody lot are excused.

BEAK: Excused? Excused? Mate, you can't excuse. Runnin's voluntary, you said that. I'm runnin Monday. Who's runnin?

ALL THE PLAYERS: Yes!! Runnin!!

EXT. RAGLAN OVAL. DUSK

Mel is waiting outside. Jimmy comes out with Luke, who sees her, melts away. She falls into step with Jimmy, takes his arm, kisses his cheek.

MEL: You're a star. Did it for me?

JIMMY: No, did it for Ben.

Mel lets go his arm, stops. Jimmy keeps walking, doesn't look around.

INT. PUB. NIGHT

Ecstatic crowd in the packed Empress of India. The new banner goes up:

ONE TO GO.

CARDIGAN WILL DO IT!

CHARGING THE GUNS!

EXT. LAKE. NIGHT

Ben is sitting on the edge of a jetty, legs dangling, looking into the water: a scene of tranquillity after the noise of the football victory. Claire comes down the jetty.

CLAIRE: Could someone like me join you?

BEN (*startled*): Someone like you? Anyone like you. You, for that matter.

Claire sits down next to him.

CLAIRE: I was going for a walk.

They look at each other for a long moment.

BEN: Very pleased that you did. Where's Rick?

CLAIRE: Kicking a football with the kid next door. We bought a football today. He went into the street and kicked it, one kick, and a boy appeared. Like magic. Never seen him before.

BEN: Amazing pulling power of the footy. The sound.

CLAIRE: Rick's changed a lot. Since you arrived.

BEN: People like him.

CLAIRE: Do you know about...about what happened to his father and brother?

BEN: I heard.

CLAIRE: I've smothered Rick. I couldn't help myself.

BEN: Sometimes we can't.

CLAIRE: I was so scared of losing him, couldn't bear to let him out of my sight. And I didn't realise how I was wallowing in sadness and how awful it was for him.

BEN: He's weathered it, he's fine. What about you?

Claire looks at Ben.

CLAIRE: In the past weeks I've started to believe that I've weathered it too. We've been here months and for the first time I'm seeing things, the place, people. I like the people.

BEN: The people in general?

CLAIRE: In general, yes. The odd particular.

BEN: And some of the particulars are distinctly odd.

From a distance, we see Ben and Claire laughing. They get up and walk home in the fading day, close together, not quite touching.

EXT. PATH BY LAKE. DAY

A picture of power and determination, the full squad, four abreast, including Jimmy and Luke, running in the rain.

INT. CARDIGAN CHANGE ROOM. DAY

Second-last game, at home, the club song on the public address system. Ben has the older players together.

BEN: You blokes've got to do the hard things. The kids see that, we can take this lot apart.

ROBBER: They thrashed us last time. More than most.

Ben is teaching them to believe in themselves.

BEN: Forget about last time. You're not that Cardigan. That was another Cardigan.

Stump appears in the doorway.

STUMP: Let's go, fellas. Ben?

BEN: Play like the first quarter's the whole game. When that siren goes, we're in front or we're history. I want you to give this bunch a first quarter they'll never forget. Put em in shock. Go hard, go forward, go straight, and...

THE TEAM: Look after each other.

INT. CARDIGAN CHANGE ROOM. DAY

Silent Players, heads down, Stump, Donkey, Ben, all in shock.

WAYNE: One bloody point. One bloody mongrel point.

EXT. CARDIGAN OVAL. DUSK

Sid, Max, Jessie and Muriel are sitting in silence in the empty stand looking at the scoreboard. It says CARDIGAN 126, VISITORS 127.

MAX: Can't believe it. These sheilas, last time I closed me eyes after they got a hundred in front of us. Now they beat us by a behind.

JESSIE: Jimmy. How many'd he get? Six?

SID: Seven. What about Robber? It's like he's bin to one of them Swiss places they inject you full of goat's…stuff. Take thirty years off you.

MURIEL: One from one now. Would it be right d'ya think to mention the players by name at the prayer circle?

MAX: Be a mortal sin not to.

INT. PUB. NIGHT

In a quiet Empress, the banner goes up:

STILL (*in red*) ONE TO GO
CARDIGAN WILL DO IT!
CHARGING THE GUNS!!

EXT. CLAIRE'S HOUSE. NIGHT

Claire comes out onto the verandah. She can see lights in Ben's cottage. She goes down the path. She is poised to knock when she hears the music. Ben is playing the guitar. She listens until it stops, knocks. Ben opens the door.

CLAIRE: That was haunting.

BEN: Deserves a better player.

CLAIRE: A letter for you.

BEN (*hesitates*): Thanks. There's wine. A decent bottle for once.

CLAIRE: It's late…

BEN: It's eight thirty.

CLAIRE: Is that all? I thought…Rick's having a sleepover with his new friend. I feel rather strange…it's the first time since…

BEN: Come in.

CLAIRE: Just for a minute. A glass.

Claire follows Ben into the sitting room, a fire in the grate. He pours wine. They stand in front of the fireplace.

BEN: Cheers.

CLAIRE: Yes. Cheers.

They drink. Ben puts his glass on the mantelpiece. Claire puts hers next to it. The sexual tension between them is palpable. They move closer. Ben goes to kiss her.

CLAIRE: No.

BEN: Why? Because I'm the handyman?

CLAIRE: No. Because I don't want to start…

Their lips meet and a feverish embrace follows.

EXT. FISH SHOP. NIGHT

Late night. Jimmy and Luke are sitting in Luke's car eating fish and chips outside the shop. They watch Gary Croker and Runt, one of the young Cardigan players, go into the shop and order. A car covered in

Lucan stickers pulls up and six youths in various states of intoxication get out.

Through the plate-glass window, they see the Lucan hoons crowding around Gary and Runt. It is clear that Gary is trying to prevent matters getting nasty. The biggest Lucan hoon pulls Runt's beanie down over his eyes. Gary says something to the youth.

LUKE: Shit comin here.

In the shop, Gary and Runt have turned their backs on the taunters. A Lucan hoon gets a tomato sauce squirt bottle and squirts some on Runt's head.

LUKE: Might need a hand.

JIMMY: Gary's a big boy. Fancies himself a fighter too.

LUKE: Not that big. I'm goin in.

JIMMY: Nothin to do with us.

LUKE: Jimmy, that thing your brother told you about Ben? You should think about that some more.

Luke gets out. Jimmy watches him going towards the shop. In the shop, Gary and Runt now have their backs to the counter. The biggest Lucan hoon is pointing the squirt bottle at Gary. At the shop door, Luke turns his head and looks back at Jimmy. There is a long moment of indecision.

JIMMY: Oh shit.

Jimmy gets out and crosses the pavement to Luke.

JIMMY: Lookin out for whitey.

LUKE: Lookin out for the team.

They go into the shop, Jimmy first. The big Lucan hoon turns at their appearance.

HOON: Famous fucken Light Brigade. Here comes the famous fucken Dark Brigade.

JIMMY: Shut your fat face. C'mon Gary, Runt, let's go.

HOON: No, no, no, no, no. Black bastard don't talk to me like that.

Silence. Jimmy wipes his lips, looks at Luke.

GARY: Who's your black bastard?

The hoon looks at Jimmy, looks at Gary.

HOON: Standin up for the coon, are you? Wouldn't do that. You and the dwarf piss off.

Gary moves towards the hoon. The shop owner screams.

GARY: Know somethin? The bloke's worth fifty white cunts like you.

Gary punches the hoon full in the mouth, sending him crashing into the plastic furniture. A brawl breaks out. The outnumbered Cardigan players are giving a good account of themselves when the two cops who arrested Ben and Jimmy arrive.

BIGGER COP: Who threw the first punch here?

No one answers. The big Lucan hoon looks at the floor. He has blood streaming down his face.

SMALL COP: Who's in that fucked Commodore?

The Lucan louts reluctantly raise their hands.

SMALL COP: Bugger off. And keep goin till you get home. See you anywhere tonight, charge the lot of you.

When they have gone, he eyes the Cardigan players.

SMALL COP: Now you fucking heroes get goin. Don't win on Satdee, I review this incident.

EXT. FISH SHOP. NIGHT

Jimmy and Luke walking back to the car.

GARY: Hey!

They turn. Gary and Runt are standing outside the shop.

GARY: Thanks, mates.

RUNT: Yeah. Thanks. See ya tomorrow.

INT. BUTCHER'S SHOP. DAY

Muriel and Jessie in Stump's butchery.

MURIEL: I bin thinkin. Max Cottee was sayin at bingo the Lord's been doin a lot of taketh away and no giveth. Well, He giveth Cardigan Ben Valentine, he's like a prophet come to lead us out of the wilderness. And then he giveth us these two dark lads, they've been sent to be a light unto us in the darkness. Like angels, really.

Stump is hacking at a lump of meat.

STUMP: Not outta the darkness yet, Muriel. Nor the wilderness. But I take yer meanin.

INT. CLAIRE'S HOUSE. DAY

MEL: I'm not anyone but I kind of, well, I loved Clarrie, everyone did, and I know he wouldn't have wanted...

CLAIRE: I don't want to sell Dick's. But we owe the bank money and we don't have it. I don't have it. If I did, I'd pay them today.

MEL: These people, CBG, they'll close Dick's, shut it down. That's what they do. I've found this stuff on them in New Zealand...(*opens bag*)...they buy local bakeries with a bit of a name, they shut the bakery, make everythin in some huge factory, put the local name on it...

Mel offers printouts to Claire. She takes them.

CLAIRE: I'll talk to Bruce Somerville.

MEL: Close Dick's, this town is finished. There's nothin.

CLAIRE: We'll get them to guarantee the future of Dick's. Put it in writing.

MEL: That would be good. Yes. If you can do that.

Mel gets up. They go to the front door.

MEL: You'll look at that stuff?

CLAIRE: Of course. Now. I'll read it now.

MEL: Thank you.

CLAIRE: No, thank you.

MEL: Clarrie loved Dick's and he loved the town and he loved the footy club and it's all sort of coming unstuck. At one...one...time.

CLAIRE: I'll read this and I'll ring Bruce.

MEL: Yeah. That would be good.

We see Mel go down the path, stop, turn.

MEL: This's not a bad town. Bit small. People...they give you a hand.

CLAIRE: Yes. I can see that.

EXT CARDIGAN OVAL. DAY

End of last practice. Dejected Cardigan players being addressed by Ben.

BEN: Being four or five kicks down it's nothing. But only if you stop thinking about the other side. Bugger them. Think about each other, where your teammates are. And don't go sideways. Forward, we only go forward. (*pause*) And two other things for Saturday. First, you may think you're Elvis, but you're only as good as your band.

JIMMY: Advice for anyone in particular?

BEN: Anyone thinks he's Elvis. Second thing...

TEAM: Look after each other.

EXT. CARDIGAN OVAL. DAY

Jimmy and Luke leaving with sports bag. Mel is waiting. Luke peels off. Mel approaches.

MEL: Gary told me what you done. You and Luke.

Jimmy doesn't respond.

MEL: On Satdee. After.

JIMMY: Need a lot of sleep after.

MEL: We'll see what you need.

EXT CARDIGAN OVAL. DUSK

Stump, Ben and Donkey leaning on the fence.

STUMP: Old Simmo Riley, he's bin runnin Nolan for about two hundred years, five Rileys in the side once, know what he says to me, Ben?

BEN: What?

STUMP: He says, Stump, he says, how'd that bloody Valentine get all your hopeless blokes to look like they belong in the same side as Jimmy Kennedy?

Ben smiles.

STUMP: Somethin else to tell ya. Signed off on ya two hundred hours yesdee.

BEN: I'm free to go?

Stump and Donkey laugh.

STUMP: And gonna give ya a surprise with this, then I thought, no, tell the bugger.

BEN: A surprise. That's nice.

STUMP: Dermie Brereton's comin up for the big one. How's that?

BEN: Dermie Brereton.

STUMP: Sal's cousin, she knows him, rang him up, told him what you done here. He says straight off, I'm comin up to have another go at the bastard, tell that Valentine he cleaned me up when I wasn't lookin. I'm comin to get him. But I'll wait till after the game. (*silence*) How's that, Ben? Dermie. That'll take you back to the glory days.

BEN: That's good. Dermie.

DONKEY: Should get some of your old Tiger mates up too. Reunion.

BEN: No, Dermie's enough. He'll be more than enough.

EXT. MAIN STREET CARDIGAN. DAY

Ben walking to the newsagent to buy the Sunday papers. Everyone he passes greets him like an old friend. People in passing cars wave.

INT. DICK'S PIE FACTORY. DAY

The factory is quiet. Mel has a pile of bank statements 20 centimetres high on her desk. Mel picks up the phone, dials.

MEL: Mr Somerville, Melanie Croker, good thanks. Sorry for ringing on a Sunday. Mr Somerville, do you know about a loan from the bank Dick's been payin off for, I dunno, twenty-five years mininum? No? And a deposit from A.H. Halliday? Okay, right. Yeah. Asked the bank Friday, they're gettin back to me soon I hope. Right. Bye.

The last run. The players warming up, stretching. Ben speaks.

BEN: Last run. Thank god. Start smoking again.

WAYNE: Nah. Don't stop. Keep runnin till next season. Then we'll show the bastards.

They set off. Wayne, Beak and Runt in the front rank. When the whole squad is in sight of the final marker, Wayne speaks loudly.

WAYNE: Eat dust, you kindy maggots.

The whole squad sprints for the finish, but with about fifty metres to go everyone except Ben slows and he is allowed to pull away from them.

At the marker, he stops and turns.

BEN: Doing favours, are we? Lucky I don't make you run another lap.

BEAK: Can't. It's voluntary, runnin.

INT. OFFICE. DAY

Claire comes in. Bruce, Cromie are standing.

CROMIE: Well, what can I say? New Zealand was a special case.

CLAIRE: Could it happen here?

CROMIE: CBG's got fifteen plants on four continents. Dick's is peanuts to us. If we shift production somewhere else, it's a business decision. Don't make any other kind. We're in business to make money for the shareholders, that's the hard reality.

CLAIRE: You won't give the assurance?

CROMIE: Let me say this. There's no plan at this time to shut this plant. Okay? Happy?

CLAIRE: But that could change?

CROMIE: This's a business. CBG's not a charity. World's not a charity.

BRUCE: Mrs Conway, no one else wants to buy Dick's. And no other buyer will give you what you want.

Claire looks at him in silence for several seconds.

CLAIRE: I need time.

BRUCE: Don't do this to me.

CLAIRE: Tomorrow. I'll give you a decision tomorrow.

She leaves.

BRUCE (*softly*): Bear with me, bear with me. She's going through a little emotional episode.

CROMIE: Fuck emotional. I thought this was done.

BRUCE: It's done, believe me, it's done, tomorrow it will be done. Now there's a very good hotel in Raglan, half-an-hour's drive, excellent food…

CROMIE (*cutting in*): For your sake, she'd better sign tomorrow. I'm going back to civilisation.

INT. PUB. DAY

Friday before the vital match, early evening. Ben is at the bar in the Empress, the only customer in the pub. Jimmy comes in, takes a stool next to him. Ben looks at Jimmy in the mirror, speaks without turning his head.

BEN: Listen, got to tell you something. I'm leaving.

JIMMY: We're all leavin. Sooner or later.

BEN: Tomorrow. Before the match.

They are looking at each other in the mirror. Jimmy's eyes narrow.

JIMMY: That's a joke?

BEN: Dermott Brereton's coming up. And I'm not Ben Valentine. Not that Ben Valentine. I didn't punch out anyone for your brother.

A long pause. Jimmy looking away.

JIMMY: I know that.

BEN: You know that?

JIMMY: Sure.

BEN: How'd you know that?

JIMMY: Guessed. Not that hard to tell you don't know shit about foot-ball.

BEN (*wincing*): The others?

JIMMY: They know about as much about football as you do.

BEN: So why'd you...

Long silence.

JIMMY: That mornin, the little cop, he sticks out a fifty, he goes, petrol money, you never saw anythin, your mate's history, any shit, you're travellin with him, so fuck off.

They sit in silence.

BEN: So?

Jimmy looks down.

JIMMY: Took it. Shoulda stuck it down his throat. You took em on for me.

BEN: No. Just pissed. Anyway, you didn't go.

JIMMY: I did. Turned around on the highway, gave the prick his fifty back. It doesn't matter, y'know, you not bein that Ben Valentine.

BEN: It matters. Done things I'm not proud of but I've never been a liar. Everything I've done here's a lie.

JIMMY: The footy team's not a lie.

BEN: Saved themselves.

JIMMY: Nah, that's not right. These blokes needed you. Still need you.

BEN: Nothing good comes of lying. My dad said that to me.

JIMMY: What about tomorrow?

BEN: You can do it without me.

Jimmy sits in silence for a while, then he slides off the barstool and walks to the door. He turns. Ben is seen in the mirror.

JIMMY: Ben. (*Ben turns*) Thanks for the lift.

EXT. CLAIRE'S HOUSE. NIGHT

Ben at Claire's front door. He leans his forehead against the door for a moment, straightens, presses the bell. Claire opens the door.

BEN: Hi.

CLAIRE: Hello. Hi.

BEN: Where's Rick?

CLAIRE: Down the street, with Dennis, his new friend.

BEN: Good. That's good. Boy needs friends. (*pause*) I wanted to say... how can I say this? The other night...

They look at each other, a moment full of emotional tension.

BEN: What happened, that was...pretty special. For me, that is.

CLAIRE: For me too. Come in and have a glass…

Long pause.

BEN: No. Thanks. I have to do things. I've got to think about tomorrow.

CLAIRE: The biggest day.

BEN: Exactly. Yes. The biggest day. Well, got to go. Goodnight.

CLAIRE: Goodnight. Perhaps you'd like to have dinner tomorrow night, that's if…

Pause.

BEN: Thank you. Better see how things…see what happens.

CLAIRE: Yes. Of course. Go Cardigan. We'll be there.

BEN: Conways must be there.

CLAIRE: You'll do it. I can feel it.

BEN: The team yes, not me.

CLAIRE: No, it's you, they'll do it because they believe in you. Can't let you down.

BEN: You can smell spring coming.

CLAIRE: I know. I feel a bit…reborn myself.

BEN: Some people can be. Well, see ya.

CLAIRE: See you there. At the footy. (*pause*) Never thought I'd say anything like that. The footy.

BEN: I should say…

CLAIRE: Yes…

BEN: Nothing. Goodnight.

CLAIRE: Till tomorrow.

INT BEN'S HOUSE. NIGHT

Ben is lying on his bed, on his back, awake, hands behind his head. He hears music, a piano, goes to the front door, opens it and looks at the house, at the sitting-room window, light streaming from it. We see the sadness on his face.

EXT. MAIN STREET CARDIGAN. DAY

People wearing Cardigan scarves and beanies streaming towards the ground.

INT. PUB. DAY

The empty bar of the Empress of India, banner on the wall. The radio is on.

ANNOUNCER (*V/O*): What's the mood at the ground on the judgement day for Cardigan, Col?

INT. CARDIGAN CHANGE ROOM. DAY

In the change room, the players are pumped up, visibly affected by the tension, stretching, handballing to each other. Donkey is massaging Gary's calves.

COL (*V/O*): Confident Robbo, confident. They're calling it Valentine's Day and that is what it will be if they get home against Lucan this arvo. This man Valentine has taken a bunch of...

STUMP: Not like Ben.

DONKEY: He'll be here.

STUMP: Christ, got to be out there in a coupla minutes.

Kevin Flynn and Max come in.

KEVIN: Where's Ben?

Stump shrugs, holds up palms.

ROSS: Maybe he don't think we can do it.

WAYNE: Shuddup, you little mongrel. Ben's the one believes we can do it. We're the fucking problem.

STUMP: OK, time to go. Do your best. You can do it. Ben'll be here any minute.

EXT. CARDIGAN OVAL. DAY

The small Cardigan ground is packed to capacity. Everyone is there. The Cardigan supporters come out with a banner reading: VALENTINE'S DAY, CARDIGAN FOREVER. We see Claire's face, Rick's excited face, the tense faces of Jessie and Muriel. The team appears. The players hesitate, unwilling to go on. We see Stump gesture and they run through the banner to huge applause.

MURIEL: Valentine's day! Where's Ben? They're goin on without Ben bein here. What's happenin?

INT. BEN'S TRANSIT VAN. DAY

Ben driving, music on the radio.

EXT. CARDIGAN OVAL. DAY

The Lucan full-forward is taking a set shot at goal. He kicks it. The Lucan supporters go wild. We see the scoreboard: VISITORS 39, CARDIGAN 2. We see the grim faces of the Cardigan supporters.

INT. BEN'S TRANSIT VAN. DAY

Ben driving. The announcer says:

ANNOUNCER (*V/O*): Update from the vital Cardigan-Lucan game brought to us by Three Triple Zed Community Radio's man on the spot, Col Jennings.

COL (*V/O*): Yes, Robbo, with eight minutes left in the second quarter, Cardigan trail by five goals. The mysterious absence of coach Ben Valentine seems to have put the team in shock, not the side we've seen in recent weeks by any…

Ben punches the off button. We see the tension in him. He reaches a T-junction with a signboard showing Melbourne to the right.

INT. CARDIGAN CHANGE ROOM. DAY

The muddy Cardigan side in postures of dejection and despair. Donkey is working on Wayne.

WAYNE: Somethin must have happened to him? Who's lookin for him?

DONKEY: Sid went around there. Looks like he packed up and left.

Jimmy keeps his head down.

ROBBER: No, crap. Why would he do that?

DONKEY: Dunno. People do things.

GARY: Jesus, what a time to dump us.

BEAK: Don't talk bullshit. Ben wouldn't dump us.

Ben appears in the doorway

BEN: Don't count on it. Take my eyes off you for a minute, you're back to your old ways.

The whole room is electrified, smiles and exclamations from everyone. Donkey crosses himself.

WAYNE: About fucken time, boss.

EXT. CARDIGAN OVAL. DAY

The crowd sees Stump with the film-star-looking Dermott Brereton and applaud the Hawthorn legend.

STUMP: Say a coupla words to em, that'd help. Not havin Ben here's knocked em about.

DERMIE: Shouldna told him I was coming. Put the fear of God into him.

INT. CARDIGAN CHANGE ROOM. DAY

Stump appears in the doorway, sees Ben.

STUMP: Jesus, Ben, thank the Lord. Well, now we can get back on bloody track. Ben, got a bloke here reckons he's got a score to settle with you. Goes back a good while.

Ben nods, unsmiling, doesn't move. Stump stands back and beckons Dermie into the room.

STUMP: Now, no violence, boys.

Dermie looks around the room, uncertain.

DERMIE: Which one's Ben Valentine?

Laughter. Dermie is still looking around. A long moment.

BEN: I'm Ben Valentine.

Dermie looks at him, smiles, smile dies, looks at Stump. Stump looks at Ben, looks at Dermie. A frozen moment. Dermie looks back at Ben.

DERMIE: Valentine, you bastard. Catch me off guard for a second, you end up a legend.

Tension dissolved, the players laugh and clap. Dermie and Ben shake hands, Dermie punches Ben on the arm.

DERMIE: Goodonya, mate. (*to the room*) Quick word. You're a couple behind, it's nothing. Just do what this bloke tells you. He's been there, he knows what it takes…Pain, that's what it takes.

The players applaud. Dermie gives Ben a mock open-handed clout to the head.

STUMP: Ben.

The room is silent, all activity ceased, all eyes on Ben.

BEN (*quietly*): Save the club. All those people out there want you to do that…all that history, all that pride. Bigger day than any day this club's ever known. On your shoulders. Scaring you, that?

The players look down, nervous, uneasy.

BEN: You're thinking, it's not fair that you have to be the last Cardigan side. You didn't ask for it. It just happened to you because you were there. The last Cardigan side…No. That's not you. This other lot, top of the ladder they can't beat you. You're not going to be the last Cardigan side. They've got no music in them. You've learned to listen to each other, to look out for each other. You can hear each other play…You're a band. You're a team. (*walks to the door, turns*) Win, lose, am I going to be more or less proud of you blokes?

WAYNE: Less.

BEN: Damn straight. Just get out there and do it. And there is one, last, small thing.

A pause. A roar.

THE TEAM (*shouting*): Look after each other!

EXT. CARDIGAN OVAL. DAY

The Cardigan supporters standing and applauding their team as it comes back on. We hear the voice of the reporter on Max's little radio.

COL (*V/O*): Cardigan crowd goin mad. Standing and applaudin, shoutin…I can't see…my bloody oath, excuse me listeners…

We see Ben walking with the players, middle of the front row. They are full of bounce and fire now.

COL: It's Ben Valentine, he's with the boys, he's finally arrived, only man who can get this Light Brigade side over the line today, save the club.

EXT. CARDIGAN OVAL. DAY

At the ball up, Luke punches the ball ten metres towards Jimmy, who takes it one-handed, swivels and sends a long kick straight down the middle of the ground. Robber marks, turns, plays on, goes for a run, jinks around a Lucan defender and kicks a goal. Cardigan supporters in ecstasy. We hear the siren, it's three-quarter time. The scoreboard: VISITORS 67, CARDIGAN 54. Ben goes out to the team. Muddy, exhausted, they crowd around him, desperation showing on their faces.

WAYNE: Jesus, throwin yourself against a brick wall.

GARY: Let me go up front, Ben.

Ben looks from face to face in silence, his own expression stony. Then he turns and walks away. The players watch him go in dismay.

BEAK: Ben, for Christ's sake, what can we do?

Ben turns, walks a few paces back, stops, looks at them.

BEN: Do? Do? Just do what you usually do.

Tired and desperate though they are, the players start laughing.

WAYNE: You bastard, Valentine.

The siren goes and they go back on. In the stand, on Max's little radio we hear Col:

COL (*V/O*): Well, I don't know what he said to them but this man Valentine can still make them laugh. In their hour of greatest need, he's got a laugh out of em and they've gone back on with a spring in the step. Remarkable.

MAX: Gonna need a lot more than a spring in the step.

MURIEL: Well, we've got more.

Luke gets the ball out to Beak, who is set upon by hordes of Lucan players. He writhes and wriggles and, from the prone position, manages to handball to Jimmy. Jimmy gets a kick in, forward. It bounces in space. Ross comes up and takes it, goes for a run, kicks long to the pocket. The receiver plays on, runs for the centre square, kicks left-footed to Wayne, ten metres in front of goal. He puts it through. VISITORS 67 CARDIGAN 66.

Then Lucan strike back. VISITORS 73 CARDIGAN 66.

Cardigan get a goal through a huge kick upfield by Luke, mark taken by Robber behind Wayne in the goalmouth. He kicks it at point-blank range. VISITORS 73 CARDIGAN 72. Closing minute. The Cardigan supporters are frozen.

CLAIRE: I can't look. I can't bear it.

RICK: They can do it.

MEL: Dear God…

MURIEL: It's not over, dear. The Lord will provide.

We hear Col on Max's radio:

COL (V/O): Robbo, ball's in the middle here. Seconds to go. Pretty much too late for Cardigan to win it. One point behind. Tension around the ground's absolutely unbearable.

Luke wins the tap-out, Beak roves the ball, is tackled, gets it away to Ross, who handballs to Jimmy lurking nearby. Jimmy takes off on a jinking run, deceiving several Lucan players, bouncing the ball on a string. The entire Cardigan side is up with play now, no one in defence. And the whole Lucan side is in Cardigan's attacking zone.

Gary comes in to shepherd and flattens two Lucan players. Forty metres out, open goal in front of him, moment of glory, crowd going beserk, Jimmy looks around, sees the running Gary. He handballs to him.

JIMMY (*ambivalent*): Your club, your history. Kick it.

Gary runs on a few paces towards goal, steadies, prepares to kick. Then he stops, swivels and kicks the ball back to Jimmy. Their eyes meet. The final siren goes.

GARY: No, mate. It's your club too. You're in the history now. Kick it for Cardigan.

Jimmy hesitates. We see the faces of all the supporters. Jimmy's eyes meet Ben's. There is absolute silence around the ground. Then Jimmy walks back, turns, looks at goal, runs three paces and puts the ball right through the middle. The ground erupts. From a height, we see Gary embrace Jimmy, spectators converging on the players from all sides, Jimmy being chaired by Cardigan players, prominent among them Gary, Wayne, Luke, Beak and Robber.

Stump and Donkey make their way through the crowd, everyone trying to pat and hug Ben. Ben embraces players, ruffles hair and they do the same to him. The players put Jimmy down and Ben is hoisted onto Wayne's and Gary's shoulders. Mel gets to Jimmy and they embrace. In the stand, Claire and Rick are embraced by Muriel and Jessie, Max and Sid.

INT. TOILET. NIGHT

Ben and Dermie, side by side, pissing in silence.

BEN: So?

DERMIE: So what?

BEN: Didn't dob me.

DERMIE: Dob you?

BEN: Dob me.

DERMIE: Never dobbed anyone in my life, mate.

They finish, zip up, go to the washbasins.

BEN: Thanks. It's over, you can do it now.

DERMIE: Me? No, mate, not me.

They finish. At the door, Dermie turns to Ben.

DERMIE: They needed a Ben Valentine, they got one.

Dermie extends a hand. They shake.

INT. CARDIGAN CLUBROOM. NIGHT

A packed room, Claire and Rick there, the end of the medal presentations by Kevin Flynn.

KEV: It's been hard, the hardest best-and-fairest I can remember, and it goes to the oldest member of the side, Robber Harris. (*tumultuous applause*) And to present it, I'd like a certain man…(*applause goes on*) You know who I'm talking about. Tomorrow, when we wake up, we'll still have a football club. O blessed day! We owe that to our heroic players and to the man who stood between this great club and the unthinkable…(*massive applause and shouting*) I give you the man: Tigers champion and our coach, the man to whom Cardigan owes its very life, Ben Valentine.

More applause. Ben hangs the medal around Robber's neck, puts out his hand. Instead, Robber embraces him.

ROBBER: Thanks, mate. For everything.

BEN: Just a few words, something I have to say before I leave. Ben Valentine didn't save this club. The players saved it. And all of you saved it because you believed in them, believed they could...Ben Valentine couldn't save it because I'm not that Ben Valentine. I didn't play for the Tigers. I haven't played a game of footy since I was fourteen. I lied to all of you. I'm sorry.

Long silence, everyone wide-eyed with disbelief.

WAYNE: Scuse me, scuse me. Your name Ben Valentine or not?

BEN: It is.

WAYNE: So you never lied to me. Any player here like to say Ben lied to him?

THE TEAM (*one by one*): Not me.

WAYNE: So we don't care about the other Ben Valentine. We don't need that Ben Valentine. Got a Ben Valentine who turned a bunch of no-hopers into a team, made them believe in themselves.

Stump begins to clap. Everyone joins in. Not a dry eye in the house.

INT. PUB. NIGHT

The celebrations are in full swing. The band assembles onstage and begin to play. It's their anthem, 'I Want to See the Bright Lights Tonight'. This time the entire number is performed as we near the end of our story. (*Intercut closing song with following scenes.*)

INT. DICK'S PIE FACTORY. DAY

Claire and Bruce are walking towards Clarrie's office. Mel is on the phone.

MEL: What? Paid off when? 1969? Jesus, so that's, what...

Mel tapping on a calculator.

INT. CLARRIE'S OFFICE. DAY

Claire, Bruce and Cromie in Clarrie's office.

BRUCE: Well, we're all here. All that remains is for you to sign the paperwork. (*produces a fountain pen*) Where the little flags are, that's where you sign.

INT. MEL'S OFFICE. DAY

MEL: You owe Dick's $129,000 plus compound interest over thirty-odd years…that's a lot of money. Come and see you? I reckon you should come and see us.

Mel puts down the phone and runs out of the office and up the stairs.

INT. CLARRIE'S OFFICE. DAY

Claire takes the pen from Bruce, prepares to sign. Loud knocking at the door and Mel comes in without being invited.

MEL: Claire, don't sign anythin. The bank owes Dick's more than $300,000, you don't have to sell.

Claire looks at her in astonishment.

CLAIRE: Bruce?

BRUCE: Um, Melanie, who told you that?

MEL: A bloke in Melbourne. High up. They admit it. They've been takin out money for thirty years after the loan was paid off. Administrative error he says.

Claire caps the fountain pen, hands it back to Bruce.

CLAIRE: I'm afraid Dick's is no longer for sale. I'm sorry to have wasted your time.

CROMIE (*to Bruce*): You stupid prick.

INT. DICK'S PIE FACTORY. DAY

Cromie walking the length of the production floor. Claire, Mel and Bruce come out of Clarrie's office.

MEL: Tell em, Claire.

CLAIRE: No, you tell them. You're the new manager.

The workers clap as hard as they can, hands above their heads, they know the town is saved. Cromie and Bruce face their defeat ungraciously.

INT. PUB. NIGHT

The last verse of 'I Want to See the Bright Lights Tonight'.

END

2007